LANDING

Before dawn on February 1 they were awakened and got ready, blacking their faces to mask that telltale patch of skin and checking their weapons. At six o'clock they filed below to the amphibious tractors that would carry them to shore. The battleships opened up with their big guns and the clamor became deafening. The barrage continued until 7:45. Heavy army air force bombers arrived over the beaches to drop 2,000-pound bombs. Dive bombers from the carriers followed them. Torpedo bombers came in low with fragmentation bombs. F6F fighter planes followed, strafing, and the battleships began firing again on the beaches. The LCI gunboats were ahead of them, spraying gunfire and rockets.

As they approached, it seemed impossible that anything could be living in that wasteland of rubble, shattered trees, and torn-up earth and sand. But from the shellholes and the wreckage came fire. Some of the pillboxes had survived, and were manned by gunners...

TO THE MARIANAS

WAR IN THE CENTRAL PACIFIC 1944

EDWIN P. HOYT

AVON BOOKS ◆ NEW YORK

AVON BOOKS
A division of
The Hearst Corporation
105 Madison Avenue
New York, New York 10016

The Van Nostrand Reinhold Company edition contains the following Library of
Congress Cataloging in Publication Data:

Hoyt, Edwin Palmer.
  To the Marianas.

  Bibliography
  Includes index.
  1. World War, 1939–1945—Campaigns—Mariana Islands 2. Mariana
Islands—History. I. Title.
D767.99.M27H69   940.54'21   79-27280

First Avon Books Printing: October 1983

CONTENTS

PROLOGUE

In the early days of the Pacific War, American forces were fighting with equipment that was vastly inferior to that of the Japanese; moreover, the American forces' equipment was in extremely short supply. From the perspective of Washington, virtually every man west of Hawaii had to be expendible for the simple reason that the United States had no reinforcements and no ships and guns to send to the Philippines or to the Dutch East Indies when the remnants of the Asiatic Fleet joined with the British and Dutch there. When the war broke out, the United States Navy had fewer than 100 vessels on the East Coast of America to combat the Nazi submarine menace, which Winston Churchill predicted would destroy the allied effort unless stopped. In the first six months of the war the U.S. lost half its prewar shipping off the East Coast. The disaster was far worse in terms of the war effort than the destruction of the U.S. Navy's aged battleship fleet at Pearl Harbor. Admiral Earnest J. King, the commander in chief of the U. S. Navy, knew that very well. In a few short months he had to try to undo myopic policies that had kept the U.S. from ever developing antisubmarine warfare (the senior commander of the antisubmarine force on Pearl Harbor Day was a chief petty officer). American shipyards had to begin turning out small fighting ships like the Canadian corvettes.

American aircraft factories had to turn out planes for search squadrons and then more planes for fighter squadrons and bombers for bombardment groups, all for the European Theater of Operations, which was given highest priority by the Americans as well as by their allies.

The Pacific Theater, then, went begging in 1942. Only a handful of ships could be brought west, and those only in desperation, as after the Battle of Midway, when Admiral King had to report to the Joint Chiefs of Staff that as things stood he would have only two operational carriers in the Pacific in the next six months. *Lexington* had been sunk at the battle of the Coral Sea, and *Yorktown* at Midway. *Saratoga* took torpedoes twice in the early months of the war and was immobilized most of the time. The *Enterprise* and the *Hornet* were the only carriers left to Admiral Chester Nimitz, and even after the sinking of four Japanese fleet carriers at Midway, the enemy still had half a dozen major carriers to those two American ships.

At Guadalcanal, the Americans were fighting with so little that when Admiral William S. Halsey took command in the South Pacific, the common term for the struggle was "Operation Shoestring." Most of the destroyers were overage fourstackers from World War I that wheezed into battle and were easy targets for the Japanese. The American torpedo bombers were clumsy and slow. The American Navy's F-4F fighters were no match for the Japanese Zeros and other swift pursuit planes. The Japanese two-engined multi-purpose Betty bomber was perhaps the most successful general-purpose plane in the war, for in addition to doing freight and passenger duty, like the U.S. Douglas Skymaster (C-47), the Betty carried guns and bombs. The Japanese Kawanishi flying boats had a longer range than anything the Americans possessed during the whole war, and they accounted for almost continually superior Japanese intelligence estimates. Even the Japanese single-engined float planes were superior in terms of search.

As for weapons, the Japanese 25-caliber rifle was a better gun than the old U.S. Springfield '03, and the Japanese light machine guns were more effective than the U.S. 30 caliber water-cooled gun. The Japanese also had the early advantage of training in night fighting and jungle warfare, which was not remedied until Guadalcanal, where the Marine Raiders came into battle, but where U.S. Marines and Army troops learned night fighting because that is how they had to fight. They learned jungle warfare because the war was in the jungle.

On the sea, the Japanese at Guadalcanal were superior tacticians as well as stronger in ships. Pure courage carried the day for the Americans, courage that began at the top, where King, Nimitz, and Halsey were agreed that they must lose ships and men to win battles. The men took their inferior ships into battle with a will. "We destroy them, but they just keep on sending more" cried one Japanese staff officer in despair as the battle for Guadalcanal was at its height. And it was true. The Japanese destroyed so many American destroyers, cruisers, and cargo ships off the beaches of the island that the water there was christened "Iron Bottom Sound." The American pilots from Army, Navy, and Marine Corps fought valiantly with inferior weapons and somehow managed to keep the Japanese air force from destroying the slender foothold that had been achieved. Their bombing of Japanese ships in many ways made up for the inferiority of American torpedoes, which had cut the American submarine effectiveness (and torpedo bombers) to improbably low levels. (Torpedo 8, the *Hornet*'s squadron, attacked the Japanese carriers at Midway, losing every plane and all but one man without scoring a *single hit*. The planes were deficient, but at least a third of the blame must be placed on faulty torpedoes, and probably much more of it.) That problem would not be remedied for many months. But like all the other problems of material, it was remedied in time. Admiral Yamamoto had gloomily predicted that unless Japan could achieve an enormously superior position in the first year of the war and force a peace settlement, the Americans would convert their economy to munitions and overwhelm Japan.

The conversion began the day after Pearl Harbor. By the summer of 1943, the major needs of the Naval forces in the

Atlantic had been met, and Admiral King could begin diverting ships to the Pacific. Half a dozen fleet carriers came out and joined together in a new "fast-carrier force" whose effectiveness was proved at once in raids on the Central Pacific islands held by the Japanese.

More important, Admiral King had the approval of the Joint Chiefs of Staff over General MacArthur's strongest objections to carrying the war up through the Central Pacific route that the Navy had always envisaged.

MacArthur wanted to strike north from New Guinea, take the Dutch East Indies, thus depriving the Japanese of oil for ships and gasoline for tanks. Then he would move back into the Philippines to redeem the promise he had made on leaving, and from there the Americans would move to Japan.

But in 1943 the invasion of Europe had not been launched, and the vast resources of the American Army had to be sent to Europe to prepare for D-Day, the invasion of France across the English Channel. The great appeal to the Joint Chiefs of the Navy proposal was that it involved only a few thousand Marines and relatively small amounts of equipment. The island chains that led back to Japan were made up of atolls and those atolls consisted of numerous small islands, most of them not fortified. By taking key atolls in the Marshalls, the Americans could provide themselves with an advanced naval base as a jumping off place for the next invasion. After the Marshalls they would move on to the Marianas, which brought them to the perimeter of the Japanese empire-proper. Here, on Saipan, lived thousands of Japanese civilians who had long before made the island their home. From this island, the new B-29 bombers could reach Japan, and the whole character of the war would change.

So the Joint Chiefs of Staff approved the Central Pacific drive as the cheapest and most effective way to get to Japan under the circumstances. The Navy, cautiously, decided to move first into the Gilberts, which Admiral Spurance felt was necessary to give advance air attack on the stronger Marshalls. The invasion of Tarawa and Betio, described in *Storm Over the Gilberts,* proved a costly lesson in amphibious warfare, but a necessary one. Going to the Gilberts, the Americans were still unsure and ragged in their planning. The Navy, for example, did not understand the absolute need for amphibious tractors and tanks to get the invaders in across the reefs until the tragedy of Betio caused by an unseasonably low tide brought it home. But by the time the Gilberts operation ended, the American Amphibious Forces were no longer unsure or ragged. They were ready for what was to come.

1
THE ROAD TO TOKYO

Almost from the beginning of the war against Japan, Allied military leaders were divided in their opinions as to the best way to defeat the enemy. The British favored a holding action until the Germans were conquered. The Americans insisted that some offensive action must begin early to keep the Japanese from continued expansion. At the end of March 1942, the American Joint Chiefs of Staff divided the Pacific war zone into two commands: General Douglas MacArthur's Southwest Pacific area and Admiral Chester Nimitz' Pacific Ocean area. The Japanese drive against Port Moresby and the invasion of the American Aleutian Islands in the spring of 1942 convinced the British that offensive action was necessary, but it did not resolve the debate over the manner in which it was to be carried out.

The battle of Midway was a defensive effort. The war in the Aleutians bogged down. The American invasion of the Solomons was a holding action, designed to deny the enemy an air base on Guadalcanal which could be used to stage bombing raids on Australia and to cut Allied communications. When it came to discussing the road back the traditional wisdom held for a drive through the Central Pacific. That strategy had been accepted in all the American war plans since the 1920s. General MacArthur

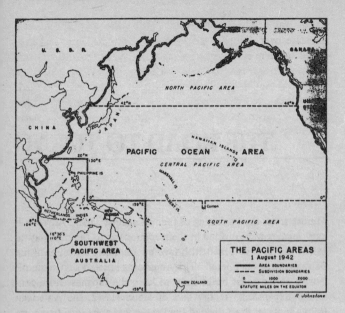

disagreed; from the moment that he landed in Australia and set up headquarters at Brisbane, he argued for a drive up through Indonesia to the Philippines. In the summer of 1942, MacArthur's army forces and Nimitz' naval forces were both ordered to remove the enemy threat in New Guinea and the Solomons, but their progress was slow and not a very convincing argument for MacArthur's island-hopping.

At Casablanca in Morocco in January 1943, the British and American leaders met to plan their joint war efforts for the coming months, and Admiral King argued for the Central Pacific offensive against Japan. General MacArthur was relegated to a supporting role ("diversionary" was the word). The major American offensive would be conducted from Pearl Harbor into the Central Pacific, and the first target would be the Marshall Islands. These islands had been a part of the old German Empire before

World War I. The Japanese had taken them and been given a mandate over them by the League of Nations. What had happened to them since was very fuzzy in the minds of the rest of the world; the Japanese had withdrawn from the League of Nations in the mid-1930s when their war policies were criticized. It was suspected that Japan had fortified the Marshalls, but so little was known about the whole area that even the naval charts had many bare spots.

What was known was that the nearest of the Marshall Islands to any Allied territory was still out of range of land-based aircraft. This was the edge of the Japanese empire; from the Marshalls the Japanese could island-hop all the way to Tokyo. If the Allies could capture the Marshalls they would take a giant step into the Pacific; the Marshalls would provide them with a base for further assault on the "Inner Empire" which began with the Marianas. The Joint Chiefs of Staff asked Admiral Nimitz for a plan of invasion of the Marshalls, but even as the request came in June, 1943, Nimitz was thinking about invading the Gilbert Islands first. His photoreconnaissance planes had discovered an airstrip on Betio Islet at Tarawa atoll and a seaplane base on Butaritari islet of Makin atoll. His chief of staff, Admiral Raymond Spruance, had suggested that the Marshalls would be a tough nut to crack, and that the American amphibious forces were not yet ready.

Spruance wanted to invade the Gilberts. The Gilberts were better known, said Spruance—which was correct; the Gilberts had been a British possession until they had been seized by the Japanese in 1941. Reconnaissance could be carried out by land-based aircraft from the Ellice Islands, which were held by the Allies.

There was another reason for Spruance's caution, aside from his innate conservatism: the only battle-tested amphibious troops were the marines of the first and second Marine Divisions. Also the Pacific forces had but one experience in landing and supply of invading forces, at Guadalcanal. The conditions there were considerably different from anything that would be faced in an

invasion of the Central Pacific. At Guadalcanal the Americans
had been backed by service bases in the New Hebrides and New
Caledonia island chains, not far from the scene of action. When
the Marshalls invasion was undertaken—and it would be Spruance
who would do the job—there would be no land-based air support
from these islands and Australia. Admiral Turner would come up
from the South Pacific to direct this new invasion, but by the
summer of 1943 he had not come yet. Nor did the Central Pacific forces even have a troop commander. The Joint Chiefs of
staff were asking for an invasion within a few months.

And so, Admiral Spruance was certain that the Marshalls invasion was too ambitious and that it would be far better to pick
a softer target than the Marshalls for the first effort. Admiral
Spruance had convinced Nimitz, and he in turn convinced the
Joint Chiefs of staff, partly with his argument about the air bases
in the Gilberts, which could harry the invaders of the Marshalls
if not first neutralized. So the Gilberts had come first as a learning operation.

The lesson was costly and bitter. At the end it was obvious
that Spruance had been dead right: they needed a learning operation. It was only too bad that they had chosen Tarawa, one of the
most fiercely defended atolls in the Pacific, and that a serious
error in calculation of the tides had left hundreds of marines out
in shallow water to brave the interlocking fields of fire from the
defenders as they tried to wade into shore on little Betio islet.
As a result of this error and the stubbornness of the Japanese
defenders, nearly a thousand Marines lost their lives. Further, the
Americans had made the mistake of attacking a group to which
they had pointed the way fifteen months earlier. In August 1942,
Lieutenant Colonel Evans Carlson's second Marine Raider
Battalion had made an attack on Butaritari in the Makin atoll.
After the raid, the Japanese set about fortifying the Gilberts,
and when the marines came again they were ready for them.

But on the positive side, the marines and the navy had learned
quickly. General Smith had fought like a tiger to secure the use
of amphibious landing craft, which Admiral Turner had said

were unnecessary. Turner had learned that without amphibious craft they might have lost the battle. He had learned that the bombardment of shore installations must be longer and *more thorough* than the Gilberts barrage had been. He had learned that the escort carriers, used to support the troops, must have better night protection. The light carrier *Independence* had taken a torpedo just before sunset on D-Day, and the escort: CVE *Liscome Bay* had been sunk by a torpedo four days later. The first torpedo had been delivered by a bomber, the second by a submarine, both at times when light and darkness were merging. This sort of attack was to be commonplace throughout the rest of the war.

Tarawa had brought about an enormous outcry in America because of the casualties. The military leaders knew, but could not say, that the campaign has to be costly. But that was the stark fact; there was no way for the Americans to learn how to storm Japanese defenses until they had tried. By choosing the Gilberts, they had driven a wedge deep into the lines of communication of the Japanese at Truk and in the southern islands. Twenty years later, historians could "prove" that the Gilberts operation might have been eliminated and the first landing staged in the Marshalls. Perhaps. But such speculations failed to take into consideration the reaction of the Japanese had the circumstances changed.

In the winter of 1943-1944, Nimitz and his commanders were too busy for speculation. The Joint Chiefs of Staff were already pressing the navy to take the Marshalls and the Carolines, for use as the base of the assault against the inner Japanese empire. But to accomplish this task, Nimitz would have to capture hundreds of islands in the 3-million-square-mile circle of Micronesia, an effort bound to be wasteful in men and equipment. It was not necessary, Nimitz insisted. Eniwetok, the principal atoll in the Marshalls, held one of the best ports in the Pacific. That was what was needed for the future buildup.

Nimitz was receptive to the requests of Admiral Turner and the demands of General Holland Smith for change. Turner

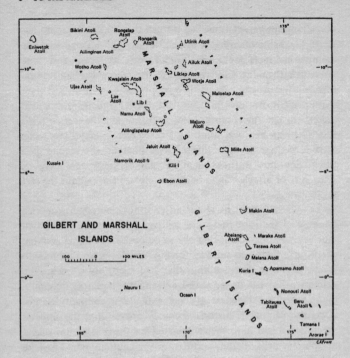

GILBERT AND MARSHALL
ISLANDS

100 |........| 0 100 MILES

expected the Japanese to build up Eniwetok's and Kwajalein's
defenses after the fall of the Gilberts. To offset this expected
action, he wanted constant observation by land-based aircraft
and constant bombing by land-based aircraft and carriers. Mul-
linix Field, named for the admiral who had gone down with the
Liscome Bay, was built on Buota. The navy built up the Betio
airstrip too. Soon daily observation and bombing flights were
begun against the Marshalls.

General Smith wanted longer naval bombardment by two or
three days, more air strikes, and better air support. To achieve
this latter, he proposed that a marine air wing be assigned to the
escort carriers so that the troops ashore could be assured of air
support from pilots who knew their problems. He also insisted

that all amphibious divisions should be equipped with amphibious vehicles capable of bringing troops, tanks, and guns in over the shallows and reefs he expected to find in the future landings—five hundred such craft to each division. That change would make sure that the first ghastly mistake of Tarawa was not repeated.

In the Gilberts invasion, Major General Holland Smith had been assigned the army's Twenty-seventh Division to attack Makin. From the beginning he had been unhappy about the choice. He had no administrative control over that division, which meant he did not supervise its training for amphibious combat. Since Smith's job just before he came to the Pacific had been chief training officer on the West Coast for the marines, he knew as much about amphibious warfare as anyone else in the United States. The army knew virtually nothing, but the Twenty-seventh Division was trained by the army under Lieutenant General Robert C. Richardson, commander of army troops in Hawaii. Richardson wanted Holland Smith's job, and that did not make things any easier from the beginning. Holland Smith laid out the plans for the operation, and handed those for the Twenty-seventh Division to the army. General Richardson then decorated his staff for the "massive planning" they had done.

In the invasion, Holland Smith had been disgusted with the slow movement and incompetence of the Twenty-seventh Division. At the end of the second day, against light opposition, they had still failed to take the airfield and link their two invading groups. Holland Smith came ashore. He spent the night at Ralph Smith's command post and felt lucky to be alive at dawn, for the area was peppered all night by rifle fire—not from the Japanese, but from wild-shooting army sentries who fired at anything that moved. Smith went back to the flagship shaken and shaking his head over the incompetence of the army. It was not the soldiers, he knew, but the training that was at fault. The secondhand notes available to the training officers in Hawaii were fragmentary. They had not covered use of tanks and other aspects. The army had not been given navy vessels to support their training.

As far as the army was concerned, one of the other ghastly mistakes was to entrust the land-based operations to a marine general. Lieutenant General Richardson, who was also the army commander in the Central Pacific, resented the way that "Howling Mad" Smith had stormed ashore at Makin and berated Major General Ralph Smith, commander of the Twenty-seventh Infantry Division, for his failure to move his troops. One of the reasons for the failure was a very late army start in amphibious training. The major literature available to Ralph Smith was printed in the 1930s and early 1940s. The best information he had was a set of notes prepared by army officers who had studied at navy training centers.

That failure was not due to oversight but rather to the nature of the Gilberts invasion. The Second Marine Division, which invaded Tarawa, had received most of its training under fire in the invasions of Guadalcanal and in the invasions of other islands of the South Pacific, and that division was shipped direct to Tarawa. General Holland Smith had expected the army to provide him with equally competent troops, and, of course, that had been impossible. But Holland Smith's principal objection to the army troops of the Twenty-seventh Division had been the failures of their officers. This objection was not forgiven by General Ralph Smith and General Robert C. Richardson. The latter was quick to congratulate Marine Major General Julian Smith and the Second Marines on their efficient work at Tarawa. "The lessons learned from our battle on Betio island will be of greatest value to our future operations." The first of these lessons, General Richardson had soon decided, was to replace the marine command with an effective army command, and he so recommended to Admiral Chester Nimitz as the invasion of the Marshalls was in the planning stage.

This recommendation was supposed to be absolutely secret. General Richardson took the precaution of preparing a "for your eyes only" memorandum to Admiral Nimitz, asking that in future General Holland Smith's duties be restricted to straight administration of marine troops only. The tactical command—

control of the troops that would invade the islands—should be given to Richardson, and he should furnish all troops for the coming invasions.

At Cincpac headquarters, Nimitz' senior officers referred privately to General Richardson as "Nervous Nellie" because he was constantly worrying about "problems" that never developed. But this memo represented something far deeper—the perennial quarrel between the army and the marines over troop employment. The navy had always used marines as its prime shock troops, and the army had always resented this. General Richardson shared this distaste for employment of marines to do what he considered to be soldiers' work. His emotions were also aroused because Major General Ralph Smith was a protégé of his, dating back before the days when Richardson had commanded the Army VII Corps and Ralph Smith had been one of his lieutenants. "Howling Mad" Smith's salty words about the military conduct and failures of Ralph Smith had gotten around Pearl Harbor, and this was Richardson's response.

No one would ever accuse Admiral Nimitz of violating a confidence, but within a matter of hours, the contents of the Richardson memorandum were known within the Cincpac staff. The naval officers were more or less amused at Richardson's gall, but the marines were furious. Fortunately for army-navy relations, very little of the Twenty-seventh Division would be employed in the Marshalls invasion. That decision was made months before the Smith vs. Smith controversy began; while the men of the Twenty-seventh Division were in action, men of the Seventh Division's Seventeenth and Thirty-second Regimental Combat Teams were preparing for the Marshalls invasion. These were the only troops of the Seventh Division that had been in previous combat (the Aleutians). They led in the training of all the other troops of the Seventh and the Twenty-seventh's 106th Infantry Regiment, which would be the army forces involved in the Marshalls invasion. The marine forces would be the Fourth Marine Division and the Twenty-second Marine Regimental Combat Team.

2
THE AIRMEN'S BATTLE

The invasion of the Gilbert Islands was completed by the end of November 1943, and the fighting troops were replaced by garrison forces. Within the week, an air strike was made by the new "fast carrier force" that had been building in the Pacific over the past few months. Task Force 50, as it was called, was commanded by Rear Admiral Charles A. Pownall. It consisted of four new *Essex*-class fleet carriers; the *Enterprise*, which was sturdy if not so new; the *Saratoga*, for which the naval word was "venerable"; and five of the new light carriers. Task Force 50 was divided into four groups, each commanded by a rear admiral.

It was the most powerful naval air force afloat anywhere in the world, and superior to the Japanese carrier group for the first time. Two of the carrier groups, Admiral Arthur Radford's and Admiral Frederick Sherman's, were in need of repairs and supply. At the end of the Gilberts battle, Sherman's *Princeton*, for example, was suffering from vibration in her propulsion system that had been exacerbated by 10,000 miles of continual steaming in the past few weeks. Three helmsmen had been injured, and the engineering department was worried about more casualties. The *Princeton* was sent back to Pearl Harbor for repairs, first having transferred all her operational aircraft to other carriers except those needed for patrol, and having taken aboard the "war wearies" damaged in the recent series of air strikes against Japanese bases in the South and Central Pacific. To a lesser degree the other carriers of these groups were in the same condition, so Admiral Pownall took with him his own group and that of Admiral Montgomery to strike the Marshalls. The force consisted of six carriers with 386 aircraft.

The two groups made an ocean rendezvous east of the Marshalls and took on fuel. Then, on December 1, they steered west and headed for Kwajalein atoll in the middle of the Marshalls. About 40 miles east of the Marshall chain they launched planes early on the morning of December 4, surprising the Japanese, who had expected the attack to come from the south and had concentrated their air power on the west side of the island chain. The Americans came down from the north. The advantage of surprise was brief. The Japanese soon had fifty fighters in the air, and a heavy barrage of antiaircraft fire came up. But the Japanese had obviously not expected an air strike quite so soon. Several warships and freighters were in the various harbors. The planes came over Roi islet in Kwajalein atoll and strafed and bombed. But the Japanese had been extremely clever in their camouflage. They had built mock aircraft of bamboo and reeds which they left on the runways and parking areas. They concealed all but their immediately operational aircraft in hidden revetments, often protected by heavy log walls and roofs. Consequently, although the Americans struck hard at Roi they destroyed only three bombers and sixteen fighters. They did not know they had left behind unhurt some forty Japanese aircraft. The cruiser *Izuzu* was at anchor in the lagoon, and they attacked it, but the *Izuzu* managed to avoid all but two bombs, which knocked out her rudder. One big transport was torpedoed and blew up with a satisfying explosion that suggested she was carrying ammunition. Other planes headed for the Japanese naval base at the southern end of the atoll. At Kwajalein atoll they struck Kwajalein, Ebeye, and Enubuj islands. At the end of the strike the American pilots reported enthusiastically on their performance as they talked to

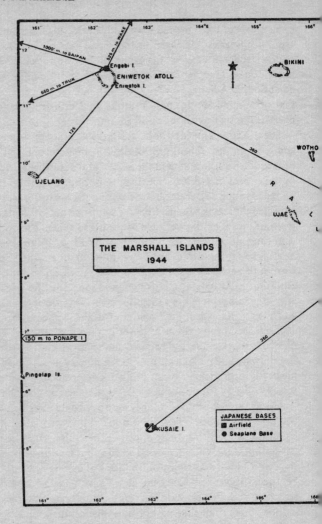

From *History of the U.S. Naval Operations in World War II* by
Samuel Eliot Morison, Little, Brown and Company.

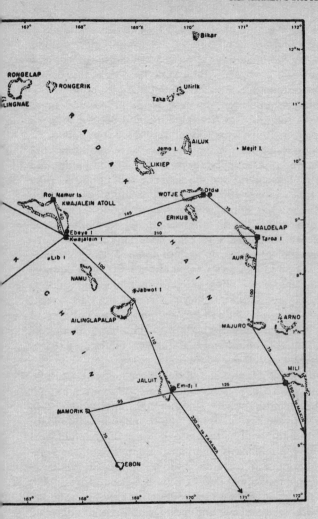

the air intelligence officers aboard their carriers. Some pilots, however, and several of the carrier captains wanted to send a second strike. That was the plan, but Admiral Pownall grew nervous here in the enemy heartland. He decided that the uncertain performance of several carriers had been caused by exhaustion. After all, the ships and planes had been in action since the early days of November. Pownall decided to cancel the second strike on Kwajalein and headed for Pearl Harbor.

Meanwhile planes from the *Yorktown* alone launched a strike against Wotje. It accomplished very little, and that failure seemed to bear out the sensibility of Admiral Pownall's decision. After all, he had no night fighters (Admiral Radford's carrier group was the only one so equipped) and he wanted to be as far out of bomber range from the Marshalls as possible by nightfall. Between 11:00 a.m. and 3:00 p.m., when the bombers were recovered and the task force steamed eastward, several Japanese planes attacked, but half a dozen of them were shot down by ship antiaircraft guns. When the carrier captains began comparing notes, they concluded that they had sent off 246 planes against the atoll and had destroyed fifty-five Japanese aircraft, most of them in the air. They also claimed to have sunk four Japanese ships. But the two cruisers in the lagoon both escaped serious damage, and so did most of the merchant ships.

The last plane landed and the losses counted (five American planes), the Task Force began to move. "Mission completed," signaled Admiral Pownall. But aboard the carriers, the photo specialists were developing film, and the films showed what the pilots had not seen, the existence of dozens of aircraft in those camouflaged revetments, and unhurt ships. Aboard the *Yorktown*, Captain J. J. Clark wanted to go back for another strike, for his photos showed how little he had done at Wotje. But Pownall said no, they were going home, and he was in command. They left, leaving behind them many Japanese aircraft that would have to be accounted for later.

As Pownall had gloomily expected, the Japanese came after them that night from all parts of the Marshalls. The "snoopers" showed up at dusk, and remained with them. In the later hours of December 4, after the moon was high, the attacks began. The Japanese had forty or fifty planes in the air attacking various elements of the force. The carrier *Lexington* took a torpedo in the stern, which killed or wounded nearly fifty men. The *Lexington* was attacked several more times, but Captain Felix Stump and his men saved the ship, and as the moon went down at about 1:30 on the morning of December 5, she could make 21 knots. The Japanese retired at moonset, and the task force relaxed. Next day, they were far enough offshore so that a large Japanese force that was launched from the Marshalls could not find the ships, and Task Force 50 steamed back to Pearl Harbor without further difficulty.

The incidents began to occur almost immediately after the carriers were moored. Admiral Pownall went off to report on the raid to Admiral Towers, but found Towers gone to Admiral John Hoover's command at Canton atoll, in the Phoenix Islands, 1,200 miles southwest of Pearl Harbor. Among General Richardson's many complaints about the navy's employment of army forces was the charge that his shore-based army bombers had been misused in the Gilberts operation. Richardson blamed the navy; Admiral Towers blamed Admiral Spruance; Admiral Hoover blamed the army for training its pilots to bomb from high altitude. When working in the Pacific islands, he insisted, Norden bombsights or not, the planes must get down on the target if they wanted to hit anything. This discussion at the Nimitz staff level had deteriorated into hot argument, and Towers had been dispatched to investigate and report to the commander in chief of the Pacific forces. (Towers reported back, but the Army continued in its own ways, and the problem was not solved.) Admiral Pownall then sat back and waited for Towers to return.

But Pownall's junior officers were not waiting. They were furious at having been called away from the Kwajalein strike because "Nellie" was nervous again. On the voyage back to Pearl Harbor the air intelligence officers had pored over the blowups of the aerial photographs and marked up the Japanese

planes they could identify in their hidden revetments. As soon
as the *Yorktown* was safely berthed, Captain J. J. Clark rushed to
Cincpac headquarters flourishing a handful of prints. He too
found Towers gone, but he then went to the office of Rear
Admiral Forrest Sherman, Nimitz' chief air officer. Sherman had
recently been brought up to that post from the job as Towers'
chief of staff, a recognition of Nimitz' increasing awareness of
the importance of the carriers.

Clark came bursting into Sherman's office that day, slapped
the photographs on the desk, and began sorting them out to
show what the task force had done—and had not done. Sherman
looked them over carefully, then got up and opened the door to
the next room, where Rear Admiral C. A. McMorris was located.
McMorris was Nimitz' chief of staff.

"Do you want to see the fish that got away?" asked Sherman.
He took McMorris into his office and showed him the pictures,
as Captain Clark stood by, expecting McMorris to show his own
outrage.

But McMorris was more interested in the photo that showed
the half-built airstrip on Kwajalein. He picked it up and took it
to Colonel Ralph Robinson, the assistant plans officer. Just at
that moment, Robinson was worrying over the planning of the
Marshall invasion. Where should they attack? Nimitz' commanders, Spruance, Turner, and Smith, all held for attacking on the
perimeter of the island group; Mili, Majuro, and Maloelap were
most often mentioned. When McMorris took the Kwajalein
photo in to Admiral Nimitz, the commander in chief decided
then and there that Kwajalein must be the focal point. Spruance
did not like the idea, because after the Marshalls invasion, he was
going to have to give up most of his ships to the Southwest Pacific
to support MacArthur's next move. There were not enough resources to do otherwise; the deciding factor in the approval by
the British-American Joint Chiefs of Staff of the Central Pacific
campaign had been Admiral King's promise that it would be
carried out with resources available and would not deny the
European theater needed supply. Spruance, always the cautious

man, did not like the idea of capturing a base in the heart of the Japanese-held Marshall Islands, then leaving it without a fleet to defend shipping that must come through the enemy-held atolls to reach Kwajalein. Turner and Smith agreed, but Nimitz said they must strike at the heart. Spruance would not have to worry about the fleet's absence. Land-based aircraft would protect the Marshalls bases from Japanese attack. Spruance, Turner, and Smith made one last argument: what about the Japanese air bases on the Marshall atolls of Wotje, Mili, Maloelap, and Jaluit? The carriers would neutralize them, said Admiral Nimitz, proving that he was far ahead of his commanders in appreciating the enormous change that the new carriers had brought to naval warfare.

If the carrier force was to succeed in neutralizing Japanese air power, it must be used aggressively. And this was the next big issue that Nimitz had to resolve. The "young Turks"—the captains of the fast carriers—were complaining about Admiral Pownall's timidity in employment of the task force. Captain Clark prepared a "White Paper" which he gave to Admiral Towers. Towers did not tell Clark, but he agreed completely. It was necessary to move quickly if a change was to be made, so Towers went to Nimitz to suggest that Rear Admiral Marc Mitscher be given command of the fast carrier force. Admiral Forrest Sherman verified everything Towers said about the problem, and Nimitz sent a message to Admiral King asking for the change.

When Admiral Spruance learned of the plan, he was upset. Pownall was just his sort of carrier commander—efficient and, above all, cautious. If Pownall was given the task of guarding an invasion force Spruance could be sure that he would not be off chasing the Japanese fleet. He was not so sure of the new breed of airmen, which Mitscher typified, men who believed the carriers should be set free to roam the seas and knock out Japanese opposition at its sources. Spruance complained, and secured Nimitz' promise that Pownall would not be replaced until after the Marshalls invasion. Perhaps, suggested Forrest Sherman, Admiral Mitscher could go along on the Marshalls operation with Pownall as an observer. Nimitz liked that idea, but events moved too quickly for it to be adopted. The Marshalls invasion was scheduled for January 31, a little over a month from the day of this discussion. It was Nimitz' habit to chew on ideas, and he worried over the problem of Pownall's command. Spruance emphasized his own conservatism by reopening the question of first invading the islands nearest Hawaii, on the perimeter. He was still loath to strike at the heart and run the danger of encirclement. A reconnaissance plane that flew over Majuro atoll saw no activity at all, and was not fired on there, and when Spruance learned of that event, he went to Nimitz to again ask for an eastern base. Nimitz relented. As long as Majuro was undefended and would require no major effort, he would allow Spruance to take it as his "protective" base. But within a few days he gave the bad news to Pownall and to Spruance. It was not Admiral Nimitz' way to mince words, and he did not this day. He told Pownall that he had been criticized for being too timid. He asked Pownall to put in writing what he would do in the future. Carriers, said Admiral Nimitz, must be risked; they could not damage the enemy if they did not go into his waters. Pownall's answers were not satisfactory. So by the end of the year, Nimitz had made his decision: Marc Mitscher would take over the carrier task force, Pownall would take over Admiral Towers' administrative job, and Towers would become Nimitz' deputy. More than anything that had happened to this point, these changes gave heart to the carrier men. Nimitz was showing his new concern and appreciation for the role of the carriers in the war.

3
THE ENEMY PLANS

The original expansion of the Japanese military effort in 1941 and 1942 had given Japan control of half the Pacific Ocean, from the Aleutians on the north nearly to New Zealand on the south. This was the populous half—except for a few dots of islands in the North and Central Pacific the only important land area in allied hands was the Hawaiian archipelago. But by 1943 the military situation had changed. The American invasion of Guadalcanal had led to a victory in the Solomon Islands. General MacArthur had moved north to New Guinea. The "campaign of attrition," as the Solomons was sometimes called, had cost the Japanese dearly in ships, in men, and especially in aircraft. The battle of the Solomons was fought largely by the Japanese naval air force, and that command lost 7,000 planes. The naval air force was still primarily responsible for defense of the empire perimeter, but its resources were shattered by the spring of 1943. The Japanese army insisted on retaining half of all aircraft produced in the Japanese factories, although the army was suffering virtually no losses. The Japanese general staff, dominated by General Tojo, the prime minister, had no sympathy for the navy. When the navy asked for more planes, the request was rejected. Let the navy show more bushido spirit to throw back the enemy, said the army.

In the spring of 1943, it was apparent that *bushido* spirit was no substitute for ships and aircraft. The Japanese Fourth Fleet was charged with the defense of the south, but the shortage of ships and planes could not be denied. Vice Admiral Masashi Kobayashi ordered a survey of the defense possibilities. His planners advised a change in the defensive line: it would run from the tip of northern New Guinea to Truk, and then up to the Marianas. This meant that the Gilberts and the Marshalls, both east of that line, would not be seriously defended. Admiral Koga, chief of the Combined Fleet, agreed with that plan, and it was adopted in the summer of 1943. The commanders of the garrisons in the Gilberts and the Marshalls had been told that they were expected to defend their positions to the death.

By the end of 1943, the Japanese were definitely off balance. In mid-October the American carrier force had hit Wake, and Admiral Koga expected an invasion there. It seemed logical that the Americans would strive to retake the old captured territory. But early in November, Koga learned of the invasion of Bougainville by General MacArthur's forces, and decided this was the major American thrust. Then came the carrier strike at Nauru atoll, west of the Gilberts, and Admiral Koga realized that the Gilberts were the target for a new invasion. He decided to send reinforcements to help the garrison, but by the time they sailed from Truk and reached the Marshalls, the Gilberts were already lost. Admiral Kobayashi had moved his headquarters from Truk to Kwajalein, and the Japanese Second Fleet had sent some units to help reinforce the Gilberts. But when all was lost, the Second Fleet and the Fourth Fleet both retired to Truk. The Gilberts gone, the Marshalls would not be reinforced. Admiral Kobayashi expected the Americans to land at Jaluit or Mili atolls in the Marshalls, and then go against the last of the Solomons, New Britain, New Guinea, and finally the Philippines. The defense line would run from New Guinea to the Palaus to the Marianas, as planned. The defense effort at the Gilberts had been a disappointment. But it would take the Americans time to assimilate their new victory, and the defenders of the Marshalls could be expected to fight bravely. Rear Admiral Monzo Akiyama knew what he was to do at Kwajalein. Rear Admiral Michiyuki Yamada, the commander at Roi, was ready too. No matter where the Americans landed, the Japanese would do their duty. They did not expect to survive the assault.

4
SOFTENING UP

For two weeks after the return of Task Force 50 from the Kwajalein strike, the carriers were in port at Pearl Harbor, refurbishing. The men had liberty, and the planes were inspected, tested, and replaced as needed. But the Marshalls were not forgotten; the airstrips in the Gilberts were used as a staging point for heavy bombers from the South Pacific. Nearly every day bombers and fighters struck the Marshalls. There was no question in anyone's mind, Japanese or American; the target would be the Marshalls. But the Japanese did have one question: which atoll?

Mili had the largest single garrison. Sitting out as it did on the southeast corner of the group, it seemed the likely candidate for invasion. But Kwajalein's two garrisons were also strong, and so were those at Jaluit, Maloelap, and Wotje. Before the strategic planners had written off the Gilberts and Marshalls in the summer of 1943, the Marshalls garrisons had been strengthened with army troops; there were an estimated 13,000 troops in the group, and no garrison equaled that of Tarawa. Mili had 2,500 men, and so did Eniwetok. Kwajalein had about 5,000, on the two islands of Kwajalein and Roi-Namur at the opposite ends of the atoll.

The Japanese had plenty of time to prepare their defenses; they had begun before the Pearl Harbor attack. Originally they had expected that an attack would come from the sea, but after the Gilberts invasion, in which the Americans had come in across the lagoon, they had moved their emphasis to the lagoon beaches. But the whole islands were prepared for defense. Once again, the blame for the defensive conditions could be traced back to the brief exploratory mission of Carlson's raiders in 1942. On balance, the Carlson raid had to be considered a disaster, for assessing it, the Japanese had created a major base at Mili, which had previously been a lookout station, and the fortifications of Kwajalein, Jaluit, Maloelap, and Wotje were rebuilt and a number of airstrips completed, although the Japanese reasoning was not entirely defensive. Until the autumn of 1943, the combined headquarters in Tokyo was still planning an attack that would wipe out the American air bases in the Ellice, Fiji, and Samoan island groups. Those plans were dropped when the events in the South Pacific caused Admiral Koga to shorten his defensive perimeter, and for the first time actually to abandon all thoughts of advances. If Midway was the turning point of the Pacific war, the Gilberts battle was the irrevocable proof that the war was lost. This shock could be concealed from the people at home—and was—but the Japanese strategists were under no illusions. In the Gilberts, in spite of the Koga plan to abandon that line of defense, efforts were made during the battle to reinforce the troops. A convoy was sent from Truk, but by the time it reached Eniwetok the battle was over, so the troops were added to the Marshalls defenses. That would be the last; in view of the outcome of the Gilberts invasion no efforts would be made to save the Marshalls.

In the Gilberts battle, the Japanese had sent air reinforcements, and these were lost to the defense of the Marshalls. But up from the big base at Truk came more planes to replace them. So there were still enemy aircraft on the fields for the American bombers to hit in December and January. Those attacks by land-based heavy bombers and fighters reduced the force, but in the last week of January, there were still more than a hundred operational military aircraft on Japanese fields in the Marshalls.

As the air attacks continued in January, Admiral Koga decided that the invasion of the Marshalls would come that month or the next. He did what he could to strengthen the defenses without jeopardizing his resources. The Marshalls would be lost, but if the defenders could stall the Americans, every day meant more time for the building of defenses elsewhere and more planes coming off the assembly lines in Japan. The last reinforcements came in December. Thereafter it was a question of moving men around within the Marshalls, with the local commanders guessing which atoll would be the target.

Captain Masanari Shiga, on Mili, was certain that his island would be hit; it was the obvious choice, since it was closest to the Gilberts. He secured 1,500 reinforcements from Rear Admiral Akiyama at Kwajalein. But after mid-December the frequency of American air raids was such that there was no further ship movement. The truth of the situation of the Marshalls defenders could no longer be concealed from the troops. It was made quite plain by one simple order: they were to plant and tend vegetable gardens as part of their official duties. So every man knew that there would be no more help from home. Except for inter-island radio communications and the regular daily news broadcast from the Domei station in Japan, the defenders of the Marshalls were alone.

By the middle of January, as Admiral Koga had predicted, the Americans were ready to launch their invasion. The fast carrier task force was dispatched to make a series of air strikes before the invasion and then to support the troops. This last was Spruance's idea, and was roundly condemned by the airmen as a waste of their efforts. Mitscher and the others had an instrument more powerful than the Japanese Combined Fleet had been at the outbreak of the war. It consisted of six big fleet carriers and six light carriers. There were also eight new fast battleships capable of speeds of 30 knots, heavy cruisers, light cruisers, and destroyers. Behind them came a fleet of oilers, repair ships, and supply ships, protected by escort carriers and destroyers. The carrier fleet could move fast, strike fast, and move again. To keep it penned up alongside an atoll, supporting ground troops, seemed to the airmen the height of foolishness—not only a waste of time, but a definite endangerment. If the Japanese had any aircraft and submarines, the invasion would draw them to the battle scene, and the carriers would be put at risk to no good purpose.

That was the airmen's argument, but Spruance was in command, and he had some support from Admiral Pownall, who would ride with Spruance in this invasion as his "unofficial" air advisor. Spruance insisted that the carriers protect the landings, and he would have his way—this time. On January 19, Spruance avoided all further argument about use of the force by sailing in the *Indianapolis* for Tarawa to consult with Admiral Hoover about the use of land-based aircraft during the invasion. On January 23, Admiral Turner sailed. The invasion was committed. Eighty-four thousand American troops were converging on the Marshall Islands to attack fewer than a quarter of their number of Japanese.

On January 29, Admiral Mitscher sent his four carrier task groups to strike the air bases of the Marshalls. Rear Admiral J. W. Reeves' group, led by the carrier *Enterprise,* hit Maloelap, but found very few planes there and almost all of them on the ground. His worst casualty was accidental: two torpedo bombers collided over Maloelap and six men were lost.

Rear Admiral A. E. Montgomery was assigned to attack Roi, one of the central positions of the Kwajalein atoll. The Japanese had apparently guessed that Kwajalein would be attacked, for most of the fighters were located here. As the Americans came in, a squadron of Zeros went up to neutralize the Combat Air Patrol, and when the American air strike came in over the airfield, more Zeros appeared. But the new American F6F Hellcat fighter plane was more than a match for the Zero. Gone were the days when that Japanese plane was the fastest and most maneuverable aircraft in the Pacific. The single greatest advantage of the F6Fs was their armor, which protected the pilots while they hammered away at the unarmored Japanese fighters. The result was predictable: the Zeros began to go down in flames. By 8:00 that morning the last fighter had been eliminated. During the invasion no more fighter planes were launched from any point in Kwajalein atoll.

Rear Admiral Frederick C. Sherman's task group was virtually unopposed when it hit Kwajalein island at the southern end of Kwajalein atoll. Antiaircraft fire was more disturbing, and the bombers were sent in to neutralize the guns. They knocked out some of them.

The fourth carrier group, led by Rear Admiral S. P. Ginder, struck the airfield at Wotje, but found little there; most of the planes had been moved to Roi. The next day Ginder moved on to Maloelap, and then divided his time between the two atolls, just to make sure the Japanese did not bring any aircraft in from southern bases. By the time the troops were ready to land the air opposition had been destroyed, there was no Japanese navy in evidence, at least on the surface, and the antiaircraft guns had been destroyed or damaged or were keeping silent to save their efforts.

Beneath the sea, the story was slightly different. The Japanese submarine RO-39 came up as the attacks on Wotje were in progress, and was ordered from Truk to take station there. Lieutenant Commander Sunao Tabata was en route to Kwajalein, filled with hope and the confidence of one important victory over the Americans. His I-175 had sunk the escort carrier Liscome Bay off Makin in the Gilberts invasion. Now he would have a chance to try again. Rear Admiral Noburo Owada, commander of submarines at Truk, also sent RO-40 to Kwajalein and I-11 up from the Samoa–Ellice Islands channel to take station east of the Marshalls. These were all the submarines he could spare. The others were being used to carry supplies to the beleaguered Japanese soldiers in the South Pacific islands.

The submarine men found this duty demeaning and protested as volubly as did the American carrier officers about their lot.

But the Japanese Navy had an even better reason for its odd behavior. The whole Japanese war effort was dominated by the army, and had the navy refused this wasteful use of its weapons, the army would have refused to supply troops to the navy defenses, and Premier General Tojo would have backed them to the hilt. The handful of submarines assigned to the Marshalls defenses certainly could not change the outcome, but this was the only assistance that Admiral Koga was in a position to give at the end of January 1944.

5
THE ATTACK: MAJURO AND ROI-NAMUR

Admiral Spruance had been worried about safeguarding his line of communications until Admiral Nimitz gave him permission to take Majuro. That way ships could thread their way by the Majuro atoll, avoiding close proximity to powerful Mili on the south and Maloelap on the north. Rear Admiral Harry Hill, one of the bright young officers Admiral Turner had brought into his expanding amphibious force, was chosen to take Majuro, and then to back up the Kwajalein invasion that would be staged that same day. He carried the reserve troops that were not expected to be needed immediately.

The landings on Majuro would be made by the Twenty-seventh Division's troops, a reinforced battalion under Lieutenant Colonel Frederick B. Sheldon, and by the V Amphibious Corps Reconnaissance Company of the marines, led by Captain James L. Jones. It was not a large force, but the absence of any activity on the island, as observed by the planes flying over in the past two months, indicated that there were few Japanese here. So these 1,500 troops should be enough to take the objective.

The first landing was made at about 11:00 on the night of January 30 by marine Lieutenant Harvey C. Weeks and a handful of men who went in by rubber boat from a fast transport.

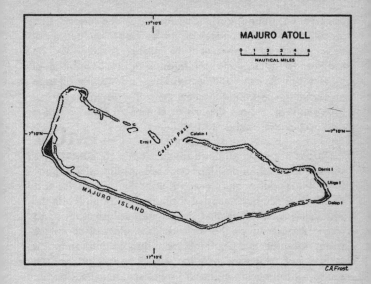

They were looking for a native to give them information, and they soon found one. The native told them there were Japanese on Darrit island, but not anywhere else in the atoll. He said the number was about 300.

Weeks and his men had landed at Catalin island, just at the channel through the reef into the lagoon. The transport then went about 12 miles to the eastern end of the atoll and landed Captain Jones and his men on Dalap island. Jones encountered natives, who told him all the Japanese but four had left the island more than a year before, and those four were on Majuro island, at the other side of the atoll.

Meanwhile, Admiral Hill had ordered a naval bombardment of Darrit, and it had begun just after 6:00 on the morning of January 31. Jones got through, and the bombardment was stopped after fifteen minutes. The captain sent a detachment to Darrit. The men found complete buildings, evidences of construction, and not too much damage from the gunfire. That evening troops landed on Majuro and captured the only Japanese there, Warrant Officer Nagata of the Imperial Japanese Navy. He had been left behind when the Japanese deserted the island, as protector of the imperial property, which included a small store of dynamite and several machine guns. The advance base had been captured without the loss of a man. Within a few days, work would be started on airstrips here.

No one had expected much trouble at Majuro, although the absolute desertion of the island came as something of a surprise. But Admiral Turner and General Holland Smith expected that Kwajalein would have many of the aspects of Tarawa, with the additional complication that there were two objectives to be taken: Roi–Namur on the north and Kwajalein island on the south. Kwajalein is a large atoll, more than 60 miles from end to end, but these ends were the only important points. The northern base would be attacked by Rear Admiral Richard L. Conolly's force, which included the Fourth Marine Division as attack troops. The division had never been in combat and had come from San Diego for this assault. Admiral Turner commanded the Kwajalein attack force himself. Indeed, General Holland Smith complained that Turner really wanted to be a general, and that when he looked at the battle plans a few days before sailing, he found that his name was not on them, a matter he quickly rectified, for the marines were not going to have an admiral running their show. The troops of this force were the Seventh Army Division, under Major General C. H. Corlett. He and Major General Harry Schmidt of the Fourth Marines would both report to General Smith once the landings were secured.

The landings would be supported by Rear Admiral Jesse Oldendorf's force of old battleships and cruisers and destroyers, which would first bombard the islands and then provide fire support for the troops on request. They, in turn, would be assisted and protected by Rear Admiral Van H. Ragsdale's escort carrier group, which would take some, but not all, of the responsibility from the fast carriers. Three escort carriers were assigned to the Kwajalein landings and two to Admiral Hill's Majuro landing—just in case of trouble. But since there was no trouble, the Hill force would be available.

Roi–Namur was so named because there were two islands here, connected by a causeway built by the Japanese. Roi was almost entirely an airfield. Namur was the defensive position where the troops lived. Nearly 21,000 marines were in the transports, prepared to move against the 2,800 Japanese defenders. Roi-Namur housed four big (12.7cm) guns, two on Roi and two on Namur, and a number of 37mm guns, antiaircraft guns, and smaller weapons on both islands. The Americans expected that the Marshalls would be more stoutly fortified than the Gilberts, but it was not true. There were not nearly so many guns, nor so careful a plan of fire fields. A number of concrete blockhouses had been built, three big ones on Roi, and the machine guns were emplaced in concrete pillboxes. But the reefs were not mined, nor were antipersonnel mines buried around the islands. There was

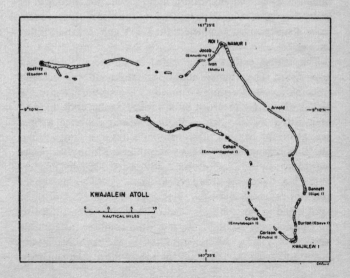

KWAJALEIN ATOLL

relatively little wire and only two major antitank obstacles except
for ditches. Admiral Yamada had organized his defenses around
seven strong points on the two islands, but he did not have the
strength to repel eight times as many assault troops as he had
defenders.

The Americans, of course, had no way of knowing the relative
strength of the Japanese defenses, and after the difficulties at
Tarawa, General Smith was taking no chances. He wanted all
the fire support the navy would give him, but once his troops
began to move, he wanted marine guns to support them too. So
the plan called for the preliminary capture of four little islands
around Roi-Namur: Mellu, Ennuebing, Ennumennet, and
Ennubirr. A battalion of marine artillery would then be brought
to each island, and from four angles they could concentrate their
guns anywhere they might be needed.

At 5:35 on the morning of January 31 the ships of Admiral
Conolly's invasion force were in place off the atoll. The battleship *Maryland* began the shelling a few minutes later, and other
ships joined in. The bombardment continued for more than an
hour, then was let up so that planes of the escort carriers could
make a strike. That completed, the ship's guns began booming
once again.

The landing craft were hampered by unfavorable wind and
heavy seas. They milled about for two hours, and several
amphibious vehicles were swamped. When they came into the
islands, they were preceded by a wave of landing craft that had
been fitted with rockets, and these vessels delivered a final
barrage on the beaches. Craft carrying tanks then came up, and
the tanks began shelling the beaches with their 37mm guns. Then
the troops landed. They stormed ashore and began inching forward. But there was little need to "inch," because Mellu held
nineteen Japanese and Ennuebing held sixteen. Most of them
were killed; a few were captured. The marines then turned to
Ennumenett and Ennubirr. By late afternoon both little islands
were taken, one by the Second Battalion and the other by the
Third, and at no time did they encounter more than a platoon

of enemy. Because of Tarawa, the marines were geared up to face lions, but the lions were not in evidence. By nightfall Roi-Namur was bracketed. The battleships and cruisers were still pouring shells into Roi-Namur: Admiral Conolly was determined that General Smith should have no cause for complaint about the navy this time. Just after noon, he sent a message to the battleship *Maryland:* " . . . move in really close this afternoon for counter battery and counterblockhouse fire . . . . " Thus was born the nickname "Close-in" Conolly by which the admiral would be known for the rest of the war.

It was midafternoon before troops were landed on Ennubirr and Ennumennet islands, not because of Japanese resistance but because of a shortage of amphibious vehicles and the marines' ignorance of the reefs and shores. These islands, too, were lightly defended. The marines ran into small pockets of defenders who fought, and they killed thirty-four Japanese on the two islands. Marine casualties were higher from accidents and drowning in the surf than from enemy activity. Last, that day, the island of Ennugarret was occupied, and by the end of D-day all missions had been accomplished. Roi-Namur was isolated and surrounded, and the marines had field guns ready to open fire. The marines had lost fewer than thirty men and suffered wounded casualties of another forty. They had killed about 135 Japanese in the process of taking the islands.

While the marines were surrounding Roi and Namur with guns, Admiral Conolly's ships were bombarding the two islands all day long. On the night of D-day three destroyers kept up the pressure, firing star shells and explosive at the two islands, to keep the Japanese off balance and prevent them from getting any sleep. The main attack would come at dawn.

The Twenty-third Regimental Combat Team would land on the southern beaches of Roi, and the Twenty-fourth Regimental Combat Team would land on the southern beaches of Namur. All this was to be accomplished by use of the vessels the Americans had developed especially for amphibious landings. Key to these was the LST (Landing Ship, Tank), a squat transport with shallow draft that was capable of coming in close to the beach (under normal conditions) and landing vehicles and men through its bow, which opened like a trap door. Inside the LSTs in these reef conditions the marines boarded LVTs (Landing Vehicle, Tank—amphibious tractors). The LSTs then moved into the lagoon as dawn neared, while the warships outside began the barrage. Admiral Turner saw the small area to be attacked, and from his readings of the aerial photographs, he predicted that Roi-Namur was going to be a tougher nut to crack than Tarawa had been. How tough a nut remained to be seen.

The barrage began again at 6:50 a.m., but the landing forces were having trouble. A number of the LVTs used the day before had sunk in the surf. Some had gotten lost in the darkness instead of finding their proper LST. There were not enough to go around, and LCVPs (Landing Craft, Vehicles and Personnel) had to be brought up instead. So the landings, scheduled for 10:00 that morning, were postponed for an hour.

Meanwhile the navy ships offshore were blasting the islands with everything that could shoot. Their targets were there on the maps: six artillery positions, eight blockhouses, sixty-five pillboxes, and about 200 buildings, including two aircraft hangars on Roi. Whatever was in those hangars represented the only Japanese airpower in the Marshalls; not a single plane was in shape to fly, and there were no enemy air attacks.

At Tarawa, one of the marines' most bitter complaints was that the navy had stood off ten miles and fired "at random—which they never hit." At Roi-Namur the cruisers moved in to just a mile off the beach, and the battleships, with their deeper draft, stood off only 3,500 yards. By naval standards this was point-blank range.

Half an hour before the new time set for hitting the beach, torpedo and dive bombers from the carriers *Cabot* and *Intrepid* bombed the two islands, and a wave of fighters swept along the beaches, strafing. Admiral Mitscher was following Admiral Spruance's ideas on use of carriers to support landing operations, no matter how he felt about it. The strike completed, the aircraft were warned away and the barrage began again. So intensive was this battering that the marine air observers, flying around in light planes to direct spot bombing, said they could not see a thing on either of the islands because of the smoke and dust raised by bombs and shells.

Just offshore the marines milled about in their vessels. Some units had lost communication with higher command; their radios had been drenched in salt water and failed. The doors of one LST jammed, and the smaller vessels could not be brought out. The idea was that the LSTs would open up and the LVTs would come out and form up into waves to land. But several LVTs of one group got lost, and had to be found. So the minutes passed and the marines were still not on the beach.

By 11:00 this confusion became a matter of concern to Admiral Conolly. One purpose of his intense barrage that morning had been to stun the enemy so that the marines could land while the defenders were still in a state of shock. But the longer it continued the more used to the gunfire the Japanese must become. Further, the small landing vehicles had limited fuel storage, and it was unthinkable that an invasion should be held up until the boats ran out of gas. In the case of LVTs, it was dangerous. These vessels shipped a lot of water and were kept afloat by pumps working all the time. But if they ran out of gas, pumps quit, and the LVTs would sink, taking down their tanks. So something had to be done in a hurry.

Offshore in his flagship, the *Indianapolis*, Admiral Spruance followed the delays imperturbably, at least as far as anyone around him could tell. Spurance's greatest asset was his "unflappability;" he had planned this invasion, then turned it over to subordinates he trusted, and now he was not going to interfere with them unless the need came for a major command decision. Not far away rode the *Rocky Mount*, Admiral Turner's flagship. His communications with the fleet were excellent; the ship was one of the new communications command ships designed to meet the needs of this war. Turner, too, listened but did not interfere.

It was Admiral Conolly's show until he got General Schmidt's men ashore and established. If they wanted any advice they would ask for it. They did not; they decided not to wait for all the forces to assemble in the proper ranks, and sent the first wave in a quarter hour after the 11:00 H-hour.

First went the armored amphibious vehicles, carrying 37mm guns and .30-caliber machine guns with which they sprayed the shore as they came close. LCI (Landing Craft, Infantry) gunboats were around them, firing guns and rockets at the beach. Behind came the infantry and the tanks. On Roi, the first to land were the men of the First Battalion, Twenty-third Marines. They hit Red Beach 2, and the Second Battalion hit Red Beach 3 on their right. Ahead of them the armored amphibians ground ashore and kept on going without a hitch, up to the first antitank trench, which stopped them. By noon the first two waves of infantry had landed on Roi. The smoke was so thick that observers on the ships offshore could not see them, and the troops could scarcely see in front of them.

On Namur, on the other side of the causeway, the Third Battalion of the Twenty-fourth Marines landed on Green Beach 1 at about the same time. The Second Battalion, on Green Beach 2, was a little faster in coming in. The invasion was launched.

The island of Roi had been so blasted by naval artillery and bombs that it looked like a wasteland. The majority of the 3,700 defenders of the Roi-Namur had been killed by the bombardment, although the marines did not know this at the time. What they saw as they came up were slow-moving, apparently punch-drunk defenders who hardly seemed capable of fighting. There were no obstacles on the beaches, and the only difficulty was with the antitank ditch just behind the beach. Soon, as the tanks came ashore, they found a spot where the gunfire had filled in the ditch and went across. On the other side of the ditch they formed into a line and clattered toward their first objective, the airfield. Behind them came the infantry.

Some of the infantry men were ready to declare a little war of their own. A number of the armored amphibians had stopped at the shoreline and let the troops go on through, then given them "support fire" from behind. Some marines were shot by their own guns, and their buddies suggested that the amphibians were more dangerous than the Japanese.

As for the Japanese enemy, the invasion of Roi was proceeding in a manner that would please even "Howling Mad" Smith, that spirited taskmaster. The bombardment had been spectacularly successful. The infantry moved up slowly, investigating every foot of ground. They had been told repeatedly of the tricks of the Japanese at Tarawa—hiding in abandoned vehicles, playing dead, and then firing on the marines from behind. They were taking no chances. Still, in half an hour tanks and troops had reached the first-day objective, a line some 200 yards inland from the beach. The Second Battalion tanks faced a dilemma there. Ahead were antitank guns in the blockhouses, according to the intelligence they had. If they stayed on the line, in the open, they would be sitting ducks for the enemy. They radioed Colonel Louis R. Jones, the commander of the Twenty-third, asking for permission to move ahead. The air was full of interference, and the message never got through. The tanks started up and began to move anyhow. On their left the men of the First Battalion also reached this line. They had expected rough going at Wendy Point, where the enemy had built a group of pillboxes. But when they got there, the pillboxes were holes in the ground, so they went on, and soon met up with the Second Battalion and forged ahead onto the airfield runway.

By one o'clock that afternoon they had gotten through to Colonel Jones. He shared their elation at the easy going and radioed to General Schmidt aboard the flagship: "Give us the word and we will take the rest of the island."

When General Schmidt had that message he was more concerned than relieved, for he was also told that the tanks and the troops had moved beyond the first objective line and scattered. Until they were reassembled there was no way an assault could be made against the north half of the island, where the bulk of the enemy were presumed to be. He told Colonel Jones to settle down and get his troops back to the line and under control. The process took nearly two hours. The marines of the Fourth Division had not been in combat before, and now it all seemed so easy they were bent on "getting a Jap" and taking some souvenirs in the process. But by 3:00 in the afternoon they were brought back, and the attack could continue in order.

Company F moved forward against a concrete building that had been untouched by the bombardment, although the buildings all around it were rubble. A marine moved cautiously up to the steel door, kicked it open, and tossed in a grenade while his companions covered his progress with a hail of fire from M-1 rifles. The grenade exploded and he looked inside. He found one dead Japanese.

The battalion continued to move. Soon the troops came to a blockhouse, three feet of reinforced concrete in the walls. It had been hit by naval shells and bombs but was far from demolished.

Lieutenant Colonel Edward J. Dillon, the battalion commander, asked for a dive-bombing attack on the blockhouse, but was turned down because the troops were too close. He ordered Company G to take the position. First a 75mm half-track was sent up to fire against the steel door. The half-track had fired five rounds when a demolition squad came up. The half-track continued to fire, and the demolition men put charges at the ports, and Bangalore torpedoes through the shell holes in the roof. When they exploded, the infantry came up and tossed grenades, and then the troops entered. They found three heavy machine guns, a large supply of ammunition, and three dead Japanese soldiers. They also discovered that the Japanese had built their defenses for an attack from the sea. The three gunports faced north, east, and west. There was no gunport at the south, toward the lagoon, through which the marines had come.

Eastward from this blockhouse ran a system of trenches and machine-gun positions that looked down on the beach. Here was the center of Japanese resistance on Roi. The marines moved along the trenches, and killed a number of Japanese, but they found far more already dead. Had the bombardment not been so effective, their task would have been far more difficult. As it was, most of the resistance was concentrated in pillboxes and blockhouses that had remained more or less intact. By five o'clock that afternoon the Second Battalion had taken its objectives and settled down.

The First Battalion moved on along the west coast of the island and found a few scattered riflemen, who fought until they were killed. In one trench they discovered fifty enemy soldiers, all dead from the bombardment. By 6:00 that night they too had secured their positions and stopped.

All that remained for the next day's work was the mop-up of the small pocket of Japanese troops that remained in the center of the airfield. After dark somebody fired off a gun, and then there was a rash of firing on Roi. The officers managed to quiet the men down, then investigated. It was not enemy, but trigger-happy marines. Luckily no harm was done, and the marines on Roi settled down for a quiet night.

Namur was a different story. The confusion of landing hurt the Twenty-fourth Regimental Combat Team more than it had the marines of Roi, for only about sixty of the 110 LVTs assigned to move the troops that morning could be found. The troops had to come in higgledy-piggledy, which was an affront to any trained amphibious officer. But in this case the confusion was not particularly harmful. The bombardment had done its job, and resistance on the beach was very slight. The troops moved up to antitank ditches similar to those on Roi. In a quarter of an hour the men of the Twenty-fourth had moved 200 yards inland except on the extreme right, where the Japanese had built a line of resistance and were manning it. The ease of their movement was illusory, for Namur held most of the troops defending the northern Kwajalein base. Nor had the bombardment been as effective on this island as it was on Roi, because the vegetation of Namur was heavy, and although many buildings were knocked down, the Japanese found hiding places in the brush.

Companies I and K came first. One of the first things they noticed was that the fire of the enemy was almost totally uncoordinated. Back at San Diego they had been warned of the Japanese expertise at building interlocking fields of fire, but in the Marshalls there seemed to be none of this, to the great relief of the Americans. Companies I and K moved along, and Company B, the reserve, came in after noon and mopped up small pockets of resistance that remained. Much of the difficulty they faced was American-made; the company had three tanks, but two of them bogged down in the sand churned up by the long bombardment and the third slid into a shellhole and slipped a track. They were not destroyed, but for the moment they were out of action.

Luckily the assault companies of the Third Battalion did not need them that morning and early afternoon, after they came in from Green Beach 1. On Green Beach 2, Companies E and F had almost the same experience—some difficulties caused by the bombardment's effects; few caused by the enemy. By 1:00 in the afternoon the marines on both beaches had reached their first objective. Before them, on the southeast or right side, was Sally Point, the southeast promontory of Namur. In planning, the marines had expected a strong resistance here, for the point commanded the beaches around it. But again the effects of the bombardment had been felt. The marines found only two machine guns on Sally Point and cleared those out in a hurry.

Early afternoon, then, found the marines moving right ahead on Namur with little indication of trouble. Then a marine demolition team moved to a large building that looked like a blockhouse. For some time the ships' guns had been silent. The fleet was ready to fire on any target given it, so thoroughly had the navy been briefed after Tarawa. But the troop commander called for a cease-fire because the marines were moving too fast. Shortly after noon all the ships had quit firing, and the only artillery heard was that of the marine guns on the surrounding islands. At 12:50 they were supposed to complete their bombardment as well. The troops were told that from this point on they would have to rely on their own field weapons.

Since the blockhouse represented a definite threat to the advance of Company F of the Second Battalion, the demolition men were told to bring down the building. They crept forward under cover from the riflemen and placed a shaped charge (plastic explosive) against the side of the building, then retreated. When they blew the charge it tore a hole in the building, and one demolition man moved up with a 16-pound satchel charge and tossed it in. Immediately the building blew up with an enormous roar and a cloud of smoke that ran hundreds of feet into the air. Debris began falling all over the island.

"The whole damn island has blown up," shouted a marine observer who was riding in a torpedo plane above the island. As the debris rained down on the Second Battalion command post, someone shouted, "Gas!" and the marines began fumbling for gas masks most had discarded on the beaches as too much trouble to carry.

But it was not gas, as investigation later showed. It was the explosion of the air base's aerial torpedo supply dump, containing scores, perhaps hundreds, of "long lance" torpedoes. The building might have been blown up by a stray shell from a late-firing gun. It might have been blown up by heroic Japanese defenders, determined not to be captured. But probably it was blown up by the satchel charge.

Down on the troops came chunks of reinforced concrete, twisted pieces of steel that had the impact of shrapnel, and the exploding torpedoes. Twenty marines were killed by the concussion or by falling debris. Another eighty were wounded. And a few minutes later came two more explosions, either triggered by the first or caused by the Japanese defenders. More marines fell, and more important to the invasion, communications between the battalion command post and the line companies was destroyed. From that point on, Lieutenant Colonel

Francis H. Brink, the battalion commander, had to rely on runners to keep in touch.

The explosions, stopping the Americans for the first time, seemed to put heart into the Japanese. All along the line the sound of the small-caliber Japanese rifles could be heard, and the characteristic "pop-pop" of the Japanese light machine guns joined in. As the Americans stopped to reorganize, and were in position for two hours, the Japanese had a chance to reorganize their own defenses. They began to fight with determination.

Colonel Franklin A. Hart, the regimental commander, hoped to capture the entire island before the end of the day. It was already growing late, but at 4:30 in the afternoon the troops seemed ready to make the push to the north shore that would complete the task. This time, however, the ground was contested. The tanks moved ahead. The infantry was supposed to move right along with them to protect the flanks, but the marines often found themselves ducking behind fallen palms and other debris and searching for snipers in the brush, in the debris of buildings, in the trees ahead, and sometimes behind them. Some of the tanks got ahead of the troops, and then there was apt to be trouble. The command tank of Company B of the Fourth Tank Battalion got out ahead of troops and its own tanks and had stopped to reconnoiter when Captain James L. Denig realized that he was alone. Out of the brush ran half a dozen Japanese, straight for the tank. One of them dropped a grenade into the open port of the turret, and it exploded inside, killing the driver and wounding Captain Denig mortally. The infantrymen who had fallen behind came up then, and killed the Japanese.

The tanks had no difficulty in penetrating, and some of them reached the road on the north shore the marines called Narcissus Street. This road ran parallel to the shoreline, about a hundred yards in from the beach. It became the last Japanese defense line that day. Darkness fell as the marines came up to the road, and they were ordered to stop and dig in for the night.

As the old hands knew, it was more than unfortunate that the island could not be taken in the daylight hours. For that night the Japanese harassed the troops. Those who had been bypassed came out to fight, which meant they were behind the lines. Those on the other side of the north-shore road began to infiltrate, and there were a number of foxhole fights for life. At dawn, about a hundred Japanese came charging against a weak spot in the line where Company I and Company B had lost contact. In this *banzai* charge a Japanese grenade came hurtling into a position occupied by half a dozen marines. Private Richard K. Sorenson saw it come and covered the grenade with his own body. It blew up, but miraculously, Sorenson was only wounded, not killed, and the others were saved. Sorenson received the Congressional Medal of Honor for this act of bravery.

Medium tanks had been landed the day before on Roi to support the Twenty-third Marines' attack on the airfield. They were brought up this morning to Namur and led the drive to clear the island. It was accomplished by 2:00 in the afternoon on February 2. When the fighting ended after two and a half days, the marines assessed their casualties and those of the enemy. They had suffered 190 dead and 547 wounded. The Japanese garrison had been almost completely wiped out, with 3,472 enemy dead counted, and fifty-one prisoners of war plus forty Korean laborers who surrendered. As it turned out, by the time the Americans attacked, the garrison at Roi-Namur was smaller than expected (about a thousand less than at Tarawa), but the relative ease of the operation was in large part due to the enormous effort of the navy in bombarding the small islands before the troops landed. When it was all over, naval officers began to refer to the Roi-Namur assault as "the perfect one."

6
THE ATTACK: KWAJALEIN

Perhaps one of the reasons that Admiral Turner did not interfere at all with Admiral Conolly's conduct of the Roi–Namur invasion was that he was personally supervising the invasion of Kwajalein island at the southern end of the atoll, and by D-Day he had his hands full.

At 11:00 p.m. on the night of January 30, the destroyer transports *Overton* and *Manley* moved into Gea Pass, the entrance through the coral reef to the southern part of Kwajalein's lagoon. Each destroyer was carrying 155 men of the army's Seventh Division, picked men who would capture the islands in the next few hours. After some confusion because of the darkness and seas made choppy by the trade wind, those troops assigned to Gea island reached shore about daylight. They found no resistance as they beached the rubber boats and moved inland. At the northwest corner of the island they did see an observation tower, and they flushed one Japanese soldier, who was killed. But as they came down the south side of the island, the Americans suddenly came under fire. Second Lieutenant Claude Hornbacher ordered his men to set up a machine gun in the crotch of a tree and lay down fire on the whole area. Sergeant Leonard Brink moved forward and found the Japanese ensconced in a shell crater. He began hurling grenades into the crater, while the machine gun fired over his head. After the resistance seemed to slacken and the return grenade fire to stop, Brink led other members of the platoon into the crater with knives and bayonets. When the struggle ended nineteen Japanese soldiers were dead, and one American was wounded.

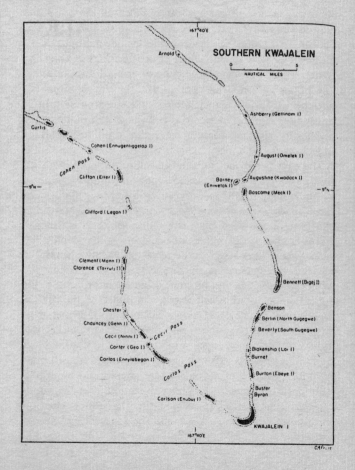

That action was the only important resistance on Gea. A few more Japanese were killed, singly, and then the island was secure.

Moving against the neighboring island of Ninna, the second force became disoriented and landed on Gehh, the next islet on the west. A garrison of about 125 Japanese was stationed here, and the American landing party ran into resistance. They stopped near a Japanese tugboat stranded on the beach and radioed General Corlett, who told them to get over to Ninna. Captain Paul Gritta, the leader of the landing party, left a detachment under Captain Gilbert Drexel on Gehh and went to Ninna, which was unoccupied. So the channel was protected. The troops left on Gehh were attacked by the Japanese, but they held them off until reinforcements could be brought in to clear the island. It was a hard task—hardest of all during the preliminary fighting, because the Japanese outnumbered the Americans and kept renewing their attacks.

The next two islands to be taken before the major assault on Kwajalein were Ennylabegan and Enubuj, the former to become a supply dump for the infantry and the latter to house the divisional artillery of a dozen 155mm howitzers and eight 105mm howitzers. These were much larger than the other islands just taken; Enubuj was two-thirds of a mile long, although only 300 yards wide. Ennylabegan was occupied easily; only a handful of Japanese were found there, and they were eliminated without any American casualties. But on Enubuj the soldiers expected stiff opposition, and four assault waves were landed on the small island. It was something of an anticlimax when they met absolutely no opposition: they came charging ashore, rocket grenadiers, flamethrower men, wire specialists, and demolition crews; the gunboats offshore battered the island as the troops came in, and carrier planes bombed and strafed; they brought in self-propelled howitzers; they moved cautiously up the island, expecting counterattack at any moment. They captured twenty-one Korean laborers. That was all. The Japanese had fled to Kwajalein.

Before the scheduled time, then, the division artillery was unloaded on Enubuj, and by three o'clock in the afternoon it was zeroing in on Kwajalein. That afternoon and evening the big guns fired sporadically on the enemy island to keep the Japanese off balance.

On the afternoon and evening of January 31, the troops of the Seventh Division moved from their transports into LSTs. The invaders were ready for anything; they sent underwater demolition teams in to destroy obstacles and mines, but there were none. It all looked very easy, but so hard had been the lessons of Tarawa that aboard the *Rocky Mount* Admiral Turner and his subordinates did not really believe it would turn out to be so simple.

All night long the artillery on Enubuj and the ships offshore kept up irregular fire. At sunrise, just after 7:00 in the morning, the ships began the heaviest bombardment that any bit of land had yet suffered in the Pacific war. At one time two shells a second were hitting in some areas. The battleships were firing 14-inch armor-piercing shells that raised havoc with the concrete blockhouses. The cruisers were firing their 8-inch guns with deadly effect on lesser targets. Battleships, cruisers, and destroyers were firing 5-inch guns loaded with high-explosive shells that tore up the brush and palm-timber fortifications. That day the ships fired 7,000 shells against the 3-mile-long island. The divisional artillery fired 29,000 rounds of 105mm and 155mm ammunition. The three escort carriers and three carriers from the fast carrier task force were supposed to fly hundreds of sorties against the island, but bad weather set in early in the day and Admiral Turner canceled air operations. He was a "battleship man" who believed that airplanes should be used to protect ships and attack ships, but that the role of attack against installations should belong to the warships. In this sense Admiral Turner was typical of the "black shoe" sailors who had not yet appreciated the role of air power in this Pacific war.

By nightfall three battalions of the 184th Regimental Combat Team and another three battalions of the Thirty-second Regimental Combat Team had boarded LSTs and were waiting.

Before dawn on February 1 they were awakened and got ready, blacking their faces to mask that telltale patch of skin, and checking their weapons. At six o'clock they filed below to the amphibious tractors that would carry them to shore. Ten minutes passed, and then the battleships opened up again with their big guns and the clamor became deafening. The barrage continued until 7:45. Heavy army air force bombers from Tarawa arrived over the beaches to drop 2,000-pound bombs. Dive bombers from the carriers followed them. Torpedo bombers came in low with fragmentation bombs. F6F fighter planes followed, strafing. Then the battleships began firing again on the beaches.

During the bombardment the LSTs had opened their doors and the amph-tracs—amphibious tractors—had come forth to begin circling as they waited for the moment to move in. They would land on the west end of the croissant-shaped island, the 184th Regimental Combat Team on the north and the Thirty-second south of them. By 9:15 they were beginning to move and the LCI gunboats were ahead of them, spraying the beaches with gunfire and rockets.

As the landing force neared the beaches, there was no question about the presence of the Japanese here. From the shore came fire from field guns, machine guns, and mortars. As they approached it seemed impossible that anything could be living in that wasteland of rubble, shattered trees, and torn-up earth and sand, but from the shellholes and the wreckage came small-arms fire; in spite of the bombardment some of the pillboxes had survived, and were manned by gunners.

The shelling was moved from the beach inland as the amph-tracs approached the surf. At 9:30 the first wave landed, and the troops ran over a dune and to shelter behind a wrecked seawall. Soon they were formed up. "Why, it's just like a maneuver!" exclaimed one soldier, but there was a difference: men did not fall and die in maneuvers, and although the Japanese were badly battered and their ranks decimated by the bombardment, they were still shooting and wounding and killing soldiers on the beach. But the waves came on. Before noon the troops had moved inland 150 yards, and the beachhead was secure. A few pillboxes had withstood the bombardment, and these were worked over with demolition charges and flamethrowers. The worst problem was with the vehicles on the beaches. The tanks were stalled by the wrecked seawall, fell into shell craters, were caught from underneath by logs and the stumps of palms.

The troops stopped at the edge of the road that encircled the island and here ran basically north and south. Ahead of them lay a broad area of marshland covered with thick brush, and to the north a palm forest. They cleared some Japanese, and some others remained hidden in underground shelters and let them pass, waiting for an opportunity to strike heavier blows than they could against the onrush.

The heaviest resistance was met by the 184th Infantry's Third Battalion, which encountered several pillboxes manned by the enemy. Company K landed on the northwest corner of the island, and the men had moved only about 25 yards inland when they came under fire from a pillbox. Private First Class Paul Roper and Private Parvee Rasberry were in this advance wave. They wriggled up to a shellhole and crawled in. Ahead of them, 15 yards away, was the pillbox, with its gunport spitting fire. They began throwing grenades. The Japanese threw them back. This game continued for several minutes, until another soldier came up with a flamethrower. They turned the flame against the pillbox, but it hit the concrete and bounced back. Private Rasberry then crawled out of the crater and up to the pillbox. From a point 5 yards away he threw a white phosphorus smoke grenade into the port. The grenade exploded and flushed a dozen Japanese from the pillbox. The riflemen of the company began shooting at them and killed several. The others rushed back into the pillbox. Rasberry threw another smoke grenade, but this time they stayed inside. Rasberry kept them busy, throwing smoke grenades until he ran out. Tech Sergeant Graydon Kickul of Company L came up and managed to crawl to the pillbox and get on top of it. He emptied his M-1 in a sweeping motion inside the port, and there was silence inside the pillbox. To make sure the enemy were dead he beckoned up an amphibian tank, equipped with a 37mm gun and a flamethrower. The tank blew its flame into the port and fired the 37mm gun.

That general technique became the method of flushing the pillboxes, and they were neutralized one by one. When this was done, the assault troops of Company L and Company I moved through the area, and Company K, which had borne the brunt of the early fighting, went into reserve. The first objective taken with the attainment of the road, the two battalions in assault pointed toward the second objective, a road running north and south near the airstrip that dominated the center of the island. The resistance stiffened here. On the south, the Thirty-second's Second Battalion took over the assault. Soon the troops came under fire from three pillboxes. Actually those points had been passed earlier by the First Battalion, but the Japanese had feigned death and after a quick look the troops of the First Battalion had ignored the "abandoned" pillboxes until the enemy riflemen began firing later in the day. At that point the Second Battalion had to stop and clear out each pillbox with the assistance of tanks.

North of the Thirty-second's drive, the 184th Regimental Combat Team's Third Battalion also encountered stiffer resistance. The troops came upon a big bunker made of reinforced concrete and palm logs. It resisted the effects of flamethrowers, so the demolition men came up with charges and white phosphorus that created dense choking smoke, to drive the Japenese out. By 3:00 in the afternoon the 184th had reached the north-south connecting road, called Wilma Road, and turned south to link up with the Thirty-second. The next step would be to take the airfield.

By late afternoon the invasion was totally secure. About 11,000 troops were ashore, and supplies were coming in steadily from the ships without difficulty. The absence of a single Japenese aircraft all day long was a blessing for which the invaders could thank the fast carrier task force and Admiral Hoover's land-based air force.

Had this been a marine invasion, perhaps in late afternoon those 11,000 men would have surged into action to storm the airfield. In his *History of U.S. Naval Operations in World War II*, Samuel Eliot Morison so indicates—an implied criticism of the army's way of fighting. But the army was doing very well, particularly in the face of mounting Japanese resistance. The defenders had built strong fortifications on the lagoon and ocean sides of the airfield to protect the runways. Three coastal-defense positions had been built on the south, or ocean side, of the island. The Japanese had also cleared away the palms around this area, to give them open fields of fire. But from the north-south road back several hundred yards, the Japanese retired swiftly in the south. On the northern side, the 184th ran into more difficulty from enemy troops in prepared positions. They were stopped by an explosion; a shell fired from Enubuj island had ignited a fuel dump, and it went up with a roar.

But around 4:00 in the afternoon the Thirty-second was also slowed when Company E encountered positions that were connected by underground tunnels. The Japanese would defend a position until the Americans were virtually on top of them, and then disappear. The farther the Americans moved toward the center of the island, the tougher the defense became. At 6:00 that evening the assault was stopped for the night and the troops dug in. The Third Battalion of the 184th had encountered far more enemy resistance than had the Thirty-second, but the Third Battalion had suffered only ten men killed and thirteen wounded. The Thirty-second Regimental Combat Team had seven killed and twenty-three wounded. They had killed about 500 Japanese defenders and taken eleven prisoners. So although by naval standards the army was slow, the caution had paid off in low casualties on this first day of the invasion.

The high number of enemy dead had to be attributed in large part to the effective bombardment of Admiral Turner's warships. In all, it had been a satisfactory first day. The troops had occupied about a quarter of the island, and were thoroughly organized. The next day they could begin to deal with the estimated 1,500 Japanese defenders who remained on the island.

That night, the problem was to protect the perimeter and prevent the Japanese from launching *banzai* attacks that could cause many casualties. The divisional artillery was given the job of providing harassing fire that night. General Charles Corlett moved ashore with his staff to a command post on Enubuj island. On Kwajalein the troops dug foxholes and waited.

It began to rain, a chill pelting rain that soaked the men in their foxholes. After dark, the Japanese began to move. Several Japanese guns at the northern tip of the island began firing into the area. The destroyer *Sigsbee* had been detailed to keep a searchlight trained on the airfield for the first half of every hour. This light bothered the enemy and brought an attempt to knock it out. *Sigsbee* was standing offshore in the lagoon, and an antiaircraft gun was depressed to fire on the destroyer. The antiaircraft gun was knocked out by the *Sigsbee's* 5-inch gun. The Japanese brought up a replacement. It was silenced. The Japanese then turned field pieces on the destroyer from Ebeye island (north of Kwajalein), but they were no more effective.

The troops ashore kept the area illuminated with star shells and flares to keep the Japanese off balance. The ships offshore were shooting again, which helped do the same. But the enemy came out anyhow, in small groups, attempting to infiltrate the American lines.

At 1:30 in the morning the Japanese launched a larger attack against Company L of the 184th Regimental Combat Team. The attack began with mortar shelling on the machine-gun positions, which the Japanese had spotted earlier in the evening. Three well-placed mortar shells fell on one 50-caliber machine gun position, wounding several men and killing one. The Japanese then attacked, and the platoon withdrew. The Japanese attacked the next platoon, but another heavy machine gun fired into them and stopped the attack. It was a momentary flurry, and reinforcements came up, but by the time they arrived the action was over.

Still, Japanese harassing fire continued all during the hours of darkness. Their mortars were particularly effective; their targets were the machine guns and antitank guns. They struck again at Company L, knocking out another machine gun that had been sent up to replace the one destroyed earlier. They dropped a shell beneath an antitank gun, disabling the gun, killing two men, and wounding another. So the night was anything but restful for the men of the Seventh Division.

On the morning of February 2, General Corlett ordered a co-ordinated attack by the two regimental combat teams. An artillery barrage would begin at 7:00 and the troops would get ready. After fifteen minutes of general fire, the guns on Enubuj would concentrate on specific targets. At 8:00 the carrier planes would strike along the line. The troops would be already moving. On the northern side, in the 184th's area, the Second Battalion began the attack. The First Battalion came along close behind in support. On the southern, ocean, side, the Thirty-second Regimental Combat Team's Second Battalion also advanced, after the artillery and the navy guns had laid down a barrage.

The 184th troops advanced about 200 yards before they encountered much opposition. At first they came under sniper fire from Japanese hidden in the ruins of buildings and among fallen logs. They passed the central pier that had served the airfield on the lagoon side and continued along the northern side of the airfield. Their tanks sprayed the trees ahead to knock down snipers. Tanks and 37mm guns stopped at pillboxes to reduce them. Most of the infantry would go ahead, while a few soldiers stood by the tanks as they pulled up to their objectives. A tank would begin firing on a pillbox, its machine gun trained on the entrance. If the Japanese decided to come out, they were mowed down before they could launch a banzai charge. Before 11:00 in the morning, this method of reducing strong points while the infantry moved on had brought the 184th to the northeast end of the airfield, and they crossed the second lateral road, called Carl Road.

On the ocean shore the Thirty-second ran into stronger opposition that morning. They called for an air strike when the

Japanese guns on the north shore began firing on them. They moved forward then, under considerable harassment from snipers, but they too were at the northwest end of the airfield and Carl Road at 11:00 that morning of the second day.

When the Thirty-second's troops had come up to Carl Road, they found they faced a clearing. On the other side of it on the south was a strong Japanese defensive position which began with a deep tank trap. Behind it were pillboxes, machine-gun emplacements, and artillery positions, all interlaced with trenches for the Japanese infantry and more antitank trenches. It was apparent to the regiment's officers that the Japanese intended to make a strong stand here to prevent anyone who crossed from the west from entering the northern section of the curved island where most of the troop installations were located. Since this would demand a maximum assault effort, the fresh Third Battalion of the Thirty-second was brought up to pass through the Second Battalion. The jumpoff time was set at 12:45.

The assault was delayed, largely by confusion between the navy and the army. Admiral Turner's ships' captains were eager to deliver spot fire in support of troops, but the army men were not totally confident in the navy accuracy and preferred to wait for their own artillery. Since that artillery was serving both the 184th and the Thirty-second, sometimes the wait was long for fire on a specific point. That day, Admiral Turner decided the army needed an air strike on these positions in the south and ordered it for 1:30, which caused the army to suspend its artillery fire. On the first day an air observer and a navy pilot had been killed when the torpedo bomber in which they were flying swooped down too low in the face of a barrage from the army artillery and was destroyed by American shells in midair. So the army was taking no chances of a repeat accident. The assault was finally delayed until 2:00 in the afternoon.

When the assault began, it moved slowly as the tanks tested the area and their ability to avoid the antitank ditch. Finally four tanks made their way around the ditch on the ocean beach and opened the way. The Japanese stayed in their pillboxes and underground defenses and would not come out even when the Americans overran the area. They were killed or committed suicide inside the positions, down to a single soldier, who surrendered. By the end of the day, this strong point, called Corn, was largely in American hands.

In the north, the 184th advanced slowly. The regiment lent its tanks to the Thirty-second to assault Corn Strong Point, and so the advance was bogged. When the tanks came back they were low on fuel and had to be sent to the western end of the island, where the gasoline dump was located. At the end of the second day, then, the American advance had gone only about half as fast as planned. The troops were supposed to have reached the third lateral road, but were only about halfway.

All day long the carrier planes had been busy. Some planes were called in to attack specific strong points near the troop lines, but the army was not particularly comfortable with navy planes flying so close. Most of the carrier-plane effort was devoted to the many installations in the northern sector of the island, where 40 tons of bombs were dropped during the day.

As night fell, the commanders counted their casualties. Only eleven Americans had been killed in action, but 241 had been wounded that day. The Japanese small-caliber rifles certainly proved the strategic contention that a wounded man is at least three times as much trouble to his army as a dead one, for all day long litter squads were taking the wounded back to battalion aid stations for first-aid treatment. They were then put into ambulances and carried along the roads to the shore collecting stations. The medical sections evacuated them by LVT to the transports, where more complete medical facilities were available.

As for the enemy, the Americans could not tell for certain what the casualties might be. Their best source of information would be prisoners, one might think, but the prisoners were enlisted men, and in the Japanese army the enlisted men were told virtually nothing about tactics and dispositions. So the estimate was that somewhere between 1,000 and 2,000 Japanese defenders had been killed and that the enemy was very near the end of his strength. One prisoner estimated that only 200 Japanese were still able to fight. General Corlett was sobered by this information, and warned the troops to be prepared for a banzai attack. It was just this sort of situation, the Americans had learned in previous battles, that brought the Japanese to an always futile but always dangerous suicide charge.

That night, however, there were no unusual activities by the enemy. A few shells were lobbed into the American positions and some grenades were thrown, but there was no suicide charge. The next day, General Corlett said, must be their last. The marines at Roi-Namur had already cleared out their islands. The Seventh Division must finish the job by 3:00 in the afternoon.

On February 3, the troops began attacking shortly after 7:00 in the morning. They had captured enemy maps, now, photographs taken by reconaissance planes, and stories from prisoners, particularly Korean laborers. It was remarkable, however, how much information these sources did *not* give the Americans. They knew where the enemy buildings had been, but not which ones were still standing, nor which strong points and destroyed buildings were being used by the defenders. The Americans had turned around the crescent so that now the line of advance was almost due north up the island. The troops of the Thirty-second expected to encounter five pillboxes and two artillery positions on their side. Their Third Battalion would lead. The troops of the 184th were not quite sure what they would meet.

After a ten-minute barrage, the soldiers began to move forward. The Thirty-second pressed forward 150 yards before coming against opposition, then found the going fairly easy for another 200 yards or so, until they came up to a concrete pillbox at the edge of the island's naval headquarters installations. Two medium tanks attacked the pillbox with 75mm shells. The Japanese ran out of the pillbox and took shelter in buildings behind, although a number were shot down by American troops. Here the Thirty-second and the 184th were almost intermingling as their drives rubbed shoulders. The 184th took on the task of clearing the defenders from the cluster of buildings. Company L and part of Company A would do the job. So the Thirty-second moved on ahead. As the two units moved up, a gap appeared between them. Under other conditions this gap might have enabled the enemy to strike a forceful blow down the center of the line and even to envelop the forward elements. But at Kwajalein, the Japanese did not now have the force to undertake any such maneuver. Their defense was stubborn and deadly, but there was little they could do except shoot and die.

The 184th's advance along the lagoon was led by Company B of the First Battalion, until they came to a concrete blockhouse. Investigation showed that this blockhouse was the center of a major defensive position, with underground shelters clustered around it. The shelters were protected by large earth mounds, and beyond the blockhouse, among the ruins blasted by the naval and artillery barrages, stood a pair of buildings that suddenly seemed enormous to the men of the 184th. These were constructed, as they discovered later, of thick reinforced concrete, steel plates, coconut logs, and several feet of sand over all. The blockhouses and shelters had remained virtually intact in spite of the rain of explosives.

Company B's First Platoon faced the blockhouse. The platoon had come up to this point without supporting weapons, which meant they had nothing larger than a Browning Automatic Rifle in hand. First Lieutenant Harold Klatt, commander of the platoon, waited for a heavy gun to come up. When a 37mm antitank gun arrived he sent it to fire against the blockhouse, but the light gun had absolutely no effect. Lieutenant Klatt decided to leave the stronghold for the tanks and demolition men to deal with and ordered his men to move around the obstruction. As they did so they broke into small groups. The Japanese, seeing that the Americans were going to bypass them, began moving out of the stronghold in an effort to make their way back to another Japanese force. The area erupted in small-arms fire, the Japanese sniping at the Americans and the Americans firing back. Tanks came up and stopped before the blockhouse, but they did not fire on it. There was no one at the point to tell them what was needed. Lieutenant Klatt's platoon was out of communication with the command post and in essence had been reduced to a group of individual squads for the moment.

Meanwhile the company's Second Platoon, led by Second Lieutenant Frank Kaplan, moved around the other side of the blockhouse, and when Kaplan encountered fire from a wharf on the beach and forward areas he asked for artillery fire. Soon it began coming in—almost in the midst of the men of First Platoon. Klatt yelled at them and got them to move back behind the blockhouse to reorganize.

All this effort was without progress, and it took an hour. Captain Charles A. White, the Company B commander, came up to see why the platoons were not moving. He had spent the last hour fielding questions from the battalion command post about the slow progress. He organized a two-platoon attack led by tanks, but this attack bogged down because the tanks could not communicate with the infantry except by opening their hatches, and all this wasted more time. The blockhouse continued to slow the troops. There were many Japanese inside, and satchel charges seemed to have no more effect on the fortification than the 37mm gun had earlier. So the advance stalled again.

Two men of the First Platoon kept on going, however. Sergeant Melvin Higgins and Private Arthur Contreras moved far ahead of their companions and dropped into a shellhole near two Japanese buildings. They radioed that they needed explosives to assault the buildings, and the company's executive officer came up with some blocks of Composition C. They made charges by putting the explosive into gas-mask carriers. Higgins and Contreras then ran forward and delivered the charges to one of the buildings. They heard the roar of the explosions, but nothing happened. They saw two Japanese machine guns near one building and directed a tank to them. The tank moved forward, and a white flag came up, but the tank began firing on the guns. Higgins moved up and found a dozen Japanese in a camouflaged ditch behind the guns. All of them were dead. Whether they really meant to surrender or were only trying to trick the Americans no one would ever know.

As Higgins and Contreras moved against the shelter, so had two other small groups. Staff Sergeant Roland Harti and Private First Class Solteros Valenzuela came up from the First Platoon, and a patrol of ten men came from the Second Platoon. Harti and Valenzuela approached the shelter, and Harti tossed a grenade in the door. They sprinted back into the brush then and waited. Just as the grenade exploded, Private First Class Harold Pratt of the Second Platoon came up from the other side and threw a satchel charge in the door, then ducked back to the patrol. The charge exploded and routed a stream of Japanese, who came out screaming, firing rifles, and hurling grenades at the shell holes twenty yards away where the Second Platoon's patrol was hiding. With the noise, Sergeant Harti and Valenzuela jumped and dove for the shell craters to join their fellow soldiers. The firefight lasted ten minutes with guns popping and grenades flying in both directions. A Japanese machine gun opened up from somewhere behind the shelter. Other Japanese suddenly surfaced from under wreckage and behind trees. At the end of the ten minutes the Americans had killed all the Japanese who had come from the shelter, but the leader of the Second Platoon patrol, Sergeant Warren Kannely, had been killed, and so had two of his men. Several others were wounded, including Valenzuela. The incident seemed to have stirred up a hornet's nest. Japanese kept appearing in all directions and firing on the patrols. Pratt crawled back to find Captain White, who sent two tanks to help. The tanks soon dislodged or killed all the Japanese in the immediate area, but the advance had been thoroughly stalled by this time and the casualties had been high. The Second Platoon's ten-man patrol had only two men left on their feet.

Company A, working to the right of Company B, moved into the navy headquarters area and came up against several blockhouses and shelters that had not been destroyed by the artillery. There was no way to go except through the area, for Company B was on the left and the Thirty-second Regimental Combat Team was on the right. Without strong weapons support the company could not go forward either. So by 11:30 the 184th drive was bogged down. A new plan was made, and by 1:30 that afternoon the troops were ready to move again. This time the 184th would begin at the middle of the island and push the defenders toward the lagoon, stopping at the point (Noel Road) where the island suddenly narrowed. The Thirty-second would drive straight along to the end of the island. Thus, the 184th would clear out the whole navy area, which seemed to be so heavily defended, while the Thirty-second finished the capture of the tip of the island.

In operation it was a different story. The 184th became thoroughly confused and the companies did not coordinate their attacks. The result was a string of small actions, with patrols and squads routing out small knots of Japanese. It was slow going, and an hour before dark it was apparent that General Corlett's call for capture of the island was not going to be delayed just a few hours, but another day. To a lesser extent the Thirty-second faced the same difficulties, and as darkness settled on Kwajalein the American troops stopped and dug in along a ragged line three-quarters of the way to the end.

The night of February 3 was an eerie one for the men of the Seventh Division. They had bypassed scores of Japanese during the day, and so the troops were intermingled. The officers could not call for artillery fire on Japanese positions, for the shells were likely to fall in American positions. Wherever a light shone the Japanese opened fire with rifles and mortars and grenades. Japanese prowled all night long in various areas. On the Thirty-second's front a group of Japanese staged a banzai charge. On the 184th's front, the Japanese charged five different times; each of these was broken up by the rifle companies and supporting artillery fire, but at 4:00 in the morning a group attacked again. More attempts were made by the enemy to infiltrate the lines. The last Japanese attack was staged at 5:30 a.m. by about forty Japanese against the line of Company E of the 184th Infantry. The machine guns began firing and the attack stopped. As the light grew bright, the men of Company E counted thirty Japanese dead in front of their position.

Offshore, Admiral Turner's commanders were growing restless at the delay. The fast carriers departed for Majuro to refuel, leaving a handful of escort carriers to support the troops. Most of the transports were unloaded. The garrison was landing, and garrison troops undertook the general defense of half the island. Everyone, it seemed, was waiting impatiently for the army to finish its job.

As the morning of February 4 dawned, the army troops still had to take a stretch of land 1,000 yards long and 400 yards wide, containing the ruins of about thirty buildings and a few strong points amid groves of trees. It seemed a straightforward task, given the strength of troops, the guns, and the tanks. But General Corlett did not know how ragged the American line had become on February 3. Before the Americans could make a controlled advance, they had to clear out the Japanese who had been bypassed and threatened their lines of communication. This need became apparent when the Thirty-second's First Battalion was moved forward to pass through the lines of the Third Battalion and carry the assault. As the troops came up in the darkness to take position, they passed a Japanese shelter and could hear the enemy soldiers talking inside. The column marched right by the shelter, and as the last men appeared, out charged four Japanese, screaming and hurling grenades. A Japanese officer came up swinging a *samurai* sword and threw a grenade from 30 feet away. The Americans could see the sparks as it sailed toward them. They scattered, but the explosion wounded two men. These Japanese were all killed but they had shown what the Americans would face all morning.

When the attack was launched, it started as raggedly as might be expected. The troops could not move forward without stopping to clear out Japanese positions, and each one took time. At 10:00 the First Battalion began to reach positions it was supposed to have made by 7:00. In the 184th sector the confusion was even greater. One company was still following the battle plan of the day before, and thus stalled the company that was supposed to come through and take over the assault. All along the line it was a case of advancing from one pillbox to the next, flushing the Japanese, and moving on. From one large shelter, they captured thirty-one Korean laborers and one Japanese. Using loudspeakers and captured prisoners, the troops began trying to talk the Japanese into surrender; Nisei interpreters managed to persuade ninety to surrender to the 184th.

On the south, the Thirty-second moved slowly, even more slowly than the 184th, since it had greater distance to cover. By noon the First Battalion had bogged down, and the Second Battalion passed through at 1:45 to take up the battle. Again it was a case of slow motion, from one pillbox to the next, using grenades, tanks, satchel charges, and flamethrowers to rout out the enemy. At 3:15 the first Platoon of Company G reached Nero Point, the end of the island, and the men sat down on the beach for a smoke. But on the other side, the Third Platoon was still encountering enemy resistance, especially from three long concrete shelters placed side by side. Staff Sergeant Raymond Borucki led the attack with satchel charges. He was planning then to bypass the shelters, but Private Elmer Collins and Private First Class Franklin Farr crawled into one shelter and found a number of live Japanese inside. They backed out in a hurry, firing as they went, and threw in grenades. The Americans stopped then and cleared out the shelters. It took half an hour for each one.

All the way, the troops faced stubborn Japanese resistance. At 5:00 in the afternoon the fighting still continued. Captain Albert Pence of Company G, walking over to talk to Captain Mark Barber of Company F, was shot down by a sniper just then, and the advance was stopped until tanks came up twenty minutes later to drive the last of the enemy out of hiding.

At his command post, General Corlett was so eager and so chagrined at the slowness of progress that at 4:10 he had already announced the end of organized resistance. The troops were just mopping up, he said. It was true in a sense. "Organized resistance" had never really materialized on the island. From the beginning it had been almost a question of mopping up, but that term, when applied to the Japanese defenders in the Pacific theater, was almost meaningless. As they had shown at Tarawa, and again on Kwajalein, they could and would exact a price in blood for every foot of ground gained. On this last day on Kwajalein the army casualties were higher than on any other day: sixty-five soldiers were dead and 252 wounded. It was a high price, but there was no escaping it if the island was to be taken. And on this last day as the Americans moved forward they were assailed by the stench of rotting bodies in this strongly defended area. The smell was a reminder of the efficacy of the naval bombardment. Had it not been for the extreme care taken in the preliminaries, it was obvious that the price of victory would have been far higher than it turned out to be.

There was other action, not nearly so heralded, in the capture of Kwajalein atoll. Most important was the assault on Ebeye island, undertaken by the Seventeenth Infantry on February 3. It took two days and cost the regiment eighty-nine casualties. About 500 Japanese troops were killed and seven were captured. The Army men captured Loi island, where about forty natives joyfully submitted to capture, and a small unnamed islet below it where twenty Japanese and Korean sailors had to be manhandled. The troops worked up and down the circular chain of the atoll, making sure that all the Japanese on every bit of sand or land were killed or captured. On February 6 the last shot was fired, and Kwajalein atoll was entirely in American hands. In the south, the battle had been fought bravely by 5,000 Japanese defenders who knew from the outset that they had no chance of victory and almost no chance of survival. In fact, seventy-nine Japanese did survive as captives, and that was all.

7
ENIWETOK

The Americans also wanted Eniwetok atoll, for it had the second-largest lagoon in the Marshall Islands and Admiral Nimitz knew it would be necessary to give shelter to all the ships he intended to send westward in the drive against the Japanese inner empire. Nimitz has expected to regroup after the capture of Kwajalein and then consider Eniwetok. That reasoning indicated the big problem of Pacific command in the winter of 1944: still a shortage of the ships. The Joint Chiefs of Staff had authorized General MacArthur to invade Kavieng in the Bismarcks, about 500 miles northeast of New Guinea. The fast carriers would have to be sent off to support this operation, and so would many of the escort carriers and the ships of Admiral Turner's amphibious force. They could not be in two places at one time, and there were not enough to stage two invasions simultaneously.

But the Kaveing operation was not scheduled for several weeks, and the capture of the Marshalls was well ahead of schedule. Just before Admiral Spruance had left Pearl Harbor, he had suggested to Admiral Nimitz that it would be possible, if they moved quickly, to take Eniwetok on the heels of Kwajalein. On February 2, with Majuro captured, the idea became a reality. The fighting at Roi-Namur and Kwajalein indicated that the 8,000 reserve troops who had been brought along would not be needed, and the amphibious tractors which were in such short supply had done their jobs and were available. So there was no reason to wait on Eniwetok. Rear Admiral Harry Hill was flown in from Majuro to confer with Admiral Spruance and Admiral Turner. That done, Admiral Hill went back to his own flagship, the *Cambria*, and began planning with brigadier General T.E. Watson of the marines, who would take charge of the invasion as soon as the troops landed. This change was precisely what the marines had always wanted. Holland Smith had been grumbling since the Gilberts about Admiral Turner's insistence on keeping command until the beachhead was "established." So the hurried planning was carried out in an atmosphere of great good will.

The Eniwetok invasion offered several specific problems. First was the need to neutralize enemy air power. After the Kwajalein invasion, the Americans could expect a reaction from the Japanese, who would have been building their resources in the south and to the north. The big problem was Truk, the major Japanese base 670 miles southwest of Eniwetok. The journalists called it the Gibraltar of the Pacific. Admiral Nimitz had a more earthy description—the Japanese *cojones*. Both epithets suggested the real respect in which the Americans held the fortress base, largely because they knew so little about it. The Japanese had fortified Truk years earlier, that much was known. But as with all the mandated islands under Japanese control, specific military information was hard to come by. Eniwetok, for example, was very much an unknown quantity. A secret Japanese chart of the atoll had been found aboard an abandoned tug on Gehh island, but it did not show any defenses. About Truk they knew even less, except that the Japanese fleet was housed there when in the south, and that its air forces were formidable. The air forces were what concerned Admirals Hill, Turner, and Spruance. Of course they were not unmindful of the Japanese fleet, still based at Truk. Altogether it was clear that an air strike was in order.

As for Eniwetok itself, Admiral Hill at first anticipated little trouble. His best sources indicated the presence of only about 700 Japanese among the thirty-odd islets of the atoll.   But at

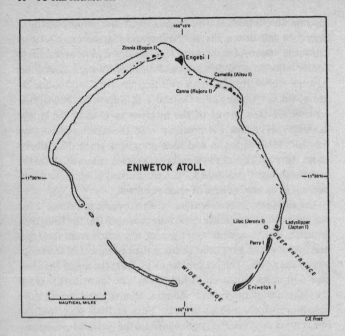

Kwajalein the army captured documents that indicated the presence on Eniwetok of the First Amphibious Brigade. The troop estimate was raised to 4,000. Original photographs, taken before the Kwajalein invasion, indicated that only the main island of Engebi was fortified, but photos taken during the invasion indicated that fortifications had been extended to Parry and Eniwetok islands in the southern part of the atoll. Even so, the Engebi invasion was to be a much less formidable and less spectacular show than either assault in Kwajalein. Admiral Oldendorf's fire support group of three battleships and three heavy cruisers and seven destroyers was retained. Hill would rely more heavily on carriers; Rear Admiral Samuel Ginder's task group of three carriers (*Saratoga*, *Princeton*, and *Langley*) would be buttressed by three escort carriers.

Since the Eniwetok invasion had not been contemplated for so early a date during the Marshalls planning, no troops had been especially trained for the task. The major units were the 106th Army Infantry, commanded by Colonel Russell Ayers, and the Twenty-second Regimental Combat Team, commanded by Colonel John T. Walker. The 106th was a part of the Twenty-seventh Division and it had not participated in the Gilberts invasion. The 106th was supposed to have invaded Nauru at that time, but the Nauru operation was called off, and so was the 106th's amphibious training. The Twenty-second Marines had been stationed in Samoa since 1942, and their training in the new methods of warfare was also extremely limited. Most of them had never seen an amphibious tractor.

After several misfires, the date of the invasion was set for February 17. Already Admiral Sherman's carriers had hit Engebi hard during the invasion of Kwajalein, destroying all the planes present on the airstrip that day. Admiral Ginder's carriers stood off Eniwetok on February 3, and for four days the bombers and fighters worked over the atoll. They returned to Roi on February 7 to refuel and rearm, but went back to strike twice more between February 11 and 13. Everyone in the Central Pacific was conscious of the need to suppress Japanese air activity, particularly after February 12. On that day the Japanese struck back at the Marshalls; six big Kawanishi flying boats from Saipan bombed the Roi airfield at 2:30 in the morning. The Japanese airmen were probably as surprised as anyone when the whole center of the island seemed to explode. They had hit the one huge dump into which the overconfident Americans had put all the supplies for the island garrison, and the explosions and fires destroyed 80 percent of the material. For two weeks the defenders of Roi lived on emergency rations, until shipments could be brought from Pearl Harbor.

Mindful of this destruction, Admiral Hill made doubly sure that Admiral Mitscher was going to carry out that air strike on Truk before the Eniwetok invasion reached a critical stage.

The carrier men were as eager to strike Truk as they had ever been on any operation, particularly after air reconnaissance showed the presence there of major elements of the Japanese Combined Fleet: battleships, carriers, cruisers, many destroyers, and submarines, as well as dozens of merchant ships. They also knew from various photographs that the six major islands of Truk atoll were alive with airplanes.

The day after the bombing of Roi the fast carrier task force was at sea heading for Truk. Admiral Mitscher had with him nine of his carriers (three were held back to cover Eniwetok) and the fast battleships and cruisers that would protect the carriers from surface enemies and could also attack the Japanese fleet if the opportunity came.

Before dawn on February 17 the Americans struck. More than seventy fighter planes appeared at sunup over the Japanese airfields. Zeros and other Japanese fighters came up to meet them, but about thirty of these were shot down while the Americans lost only four. The enormous superiority of the F6F Hellcat was already showing. Some of the American fighters were assigned to strafe the airfields and they destroyed more planes on the ground. As they returned to their carriers, bombers loaded with fragmentation bombs and incendiaries arrived to smash the airfields and plane-storage areas. The strike was totally effective. Later the Americans estimated that there had been 365 Japanese aircraft on the fields of Truk atoll and that they had destroyed all but 100 of them.

To temper the airmen's elation, however, came one big disappointment. With the capture of the Gilberts in November, Admiral Koga had grown nervous about having the Combined Fleet so far south and so close to the enemy. When it became apparent on February 3 that the Marshalls were also lost, he gave the order to the fleet: Truk was to be abandoned and the ships were to sail 1,000 miles west to the Palaus and base there. So when Admiral Mitscher's carrier planes arrived over Truk the fleet was gone and only a handful of destroyers, a number of service ships, and two auxiliary cruisers (converted merchant ships) remained in the harbors.

Still, there were enough ships to provide many targets. The carriers sent their bombers, loaded with torpedoes and bombs, to strike the ships all day long. In two days they flew 1,250 sorties and dropped 400 tons of bombs on ships and 94 tons on airfields and shore installations. Altogether they wrecked 200,000 tons of Japanese shipping, including a destroyer, the two auxiliary cruisers, and half a dozen tankers, which were probably the most valuable ships in the harbor as far as Japan's needs were concerned.

The Japanese did strike back on the first night. Here at Truk they had some planes equipped with radar. One of these got through to the carrier *Intrepid* and torpedoed her. The *Intrepid* did not sink, but eleven men were killed and seventeen wounded, and the carrier was out of action for the next six months.

While the carriers struck the harbors and airfields, Admiral Spruance, who had come along in charge of the whole operation, led the surface ships on a run around the islands, hoping to catch some warships as they escaped. With him were the new battleships *New Jersey* and *Iowa*, the heavy cruisers *Minneapolis* and *New Orleans*, and the destroyers *Izard, Burns, Bradford,* and *Charrette.*

They found a prize: the Japanese light cruiser *Katori* and destroyers *Maikaze* and *Nowake* had escaped the confined waters of the atoll and were steaming away. They were spotted first by carrier planes and attacked by them, but the surface ships took over. One could scarcely call it a battle, two battleships and two heavy cruisers against a light cruiser. Admiral Spruance ordered the *Minneapolis*, the *New Orleans*, and two destroyers to sink the light cruiser. As they came up she was already badly hurt by the bombs of the carrier planes; they finished her off in about fifteen minutes. The Japanese crew of the *Katori* fought valiantly, manning the guns as long as they were above water and launching all her torpedoes. Even as she rolled over and sank, her 5-inch guns aft were still firing.

The two American battleships and two destroyers went after the destroyer *Maikaze*, but she seemed almost indestructible. The shells hit time and again, yet she remained floating and her guns fired back. She launched a spread of torpedoes, and they were well aimed, but a carrier plane warned the American ships of their approach and they managed to avoid them.

The *Maikaze* went down at 1:41 in the afternoon, and that was almost the end of the surface action. The Americans had spent so much of their superior firepower concentrating on these two ships that the destroyer *Nowake* managed to escape and was 20 miles away before the battleships discovered it. They began firing, but the distance was too great, and the *Nowake* got away to tell the tale of the unequal struggle off Truk. After that battle, for the first time during the war, Radio Tokyo raised the specter of possible Japanese defeat in the war. "The attacking force is already pressing upon our mainland," said one broadcast. It was a big change from the jingoism that had dominated the Japanese government's public statements for a dozen years as the Japanese people were fed the propaganda from the cradle up that the gods had ordained Japan's rulership of "the eight corners of the earth."

At Eniwetok, Major General Yoshima Nishida was preparing for the attack he knew must come. The defeat at Kwajalein and the subsequent heavy bombing of his own atoll left no doubt in his mind that the Americans were moving against Eniwetok. General Nishida had very little with which to work. In the first place, he had arrived only on January 4, with about 3,000 troops assigned to the Eniwetok defenses. Another hundred defenders had come in to augment the small garrison from the airfields of the eastern Marshalls. After the first series of air attacks in January the Japanese high command had ordered all pilots and aircrews whose planes had been destroyed to move to rear areas. The Japanese were well aware that one of the reasons for their growing inferiority in the air was the quality of their pilots; since the disaster at Midway in which four carriers had been sunk and all their planes lost, the Japanese naval air service had never recovered. Pilots were regarded as a precious resource, but these hundred men were unlucky enough to be trapped on Eniwetok and they would have to die here.

Having studied the American amphibious technique, General Nishida knew what to expect. He built his defensive positions on the lagoon side of the islands, knowing that the Americans preferred to come in this way. He had no reinforced concrete or steel framework and plating for defense, but his men were put to work building trenches and dugouts protected by coconut logs. They had enough cement to build thick concrete pillboxes.

General Nishida also knew it was the American plan at Kwajalein to first attack the outlying islands and then use them as a base for artillery to prepare for the attack on the major defenses. So he put more troops on little Parry island, north of Eniwetok, than anyone had expected. The strongest defenses were constructed at Engebi, which held the airfield. And although he could not build little fortresses as he would have liked, he could make use of camouflage, at which the Japanese were expert. The American ships and the American bombers would have to find the defensive positions before they could destroy them. For the Japanese to have so much accurate information about the American attack, given the paucity of their communications, was quite remarkable. Not that it would help much, for the only coastal-defense guns were a pair of 4.7-inch British antiquities mounted on the northern tip of Engebi. The general had some antitank mines, which were placed in strategic positions. He had some beach mines, but neither the trained manpower nor the time to establish underwater defenses. Otherwise the troops were equipped with standard infantry weapons, machine guns and mortars, and the immutable demand that they die gloriously for their Emperor.

On February 15, Admiral Hill's Eniwetok Expeditionary Group sailed from Kwajalein lagoon. The force had been slightly changed: Admiral Oldendorf's fire support force consisted of the old battleships *Pennsylvania, Colorado,* and *Tennessee* and the heavy cruisers *Indianapolis, Portland,* and *Louisville,* with fifteen destroyers.

On February 17 the force approached Eniwetok and moved around southeast to the channel known as Deep Entrance, which runs between Japtan and Parry islands. Oldendorf's big ships opened fire on Eniwetok and Parry, but the Japanese gave no sign of life. General Nishida had issued strict orders that no man was to give the enemy the slightest indication of the troop disposition. General Nishida remained in his headquarters on Parry island, waiting. Meeting no opposition, the naval force brought in the minesweepers, and they worked over Deep Entrance and Wide Passage on the southwest side of Eniwetok island. The sweeping effort was rewarded: for the first time in the Central Pacific campaign the sweepers discovered a mine field inside Wide Passage. They were two hours in clearing a channel for the big ships. Then the *Tennessee* went through and the transports, loaded with 8,000 troops, followed. Already the invasion was two hours off schedule. Matters grew worse. One submarine chaser was assigned to guide the convoy to little Aitsu island, where the marine artillery would land. The ship's captain took station off the wrong island, the marine artillery got mixed up, and three more hours were lost.

Aboard the *Cambria,* tempers were short. Colonel Ayers, commander of the 106th Infantry, asked Admiral Hill if he could not land his own artillery on one of the small islands. That was army procedure, and (although he did not say it) the colonel would obviously be more comfortable under army guns than navy and marine. Admiral Hill had rejected the request on the basis that it would occupy most of another day and stall the invasion. And now the navy and marines had fouled up and lost most of the day already. It made Colonel Ayers more unhappy. Admiral Hill was unhappy because he realized he could not look very competent in the eyes of Admirals Turner and Spruance at this moment, and this was his first independent operation. As Hill considered the confusion he grew so angry that he relieved the captain of the subchaser. General Watson relieved his artillery commander. Admiral Hill sent a hot message of criticism to Captain D.W. Loomis, an officer with far more experience in amphibious landings than his critic.

Actually the fits of temper aboard the *Cambria* were unnecessary; the first day's objectives were met anyhow, since the Japanese refused to be tempted forth to fight just then. The marine and army guns were landed safely on Aitsu and Rujoru islets, and they fired their sighting rounds before dark.

Next morning the American troops would invade Engebi island, where they expected to find stout resistance. Actually their intelligence was sadly in error. The total garrison of Engebi consisted of about 1,250 men under Colonel Toshio Yano. The weapons at his disposal were two flamethrowers, thirteen grenade launchers, twelve light machine guns, four heavy machine guns,

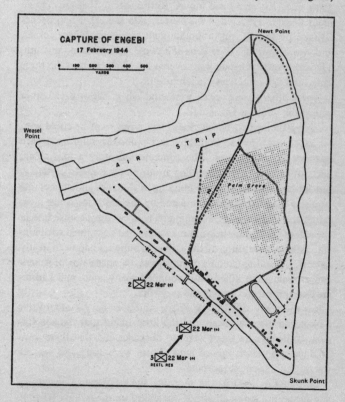

CAPTURE OF ENGEBI
17 February 1944

twelve mortars, six field guns ranging from 20mm to 12cm, and three light tanks. It was not much of a defense, but whatever there was, Yano was certainly competent to make the best use of it. A week earlier he had written a situation report predicting the manner in which the Americans would come. They would bombard Engebi, and bring up heavy ships to fire on the island. After the naval bombardment would come the landings, and they would be on the lagoon side.

Colonel Yano's defense, then, would concentrate on the lagoon side. His men were moved to this shore. Half the detachment was concentrated in the center, with the beach approaches flanked by two 75mm mountain guns on the northwest corner, and two 20mm rapid-fire guns and two 37mm guns on the south. The front on the beach was covered by 37mm guns in the three tanks and light and heavy machine guns.

Three other strong points were established, one on each corner of Engebi, which is triangular.

Along the lagoon beach, Yano had done what he could with his resources. He had built concrete pillboxes, reinforced with coconut-log embrasures. The concrete was only a foot thick, and not capable of withstanding armor-piercing shells, certainly, but he had commanded the building of trenches and connecting tunnels. His efforts were hampered by the condition of the men. After the Japanese high command re-drew the defense line in the fall of 1943, supplies and medicines had continued to diminish. After the capture of the Gilberts, supplies had been nearly cut off. To add to Colonel Yano's woes, the succession of American air raids had killed and wounded many men, and had increased the tension among the survivors.

On the night of February 17 the American navy's underwater demolition men swam around the little island that flanked Engebi, to make sure there were no obstacles and that there were no Japanese on the bits of land. There were none. All was set for the landings next morning.

Just before 7:00 in the morning the navy guns opened up, and an hour later an air strike was staged on the island. When it ended the guns resumed firing, joined by the artillery from the shores of the two little islands. At 9:30 the landings began.

The troops who came ashore at Engebi were the marines of the Twenty-second's First and Second Battalions, led by LCIs firing guns and rockets to discourage the defenders. Those defenders could scarcely be discouraged more than they were already. They had been left alone to die, and their commander had made that quite clear. In the past few days their numbers had been reduced by a third through the bombings, and of the 800 men who remained on their feet, half were scarcely fit for action. All that sustained them was the discipline of the Japanese military and their ingrained acceptance of the need to die fighting.

The marines landed easily. The worst loss occurred when a tank-carrying LCM (Landing Craft, Mechanized) lowered its bow ramp too soon, the craft filled with water, and the LCM and its tank sank in 40 feet of water. The tank crew had "buttoned up"—they had the hatches all locked—and apparently none of the crew heard the frantic shouting of the LCM crew. Only one tank man got out before the sinking.

On the beach itself, opposition seemed very light. A few guns began firing from "Skunk Point," on the southeast corner of the island, but that was all. On the left the Second Battalion moved swiftly, bypassing the pillboxes, leaving them for later cleanup. They overran the airfield in less than an hour. Tanks moved up to the northern part of the island. Half an hour later the Third Battalion was landed and given the onerous task of flushing the Japanese from the bypassed defenses. These consisted of "spiderweb" fortifications, trenches fanning out from a central pillbox. The simple concrete was no match for 75mm guns, satchel charges, and flamethrowers.

There was one area of strong resistance—the southeast corner of the island. The Japanese here put up stubborn fights, retreated along the northeast shore a little, and stopped to fight again. The marine advance was hampered by the dense growth of underbrush, but on all sides the marines kept moving, and by 3:00 in the afternoon, they reported the island secure.

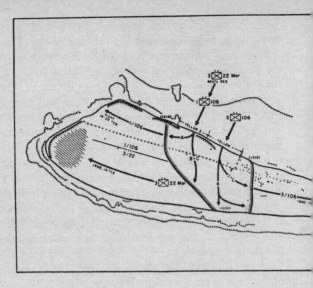

The Americans had expected Engebi to be the difficult operation, and the plan called for capture of Parry and Eniwetok islands on the day after Engebi was secured. But when the troops searched the papers on Engebi, they learned that the garrisons of the other two islands were stronger than they expected. Several natives confirmed this finding, although none of them were quite sure of the actual numbers involved.

This intelligence caused Admiral Hill to change the plan. The army's 106th Infantry would attack Eniwetok as planned, but the invasion would take more troops, so marine tanks and the marine regiment's Third Battalion would support the 106th's three battalions.

The rapid change of plan did not percolate entirely through the system. Admiral Hill and General Watson obviously felt that Eniwetok was going to be difficult, since three battalions were to be landed instead of two. But the bombardment of Eniwetok had been set up to be lighter than that of Engebi or Parry,

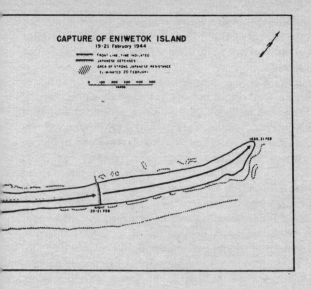

CAPTURE OF ENIWETOK ISLAND
19-21 February 1944

and that part of the plan remained. The bombardment was carried out followed by an air strike, and then the troops landed. Lieutenant Colonel Harold Mizony's Third Battalion was to land on the northwest side of the island, which was the widest area. Mizony would then move to his right down to the southwest corner, and control half the island. Lieutenant Colonel Winslow Cornett, commander of the First Battalion, would land to the left of the Third Battalion and turn left, driving to the northeast end of the island.

The troops reached the beach shortly after 9:00—and ran into trouble. The island rose sharply up just in back of the beach, and the amphibious tanks could not manage the slope. They dropped back and began to clutter the beaches. The Japanese opened fire, and the troops dropped behind the LVTs for protection. Behind them the following troops began to back up, and then to come around the stalled area, which put them out of their assigned positions. The ease of the landing at Engebi had not prepared the invaders for the fierceness of beach opposition here. As at Tarawa, the defenders of Eniwetok had established fields of fire from well-concealed positions on high ground behind the beaches.

Company B on the east side of the beach ran into difficulty when it came up against one of the spiderweb fortifications its men knew nothing about. This web was made up of a network of firing pits and radiating trenches, linked by underground tunnels and all artfully concealed by camouflage made of vegetation. As the troops moved inland the Japanese attacked from one flank, then scurried underground and attacked from the other. Second Lieutenant Ralph Hills and Private First Class William Hollowiak were caught within the center of the strong point. They lay prone and shot at the Japanese as they rose up in the firing pits to shoot at the beach. Hollowiak decided this was a slow method. He asked Lieutenant Hills to cover him while he moved forward. He found a hole, fired into it with his M-1, and then threw a grenade. Then he covered Hills while he did the same at the next position. They ran out of ammunition, so Hollowiak picked up a Japanese rifle and searched Japanese bodies for cartridges until he had enough. They searched the American dead for grenades. They kept moving until they had knocked out seven of the positions and neutralized the east side of the spiderweb. After a while other troops came up to help them, and they brought an amphibious tank and a 37mm gun. With these weapons the spiderweb was soon clear of spiders. Lieutenant Hills pushed across the island to the other side.

One of the most difficult landings was made by First Lieutenant Robert Bates' Company C. When the company came in on the sixth wave of landing craft, the beach was badly congested because of the backup of the tracked vehicles, so four boatloads landed west of their assigned area, and three of them came under heavy fire for the last 150 yards. The enemy had mounted machine guns on jutting points on both sides of their landing place, so the crossfire was intense. The Japanese also had mortars zeroed in on the beach, and when the Americans hid behind their boats the mortars began firing. There were fifty-three men in those three boats; twenty were killed and fifteen were wounded. The other eighteen were saved by the advance of Company A along the lagoon shore, when that company flushed out the Japanese from the side and rear. This Japanese defense was more reminiscent of Tarawa than any action yet in the Marshalls.

By noon the front line of the 106th's First Battalion wove like an S from the lagoon beach to the ocean side of the island. On the lagoon side, the men of Company A were facing a series of spiderweb defenses, each of which must be flushed out in a wearying process. On the ocean side, Company B and part of Company K had captured a Japanese position and were digging themselves in. Along the S line were elements of Company C and Company B and Company K, intermingled with two 75mm guns. The Japanese suddenly counterattacked with a force of 400 men. The first indication, just after noon, was an intense mortar barage laid down in the center of the line. It was followed by troops firing and moving up. The Japanese charge actually broke the American line in several places, but the machine gunners held their positions and swept the field with fire, killing the enemy who had broken through. The machine gunners continued to hold, and finally stopped the advance. The Japanese diverted their assault to the left side of the line, hoping to flank the Americans. They came up against parts of K Company and B Company. The machine gunners and riflemen were engaged in hand-to-hand combat for a few minutes, some of them using knives and grenades. They held, the Japanese attack lost its force, and the firing stopped.

The Americans then continued the move west, and as they went they discovered that they had landed and penetrated at the beginning into the heart of the Japanese defenses. General Nishida had expected the Americans to land at the broad west end of the island, and the defensive positions were emplaced to give best protection to that end. By landing toward the end, but on the side, the Americans had threatened the Japanese positions from the beginning, and that was why the counterattack had come so quickly. What they faced now, as the First Battalion tried to move west, was the center of that line, made up of concrete pillboxes interconnected by trenches and tunnels. The American troops reduced one Japanese position after another but they were making no progress west, and so at 12:45 Colonel Ayers called for his reserves, the Third Battalion of the Twenty-second Marines. Major Clair Shisler brought the marines ashore at 2:25, and made contact on the line at 4:00 in the afternoon. Within the hour, the offense began moving. By 6:30 the marines had driven to the southwest corner of the island, leaving the army troops behind.

As darkness began to lower, this gap became a serious problem, so Colonel Ayers adopted the unusual army tactic of ordering a night offensive. But the army attack was confused, with Company A and Company B failing to reach the marine right flank by 100 yards. At 9:00 that night the Japanese attacked along the gap. They were repulsed, but not before they had succeeded in reaching the marine command post. They killed ten officers and men, including the battalion operations officer, Captain L.M. Clark. Sergeant C.E. Green was shot in the leg and fell. He saw Japanese all around him and played dead until their attention was diverted. Then he got up and mowed down fifteen of them with an automatic rifle. He rallied the remaining men in the area, and they killed seven more Japanese and routed the attack.

The rest of the night was a nightmare for the marines. They had learned how best to cope with Japanese tactics, beginning at Guadalcanal. At night, the marines dug in and remained quiet, never firing their weapons unless there was cause. They knew that unnecessary firing did nothing but give away the positions of the troops. That was obviously how the Japanese had learned of the gap between the lines, for all evening the soldiers had been firing at anything that moved anywhere, including some marines. The soldiers continued their senseless barrage all night long.

When morning finally came, the marines again carried the assault. The major Japanese position was a spiderweb at the southwest corner of the island. The army helped by sending up some tanks and a rifle company, but the marines carried the day, took the position, and cornered fifty Japanese at the end of the island. When the enemy launched a banzai charge, the marines "cut them down like overripe wheat and they lay like tired children with their faces in the sand." The battle for the western half of Eniwetok was over, or almost over. The First Battalion of the 106th still had one small pocket of resistance to overcome on the lagoon side by day's end. But there were so few Japanese in the position that they offered no problem. The marines would not be needed.

On the eastern side of the island, the troops of the 106th made such slow progress that even the riflemen despaired. "If only someone would tell us what to *do*," one soldier cried. But their officers did not know what to do, and so the Third Battalion drive was stalled time and again by tiny pockets of resistance that the marines would have driven straight through. One light tank struck a land mine on the second day and lost a track. The men in the tank buttoned up and sat tight. Riflemen from the battalion came to try to rescue them, but the tankers would not listen to their calls, thinking they were Japanese. The patrol retired. Just before dark, the tank commander was so foolish as to open the hatch and crawl out to inspect the damage. As he hit the ground a crowd of Japanese attacked, and he was wounded. He crawled under the tank and played dead. The Japanese came up and dropped grenades in the turret hatch. Only one man inside survived. The Third Battalion was ordered to advance that night, and at 2:00 in the morning reached the tank. The Japanese used the tank as a pillbox then, and it took hours to drive them off, stalling the whole advance again. Finally, on the third day, the troops of the 106th reached the eastern end of the island, only after the ships had laid down a heavy barrage of fire.

Admiral Hill and General Watson were thoroughly disgusted with the shabby performance of the army troops on Eniwetok, and so, although the marines of the Twenty-second Regimental Combat Team were tired from bailing out the army on Eniwetok, General Watson decided he must use them to attack Parry island rather than depend on the army. Hill had learned also that the intelligence estimates had been as wrong about the defenses of Parry as they had been about Eniwetok island, so the troops got the benefit of a much heavier advance shelling of Parry. The accuracy of the barrage was aided considerably by captured maps which showed the Japanese defense positions in detail. Japanese troops on Parry numbered 1,350, as compared to the 800 on Eniwetok.

The preparations for the Parry landings began on February 20, when marine artillerymen were landed on Japten islet, across the Deep Passage from Parry. For three days they fired against the Japanese positions. The artillery was augmented by fire from the three battleships, two heavy cruisers, and planes from the three escort carriers, *Sangamon, Chenango,* and *Suwannee.* The army's 104th Field Artillery Battalion landed on Eniwetok and joined in.

On the morning of February 21, having made sure the west end of Eniwetok was cleared, the marines of the Third Battalion of the Twenty-second Regimental Combat Team were taken back to the transport *Leonard Wood* for a few hours of rest and the rehabilitation of their weapons before the Parry landing. The troops of the First and Second Battalions of the Twenty-second were brought down from Engebi, where the garrison forces had taken over. The army's Third Battalion of the 106th would be held in reserve, but General Watson was so unsure of them that he organized a battalion of 500 marine riflemen from the Tenth Marine Defense Battalion who would also be in reserve.

Just before the invasion, it was discovered that the planning had been so inaccurate that the expedition was running out of ammunition. This lack was really no one's fault; there was no way the Americans could have known how many Japanese defenders they would meet on these islands. They had made the obvious guess that Engebi would be the major base, and General Nishida had outfoxed them by putting his major defenses where they least expected them. So a hurried call was made to Kwajalein and grenades and percussion caps for demolition charges were flown in.

Parry island is shaped like a raindrop, with the big end on the north. The Japanese had built two major defense works (among eight) on the northwest side of the island. The Twenty-second's

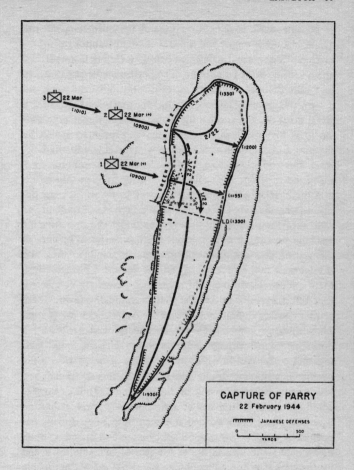

CAPTURE OF PARRY
22 February 1944

JAPANESE DEFENSES

0   500
YARDS

Second Battalion would land near the north end on the west side and drive north to the end of the island. The First Battalion would land south of them and drive to the south end. Their tanks and infantry would cross the island to the ocean side, and cut it in two, thus isolating the five defensive areas in the south. The navy and the artillery would lay down a barrage on the south to prevent reinforcements from coming up until the north end of the island was secure and the troops could turn south.

The barrage opened at dawn on February 22. The troops landed at 9:00 in difficult conditions. The barrage had been so heavy for hours that the island was covered with smoke and haze, and it blew out over the lagoon, blinding the gunners of the cruisers and destroyers. Thus, when the troops came in, three of the leading LCIs that came ahead firing guns and rockets were hit by shellfire, and sixty men were killed or wounded by "friendly fire." When the troops landed some of the landing craft got out of position and the front was widened. Unfortunately, instead of hitting the beaches between the two major northeast Japanese positions, the marines landed in the middle of both of them, so well were they concealed. They came under fire by enfilading machine guns at the water's edge. These guns were soon enough silenced by grenades and shell from the amphibious tanks, and the marines pushed inland. Again the Japanese retreated into their spiderwebs—so many of them, and so artfully connected, that the marines compared Parry to a prairie-dog town. These were the most elaborate spiderwebs the Americans had yet seen. The center of a spiderweb was an underground shelter for a dozen men, lined with coconut logs on the sides and roofed with logs and corrugated iron, covered by sand. Tunnels were made by opening gasoline drums and placing them end to end, and each tunnel led to a foxhole on the perimeter. Thus a Japanese could leave the central shelter and crawl to a foxhole that the Americans had bypassed and not seen because it usually was opened by a hatch cover concealed by a piece of brush. The soldier would stand up and fire at the rear of the Americans, and by the time they turned around he was down again, the foxhole covered, and crawling back to the central shelter to move out into another tunnel. There was only one way to clear the Japanese out: find the central shelter and destroy it, and then find each Japanese who might be in a tunnel or a foxhole and destroy him.

Through their experience on Engebi and Eniwetok islands the marines had developed an efficient tactic of dealing with these defenses. A tank went ahead, firing its 75mm gun and machine guns. Immediately behind this shock force came demolition and flamethrower men, who stopped at each enemy nest and burned or blew it up. The system had worked well on Eniwetok. It worked less well on Parry, for the Japanese had put down land mines, which knocked the tracks off tanks and blew men apart.

Until 11:00 the invasion was supported by naval gunfire on the southern part of the island, but the troops moved swiftly and the gunfire began hitting their positions, so it was stopped. The Japanese resisted firmly; at 1:00 in the afternoon the marines had to call for reinforcements, and marines from the boats came on in to help. At 1:30 the marines reached the north end of Parry and isolated one last enemy position near the pier on the lagoon side. The First Battalion moved southward behind the tanks, and kept slogging, using those same tactics—tank, flamethrowers, demolitions; riflemen taking a position and then moving on to the next, taking casualties, with replacements coming up to carry on as the wounded were carried back to the aid station; and the dead were left, with their rifles stuck in the sand to mark the place for the burial parties.

The marines did not wait for big guns to come up and blast positions, or waste any time. They formed a skirmish line that extended across the island, and like beaters pushing the game ahead of them, they pressed on. Late in the afternoon they came to an area of thick underbrush, where the Japanese had strewn scores of land mines. The marines took heavy casualties, but they did not stop, and the resistance seemed to give them a sense of urgency. They pushed harder and faster until 7:30 that night, when they reached the end of the island and dug in for the night. Next morning they would mop up those Japanese left in their holes in the spiderwebs.

That night destroyers kept the island lighted up with search lights and starshells. The Japanese tried to launch several counter-attacks but were quickly discovered in the light, and group after group was destroyed.

When morning came, the tanks and infantry went over the whole island, looking for little pockets of resistance. They found a few Japanese in their holes, but most of them had either been killed or killed themselves the night before. So by midday the island was quiet, and the marines went back to their ships, leaving the troops of the Third Battalion of the 106th army infantry to take up garrison duties. In the marines' opinion that was about all the army troops were good for, an opinion they were not bashful in expressing after the Eniwetok island invasion. Admiral Hill shared that opinion, and so did many of his officers. Their own errors were forgotten in the success of the Eniwetok assault, but those of the army were not, and the irritation between the army and the naval services was increased when Hill and General Watson expressed their opinions to "Howling Mad" Smith, who already had a very bad impression of the army 106th Regiment's parent division, the Twenty-seventh Infantry Division, and Major General Ralph Smith, the divisional commander.

As far as the American public was concerned, this animosity was scarcely known, nor was it widely broadcast outside Pacific Command Circles. Had the army authorities in Washington been fully aware of the uncertainty of the Twenty-seventh Division they most certainly would have taken action at this point to make changes in command and training that would have prevented the chain of events that was to follow very shortly.

8
CENTRAL PACIFIC
STRATEGY

The spring of 1944 saw the consolidation of American gains in the Central Pacific and the slow but sure capture of various atolls in the Gilberts and Marshalls. Not all these island groups were taken by far; Jaluit, Mili, Wotje, and Maloelap remained Japanese until the end of the war. All of them were occupied by fairly large garrisons. Since the Japanese were cut off from outside assistance, the garrisons were doing no harm to the Allied effort, so they were let alone, and many American lives were saved by not forcing the issue (as well as Japanese lives).

In the south, General MacArthur was definitely relegated to a supporting role. He wanted to strike New Guinea, and after occupying the Dutch section of the island in the north, to leap off from there to recapture the Philippines. In a series of landings between April and August, MacArthur accomplished his first goal, but the eyes of the Joint Chiefs were not focused on the MacArthur operations, as he had hoped. The Joint Chiefs were enormously impressed with the effectiveness of the fast carriers and the speed with which the Central Pacific invasion operations had been accomplished. Further, the MacArthur strategy had called for a three-prong attack. He would drive up from the south. Nimitz would come from the east across the Central Pacific. The

British and the Americans would reopen the Burma road into China, and then drive to Hongkong. But the British in 1944 were totally occupied by the coming invasion of the European continent across the English Channel, and by their commitments in the Mediterranean. MacArthur's operational technique—the army way—was far slower in motion than the marine and navy way. And in the spring of 1944 the Americans had a brand-new weapon, the B-29 Superfortress, which could carry 10,000 pounds of bombs and take them farther than any aircraft in the world. The Americans built bases in western China, but it soon became apparent that the problem of supply of those bases and the distances were so great as to make the use of Hsian and nearby areas of western China less than optimal. A very logical base for the new B-29s would be Saipan in the Marianas, and this was also logically the next invasion point for the Central Pacific forces. By the spring of 1944 Admiral Nimitz and King were certain that they could defeat Japan without the necessity of invading the Japanese home islands. The strategy called for movement into the Marianas, then toward the China coast. They might take Formosa on the way which would give the U.S. an enormous land base for air operations against Japan. But in all this, the Marianas were the next stop. With the coming of the B-29, Admiral King gained a new ally, General H. H. Arnold of the Army Air Forces, and this turned the trick. King could argue cogently that the Marianas represented the perimeter of the Japanese inner empire and that their capture would aid immeasurably in bringing the war to a close.

All this discussion occurred before, during, and after the Marshalls invasion. General MacArthur tried to stop the plan. His chief of staff, Major General Richard K. Sutherland, appeared at the Cairo Conference shortly before the end of 1943 and presented the Joint Chiefs of Staff with the MacArthur plan. MacArthur was to take over; Admiral Nimitz was to assist MacArthur (with MacArthur in charge) to attack Mindanao after the Marshalls. A Central Pacific offensive simply would not work, said General Sutherland.

But the Joint Chiefs of Staff knew General MacArthur very well, and the Central Pacific drive was approved. MacArthur made one last stab in February, but the Marshalls invasion was so successful and so swift that General Sutherland's visit on behalf of his superior was unsuccessful. The JCS, in effect, told MacArthur to shut up and take orders. On March 12 the Joint Chiefs issued a directive, backing the Central Pacific approach to Formosa, Luzon, and China by way of the Marianas, the Carolines, Palau, and Mindanao. That order meant there would be two separate drives, one by Nimitz through the Central Pacific, and one by MacArthur up through the Philippines. Truk, which had been singled out for invasion after the Marshalls, was discarded as a target after the Japanese Combined Fleet moved its headquarters north and west. Nimitz would invade the Marianas, and after that the Palaus, which had become the new Combined Fleet base.

As the Americans planned, so did the Japanese. Admiral Koga, chief of the Combined Fleet, went to Tokyo in February to confer with the Imperial General Staff, and he was there when the bad news came about the Marshalls and Truk. As the general staff considered the fleet it became apparent that the name "Combined Fleet" had become meaningless in view of the ship losses suffered by the Imperial Japanese Navy in recent months. In the battle for Guadalcanal the navy had lost two battleships, one light aircraft carrier, three heavy cruisers, eleven destroyers, and six submarines. There was talk of brave plans to build fifteen light carriers and five heavy carriers and convert the big battleship *Shinano*, one of the largest vessels in the world, to a carrier. But the construction was moving at a snail's pace because of lack of materials. In the months after Guadalcanal, the attrition to warships had been constant. To be sure, the Americans did not escape unscathed; they lost destroyers and cruisers and other vessels. But the Americans were building ships with ever-increasing speed. (After the fall of 1943, shipbuilder Henry A. Kaiser turned out escort carriers in less than ninety days, and in 1944 was turning out escort carriers in just over seventy days from keel-laying to completion.)

Admiral Koga, who had succeeded Admiral Yamamoto as chief operations officer of the Japanese navy after Yamamoto was ambushed by the Americans, knew as well as his predecessor that time was the enemy of Japan. The navy's one chance of influencing the outcome of events was to attack the major elements of the American Pacific Fleet and win a great battle. After that, went the line of reasoning, the Americans would be stopped, and would have to listen to reason, granting Japan an "honorable peace." There was no more talk about winning the war in the private councils of the Imperial General Staff. That sort of verbiage was for the public. Koga offered a program of reorganization which showed the desperate straits of the navy:

1. For all practical purposes the Combined Fleet would cease to exist. The Mobile Fleet would become the main body of the navy.
2. The navy must expend its land-based air forces in the absence of adequate carriers, and make Tinian island in the Marianas the main base for the new force.
3. The navy must also move its fleet headquarters to Saipan, which would become the point beyond which the Americans must not be allowed to pass.

But not even this program could be carried out. The fuel shortage had grown so severe that the Mobile Fleet could not be accommodated at Palau or at Saipan. Tokyo simply could not guarantee the tankers to keep the fleet in oil. So part of the fleet would be kept in the Singapore zone, close to the Dutch East Indies oilfields. Most of the rest of the major units would be retained in Japanese home waters for training. Admiral Koga, in his flagship *Musashi,* would remain at Palau.

This agreement reached, Admiral Koga returned to Palau that month. He prepared a new defensive plan. The zone of inner defense of the Japanese Empire now extended on the east from the Kuriles in the north, down the east of Honshu Island in Japan, to the Nanpo Shoto islands, then the Marianas, and the Carolines, to the west end of New Guinea. Any enemy vessels or invasion groups that passed that line would bring forth the maximum effort of the fleet and the Japanese air arm.

The admiral then drew up plans on paper for the formation of a Third Aircraft Carrier Fleet, in three divisions, each composed of three carriers. It looked very impressive, unless one knew that the third division consisted of two converted tankers (*Zuiho* and *Chitose*) and *Chiyoda*, a converted naval auxiliary ship. Also, while the Japanese navy still did have the big and impressive carriers *Shokaku, Zuikaku,* and *Taiho* (brand new) when Division One began training at Tawi-Tawi at the south end of the Sulu Sea, east of North Borneo, the three carriers had virtually *no* pilots who had taken part in earlier carrier operations. So many pilots had been lost at Midway and in succeeding operations that the supply of trained men was extremely short. Further, because of the need for skilled pilots to oppose the Americans in the South and Central Pacific, carrier pilots had been sacrificed wholesale in the past year. Between November 1943 and April 1944, almost the whole First Carrier Division had been lost in the Rabaul area. The Second Division had been decimated in the preliminaries to the Marshall landings. The pilot force of the Third Division had not been organized until February 1944, and the men had only about three months' training, whereas their predecessors had had nearly a year (as compared to the American system of training for eighteen months or two years before going into combat). The twenty-second Air Squadron, for example, consisted of ten pilots with some experience and thirty students. The squadron lost some planes in the American carrier attack on the Marianas of February 22, but within a matter of weeks the Japanese were building up their air force there once more. Between February and May the navy would fly in 600 new aircraft of the First Air Fleet for the defense of the Marianas. Training was still a problem, but at any given moment the Japanese were ready to put 400 planes in the air.

The navy was vying with the army for aircraft, but Japanese industry was responding very well: by March 1944, 1,700 planes per month were being produced.

All this effort was preparation for the major sea battle Admiral Koga expected and wanted. He developed Z Plan, a strike against the American fleet the moment it entered the Philippine Sea, either from the south, along the New Guinea coast, or the northwest, via Palau or in the Marianas. Pilot recruiting led all branches. Admiral Koga wanted to be prepared to use 500 planes on the carriers, and another 500 on the islands. The Z Plan envisaged the use of island bases as shuttle stations for aircraft. Some planes would take off from the carriers, strike the American enemy, and then land on the islands to refuel. The island planes would do the same, landing on the carriers. Thus the effectiveness of the Japanese air force would be increased by about 50 percent.

The Koga Plan also called for a strong defense force in all the perimeter islands. For years the Japanese had maintained the cream of their military in Manchuria, on guard against Soviet entrance into the war. But the Soviets seemed totally uninterested in Manchuria these days, so the Imperial General Staff agreed that several divisions of troops could be moved to the defense of the Pacific perimeter. This reinforcement began in February. It was expensive in ships and lives, for the American submarines were becoming ever more aggressive and destructive even inside the Japanese perimeter. On February 27, the American submarine *Grayback* encountered a big convoy bringing troops down from Korea to the Marianas. The *Grayback* damaged one big transport but was sunk herself that day. Two days later the *Trout* attacked the convoy and sank one ship that carried 4,000 troops. The Japanese were swift in vengeance—they sank the *Trout* that day—but the loss of the trained soldiers was something not to be remedied.

In March 1944, Admiral Raymond Spruance was at Kwajalein, planning his invasion of the Marianas. He spent part of the month

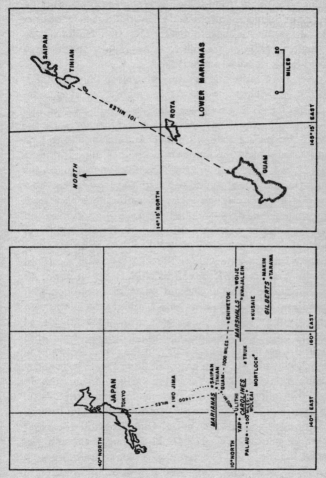

Pacific and Lower Marianas distance charts.

at Majuro and part of it at Pearl Harbor, checking details, conferring with Admiral Nimitz. He interrupted the planning toward the end of the month when General MacArthur asked for a carrier raid on the Palau Islands, to prevent them from reinforcing the Japanese in New Guinea. MacArthur was just then ready to move against Hollandia on that island.

On March 22, Admiral Spruance went along with the carriers and fast battleships on the raid. It was more or less of an excursion for him. True, he was the commander of the Fifth Fleet, but functioning as it was on a raid, the carrier force was not looking for surface action. The ships left Majuro on the 22nd and skirted around the Carolines in order to miss Truk by a margin, and escape sighting by Japanese search planes. The Americans had a tendency to underestimate Japanese watchfulness. On the third day out they were spotted by a plane from Truk, and the next day Admiral Spruance was sure they had been seen. He advanced the day of the raid from April 1 to March 30. As the fleet came toward the Palaus, so did a number of American submarines, and on March 29 the *Tunny* torpedoed the *Musashi,* Admiral Koga's flagship. Next day at dawn, the carrier planes of three of the four American carrier groups hit the Palaus. For the next day and a half the Americans flew hundreds of sorties over these islands, striking the airfields and shooting down all planes they could find. Admiral Koga called for help from neighboring islands, but the planes that came in from Peleliu and Yap were nearly all shot down. The next day Admiral Reeves' group hit Yap and destroyed more precious aircraft. The other American planes continued to strike Palau, and laid traps for the Japanese shipping in the inner harbors. The torpedo bombers sowed mines. Others found the destroyer *Wakatake* and the repair ship *Akashi* and sank them both. On April 1 the carriers hit Woleai in the Carolines. Scarcely a week later they were supporting General MacArthur's move into Hollandia, and knocking out more planes of Admiral Koga's defense force. By that time, however, the losses meant nothing to Koga. He had anticipated the western New Guinea landing and made arrangements to send all available planes there, plus aircraft from Admiral Ozawa's carriers at Singapore. Koga left for Davao on the evening of March 31 to organize the force. Behind him in another plane came Admiral Fukudome, his chief of staff. The Japanese officers of the high command were careful not to travel together, and the proof of the wisdom of that caution had come when the Americans ambushed Admiral Yamamoto the year before. His chief of staff, Admiral Ugaki, had been able to pick up and carry on until Admiral Koga was chosen as successor to the Combined Fleet command.

Admiral Koga was traveling in a two-engined general-purpose bomber, the usual command aircraft for the Japanese. On route, the air convoy ran into a violent storm. Admiral Fukudome's plane made an emergency night landing near Cebu city, and crashed on the beach. Admiral Fukudome was captured by Filipino guerillas and held hostage for several months until he was rescued by Japanese troops. Admiral Koga was killed, presumably by the storm, for the plane was never seen again. Koga had vowed that he would hold the line from the Marianas to Palau to the death, for if that was pierced, he said, Japan was lost. He had kept his vow, and his prediction remained.

9
CENTRAL PACIFIC
REAFFIRMED

The occupation of the Marshall Islands had advanced the American drive through the Central Pacific by months. Coming quickly after the Gilberts victory, it also played an important public role, for these victories plus the Truk strike were announced by a U. S. Navy Department that had suddenly grown public-relations-conscious. General MacArthur was more responsible for this change in Navy policy than any other man. In Washington and from Australia MacArthur lobbied incessantly for his own war plan. Secretary Frank Knox, a newspaper publisher in private life, was finally stung into revamping the navy's press program, and a directive was issued to Nimitz to be more "cooperative" with the press. So the public had access to such close-mouthed commanders as Nimitz himself and Spruance for the first time.

Yet the most important value of the quick successive victories in the Gilberts and Marshalls was its effect on the Japanese. A year earlier they could not envisage a cracking of their defensive line to eliminate Truk as the central point. In less than twelve months this change had come about, so swiftly that the Japanese had to live with the defenses they had constructed in those pre-war years and in the flush of victory in 1942 when "defense" was a word almost unknown.

The decision to strike the Marianas had been made at the meeting between Admiral King and Admiral Nimitz in San Francisco in January. The commander in chief of the navy and his Pacific fleet commander met about every six months—more often if necessary—to make basic decisions about strategy. These decisions, of course, were subject to ratification by the Joint Chiefs of Staff on major issues, but so far the Joint Chiefs had seen the King point of view on most matters. At San Francisco in January, King and Nimitz talked about the Marianas for the late months of 1944 or early 1945, not realizing then that Eniwetok would fall to them long before the May date they had established.

In the spring, with General MacArthur growing more aggressive in Washington to push his own war plan, the Marianas loomed as the last great naval operation in amphibious warfare that would be completely under naval command. King and Nimitz sensed the growing irritation of the army over supplying troops to be commanded by a marine general. As long as the operations continued to be "shock" invasions, the use of marines could be justified. But when they moved to Formosa, as they expected, or the China coast, Nimitz would have to turn over land operations to the army. What he and King intended was to use the marines to land, and then bring in the army generals to work under Nimitz. It was apparent early in 1944 that the system of command was in for change once the Americans were faced with assault on a major land mass.

In March, Admiral King took the Marianas invasion plan to the Joint Chiefs of Staff and announced that the navy was ready to move. He outlined the navy reasons: need for Guam and Saipan to become advance air and naval bases and the strategic consideration that capture of Saipan would leave the Japanese worried and unsure about the next American move. It opened the options of striking the Philippines, Formosa, or Okinawa. King called Nimitz to Washington, and when Nimitz returned to Pearl Harbor at the end of March he ordered Admiral Spruance to begin the official planning. Actually, the work had already begun. Admiral Turner had come up from the Marshalls at the end of the third week of March. He had looked over the maps and decided that Saipan would be their first objective, Tinian the second, and Guam the third. Spruance and Nimitz agreed, and the work began. The date would be June 15.

When Admiral Turner looked at the maps and charts of the Marianas he saw that once again the long period of Japanese mandate over these islands had produced the same difficulties he had faced in the Marshalls. He did not know the condition of the beaches, or the defenses. He was short of information about tides and water depths and natural and man-made obstacles. Some of these deficiencies could be remedied by photoreconnaissance. In April a group of Navy B-24 Liberator bombers at Henderson Field, Guadalcanal, was assigned the task of photographing every inch of the target islands. It meant flying 2,000 miles from their base with a halfway stop at Eniwetok. It was done, and the photographs arrived at Pearl Harbor in plenty of time.

In mid-April, Admiral Nimitz decided a preventive strike was needed against Truk to be sure the Japanese did not build up their air power there before the Marianas invasion. Intelligence reports indicated that the Japanese had been rebuilding their strength, and the reports were correct. Even though no new tactical commander had been appointed to replace Admiral Koga, the staff continued to function in pursuance of his planning.

On April 29, an American Task Force 58 was off the Caroline Islands, and the first strike was launched against Truk. The Japanese put up more than sixty fighters to meet the eighty-four planes the Americans had sent out, but they missed one another in bad weather, so that the initial impact was lost. The American fighters swooped down on the airfields and strafed installations and planes on the ground. The Japanese came back to attack, but again the superiority of the new American fighter planes and the excellence of the longer U. S. pilot training made the difference. The raid lasted two days, and at the end of it only a dozen of those Japanese aircraft were still operational. The American losses in planes were not so heavy—twenty-six in combat and nine operationally. Half the airmen shot down were rescued by planes or by submarines. This factor, too, was important in the increasing vigor of American attacks. The American airmen had grown to expect that even if they were shot down in enemy waters their chances of being picked up by their countrymen were excellent. In this operation, the submarine *Tang* picked up twenty-two airmen who otherwise would have perished in the sea or fallen into Japanese hands.

Having smashed Truk so that it would never again be an important factor in Japanese defenses, the task force turned to Satawan island in the Carolines, and Ponape, the largest of the group. There was nothing very important to the Japanese on either island, but Admiral W. A. Lee, the commander of the battleship force, felt his men needed some target practice. It was a measure of the state of the war in the Pacific that the American ships were using Japanese-held territory for target practice, without fear that the enemy fleet or enemy air force would bother them. The fact was that the Japanese just then were totally occupied in this area by General MacArthur's invasion of central New Guinea.

Admiral Soemu Toyoda, former commander of the Yokosuka naval base in Japan, was chosen early in May to replace Admiral Koga as operational chief of the Japanese fleet. His first move was to lay a major plan for battle. He expected the Americans to try to breach the internal defenses of the empire quite soon. He developed a plan to replace Koga's Z Plan. The Toyoda plan was called A-Go, and it met the instructions of the Imperial General Staff: the navy was to seek a decisive battle in the near future if it could be waged under "favorable" conditions.

The first major change made by Toyoda was the reorganization of the fleet. The effective fleet was now called the Mobile Fleet and was commanded by Vice Admiral Jisaburo Ozawa, whose flagship was the carrier *Taiho*. The Mobile Fleet consisted of the Third Fleet of carriers, and the Second Fleet, made up of battleships and cruisers. Ozawa commanded the Third Fleet and Carrier Division One himself, which meant he directed the activities of the *Taiho, Zuikaku*, and *Shokaku*, the best of the Japanese carriers. Carrier Division Two was led by Rear Admiral

Takaji Joshima. It consisted of the carriers *Junyo, Hiyo* and *Ryuho,* inferior to the bigger ships of Carrier Division One, but still powerful fighting instruments. The third element was Carrier Division Three, under Rear Admiral Sueo Obayashi. His force was the equivalent of an American escort carrier group, more or less; all the ships were converted vessels. Vice Admiral Takeo Kurita in the cruiser *Atago* commanded the Second Fleet, which included the battleships *Yamato, Musashi, Nagato, Kongo* and *Haruna,* and the cruisers *Atago, Takao, Maya, Chokai, Myoko, Haguro, Kumano, Suzuya, Tone,* and *Chikuma.*

It was a considerable force, augmented by light cruisers and several dozen destroyers. Given the plan devised by Admiral Koga, to use the airfields of the Pacific islands as shuttle points for carrier operations, and enough airplanes, that Japanese fleet could be a formidable enemy even to the powerful Fifth United States Fleet with its fast carrier force. It all depended on the Japanese ability to produce aircraft, man them effectively, and bring them to the proper place at the proper time. To do this, Imperial Headquarters moved the navy's First Air Fleet to Tinian and placed it under the direct command of Naval General Headquarters. The change meant the airmen had direct access to Tokyo, which could be all-important in the matter of supply. Vice Admiral Kakuji Kakuta was appointed commander in chief of this force, and he was promised nearly 2,000 aircraft for the bases of the Inner South Seas: Tinian, Guam, Saipan, Rota, Iwo Jima, Yap, and Palau. This force was an addition to Admiral Ozawa's 450 carrier planes, so it was not surprising that the Japanese strategy depended so heavily on the success of the shuttle operation.

But by mid-April, the planning developed kinks. The capture of the Marshalls and the subsequent U. S. move northward in the South Pacific confused the Japanese. Where would the Americans strike next? Admiral Kakuta shifted his planes from the Southern Philippines to the area north of Australia to meet the threat at Hollandia. He shifted them from Biak to Palau when Biak was attacked. He shifted from Halmahera to Tinian and to Saipan to meet the threat he saw against the Marianas. All this shift had to be accomplished by air; the sea lanes were so devastated by American submarines that the shipping of planes was abandoned. The air route was a reasonable alternative, given skilled aircrews. But the fighter and bomber pilots were not skilled as they came out of Japan these days. Even when pilots were sent to the battle fronts, they seldom had more than a few hours of solo flying time behind them, and almost no combat instruction. The result was that although the Japanese were producing fighter and bomber aircraft that were superior to those they had employed in the first three years of the war, fully 80 percent of them were lost before they ever saw military action. Some were shot down by American planes en route to their destinations. More were lost through accident and pilot error.

In April, the carriers were virtually immobile, since the fleet had no commander. In May, when Admiral Toyoda took over, the fleet was stationed at Tawi-Tawi on the northeastern tip of Borneo, so Admiral Ozawa could counter an American threat either to the Palau-Marianas area, or farther south. Fuel was in such short supply that its use governed every activity. In May all training flights were suspended because of lack of fuel, so the green pilots who had expected to learn combat techniques "on the job" were denied the opportunity. Everything had to be saved for the coming "decisive battle."

What was most discouraging to the Japanese was the breadth of the American attack. It was quite enough to contemplate the thousands of American aircraft in the South and Central Pacific. They alone prevented ship and troop movement. It was equally discouraging to see the results of the American submarines, whose numbers seemed to increase every day. For example, late in April, after General MacArthur had landed in the Vogelkop area of Dutch New Guinea, the Japanese army sent an entire convoy south from Shanghai, with troops and supplies to reinforce the Japanese positions in New Guinea. More than a division of troops was involved. The convoy lost one transport to an American submarine off Manila Bay. On

May 6, the convoy ran into the submarine *Gurnard*'s path in the middle of the Celebes Sea. The *Gurnard* sank three more transports. Thousands of soldiers were drowned, and the strength of the division was destroyed before it ever landed in the combat zone.

Were these threats not enough, the Americans in the spring of 1944 were moving so rapidly that the Imperial General Staff had difficulty keeping up with them. Just then, General MacArthur was attacking in New Guinea and pressing the whole area. They struck Aitape, and then Humboldt Bay, and then Tanahmerah Bay. A few weeks later they attacked the Wakde-Sarmi area, 120 miles west of Hollandia. Then they attacked Biak, one of the Schouten Islands across Japten Strait and Geelvink Bay from the Vogelkop. The Japanese had 10,000 troops on that island, but as soon as the Americans and their allies seemed to be successful in the first invasions, Imperial Army Headquarters in Tokyo announced that it intended to abandon the troops on Biak to fight to the last man. That word was communicated throughout the general staff on May 9 (and, of course, not outside it). The navy, in particular, was shocked. This was the largest force yet abandoned to certain destruction.

As the navy planners in Tokyo considered the situation in the south, they decided that the opportunity for the fateful "decisive battle" was offered them in New Guinea. Rear Admiral Daniel Barbey, commander of the U. S. amphibious operations for MacArthur, had borrowed ships from Admiral Turner's amphibious force, and in those three initial landings he put together a fleet of 215 vessels. They were protected by eight escort carriers during the landings on April 22, and for several days the fast carriers and battleships of Task Force 58 roamed these seas. It was reasonable, then, for the Japanese to believe that the American naval force could be drawn into major action off New Guinea.

The invasion of Biak on May 27 triggered the Japanese plan. The navy would fight at Biak. The army quickly reconsidered its abandonment of the Biak garrison and began assembling reinforcements. The navy ordered nearly a hundred planes from

Philippine and Marianas bases down to Sorong, on the northwest coast of New Guinea, where Rear Admiral Yoshioko Ito's Twenty-third Air Flotilla was located. A few days later another seventy-five fighters and bombers were sent from the Carolines. Admiral Toyoda put aside the A-Go operational plan and quickly devised a new plan to meet this new situation. It was called the Kon Plan. The Second Amphibious Brigade of 2,500 troops would be transported from Mindanao in the Philippines to Biak. The transports would be guarded by battleships, destroyers, and cruisers. The reinforced air flotilla would smash the American landing at Biak, the troops would come in to help the Biak garrison drive the American soldiers into the sea, and the battleships and cruisers would destroy Admiral Kinkaid's Seventh Fleet. All these forces were in motion on May 30. The cruisers *Myoku* and *Haguro* went to Davao, and the *Aoba* and the *Kinu* went first to Zamboanga to pick up the laden troop transports and then met the first two cruisers. The force turned south toward Biak.

Then, on June 1, Lieutenant Takehiko Chihaya made a report on an aerial reconnaissance flight he had completed in the teeth of the enemy, without detection. The Americans had built up Majuro in the Marshalls with an enormous number of ships of all sorts. It seemed obvious that a new invasion was just days away.

The Imperial General Staff reeled with the shock. Where was the major action? It could be coming from Biak. It could be Palau. It could be Saipan. With so many U. S. ships in the New Guinea area and so many in the Marshalls, which was the major force?

Aboard Admiral Toyoda's flagship *Oyodo* in Tokyo Bay, the naval staff debated, and the debate degenerated into argument. The truth was that no one knew, and no one had a "feel" for the American strategy except one lone staff intelligence officer, Commander Chikataka Nakajima. He said it would be Saipan. But his fellow staff members scoffed. Even the Americans did not have such power that they could mount an operation the size of the three-pronged New Guinea strike as just a feint, they said. No, Biak was the place. If the Americans consolidated their landings they could build an airfield. From that field they could bomb the Philippines and Palau with their long-range B-24 Liberators. And the American carriers were in evidence off New Guinea. There were no carriers mentioned at Majuro. (The carriers in New Guinea waters were escort carriers, which the Japanese often mistook for the big fleet carriers of Task Force 58. The task force was in Hawaiian waters, taking on supplies and training for the Marianas invasion.) Commander Nakajima must be seeing things. It was either going to be Palau or Biak, and they were about evenly divided on that. Admiral Toyoda decided that Biak was the place, and the Kon operation continued. The enemy fleet would be met here and defeated once and for all.

10
THE GUESSING GAME

While the Japanese reacted to the Biak landings and debated the next course of action, at Pearl Harbor Admiral Spruance was assembling the largest force yet employed in the Pacific. A fleet of 535 ships would be engaged—everything from battleships to tugs—and this did not count the support available at Pearl Harbor and in the Marshalls on short notice. The ships would carry 127,500 men. First they would capture Saipan, and then Tinian, with the Second and Fourth Marine Divisions. The Third Marines and the First Provisional Marine Brigade would attack Guam. The Twenty-seventh Army Division would be held in reserve for Saipan. The Seventy-seventh Army Division would be in reserve for Guam.

In May the Hawaiian Islands were the scene of many mock battles. The troops were given practice in "invading" beaches of the neighbor islands. The carriers and escort carriers sallied forth from Pearl Harbor to carry on mock battles and learn the techniques of supporting troops on the beaches. For many of the men of the escort carrier force this would be the first entry into battle. The same was true of the men of other ships, some of which would sail directly from the United States to join the expeditionary force at sea.

The big battle rehearsal for the Saipan invasion was held between May 14 and May 20, at Maalea Bay on Maui island and Kahoolawe, a deserted island used for bombardment and bombing practice. Admiral Turner's second-in-command, Rear Admiral Harry Hill, was particularly eager to try out a new weapon he had devised. He was so impressed with the success of the rocket-firing vessels in the Marshalls invasions that he had equipped three tank landing craft (LCTs) with half a dozen 4.2-inch mortars. These gunboats were to protect the left flank of the landing force on Saipan from reinforcements that might come down the beach. The final test would be their performance in the maneuvers.

On the night of May 14, when the invasion fleet sailed for Maui, the weather was very rough off Pearl Harbor. Two of the special LCTs carried away from their lashings aboard the LSTs that were transporting them and sank. A number of lives were lost, and Admiral Turner scrubbed the whole proposition, since it was too late to build up another pair of LCTs and reorganize the safety procedures for shipping them.

After the exercise was over, *LST-353*, which was carrying the last of the experimental gunboats, was ordered into Pearl Harbor's West Loch to unload 2,500 mortar projectiles that had been put aboard for the gunboat operation. *LST-353* moored in West Loch near the Naval Ammunition Depot, next to sixteen other LSTs which had been designated as ammunition ships. The mortars and the ammunition belonged to the army, so trucks were sent down from Schofield Barracks to pick up the ordnance, and a black labor battalion was sent down to move the material. It was a hard and heavy job, since the LCT had been loaded with 40 tons of ammunition.

The civilian dock workers at Pearl Harbor were not always as careful as they might be about smoking around live ammunition. That day one of the officers of *LST-353* had to order two civilians on deck to stop smoking. But nothing untoward occurred until just after 3:00 in the afternoon. Then, as members of the labor battalion were loading ammunition onto one of the trucks, there was an explosion, followed by two more explosions, and debris rained down on all the LSTs nearby. They were loaded with ammunition and with gasoline drums on deck, and one burning fragment ignited a gasoline fire, and then there was an enormous explosion aboard the LST involved. Others began to burn. The sky above Pearl Harbor was black and gray with smoke, and flames were shooting hundreds of feet in the air. Aboard *LST-353* and others the men tried to fight the fires, but the power was out and the hoses would not work. The explosions and fires continued, and in Honolulu many people believed the Japanese had attacked again by air. (This belief continued for years; in 1979 the Gannett news service in Washington reported erroneously on the "second Japanese bombing of Pearl Harbor" on May 21, 1944.) Admiral Turner, whose invasion was at stake in the ammunition ships, came to West Loch and supervised the firefighting personally. He became so emotional that when a boatswain's mate commanding a yard tug backed away from the ammunition dock the admiral threatened to shoot him. By the time the fires were out and the smoke cleared away, the navy had lost six LSTs loaded with ammunition, and 163 men killed and 396 injured. It was a serious disaster; coming just on the eve of the invasion made it even worse, because Admiral Turner was not certain enough other ships could be found to replace these. But the ships were found and loaded in fast time, and the Saipan invasion proceeded on schedule.

On June 6, Admiral Spruance sailed in the *Indianapolis* for Eniwetok. The slower ships were already on their way, protected by the escort carriers, and other ships were coming in from the West Coast, all to converge in the Marshalls and then move to the Marianas. Admiral Spruance learned that a Japanese search plane had reconnoitered Majuro. Since the carrier task force had arrived there, the Japanese must know about the fleet, but they still did not know where the Americans were headed, and Admiral Toyoda was still betting that the point of action was south around Biak.

On June 8, Admiral Turner's Saipan expeditionary force arrived at Eniwetok. Spruance conferred with Turner briefly, and then the *Indianapolis* sailed, taking him to join Task Force 58, which would open the invasion by air strikes against the Marianas.

The next day, Spruance approved Admiral Mitscher's plans to make a 208-plane fighter sweep over Guam, Rota, Tinian, and Saipan islands. Mitscher knew the Japanese had been reinforcing the Marianas with new planes, and he wanted to hit them hard before the invasion forces were seen and could get into trouble. D-Day was set for June 15. Mitscher wanted this first sweep at D-4, and the second the next morning at Tinian and Saipan, which he concluded had the most planes.

On June 9 another enemy search plane was spotted over Majuro, so Admiral Spruance had to conclude that the Japanese knew the carrier force had sailed. But to confuse the enemy, air strikes by Admiral Hoover's land-based air force were arranged on Palau, Truk, and other areas in the south. The bombings helped keep Admiral Toyoda guessing.

On June 10, the Central Pacific command perceived much greater air activity by the Japanese in all areas, and Admiral Mitscher asked permission to launch his strikes a day early in view of the apparent Japanese discovery of the American plans. But the Japanese on that day were still occupied with the Kon operation, half expecting to see the American fleet come forth in strength to challenge them. Admiral Kinkaid was sure the Japanese were planning a major naval move, and in the first week of June he was certainly correct. The Twenty-third Air Flotilla had been augmented by 200 aircraft, and the pressure on the American landings and the American ships off Biak was heavy. The cruisers *Australia, Phoenix, Boise,* and *Nashville* and fourteen American and Australian destroyers were out scouting to fight if they met equal or inferior forces, and give warning if they met superior forces.

On June 5, Japanese planes attacked Allied aircraft at Wakde island, where they were packed on the runways, and did such severe damage that Wakde was useless for most of the next week, but the Japanese destroyer force and the Allied cruiser force met only in a brushing action on June 8, and the Japanese retired before superior strength. The destroyer *Harusame* was lost to a flight of American medium bombers, but the fleet action was inconclusive when the Japanese ran north. The information about this action reached Tokyo, and persuaded Admiral Toyoda to commit his major forces to the Kon Plan. The big battleships *Yamato* and *Musashi* with their 18-inch guns were ordered to sail from Tawi-Tawi to join the cruisers and destroyers. Admiral Ugaki in *Yamato* sailed that afternoon. On the evening of June 11 a large force had assembled at Batjan, the Japanese base south of Halmahera, about 200 miles west of New Guinea. But that night Admiral Toyoda had the news from Saipan of the air attacks that day. Next day it was the same. Toyoda knew then that the major attack was going to be on the Marianas, and he switched gears. Operation Kon was suspended. Operation A-Go was to be carried out immediately.

Admiral Ozawa, commander of the Mobile Fleet, had remained behind at Tawi-Tawi with the nine aircraft carriers, waiting for the definitive word on the direction of the big battle. On June 13 he sailed. There was no further question in anyone's mind about the objective of the Americans: Admiral Turner's pre-invasion bombardment of Saipan had begun. Ozawa sailed north for the Philippines. He stopped long enough at Guimaras Strait between Panay and Negros to take on fuel from his seven tankers. Enroute his force was intercepted by Admiral Ugaki's battleships, and the cruisers and destroyers, hastening northward from the New Guinea area, began to join up. The guessing game was over. The American fleet would be found somewhere around Saipan, and the decisive battle would be fought there. The Americans had played into the hands of the devisers of Plan A-Go.

11
THE OBJECTIVES

From the beginning of the plans stage of the Marianas operation the Americans knew they were moving into a wholly different sort of combat than they had known on the coral atolls of the Gilberts and the Marshalls. The latter were bits of sand created by living coral reef. The former were mountain tops rising up above some of the deepest sea gulches in the world. Back from the shore the land was fertile, wooded, and rugged, serrated by hills and valleys. The people of the Marshalls and Gilberts were Melanesians, dark, primitive, and friendly to the Americans. When the marines had taken Betio island in Tarawa, they encountered a few islanders who led them to the Japanese on other islands. When the marines and soldiers landed in the Marshalls, they were also assisted by the islanders. They could expect no such help on Saipan or Tinian, the two major objectives. Guam was an exception—the island had been an American territory since 1899, and the Chamorros there were mostly loyal to the United States after the fall of Guam to Japan in 1942. But the other islands of the Marianas had been first Spanish, and then German possessions. The Japanese captured the islands in 1914, and the League of Nations gave Japan a mandate to rule them in 1920. The Japanese had come to the Marianas in force, and by 1941 Japanese outnumbered Chamorros two to one in the fourteen

Marianas aside from Guam. The islands had been made an essential part of Japanese planning; much of Japan's sugar was grown here. The Suntory distilling company made whiskey here. The Japanese built roads and railroads, grew corn and vegetables; and by the time war broke out the islands were thoroughly "Japanized." The houses, language, culture, and most of the people

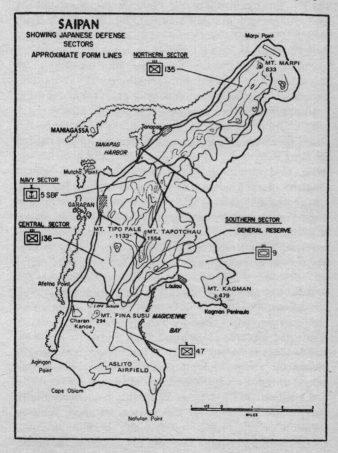

were Japanese, so the Americans could expect to find people here who would fight for their "homeland."

Saipan—the most important of the objectives, because the Army Air Forces wanted it for B-29 base—is 13 miles long and 5 miles wide at its widest point, about the size of Nantucket Island off Massachusetts. In the middle of the island at its widest point lies Mt. Tapotchau, which rises 1,500 feet above sea level. At the southern end was Aslito airfield, Japan's major military staging air base for planes going south, and the most important field between Tokyo and Truk. Tinian is a smaller island, lying in the shadow of Saipan and quite visible from the larger island; it is less than 3 miles away across the channel. It was an important factor in the Japanese defense of Saipan, with four airfields.

During the American planning for the seizure of the Marianas, Admiral Turner had gone over every detail. The objective, he said, was to take the Marianas to control sea communications through the Central Pacific for the support of further attacks on the Japanese. To do this was going to be difficult, as General Holland Smith could see. The east coast of Saipan was mostly free of reef, except around Magicienne Bay, but the beaches were narrow, and rose up sharply to rugged heights, which meant the defenders had an enormous natural advantage. The west coast seemed much easier, with flat beaches and gently sloping land. The catch was that the whole west coast was surrounded by a barrier reef, except at two points: a channel off Charan Kanoa, a small town surrounded by sugar fields and sugar mills; and Tanapag Harbor, which served the big town of Garapan. After much discussion, Admiral Turner and his staff decided they would choose the more constricted west side of the island. They were to go in over the reef, as they had learned to do at the Gilberts and Marshalls. The Second and Fourth Marine Divisions would land side by side around Charan Kanoa, and drive across the island, then capture Aslito airfield. After that they would turn northeast and drive the Japanese up the island. This, as everyone knew, would be almost as difficult as the original landing, because the central and northern parts of the island were extremely mountainous.

On June 15, then, the operation would begin with a feint. The reserves would pretend to make a landing 4 miles north of the real beaches, hoping to draw the Japanese defenders to that area in force. Landing craft would be run in to within 4 miles of the beach.

The American carrier strike of June 11 against the Marianas destroyed an estimated eighty-two planes at Saipan and Tinian and twenty-five at Guam. From that point on the carrier force was shadowed by Japanese planes, but no attacks were launched. The next day the carrier planes struck again and destroyed another seventeen Japanese aircraft. The American losses were twelve fighters and eight bombers.

On the morning of June 13, Admiral Lee left the task force with most of the battleships and cruisers to begin the two-day naval bombardment of Saipan. The carriers continued to harry various islands in the Marianas, and land-based planes all over the South and Central Pacific struck at Palau, Truk, and other airbases to keep the Japanese from mounting any massive air relief. On the night of June 13, the submarine *Bowfin* reported that the Japanese fleet was on the prowl. She had encountered four battleships, six carriers, and eight cruisers accompanied by a number of destroyers in Philippine waters. So Admirals Spruance and Mitscher knew the enemy was seeking naval battle.

On June 14, Admiral Mitscher sent two task groups to Iwo Jima to strike airfields there and prevent the Japanese from bringing reinforcements down the island chain from Japan. But the carrier groups were warned that the Japanese fleet might appear in Marianas waters on June 17, and they must be ready for a quick run back if needed. Back at Pearl Harbor, Admiral Nimitz, who had copies of all these messages, asked General MacArthur to widen the search patterns of his land-based heavy bombers and scout planes, to try to find and track the Japanese fleet. Nimitz never missed a bet in matters of this sort. He chose his commanders, let them have their heads, but watched every move and if anything was undone he made sure the necessary action was taken before the omission became an error.

The carrier planes learned one new fact at Tinian and Saipan: the Japanese were very good antiaircraft gunners when given the weapons. Around these major Japanese air bases they had rings of guns, and the American plane casualties were mostly due to antiaircraft fire. Planes from the *Lexington's* air group suffered badly. Lieutenant Commander Robert Isely, the group's bomber commander, went in to attack Aslito airfield with a new technique: wing rockets. He was shot down, and so was another TBM pilot. The reaction of the carrier officers was to abandon the rockets as not useful for the relatively slow torpedo bombers. But the fact was that the new carriers had been having the war so much their own way until the Marianas that they were not used to effective opposition.

The bombardment fleet also encountered something new. At the Marshalls the ships had stood offshore and peppered the land as they pleased. At Saipan the Japanese shore guns began firing back. The destroyer *Braine* was severly damaged by a 6-inch shell. The battleship *California*'s main battery director was knocked out by a 5-inch shell. The cruisers *Birmingham* and *Indianapolis* were also hit by shore gunfire, though neither was seriously damaged.

The bombardment on June 13 by the new fast battleships was not very successful; they did not know the technique. But on the 14th, Admiral Oldendorf's old battleships and accompanying cruisers came up and did a better job. They had the experience and were effective at blowing up roads and knocking out some enemy installations. On the whole, however, the bombardment could not be as effective as it had been in the Marshalls for the simple reason that Saipan was too large an area, and they also had to work over Tinian. The Marianas, from the outset, represented a new challenge to the amphibious forces.

On the morning of June 15, the transports carrying the expedition's reserve troops moved in off Tanapag Harbor, and the landing craft began buzzing about, in what seemed to be an attempt to land there. But after the landing force had come in to within its prescribed 4 miles from the beach, the craft turned about and headed back to the ships. If the Japanese were fooled, they gave little evidence, for they did not fire on the decoys. Later, in the day, however, Radio Tokyo broadcast that the Americans had tried to land off Garapan and had been thrown back into the sea by the stout defenders of His Majesty's Empire. Radio Tokyo had very little to say about what was happening elsewhere along the beach.

12
THE DEFENSES

The relative importance of the Marianas to Japan was indicated in the ranks of the officers chosen for its defenses. The senior of these was Vice Admiral Chuichi Nagumo, commander of Japan's carrier force at the battle of Midway, whose failure there had caused him to be demoted to a defensive command where the Japanese expected never to have to make a defense. The defense of the Marianas, however, was not regarded primarily as a naval matter (as were the defenses of all the island outposts outside the empire's inner perimeter). Saipan was Japanese soil, and the land area was large enough for the army to maneuver. So it was primarily an army command, a part of the area of Lieutenant General Hideyoshi Obata, whose headquarters was located on Palau. The Saipan army garrison was under command of Lieutenant General Yoshitsugo Saito.

The Americans made one serious mistake at Saipan: they underestimated the number of Japanese defenders on the island by more than half. The U.S. estimate suggested that Saipan would house about 15,000 defenders, including several thousand construction workers. In fact, there were more than 30,000 soldiers and sailors on Saipan. The Americans never did discover the exact number, for reasons that will become apparent, but the error in intelligence was costly in time and the effectiveness of the American battle plan. One reason for so great an error was Japan's hasty effort to shore up the Marianas perimeter after the fall of the Marshalls. A Japanese transport carrying 4,100 troops was dispatched from the homeland in February but was sunk. None of those men ever reached Saipan; about half arrived in Guam, confusing that picture too. Early in June the army sent a seven-ship convoy to Saipan to reinforce the garrison. Five of the ships were sunk by American submarines, and there was no accurate count of the survivors. There were also many survivors of other sinkings, who had not yet been moved back to Japan. But survivors do not make an army, and this was the major problem that General Saito faced. After the Marshalls invasion, when Admiral Ogaki moved the Combined Fleet headquarters, the Sixth Fleet (submarines) moved its headquarters to Saipan, and General Saito was constantly complaining to Admiral Takagi, the submarine commander, that he could not provide a defense if Takagi kept letting the American submarines sink the supply ships. Most of the survivors of such sinkings arrived on Saipan with little more than the clothes they wore. Saito had issued a call for construction materials and heavy weapons, and complained bitterly that he did not get them because of the sinkings.

The result was that General Saito's defenses were totally inadequate for the island. He had only eight 6-inch guns, seventeen smaller field guns, and a few mortars. His plans called for a far stronger defense, dozens of guns, and scores of pillboxes and highly fortified blockhouses, but the Americans had moved so rapidly since the fall of 1943 that these had never been built. The American submarines could be thanked for that failure.

One of the main lines of defense for the island was to be Admiral Takagi's submarine force. Eight Japanese submarines were stationed on a picket line east and southeast of Guam. Ten were strung out east of Saipan and two more stationed to the west. They were supposed to watch for the appearance of an American fleet and give plenty of warning to the islands and to Admiral

Toyoda so the A-Go Plan could be put into effect. But American warships interfered.

The most effective interference was that of Commander Samuel Dealey in the submarine *Harder*. On the night of June 6, the *Harder* came across three big transports guarded by two destroyers, near Tawi-Tawi, the Japanese base. He sank the destroyer *Minazuki* that night. Next morning the Japanese conducted an intensive search for the submarine, and it was discovered by the destroyer *Hayanami*. Sam Dealey sank the *Hayanami*, too. Two days later he fired on two more destroyers; he sank the *Tanikaze* and claimed the second, but apparently it was only damaged. A day later he had another encounter and submerged hastily after firing several torpedoes. Inside the submarine the crew heard torpedoes strike and the sounds of a ship breaking up, but no records were found to substantiate a sinking there.

General Obata had told his subordinates earlier to convert Saipan into an "invulnerable fortress." Like so many declarations of the higher commands, the plan was separated from the reality by deficiency in force. The coastal defenses had been completed before June. Five gun positions guarded the approaches to these beaches between Agingan and Marpi points. One 120mm gun and one 150mm gun were placed to hit targets off the northwest coast. Marpi Point had a battery of 40mm guns. Magicienne Bay was protected by four batteries, among them 200mm guns. Nafutan Point had two 150mm guns. There were many dual-purpose antiaircraft guns, which could be trained on surface targets.

As the generals had promised, the finest fighting troops were entrenched along the beaches. Behind them were tanks, on the edge of the mountains, and more troops. General Obata had prepared a second line of defense, and behind the second line the Japanese had scouted out caves and thickets and deep ravines, which would be used defensively if all else failed. The plan had been to build up every available position, but the shortage of materials in the winter of 1943–44 and the speed with which the Americans were moving had prevented General Obata from achieving his goals. He had come, perhaps, halfway along in his plan.

Although Admiral Nagumo, called the Hero of Pearl Harbor before Midway's disaster, was the senior officer present, the defense of Saipan was to be an army matter largely because there were 25,500 soldiers on the island and only 6,000 sailors. There was no trouble about that. Admiral Nagumo yielded gracefully to General Saito, and Saito was in command. He divided Saipan into four sectors, three under the army and the fourth under the navy. The northern sector was protected by the 135th Infantry Regiment. The navy's Fifth Special Base Force was responsible for the area around Garapan, including Mount Tapotchau, the highest point on the island. Among the naval contingent were men of the Fifty-fifth Guard force and the equivalent to the marines, the Yokosuka First Special Naval Landing Force. Beyond them in the landing area were troops of the 136th Infantry Regiment. Back in the hills were the artillery, the antiaircraft units, and a mixed bag of survivors of sunken ships and stranded soldiers.

On June 10, the U. S. S. *Taylor* discovered the Japanese submarine *RO-111* on the surface and sank her. Three days later, the destroyer *Melvin* discovered the *RO-36* and sank her. Before the Americans ever reached Saipan waters, the naval defensive ring had been shattered, and communications between Takagi and his submarines were lost. This was partly the fault of the navy; Takagi had moved to Saipan without adequate communications facilities. It was partly the fortunes of war; the Americans had prevented the shipment of new communications facilities and the weather turned bad for Admiral Takagi. But whatever the reasons, the result was that contact with that American force seen at Majuro was lost and the intensive activity around Tawi-Tawi indicated that the Americans might be moving in the south—which added to the Japanese confusion. By June 13, when the reports of the ship bombardment of Saipan and Tinian were available, it was too late to do much about any defenses except air. Still, as the American fleet lay offshore on June 15, and the invasion troops moved into their landing craft, General Saito had but one order for his defenders: "Destroy the enemy on the beach," he said. How that was to be done, he did not indicate.

13
THE LANDINGS ON SAIPAN

Everyone concerned from General Holland Smith down to the last marine private had worries about the landing on Saipan. It was the largest landing to date, and the conditions were anything but ideal. The marines had to go in over a reef that in some places was 700 yards across, and 8,000 of them were supposed to be ashore on a beach 3.5 miles long within the first hour. The reef side of the island had been chosen because of those beaches, and the fact that behind them was relatively flat land, rather than the steep hills of the other side.

On the day before the assault, underwater demolition teams had scoured the area and come back to report that it was clear, free of man-made obstacles. Small boats came in to plant buoys that would guide the landing craft in along the lanes established on paper. That night the Japanese came out in small boats and planted flags in the area between the reef edge and the beaches, to help guide their machine-gun fire and mortars when the Americans landed the next day. The Japanese artillery, back in the hills, was already zeroed in on the beaches.

Very early in the morning, the Americans formed up. As the transports moved over to Tanapag Harbor to try their bluff, the assault forces that would carry the Second and Fourth Marines into land began making ready. At 5:20 they were on station. Admiral Turner ordered the landings to begin at 8:40. For the next three hours the preparatory bombardment brought man-made thunder and lightning to the island. The naval barrage continued until 7:00, with two battleships, two cruisers, and six destroyers throwing shells over the heads of the marines into the beaches. The marines moved out of the LSTs and transports into the small landing craft, and the little boats bobbed and pitched in the sea, the marines watching the spouts of sand go up as shells hit on the beach, and the palm trees go down as they were struck and splintered. At 7:00 the thunder ended, and then bombers from the escort carriers came in to swoop down and plaster the beaches with high explosives. Sand and smoke filled the air, and for a few moments the beach was obscured.

By H-hour minus 30 minutes, the marines were in their boats, which jockeyed around, waiting for the signal to move in. Behind them, the naval bombardment began again. The battleships concentrated on Agingan Point, which would be at the right end of the marine line; on Mutcho Point, at the other end; and on Afetna Point, in the middle. The first wave would contain nearly a hundred LVTs (Landing Vehicle, Tank) and nearly seventy armored amphibious tractors, those amph-tracs for which Holland Smith had fought so hard after the difficulties at Betio. They could go in over the reef, and carry the men up onto the beaches. Ahead of all were twenty-four LCI gunboats which would rake the beaches one more time with gunfire and rockets before the troops landed. Behind them were the second and third waves of troops, and out beyond them were the reserves, who would be brought in by the landing craft on a second trip.

At 8:12 that morning the first wave began to move. General Watson's Second Marine Division would attack on the left. The Sixth Marine Regiment would take Beaches Red 2 and Red 3. The Eighth Marines would take Beaches Green 1 and Green 2. That would put them on the beach just north of Afetna Point. South of the point, the Fourth Marine Division would land—the Twenty-third Marines on beaches Blue 1 and Blue 2, and the

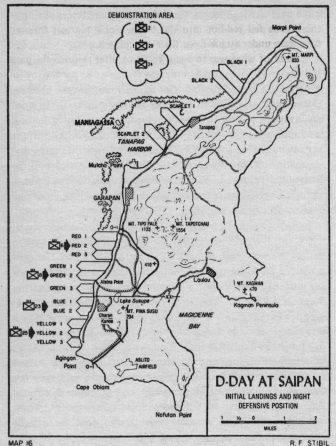

DEMONSTRATION AREA

Marpi Point

MT. MARPI
833

BLACK 1

BLACK 2

SCARLET 1

MANIAGASSA

Tanapag

SCARLET 2

TANAPAG
HARBOR

Mutcho Point

GARAPAN

O-1

MT. TIPO PALE
1133

MT. TAPOTCHAU
1554

RED 1
RED 2
RED 3

410

GREEN 1
GREEN 2
GREEN 3

Afetna Point

Laulau

MT. KAGMAN
479

BLUE 1
BLUE 2

Lake Susupe

Kagman Peninsula

MT. FINA SUSU
294

MAGICIENNE
BAY

YELLOW 1
YELLOW 2
YELLOW 3

Charan
Kanoa

Agingan
Point

O-1

ASLITO
AIRFIELD

Cape Obiam

D-DAY AT SAIPAN

INITIAL LANDINGS AND NIGHT
DEFENSIVE POSITION

1   ½   0   1   2
MILES

Nafutan Point

MAP 16

R. F. STIBIL

Twenty-fifth Marines on Beaches Yellow 1 and Yellow 2. Each
battalion would have a 600-yard front, which took the Fourth
Division down almost to Agingan Point.

As the landing craft moved inward, a final assault was made by
the planes of the escort carriers, fighters this time. They flew in
at treetop level to strafe, scaring the marines half to death as they

came over the landing craft and the shell casings from their machine guns fell red-hot into the boats. Some marines thought they were under attack from their own planes.

A taste of what was to come began to filter through the haze and smoke as a handful of Japanese shells burst near the line of departure of the amphibious tractors and landing craft. They did little damage—the awesome bombardment and air strikes seemed much more significant. But at the Marshalls the Japanese had not used their artillery so early in the game. The geysers in the water gave an indication that this invasion was not to be the same, and the marine observer flying above the island in a "grasshopper" observation plane radioed down to the men in the boats: "This is not like the Marshalls. Not at all." Robert Sherrod, correspondent for *Life*, who had been at Tarawa, scribbled in his notebook: "I fear all this smoke and noise does not mean many Japs killed."

But the tractors pushed ahead. The battleships and cruisers and destroyers continued to fire, and as the landing craft reached a point 300 yards from the beach they shifted their fire to the obvious strongpoints, Afetna Point in particular. The carrier planes continued to strafe along the beaches, and would until the marines were ashore, trying to be careful to stay a hundred yards from the beach itself.

In the landing craft, the marines waited nervously. Some smoked and kept their heads down. One man got sick on the steel deck. A few appeared to be reading paperback books, but their buddies would have bet no one was remembering what he read. The tractors bucked up and down in the choppy sea. There was a stir when they were halfway in: the Japanese fire became heavier, and the word was passed to a battalion of the Twenty-third Marines not to land on Blue Beach One, as planned, but on Blue Two, where the fire was less—or seemed less.

So the marines, those who had been at Tarawa and at Kwajalein and Eniwetok, knew very well that the observer overhead knew what he was talking about. It was not going to be like the Marshalls. Not at all. The marines did not know it, but General Saito had planned to expend 15 percent of his ammunition on the approaching landing craft, and another 15 percent on the landing force after it hit the beaches. So when the Americans hit the 300-yard mark, the shells were coming thick and fast, and they seemed to have a pattern: every 25 yards the boats went in—every 15 seconds—another shell would burst.

A few marines stuck their heads up over the sides of the tractors. They saw that some of the amph-tracs had been hit and flopped over. But at 8:43 the first wave hit Beach Red 2, and within eight minutes there were troops on every beach. The Second Marine Division had landed out of position, the landing craft pulled by a strong current and the drivers facing deadly fire on the left. The Sixth Marine Regiment and the Eighth got jammed up, and the troops were concentrated on Beaches Red 2, Red 3, and Green 1, which gave the Japanese a massive target. The casualties in these first minutes were heavy. Down the beach, the Fourth Marines were more fortunate on the other side of Afetna Point, and landed in more orderly fashion. They were supposed to push forward and overrun Agingan Point, Charan Kanoa, and the ridge line above, but the Japanese fire prevented a coordinated attack. Some troops were stuck on the beaches under fire, and the attack began to bog down. This could be fatal.

Coming in, the amph-tracs began firing with their cannon and machine guns. But they were firing at areas, not at troops, for they could see virtually no Japanese. One machine gunner turned to a buddy: "It gives me the creeps," he said. "Like fighting a bunch of ghosts." Then he turned back to his weapon and did what he had been told to do: rake the trees up ahead, they might be full of Japanese snipers.

The Sixth Marine attack stalled about 100 yards inland under the pressure of Japanese machine-gun fire and shellfire. The captured sand was unrecognizable as a sloping beach. The shells and bombs of the morning had torn huge craters in the sand, and smashed and burned-out amph-tracs littered the beach. Behind them, in the little shelter they gave, the wounded lay awaiting evacuation. A few yards inland a Japanese tank lay among the American vehicles, apparently abandoned. But after the first wave had passed, and the reserve First Battalion of the Sixth Marines was coming in to shore, the tank suddenly came to life and began firing on the amph-tracs. Lieutenant Colonel William K. Jones sent up a rocket launcher and riflemen with grenades. They fired, and the tank erupted in smoke and flame. This time it *was* abandoned by all the living Japanese.

Ahead the going was very difficult for the Third Battalion of the Sixth Marines. Machine guns fired on them, causing them to stay low. Up on the ridge behind, spotters called for mortar fire, and it began to arrive, the kind of fire that ducking did not help. The marines were waiting for *banzai* charges, but they did not see any. Once in a while they saw a Japanese figure rise, fire a rifle and duck down. But General Saito had ordained a defense in depth; there would be no *banzai* charges, not yet.

The marines had been on the beach about an hour when the Japanese infantrymen staged a counterattack. Two dozen grey-green uniforms appeared as Colonel James Riseley was establishing his command post on Beach Red 2. The enemy knew the command post was important; if they could knock it out they could confuse the American attack. But the marines were ready. The Japanese came forward stubbornly, and the defenders cut them down with M-1 rifles and machine guns. In this sort of attack the enormous firepower of a dozen M-1 semiautomatic rifles made all the difference.

At noon, the Japanese sent two tanks down from the foothills to help stem the advance. But the commander of the tanks became disoriented, perhaps by a landscape quite changed with the distruction of the morning, and stopped shortly after he had passed through the American forward line. The turret hatch of the leading tank popped open, and a Japanese helmet came up. The commander was having a look around. Stopping was his first mistake. The marines brought up rocket launchers and rifle grenadiers, and they made quick work of the two tanks.

Early in the afternoon, the Japanese tried again to thrust the landing force back into the sea. Three more tanks came down, headed for Risely's command post. Two were stopped by rockets and grenades before they reached the line, but the third came on and reached a point 15 yards from the command post before the marines could smash it.

The constant artillery and mortar fire from the defense line was extremely effective. By 1:00 in the afternoon, Colonel Riseley estimated that 35 percent of the regiment were casualties. It was apparent that the Japanese had a strong force up ahead. But the marines had expanded the beachhead, and it extended 400 yards inland in a place or two. Riseley tried an assault on the ridgeline ahead, where the Japanese mortars lay, but it was thrown back. The reserves were needed to hold the positions they had taken.

On the right of the Sixth Marines, the Eighth Marines were to take the Green Beaches and Afetna Point, the Japanese stronghold. Lieutenant Colonel H.P. Crowe's Second Battalion and Lieutenant Colonel John C. Miller, Jr.'s Third Battalion were supposed to land on different beaches, but the current and crossfire had brought them both to Green 1. The sorting out of companies took a little doing, but it was done, and soon the marines were fanning out to attack the positions assigned. At this point the Charan Kanoa airstrip came very near the sea, and the strip was a point to be taken by Crowe's battalion. They advanced along the strip edge toward Afetna Point, and were met by Japanese riflemen firing across the runway from prepared positions on the other side. On the edge of Afetna Point stood nine small field guns, which were trained on the beaches. The Japanese fired on the incoming amph-tracs, and when the Americans began to approach from their flank, they continued to fire on the boats. The marines cut the gun crews down, one by one. Until noon, there was still considerable confusion, with heavy mortar and artillery fire concentrated on the Red and Green beaches. Shortly after noon, however, Brigadier General Merritt Edson, assistant division commander of the Second Division, came ashore to visit the command post of the Eighth Marines, and correspondent Sherrod came with him. Later Sherrod wrote a description of what he saw, a word picture of death and destruction; at one point on the beach he counted seventeen dead marines within a few yards, many of them in that position so common in warfare; fallen as they ran forward, sprawled with arms and gun outstretched and legs tucked beneath them. He saw dead Japanese defenders, and wrecked amph-tracs and an abandoned Japanese field gun and ammunition carts. He saw a goat sitting under the front of an abandoned amph-trac. Around him, and up front was the popping of guns and the heavier noise of artillery fire and the plopping of mortars. And there was the goat, a white goat, looking up at him.

Up near the command post, Colonel Wallace was directing the advance of his troops. The fighting was vigorous, and the commanders of both assault battalions were wounded that day and had to be evacuated. The regimental reserve, the First Battalion, was ordered ashore almost as soon as the assault battalions got their feet dry. Early in the afternoon, the division reserve was committed here, too, for the capture of Afetna Point was that important. The real problem was effective Japanese artillery fire which prevented the troops from moving inland. The Eighth Marines battled inland to the swamps below the point, but could go no further. In midafternoon Colonel Wallace assessed his situation. He had lost 35 percent of his effective troops, too.

On the south side of Afetna Point, the Twenty-third Marines attacked on the Blue beaches. Here the amph-tracs went straight ashore and kept on going. They advanced up to the road that led to Charan Kanoa, a village of single-story white concrete buildings ablaze with bougainvillea. Soon they were in the town, which had been badly mauled by naval gunfire. They were fired on by snipers from the ditches, but went on through, past a baseball diamond and a Buddhist temple. They were heading for the ridge a mile away, which was a key to the Japanese defenses.

The advance troops reached Mount Fina Susu, which stood out from the ridge, and occupied the hill. The trouble was that this hill was totally exposed to Japanese fire from behind, and the marines were under fire all day. Other troops were supposed to come up from the road to help, but instead of bringing up the amph-tracs, which carried cannon that might be useful, the troops came up on foot. They held the hill all day, but at night they were ordered to pull back. The troops who were supposed to come up on the flanks had not made it that day. On the north the swamps of Lake Susupe had stalled them, and on the south, the troops had run into a sharp incline, not visible on the aerial photographs, which had stopped the amph-tracs cold.

On the Yellow beaches, Colonel Morton Batchelder's Twenty-fifth Marines landed in a barrage of enemy artillery fire. One amph-trac after another was hit and stopped; only half of them finally reached the railroad embankment, an objective that ran diagonally inland, 500 yards from the shore at its nearest point. The Japanese artillery fire continued to be heavy, and so was fire from a pair of mortars that had been bypassed near the beach and now turned on the rear of the Americans. The mortars were silenced by a strike from one of the escort carriers off-shore. On the south, where the First Battalion landed, the Americans came under heavy enfilade fire from Agingan Point, which was the focus of Japanese resistance in this area. The whole position was heavily fortified, and a number of artillery pieces kept firing on the beach. Less than an hour after the troops were ashore, the Japanese heightened the barrage, and then an infantry unit counterattacked, hoping to push the marines back into the sea. But the battalion commander called for an air strike and support from navy guns on the point, and this helped stop the counterattack.

That first Japanese counterattack came at 9:30 in the morning. A second was launched early in the afternoon, involving two companies of Japanese troops. They attacked against the Twenty-fifth's flank, and threatened the whole position on the beach. But the marines brought up tanks from the Fourth Tank Battalion, and they drove the Japanese back. Many of the defenders were killed in this foray, and the remainder retreated into spider-web fortifications of the sort that the Americans had encountered in the Marshalls. All afternoon the marines routed them out, and by the end of the day one company reported that it alone had killed 150 Japanese.

As the day lengthened, the tanks became more evident and more useful. By 3:00 in the afternoon, the Second Tank Battalion was ashore, and one company of fourteen tanks played a decisive role in destroying Japanese defenses at Afetna Point. It was not an easy job; eight of the tanks of the company were damaged at some point, and one was put out of action altogether. When the Fourth Tank Battalion landed, several tanks were stopped by short-circuiting of their electrical systems. Seawater had gotten in. Company B's tanks were split up. Some were sent to the Blue beaches and some to the Green. Half a dozen were lost in deep water. Only Company C, which landed on the Yellow beaches, managed to get all its tanks ashore safely.

The artillery was supposed to come ashore on this first day, and several pack howitzers were brought in. But the 105mm guns did not make it until very late in the day. The casualty rate of the artillerymen was so high that on the Blue beaches three 75mm howitzer batteries were merged into two. When the 105s did come in, four of them were hit almost immediately by Japanese mortar fire. That meant more time lost in repairing the guns. As evening neared, many Japanese guns had been silenced, but the beach was littered with amph-tracs and dead marines and knocked-out tanks. As if to show that the fight was still in progress, the Japanese continued their shelling of the beaches, and the casualties among the marines rose. The wounded were often hit again by artillery and mortar fire as they lay beneath wrecked vehicles or in the shelter of wrecked enemy defenses. Many who had survived one wound died from another, incurred as they awaited transportation back to the ships. One estimate at the end of the first day put the casualty toll of the marines at 2,000.

By the time night fell at the end of D-day the marines were ashore and established, but they had not accomplished their plan. The enemy still held half the territory they had hoped to occupy by day's end, and his presence on the ridges above the beaches constituted a serious threat. The Second Division held a line from the coast, about a mile south of Garapan, to the middle of Afetna Point. Its deepest penetration inland was about two-thirds of a mile. But the position was regarded as well enough established that General Thomas E. Watson came ashore and established his command post in a captured ammunition dump on the inland side of the coastal road. The Fourth Division had moved forward during the day to the ridgeline, but the salient had to be withdrawn with nightfall, lest the marines be surrounded during the night. The Japanese were still entrenched on Agingan Point, but General Harry Schmidt had moved his command post ashore too. The marines planned to stay.

As night fell, the Japanese planned to counterattack. They slipped down from the ridges and moved toward the American lines in small groups. From their concealed positions in the hills, Japanese tanks came forward, and the troops joined behind them. The major attack was aimed at the Sixth Marines. They had dug in for the night and were in their foxholes when the sounds of movement came to warn that the enemy was coming. At 3:30 in the morning the enemy moved, and within a few minutes had overrun one 60mm mortar position. A tank passed right over another foxhole occupied by mortarmen, and went on, dripping oil on the marines as it went by. In fifteen minutes the tanks had penetrated deep behind the marines' line, but this did not prove to be totally beneficial to the Japanese attack. The marines stayed in their tankproof foxholes and attacked the vulnerable rear ends of the tanks after they had passed. One marine with a bazooka disabled four tanks that way. The Japanese tanks came on, with the infantry behind them, and some stalled. The tank troops would jump out, look over their vehicle, and clang their long swords on the metal and make fearsome noises. The marines responded with grenades and machine-gun fire then mowed them down. One pair of marines, Private First Class Charles D. Merritt and Private First Class Herbert J. Hodges, took their bazookas around on a tour. They fired at seven tanks and hit seven tanks.

When the tank and infantry attack began, the marines called for help from the navy, and soon starshells began illuminating the perimeter of the Sixth Marines. The battleship *California* fired at the base of the ridge to halt tank reinforcement. Reinforcement came up from the beachhead to help the beleaguered battalion, and a platoon of American medium tanks rumbled up. By morning the fighting was intense, for the Japanese had sent a battalion of the 136th Infantry to drive the marines back. But the drive failed, and when the last stalled tank had been investigated to be sure there were no living Japanese inside, the Japanese casualty count came to more than 700.

All along the line, the Japanese made some sort of effort that first night to halt the American invasion. The Eighth Marines were harried by attacks along the front of the swamp that marked their perimeter, but the swamp inhibited the Japanese attack as much as it had the marine attempts the day before. The Twenty-fifth Marines were hit by a counterattack at 3:30. At first they saw a party of civilians coming toward them, hands up, asking for refuge from the fighting. But immediately behind the "refugees" were Japanese riflemen. The marines' sympathy evaporated and they called in artillery to support the ground troops. The 105s were ashore by that time, and they put down a very effective barrage that put an end to the "civilian" effort. In the fighting a Japanese shell set fire to a self-propelled 75mm gun, which lit up the area. When the ammunition in the vehicle began to explode the marines had to move back 200 yards, but they held there.

As dawn broke, the front quieted down. The Japanese had tried their best, but they had failed to dislodge the marines from the beachhead. The chief of staff of the defending forces reported to General Saito that the efforts had not been successful. But he was not dismayed, he said. The troops would reorganize during the morning, and they would attack again. The A-Go Plan had been activited. Admiral Ozawa was on his way with the Japanese fleet to destroy the American force at sea. From the Japanese carriers and from the air bases at Tinian, Rota, Guam, and the Palaus the indomitable Japanese airmen would arise and strike the enemy. And on Saipan, as the

American fleet and air arm were destroyed, the soldiers would mass and drive the miserable remnants of the marines back into the sea to drown. *Tenno Heika Banzai*! May the emperor live 10,000 years!

14
ADMIRAL OZAWA'S RUN

Admiral Ozawa was a brilliant naval officer. There was no question about that. From the beginning of the war his conduct, from Japan's point of view, had been irreproachable. He had commanded the Japanese forces that assured the capture of Malaya, and he had led in destruction of the remnants of the American Asiatic Fleet in the waters of the Dutch East Indies. When Admiral Nagumo had been disgraced by the failure at Midway and been exiled to Saipan, Admiral Ozawa had been promoted to command the carrier force. In the changes made since the Americans began charging across the Pacific, Ozawa had also gained command of the First Mobile Fleet—the Japanese euphemism for the remainder of the once-mighty Combined Fleet.

On the morning of June 15, as the Americans began streaming ashore on Saipan, Admiral Ozawa was aboard his flagship *Taiho* at the entrance to Guimaras Strait, waiting for the Mobile Fleet to complete fueling, and waiting also for some word as to the whereabouts of the Americans. The loss of so many of Admiral Takagi's submarines had dealt a serious blow to Admiral Ozawa's intelligence system. The single-engine float planes and four-engine flying boats that were used for observation too often did not make it back to base, so full of American aircraft were the skies these days. But on June 15, Admiral Ozawa did not need that sort of intelligence. Admiral Nagumo had the word for him: the American fleet was at Saipan. Just before nine o'clock that morning, the admiral approved a message to the fleet, and it was sent to every commanding officer of every vessel, from the proud *Taiho* (which was second in carrier size only to the American *Saratoga*) down to the last oiler, on whose services Admiral Ozawa depended for survival. The navy had emptied its barrels for this operation. The amount of refined fuel given the fleet was far in excess of its ration; earlier Tokyo had said the fleet must stay in Indonesian waters and burn unrefined crude oil for maneuvers, so serious was the shortage of refined oil. But Operation A-Go was considered so important at the highest levels that Admiral Ozawa could have anything Japan could give him. A-Go was the navy's last great hope. If it worked to perfection, the American carrier force would be wiped out, and the American drive across the Pacific set back at least a year or two. In that time, Japan, too, could augment its naval forces, completing those ships already on the way. No senior Japanese officer liked to consider the future; those who remembered Admiral Yamamoto's pre-Pearl Harbor warnings about the long-term American potential for production of war materials knew that Japan's dream of an Asian and Pacific super-empire had vanished, but even the most conservative officers had hope that Operation A-Go would bring a victory that would bring respite, which, in turn, would bring an honorable peace.

". . . A strong enemy force began landing operations in the Saipan-Tinian area. The Combined Fleet will attack the enemy in the Marianas area and annihilate the invasion force." This was Admiral Toyoda's message to Admiral Ozawa that morning. The fueling process was stopped. The fleet sailed, heading eastward. Admiral Ugaki's battleships and cruisers were coming up east of the Philippines, and Ozawa would meet them and fuel them. On June 16 and 17 the two forces topped off their tanks and the tankers set course for a rendezvous point. Admiral Ozawa's intelligence about the enemy was much better than the Americans knew; he knew that four carrier groups were involved, and that the landing force on Saipan was heavily protected by escort carriers and seemed to have its own battleships and cruisers. The fleet he would engage, then, was Admiral Mitscher's carrier force, and he knew it was Mitscher in command. He also knew that the commander of the whole fleet was Admiral Spruance, and so Ozawa felt no concern about being surprised. Spruance's reputation for extreme conservatism had spread to Japan. Ozawa knew that Spruance would never let the carriers loose to attack outside the Saipan area, so he would have the advantage of the initiative. By nightfall on June 17, Admiral Ozawa had a good picture of the American disposition, acquired by the risk of sending out sixteen seaplanes, thirteen fighters, and thirteen bombers to observe the enemy activity. They counted seven fleet carriers, eight light carriers, fourteen escort carriers, fourteen battleships, ten heavy cruisers, fifteen light cruisers, and eighty-six destroyers. Here was the American fleet. If Admiral Ozawa could work the A-Go Plan, its power would be destroyed.

The basic assumption of the A-Go Plan was that the Mariana Islands themselves provided Japan with the material for victory. To be sure, the Americans had fifteen aircraft carriers of various sorts, as opposed to Ozawa's nine. They had 1,000 carrier planes, as opposed to Ozawa's 430. But Saipan's and Tinian's air strips were better than carriers, and made up for the difference. If one counted the 500 aircraft shipped into the area by Imperial Headquarters in the past two months, then it was easy to see, if you were Japanese, that the statistical edge of the American fleet was not nearly so important as it appeared. If one added to that the *bushido* spirit which made every pilot a hero, then one could say, if one were Japanese, that there was no question of victory, it must come. That was the official view. In Tokyo at Imperial Headquarters, admirals and generals were telling one another quite seriously that the American invasion of Saipan did not really matter, for as soon as Ozawa had disposed of the carrier fleet, the army would drive the invaders into the sea.

There was the question of aircraft, a little troubling to the Japanese. They had developed radar for their planes, but few were yet equipped with it, and even fewer of the pilots knew how to use it. That was the main trouble at this moment, the lack of skilled pilots. There simply had been no respite from the Americans since Guadalcanal, so that the losses suffered at Midway were never made up. Each time a class of pilots was graduated from a flying school, most of the class was rushed down to the South Pacific to replace men lost, and most of these pilots, too, were lost. On the face of the matter, that was a fatal difficulty, but again the senior officers of Japan's armed forces comforted themselves by believing that superior dedication—*bushido* again—at least compensated for inferior training. There were some realists in the Japanese military ranks, but they were not encouraged to air their views, and if they were so impolite as to press objections, they would find themselves reduced to some position where they were not heard. On the positive side, Admiral Ozawa's light, unarmored planes had a flight range of nearly 600 miles, while the American range was closer to 300. That difference meant that with any luck Ozawa was certain to know where his enemy lay and be able to launch a strike against him, perhaps hours before the Americans had any indication of his fleet's position. This first-strike capability could be the difference between victory and defeat. If coupled with assistance from the land-based planes on Saipan, Tinian, Rota, and Guam, a first strike could knock the Americans out before they found the Japanese fleet.

Ozawa had one advantage that applied to carriers in a way that it had not applied to modern navies since the sailing days. He had "the weather gauge"—the eastern trade winds were blowing at his bows as he headed toward the American fleet. He would not have to circle about to launch planes into the wind, which Admiral Mitscher would have to do. That meant precious minutes saved, which, again, could make all the difference. And there was one other advantage: as searchers of these waters, the Japanese were extremely effective, a fact already proved in the amount of intelligence Admiral Ozawa had.

The search planes were launched all morning on June 18. At 3:00 in the afternoon, Admiral Ozawa's fleet had reached a point 500 miles west of Saipan, and had landed several of the Type 92 fighters, Tenzan torpedo bombers, and Suisei bombers, all bearing bits of information that indicated his enemy was about 150 miles west of Saipan, steaming toward him. Half an hour later, Rear Admiral Sueo Obayashi, commander of Carrier Division Three, suggested that they launch a preemptive strike that afternoon. He was so eager and so sure that Admiral Ozawa would proceed that he began launching planes after sending his message. But Ozawa ordered Obayashi to stop launching and recall his planes. It was too late in the day for his planes to attack the Americans and return to the carriers. They would have to land on the islands of the Marianas, and that meant there would be fewer aircraft for the dawn strike that Ozawa now planned. He wanted that first blow to be aimed at a knockout. Admiral Ozawa headed south then, instead of continuing his eastward course. Thus he would preserve the distance factor to his advantage, and next day launch planes again as he moved toward the enemy. He sent the major part of his fleet due east still, but the six largest carriers headed south.

Late that night, Admiral Ozawa broke radio silence to communicate with Vice Admiral Kakuta on Tinian, commander of the land-based air forces in the Marianas. He announced—in code, of course—that he was preparing to strike in the morning, and called on Kakuta for supportive action from the land.

That night, Admiral Ozawa found his fleet in an area of squalls. Low clouds hung over the carriers, which was certainly a defensive advantage, but if they extended west to the enemy, it was also a disadvantage. An hour before dawn he dispatched a group of sixteen seaplanes to scout out the enemy. A second group of fourteen planes and a third of eleven bombers were launched within the hour. Just after 7:00 in the morning, the scouts began to report. They had found the enemy in three groups, it seemed, with the nearest group 300 miles east of Obayashi's carriers.

Admiral Ozawa gave the order to attack. Aboard the *Taiho*, the flight leaders had asked permission to speak to the admiral, and when it was granted they came forth emotionally to announce their determination to wipe out the shame that had fallen on the carrier forces at Midway. They were going out to destroy the enemy this time, said Lieutenant Takashi Ebata, and they would bring Admiral Ozawa a victory on the wings of their triumphant planes. On the other carriers, the pilots were conducting similar little ceremonies. As well as any admiral, every pilot knew that this battle was to be their moment of decision, when the future of Japan rode in their cockpits. They were supremely confident that the superior Japanese spirit would triumph. So saying, the pilots manned their planes.

At 7:30 the first attack wave of forty-eight fighters, fifty-four bombers, and twenty-seven torpedo bombers was launched, and the formations assembled over the carriers. Admiral Ozawa stood on his flag bridge, with his chief of staff, Captain Matake Yoshimura, and his senior staff officer, Captain Toshikazu Ohmae, and watched. They were very pleased, for they, too, expected a victory this day. If they did not get it they also knew that the fleet was finished as a major arm of Japanese defense and that the war, already lost, could not be turned around even enough to assure an honorable peace.

Admiral Togo had overstated his case in May 1905 when he told the fleet: "The fate of the empire rests on this one battle. Every man is expected to do his utmost." But when Admiral Toyoda repeated the statement thirty-nine years later, he was not exaggerating, and when Admiral Ozawa transmitted the word to the fleet every man sensed that somehow the fate of the empire lay in his own hands.

15
SPRUANCE HESITATES

On June 15 Admiral Spruance was waiting for the Japanese to show their hand. He had asked for more and longer searches from General MacArthur's land-based aircraft in the Southwest Pacific, since he knew that a number of Japanese ships had been operating in the Biak area. General MacArthur obliged, but the planes did not find the Japanese fleet. Neither did those of the American fleet. Admiral Ozawa had anticipated this activity and had taken a route that kept him outside the range of American air search. Spruance's only reliable sources of information were reports from the American submarines scattered all over the area.

The moment the navy's fighting men had prayed for was approaching. From the American point of view, Saipan represented Midway in reverse; this time the Americans had the overwhelming advantage in ships. By assaulting Saipan, in the inner ring of the empire, they had lured the Japanese fleet out to fight, just as Admiral Yamamoto had done with the Americans in 1942.

There was another similarity to Midway in a small way: the Japanese intelligence, with all the material deficiencies, was superior to the American. The fact is that as of 2:00 on the afternoon of June 15, Admiral Spruance did not know where his enemy was, and Admiral Ozawa did know where the Americans were, and how many of them there were. In every way, Japanese air reconnaissance was superior to American.

The trouble was that there were so many reports and so little information. The *Flying Fish* reported a Japanese fleet coming out of San Bernardino Strait on the evening of June 15. An hour later the *Sea Horse* reported a battleship force heading north east of Surigao Strait. That meant the Japanese were in two forces, and to Spruance that meant trouble. The invasion of Guam had been set for June 18. Spruance canceled it. He did not want to have to protect two invasions at the same time. On the morning of June 16, Admiral Spruance went to Admiral Turner's flagship, the *Rocky Mount*, to confer. They agreed that he should detach eight cruisers and twenty-one destroyers for Turner, and then he was free to pursue the Japanese fleet. Turner was satisfied that with his own large force of old battleships, cruisers, destroyers, and seven escort carriers, he could protect the landings from any Japanese attack other than that of the main carrier force. Since Spruance was going after the Japanese carriers, Turner was not worried.

So on the morning of June 16, Admiral Spruance seemed to have decided to take the initiative and destroy the Japanese fleet. He ordered his flagship, the *Indianapolis*, to sail out and join the carriers.

Just after 2:00 on the afternoon of June 17, Admiral Spruance issued a battle plan worthy of a Nelson. The carrier planes, he said, would first knock out the Japanese carriers' ability to operate. Then they would leave them as cripples if not sunk and attack enemy battleships and cruisers to disable them or slow them down. The battleship fleet would come up and destroy the enemy in a fleet action if the enemy elected to fight. If the enemy ran, Admiral Lee's battleships and cruisers would chase and sink the cripples. "Action against the retreating enemy must be pushed vigorously by all hands to ensure complete destruction of his fleet. . . ."

Admiral Mitscher was riding in *Lexington*, and when he had the stirring battle call from Spruance he was elated. He asked

No one quite knew what to expect after the heavy bombardment that was supposed to soften up the Japanese on Roi-Namur island in the Marshalls. The landings were easier than expected, as this beach scene shows. At least the landing craft made the beach . . . .

The Marines called them "darlings," those torpedo bombers above on Roi-Namur, that bombed the enemy on request. Even after the landings, the carrier bombers continued to give air support.

At least he could get his head up. The sand of Eniwetok was sprinkled with sticks and pieces of metal after the hammering by the bombers and the snips before the marines landed. When the marines came in, they advanced, and rapidly.

The Japanese died bravely. When the end came on Kwajalein, and there was no further place to retreat, many followed the dictates of their officers and the *bushido* code, and used their rifles or grenades to kill themselves rather than be captured.

The men in charge. Once the Saipan beachhead was secured, General Thomas Watson (center) moved his command post ashore. General Holland Smith (left), the commander of the land forces, came with Admiral Raymond Spruance (right), commander of the whole invasion force, to confer.

When the Americans approached Saipan, they sent in the bombers first, then the fighters to strafe, and the naval ships offshore delivered the bombardment. As the first wave of marines headed for the beach, the fires on the island were burning fiercely.

Troops kept coming ashore on Saipan long after the beachhead was secured and the supplies built up. In the background lies Tinian island, the second of the Marianas group to be attacked, just as soon as Saipan was secured.

The small escort carriers stood offshore at Saipan during the landings, giving air protection to the troops ashore. In the first day or two, as night came, so did the Japanese bombers, heading instinctively for the carriers. This one streams smoke across the *Kitkun Bay* as it attempts to crashdive on the deck after being dealt a mortal wound.

As the Marines fought for Saipan, the planes of Admiral Spruance's Task Force 58 engaged the Japanese fleet hundreds of miles away. The Japanese had hoped here to win a victory that would change the course of the war. But when it ended, the Americans called it "the Marianas Turkey shoot" because they had destroyed so many aircraft. Here the carrier *Shokaku*, one of the attackers of Pearl Harbor, burns as she fights for survival, turning to miss American torpedoes. She sank that afternoon of June 19.

The naval gunfire delivered on Saipan was important until the marines could get their artillery ashore, and it still helped after that to silence Japanese guns.

For the first two days the fighting on the beach and just beyond was very hard. These marines have crawled around the end of an amphibious tractor to move up on a burning Japanese oil dump.

When the battle began, Garapan, Saipan's largest city, was intact. When the battle ended, it looked like this.

Most of the houses in Garapan had corrugated roofs, made from Japanese steel. As the battle sounds stopped, the roofs were all that was left of most buildings.

This wreck had been a Japanese Zero fighter a few hours before. When the invasion began, the carrier planes bombed and strafed the airfields of Saipan, so that most planes did not ever get off the ground.

This sort of concrete blockhouse was common in the Japanese defenses of the Marianas. But in this case, the blockhouse was left undefended at the edge of the Aslito airfield, as the Japanese moved up to the hills to consolidate their defense line.

Long after the marines had taken the beaches, they were still fighting a foxhole war, moving cautiously against strong enemy opposition through difficult terrain.

Saipan's coastal plain was surrounded by jungle, and it made excellent concealment for Japanese snipers, as these marines had already learned.

As the marines drove north, the land changed, and toward the northern tip of Saipan island, the going got much easier.

But, no matter the terrain, the Japanese used every nook and cranny for defense. This marine is about to throw a grenade into one of the caves in which the Japanese held out to the last man.

The Japanese staged several tank attacks like this one, which is observed by a marine who found a shellhole useful for shelter. But each attack was broken up by American tanks and bazooka teams, which fired rockets at the enemy.

A Bazooka team on Saipan wipes out a Japanese machine gun nest on the drive north on Saipan.

The 37mm gun could be used against light tanks, and against enemy positions. Here the gun is employed to give cover to marines advancing against the strong point at right center.

As the marines moved north on Saipan the Japanese resistance made up in fury what it lacked in weaponry. The Japanese charged into the teeth of American guns, shouting *banzai* (may the emperor live 10,000 years), and were mowed down like wheat.

Once Saipan was taken, the marines and the navy moved against Tinian. First the ships opened up, like this cruiser . . . .

As soon as the marines left the beach in Tinian the going got rough. The Japanese had all the advantage of this terrain.

The Guam invasion had been delayed by the sally of the Japanese fleet, but finally weeks after schedule, it began with the usual roar of the big American naval guns. Ashore the Japanese said they were deafened by the barrage.

This is the beach at Asan point, Guam, with the marines coming in. The coral reef stopped the boats offshore, and the men had to wade for it.

The Landing Ship Tank (LST) could come into remarkably shallow water to land its cargoes. Here a DUKW, or amphibious tractor, comes out of the bow of an LST at Guam.

Amphibious tractors make their way across the coral reef at low tide. These vehicles made the landings in the Marianas much easier than the first landings had been at Tarawa in the Gilberts, when Amphtracs were in short supply.

The amphibious tractor was fine on the water and on the beach, but too valuable to take inland. So the marines scrambled off on the beach and began the foot-soldiers slogging drive forward.

American tanks made the assault on Guam move quickly, but it still took riflemen along the sides of the road to flush out the Japanese defenders, one by one.

The Navy's corpsmen and the Marine stretcher bearers worked steadily and in great danger to save comrades wounded in the line and bring them back to hospital ships and aid stations.

Finally the Marianas were all secured under American control but the price, as always, was higher than anyone cared to contemplate.

Spruance for further orders. Spruance answered: "Desire you proceed at your discretion selecting dispositions and movements best calculated to meet the enemy under most advantageous conditions. I shall issue general directives when necessary and leave details to you and Admiral Lee."

So they were really going into battle! Mitscher and Lee were given a ticket to go out and destroy the enemy. The elation spread through the carrier fleet.

On the evening of June 17, the *Cavalla* reported that she had seen the Japanese fleet but all she could report was "fifteen or so large combatant ships" heading east. When Admiral Mitscher had that report, he did some calculating. Rear Admiral J.J. Clark's four carriers, including the *Lexington*, in which Mitscher was riding, were just coming down from an attack on Iwo Jima. Rear Admiral W.K. Harrill's carriers were doing the same. All the task force ought to be assembled that evening and could steam directly toward the enemy. To be sure, the Japanese appeared to be about 800 miles away, but the two forces, heading toward one another, could eat up that distance in amazingly short time (at perhaps 50 knots). They had the go-ahead from Spruance. If Admiral Lee agreed, they could strike the Japanese that night. He sent a message to the battleship commander: "Do you desire night engagement. It may be we can make air contact late this afternoon and attack tonight. Otherwise we should retire to the eastward."

What Mitscher wanted to do was obvious. But when Admiral Lee had the message, he was alarmed. At Guadalcanal the Americans had learned that the Japanese were far superior to themselves in night naval actions. To be sure, the Americans had every material advantage, including radar, which could find the enemy long before any visual contact, especially at night. But the Americans just did not fight at night, and they had not —even after Guadalcanal—been properly trained to do so.

Admiral Lee wanted no part of a night engagement in which skill might be the deciding factor. He replied swiftly. "Do not, repeat NOT believe we should seek night engagement. Possible

advantages of radar more than offset by difficulties of communications and lack of training in fleet tactics at night. . . . " He
added that he would be willing to pursue a damaged or fleeing
enemy anytime, including at night, but he did not want to get
involved with an undamaged, attacking enemy.

So the Americans lost their first chance to destroy the Japanese fleet. Instead of heading west toward Ozawa, they made
a course south and east toward Saipan.

On the morning of June 18, land-based bombers scoured the
air hundreds of miles west of Saipan, and so did navy flying
boats, but they found nothing. At 4:30 in the afternoon, when
Admiral Obayashi had to be restrained from sending his planes
out to attack, the Americans still did not know where the Japanese fleet was located, or how many ships were involved.
Spruance was satisfied that the Japanese had not come within
400 miles of Saipan. He was right, but for the wrong reason.
When Admiral Ozawa's search planes found the American fleet
that afternoon, Ozawa turned, so that he could maintain a 400-
mile distance between his forces and the Americans. At dawn,
when the planes flew off, they had that great advantage. They
could attack the American fleet and return, but the Americans
could not reach them and return to their own carriers.

Aboard the *Indianapolis*, Admiral Spruance had completely
changed his mind. The brave words of the battle plan were
forgotten when he learned that Admiral Mitscher had suggested
going after the Japanese even at night. He was much relieved to
have Admiral Lee's message of refusal of a night action, but he
felt it necessary to be sure that Admiral Mitscher was kept under
control. All those reports of various Japanese units, and not one
recent sighting, had Spruance worried. What if the Japanese
split up, lured him off, and destroyed the Saipan landings? Turner
had said he could manage, but not if the carriers came after him.
That much seemed certain. Spruance sent Mitscher a long, lame
message, noting that the Japanese might come from the west,
but also they might come from the south or maybe from the
north. In other words they might come from anywhere. And it

was not Task Force 58's role to hit the enemy fleet (as Mitscher had been led to believe by the brave battle order) but to protect the invasion forces on Saipan. Mitscher must steam westward in the daytime, and then east at night, and he must not attack the Japanese at night, but just hang around and wait for them. Of course it was important that he find the carriers, and make the strike against them at the earliest possible moment.

Perhaps if the American air-search technique had been more skillful, Spruance's fears of being hit by two or three Japanese forces at once would have been allayed, and he would have allowed his aggressive admiral the chance to destroy the Japanese. But that did not happen. The American planes never did locate the Japanese; Admiral Nimitz did it for them at Pearl Harbor. When Admiral Ozawa broke radio silence to call on Kakuta for all assistance from the Marianas land-based air forces the next morning, Admiral Nimitz was able to get a fix on the location of the transmission, through a technique developed by the British as a weapon against Nazi submarines— the "huff-duff" radio direction finder. Powerful stations in the Aleutians, at Pearl Harbor, and in the South Pacific reported the transmission. At Pearl Harbor, Nimitz' intelligence officers could triangulate the beams and fix the spot from which they came with remarkable accuracy. So Admiral Nimitz saved the day for the Americans.

When Admiral Mitscher learned that the Japanese fleet had been found, he was sailing directly away from them. In a few hours he would be so far away that no attack could be launched. If he turned, and attacked, he could launch his planes at daybreak and they could attack the Japanese and still make it back to their carriers. Mitscher asked Spruance for permission to attack.

Spruance was dismayed by this temerity. For an hour he worried with the problem and talked it over with his staff. Then he seized a last remaining straw of negativism: a message from Admiral Lockwood to the submarine *Stingray* saying that Lockwood had been unable to read the *Stingray's* most recent report because of garbling. What if that report contained information that the Japanese had another fleet someplace coming to attack Saipan? Completely forgotten now was that conversation with Turner in which the amphibious commander had told them to go ahead and get the fleet; he would take care of Saipan. Spruance sent Mitscher a message: no, he could not attack. The Japanese might have other carrier groups ready to pounce.

This estimate, of course, showed how little Spruance knew of his enemy, in one sense. But it was completely in character. Ozawa *knew* that Spruance would never attack him first, for everything in Spruance's career showed him to be the sort of man who never took a risk. Later he compared himself to Admiral Togo waiting at Tsushima for the Russian fleet to appear. Given the circumstances, it was not a very apt comparison, for the very essence of carrier war was to seek the first strike. Apparently Spruance never did learn that basic fact, for his postwar reminiscences always justified his actions in the only way he knew: as a traditional battleship admiral given just another new weapon among weapons. It seems likely, given Spruance's whole deportment during the battle, that the initial battle order represented the thinking of someone else on his staff.

For the second time, then, Admiral Mitscher had suggested that he be allowed to carry the battle against the Japanese, and for the second time he had been refused. Now he must wait, make sure that his pilots were constantly alert for the first strike that Spruance was allowing the Japanese to make, and win the battle anyhow. It was quite an assignment.

16
OZAWA STRIKES

Task Force 58 was prepared for attack by the enemy. On the front line were the three carrier groups of Admiral Clark, Admiral Reeves, and Admiral Montgomery, the four carriers of each group in the center of a wide circle with destroyers and cruisers around the perimeter to provide antiaircraft and antisubmarine protection for the vulnerable flattops. Clark was on the north, Reeves in the middle, and Montgomery on the south. About 12 miles of open sea separated each group. Behind Clark by about 15 miles came Admiral Harrill's carrier group of three, also arranged protectively. Twelve miles south of Harrill was the battleship force. *Indiana* was in the middle, and the others were around her in a circle, interspersed with destroyers and cruisers. In front and behind the force were picket destroyers whose function was to give advance warning of enemy aircraft.

Spruance, whose demeanor now seemed totally defensive, suggested that in the morning Admiral Mitscher send a force to strike Guam and Rota islands, to knock out more Japanese aircraft. Mitscher, who was determined not to disperse his forces thus, answered placatingly but nebulously; he would keep the islands under surveillance, he said. Admiral Montgomery, one of the new breed of carrier men, was outraged by Spruance's suggestion that they begin splattering their strength all over the lot, and said so in a message to Mitscher. Everyone concerned understood that Montgomery was talking to Spruance when he said, "I consider that maximum effort of this force should be directed toward the enemy force at sea; minor strikes should not be diverted to support the Guam-Saipan area." If Spruance wanted to dilute their efforts still further, then why did he not detach some of the carriers, and let the others get on with the battle? The message was not insubordinate, because it was not addressed to Spruance, but it was as close as Montgomery could come to telling Spruance to lay off and let them win his victory.

The air searches launched aroung 1:30 on the morning of June 19 and again around 5:30 still produced no results for the Americans. Ozawa had really outfoxed them; they did not know where he was, and yet he had a striking force already poised, and was simply waiting for the word from his early-morning searches. The word came at 7:30—one of the float planes from the first search group, provided by the battleships and cruisers, reported the sighting of American carriers, and gave the position. Admiral Ozawa gave the order to launch and the strike began.

The Americans were two and a half hours away in flying time, so Ozawa had nothing to do but wait. Meanwhile, the battle had already been opened by Admiral Kakuta. During the night, after receipt of Ozawa's message, Kakuta had been bringing up planes from Truk and other areas to Guam and Tinian. At dawn the fighters and bombers took to the air and headed for the American fleet. A Zero fighter appeared suddenly out of a cloud and dropped a bomb on the picket destroyer *Stockham*. The bomb missed, and the fighter was shot down by the destroyer *Yarnall*. Either that plane or another must have warned the Guam command of the location of the carriers, for half an hour later, the task force radar screen began picking up a number of blips— "bogies" or unidentified aircraft—and part of the combat air patrol of the carrier *Belleau Wood* was sent to investigate. Lieutenant G. I. Oveland was in command of the six fighters of the division. They flew the 90 miles from their carrier and arrived over Oroto airfield on Guam at about 6:30. Below they saw furious air activity. The Japanese saw them too and began firing with antiaircraft guns. But the range was too long for them; the bursts exploded 2,000 feet below the planes, which were high, at 15,500 feet. A moment later, however, they came under attack from a flight of four Zeros that swooped down from even higher altitude. On their first pass, Lieutenant Oveland shot down one Zero, and Lieutenant (j.g.) R. G. Tabler shot down another. More Japanese kept coming, however. As Oveland called on his F6F Hellcats to form up again in tight echelon, the Japanese came swooping in, four of them straight for him. Oveland pushed over in a dive and screamed down to 8,000 feet, then pulled out and climbed back to 15,000 feet. He had lost the Zeros in the dive. Oveland called for help and warned that the Japanese had a large force of planes on the island.

One of the Zeros got on the tail of Lieutenant Tabler, but his wingman, Ensign E. Holmgaard, shot him down; his fire blew half the Japanese plane's starboard wing off, and the plane spiraled down to crash in the water. But the action was getting hot, even as Oveland called for assistance. Lieutenant Tabler saw two Zeros on his left and went after them, then out of the corner of his eye saw four more on his tail. He shouted, and the whole section dived for the deck at full throttle to shake off the enemy. Ensign C. J. Bennett got separated from the others and found himself surrounded by Zeros. He could feel the shock as the Japanese bullets struck the Hellcat. The superiority of the aircraft now saved him; the Japanese Zeros had been built light for speed, and the pilot of that plane shot down by Tabler had suffered the consequences when the .50-caliber machine-gun bullets severed his wing. But Bennett was saved by the heavier construction of the Hellcat and the steel plate behind his seat that fended off the accurate enemy fire. In a few minutes he managed to join up with two other Hellcats. Zeros attacked, and he shot at one. It began smoking and turned away. He did not see what happened to it; he was too busy. Planes from the carriers *Cabot, Hornet,* and *Yorktown* arrived. The sky was full of vapor trails crossing and crisscrossing—vapor trails were not characteristic of carrier warfare, but the meteorological conditions of that day produced them. The danger of collision seemed as great as that of gunfire as the Americans and Japanese rushed at each other. Lieutenant Oveland nearly collided with two Zeros when they attacked. The Japanese were extremely aggressive, but soon discovered that they could not dive with the Hellcats, nor compete with them in a head-to-head firing contest. The superiority of the new American fighter was complete.

The action did not let up. Admiral Kakuta was doing his best to help Admiral Ozawa, and just after 8:00 in the morning the carrier radar screens showed a large group of blips coming up from the southwest toward Guam. Obviously Kakuta was sending reinforcements. Mitscher ordered three task groups to send fighters, and soon another three dozen Hellcats were heading for Guam. Lieutenant Commander E. S. McCuskey led the flight from the *Bunker Hill*, and his planes were over Oroto airfield an hour later. Below they saw many Japanese aircraft landing and taking off. Lieutenant Heinzen's division was selected to strafe the field, while the other eight planes of Squadron VF-8 flew cover. They were at 16,000 feet, but dived to 5,000 and then began firing. They fired until they hit 500 feet and then pulled up. Lieutenant (j.g.) Hobbs and Lieutenant (j.g.) Hanenkratt fired on a single-engine plane as it was taking off. The Japanese plane ground-looped and crashed. Lieutenant Heinzen and Lieutenant (j.g.) E. S. Dooner also strafed, and damaged two other planes. As they came out of the run, Heinzen saw two planes making approaches to land on Oroto field, and they jumped on them. Heinzen overshot, but Dooner shot down one Zero, which crashed into parked planes on the field, doing more than double damage. Heinzen put a long burst into the second plane, and it crashed on the field.

In a moment, Heinzen's flight was under attack by a swarm of Japanese fighters, and the Americans were surprised to discover that these Japanese pilots were extremely skillful. Lieutenant Hobbs got on the tail of one Zero down on the deck and managed to shoot fabric off the tail section. But then the Zero led him in over the field and he had to break off when he realized that in a moment he would be a very low-flying duck for the antiaircraft guns. McCuskey got on the tail of another fighter; as he closed the range the Japanese plane seemed to be just waiting to be shot down, but the moment his guns opened fire, the Japanese pilot made a sharp diving turn and headed straight for the Hellcat, guns blazing, then seemed to cut the throttle and slow. McCuskey overshot, and the only way he could recover was to turn over on his back. They were at low altitude, and if he did so he was very likely to go into the sea. McCuskey climbed and attacked another fighter, and this Japanese pilot used the same maneuver—the diving turn. When McCuskey did roll over this time with plenty of altitude, the Japanese was immediately on his tail. McCuskey came back from the mission with a much higher estimate of the enemy's skills than he had had before. The Japanese had obviously been studying the tactics of fighting F6Fs and were using their superior speed but inferior turning ability against the Americans by using the diving turn.

The twelve pilots of the *Bunker Hill*'s fighter squadron accounted for fifteen Japanese planes in the air that morning, and several more on the ground. But the squadron did not escape unscathed. Lieutenant (j.g.) Brownscombe's Hellcat was riddled just forward of the tail section and the left wing was badly damaged by an extremely proficient Japanese fighter pilot. All that saved Brownscombe was the strong construction of the F6F. He ducked into a cloud and hid for a while, and then found a Japanese fighter in the cloud. He shot, and the other fighter's engine began to smoke. The Japanese pilot bailed out. Brownscombe ducked back into his cloud, and as he did so he saw another Zero on the fringes. He made an approach on the tail, fired, and the Zero spun off and crashed into the sea. Brownscombe climbed to the top of his cloud, and saw the rest of his division on the other side of the island. He managed to join them, and they nursed his plane home. Another violent maneuver or two and the tail might have broken off, but they met no more enemy planes.

Lieutenant Dooner called McCuskey and said he had a broken oil line and was going to have to head back. McCuskey joined him, and they headed for the *Bunker Hill*. But Dooner did not make it back. The plane had been hit in the gas tank, too, and either ran out of gas or the engine froze. He announced that he was going to land in the water. McCuskey circled and saw the F6F hit the water and explode. The wreckage broke up, and McCuskey looked for a bobbing head. But no head came to the surface, so he turned and joined the others. They landed on the *Bunker Hill* without incident.

Just after ten o'clock, the radar operators saw Admiral Ozawa's strike force coming, 150 miles west of them. Mitscher had less than half an hour to prepare. He called in all the fighters that had been vectored out on search and combat missions, and ordered the carriers to launch all available fighter planes. At 10:20 they were launching, as the Japanese arrived. But the Japanese, instead of boring in to take advantage of shock and surprise, began to circle and regroup as they came into sight of the carriers. This delay gave the carriers time to get all the bombers off the decks and to launch more fighters, and for the American fighters in the air to prepare.

Aboard the *Bunker Hill* the word came to launch fighters, and Lieutenant Commander R. W. Hoel led a dozen F6Fs into the air. They headed toward the enemy, climbed to 12,000 feet, and orbited, awaiting orders. Immediately after the fighter contingent had left the *Bunker Hill*'s deck, Captain T.P. Jeter launched a bomber strike against Guam. By this time Admiral Mitscher was cognizant of Admiral Ozawa's strategy and was determined to deny the Japanese any advantage from the shuttle technique. He sent bombers and fighters to hit the airfields again.

Hoel's group of planes orbited for fifteen minutes, while the fighter director decided where to send them. They were told to climb to 23,000 feet and head southwest (260°). Fifteen miles out at 20,000 feet they would encounter a group of Japanese planes. Hoel's radio was out, but Lieutenant Beauchamp heard, and he lifted the nose of his plane and headed up and in the proper direction. Hoel and the others followed. Soon they saw several Japanese planes splash in the water below them. The main attack had come in several thousand feet lower, and had been intercepted by other fighters. Those others were fighters from the *Essex*, *Princeton*, *Lexington*, and *Enterprise*, all of which had sent planes out, and they were busily decimating the Japanese fighters and bombers.

Lieutenant Beauchamp and seven other *Bunker Hill* fighters were too high and soon too far away to get into the action. But Lieutenant Commander Hoel had never quite caught up with them, and his division had remained with him. When he saw the splashes, he was several thousand feet below and behind his shipmates. He nosed over and the other three planes of his division followed, and they got into the fight. Hoel made a run on two Zeros; they split off and he followed one and shot it down. The other got away. The *Bunker Hill* planes then attacked two more Zeros, and one of them dropped, smoking, but pulled out above the sea and headed away. They saw two dive bombers and attacked them. Hoel shot one down; it made a steep diving turn and fell into the water.

Just then, a Zero attacked Hoel and fired several bursts into the plane, damaging the wing and tail. Some shots struck the gun-firing mechanism; Hoel's guns began to fire and kept firing until the ammunition was exhausted. He was having trouble with the stick, which tended to jam, and he decided to try to make it back to the carrier. He found the *Bunker Hill*, saw the big numbers CV-17 on the flight deck, and circled. Then the stick jammed all the way forward and the plane went into an inverted power spin. He took one yank at the stick and nothing happened, so he pulled the canopy release and bailed out at 4,000 feet. A destroyer picked him up and delivered him back to the *Bunker Hill*. He had two cracked ribs, but he was alive.

The second section of Hoel's division found several Zeros and attacked. Lieutenant (j.g.) Kirk and Lieutenant (j.g.) O'Boyle each shot down a Zero. They saw a dive bomber below them and attacked. But as they approached, before either could fire a shot, the divebomber exploded in midair, and pieces of wreckage trailed down to the water. It must have been hit by one of the planes from the other carriers, and blown up like a delayed-action bomb.

By this time, Admiral Ozawa's second strike had reached the American force. The first strike had exhausted itself, without doing much damage. The battleship *South Dakota* was hit by one bomb, which killed and wounded fifty men. The cruiser *Minneapolis* was damaged by a near miss, and several destroyers had narrow escapes. But by 11:00 the first raid had broken up, and not one plane had reached its primary target, the carriers. Just about a third of the strike force headed back for their carriers; of the total sixty-nine planes, forty-two were either shot down in this raid or managed to land on Guam or Tinian. Saipan was no longer open to air traffic. The Japanese garrison had retreated from Aslito airfield the day before, and the runways were under fire if anything moved. The marines were bent on its capture in the next few hours.

The *Essex* had sent up its fighters to meet that first raid, and they had shot down more than twenty planes. The leader of the flight, Commander C. W. Brewer, accounted for four, and so did Ensign R. R. Fowler, Jr.; Lieutenant (j.g.) G. R. Carr shot down five. Commander David McCampbell and eleven other *Essex* pilots were also launched to meet the second strike, which was larger than the first. More than a hundred planes were coming at the task force, and when they were observed by the picket destroyers out in front, they were identified as mostly dive bombers and fighters. McCampbell's planes were at 25,000 feet when they saw the enemy approaching. He picked a dive bomber halfway back in the formation. He planned to dive down on the plane, fire at it, and then duck under and attack another plane on the other side of the formation from below, but when he fired on the first bomber, it exploded almost in his face and caused him to yank the stick back to avoid collision with the debris. He had to pass above the formation, and he had the feeling that every rear gunner in every one of those dozen dive bombers had his gun trained on the Hellcat. But he made it across safely, and put a long burst into another dive bomber, which began to burn and fell over out of formation to the sea. He chased another dive bomber and shot it down from the rear, then made an attack on the leader of the formation. His attack produced no visible damage, so he came around and took a shot at the leader's wingman on the left, and the plane burst into flames.

Then he came back and got on the leader's tail, firing long bursts until the plane began to burn and spiraled down out of control. His guns jammed, but he managed to clear those in the right wing and they fired. The result, however, was hardly what he wanted: The uneven firing caused the plane to skid violently to the left, and he missed the enemy plane. He came around again, charging his guns, trying to make them work, and began firing. Still only the right-wing guns fired, but he managed to correct the angle and shot down this one more plane before his guns quit completely. He headed back to the carrier. As he went he took a look around. His squadron mates had been busy too, and the sea below was dotted with oil slicks and oil and gasoline fires marking the points where aircraft had fallen, for a distance of a dozen miles. McCampbell estimated that they had shot down 90 percent of the Japanese bombers in that formation.

Lieutenant (j.g.) Symes was leading the Third Division when his radio cut out and he turned over the lead to Lieutenant (j.g.) Milton. Symes shot down one bomber and then saw fighters coming at him. He made a pass and shot down a Zero, in company with another F6F, so he claimed a half plane destroyed. They were so close that ejected cartridges from the other Hellcat smacked into Symes' windshield. That plane was flown by Lieutenant Milton, who had already shot down one bomber but was determined not to miss any chances, so he kept boring in until the end. This was the last of their action, for as Commander McCampbell later wrote, "the sky was getting short of enemy planes."

McCampbell's wingmate, Ensign R. E. Foltz, shot down one dive bomber and then was attacked by a Zero that got on his tail.

The superior speed and diving capability of the F6F let him escape quickly and he was soon back at the fray. But the Zero had done him some damage, for oil started spurting from the engine and clouded his windshield. He could see a dive bomber ahead, very dimly, through the streaks, and he began firing. He was lucky—the bomber exploded and he pulled up through the debris. But the oil pressure of the F6F began to drop, and he turned and headed back to the carrier.

Ensign Plant peeled off from the others and went after the fighter cover of the dive bombers. He shot down one Zero, and then another. He saw a third Zero on the tail of an F6F and gave chase, caught it, and shot it down. He then attacked two Zeros. One sheered off, but the second was in his gunsight. He began to fire and fired several long bursts, but the plane did not burn. Instead it went into a falling-leaf pattern, and finally tumbled into the water and sank. Plant was watching when suddenly he heard and felt the impact of bullets on the Hellcat. A Zero was on his tail, and firing. He pulled into a tight circle and escaped, but another Zero got on his tail and began eating away at the empennage with 7.7mm guns and 20mm cannon. He could feel the impact and hear the bullets splattering off the armor plate behind his seat. Just then another F6F saved him, attacked and shot down the Zero, and they joined up. The other Hellcat was also badly damaged. They could not communicate, since both their radios were shot out, but they headed back to the carrier formation. When Plant landed his crew chief counted 150 bullet holes in the plane, from tail to propeller.

Ensign Power of this formation also went after the Zeros. He got one in a surprise attack on his first pass, but then another turned directly at him and they came head-on, firing furiously. Power put shots into the Zero's wing roots, and the Zero flamed up and crashed. The difference: Power's plane was also hit in the wingroot by a 20mm shell, which threw off a piece of shrapnel that hit the pilot in the leg. He dove down to the water and turned back toward the carrier.

Ensign Slack was flying above the formation to cover the others. He shot down a dive bomber and then got into a dogfight with two Zeros. He fired steadily at one, but it did not burn or fall. The second Zero got on his tail and shot the F6F full of holes before another fighter came up and shot down the Zero. Slack and the other plane joined up and headed back to the carriers.

Suddenly the attack was over, and only a handful of Japanese planes turned back to their carriers. A few limped into Guam, Rota, and Tinian, but the great majority were shot down, seventy by the aviators' estimate.

Some Japanese planes got through the fighter screen. About twenty struck at the battle line. Fighters from the carriers were hurriedly sent out, and they began attacking. The ships put up an intense antiaircraft barrage, but the Japanese came on. One torpedo bomber pilot, apparently hit, and unable to release his torpedo, crashed his plane into the side of the battleship *Indiana*. Fortunately for the Americans, the warhead did not explode. Several bombers got through to the carriers this time. The *Wasp* was attacked, and several casualties were incurred when a bomb exploded on the flight deck. The *Bunker Hill* was damaged by two near misses which started fires and punched a hole through the hangar deck. The carrier suffered seventy-six casualties in that attack.

Other bombers attacked the *Enterprise, Princeton,* and *Lexington,* but the carriers managed to escape damage. Half a dozen pilots were shot down from the American carrier force, but that was a small price to pay for the destruction they had wreaked on Admiral Ozawa's aircraft.

By the time the second strike reached the American fleet, Admiral Ozawa was still unaware that the A-Go Plan was in trouble. The American submarine *Albacore* had discovered the Japanese fleet early on that morning of June 19 and had immediately turned attention to the *Taiho*, not because she was the flagship or because she was the largest carrier that Commander J. W.

Blanchard had ever seen (she displaced 33,000 tons and was 850 feet long) but because Blanchard had the best shot at her. In enemy waters, surrounded by the enemy's destroyers, Commander Blanchard scarcely had time for niceties.

Just as the last planes were being launched for this second strike, Commander Blanchard fired a spread of six torpedoes at the carrier. Warrent Officer Sakio, flying one of the new, much improved navy fighters known to the Americans as a "Hamp," had just taken off and was circling when he saw a torpedo heading directly for his ship. He turned into a dive and crashed into the torpedo, which blew the Mitsubishi fighter to pieces. Sakio saved the ship, but only for a moment. Another of that spread of torpedoes ran true, and even as Admiral Ozawa and his staff were speaking admiringly of the brave pilot, the *Taiho* was smashed by that second torpedo on the starboard side. The explosion came near the forward gasoline-storage tanks. At first Admiral Ozawa was merely disconcerted, and then even that passed. A single torpedo could scarcely stop the *Taiho*, which had been engineered and built for maximum safety. Watertight compartments would control the damage to a limited area. The flight deck was unaffected, and having launched planes, the carrier was waiting to participate in more fighting and to recover the planes, which could be expected to return in about five hours. No one expected to see all the planes, for the pilots had instructions that in case of difficulty or shortage of fuel, they were to land on Guam, Tinian, or Rota. But those planes that experienced no difficulty would return to the carriers. Now that Admiral Ozawa had come to a point two and a half hours from the enemy fleet, the planes of the first strike should be returning at about noon, and then he would have a good idea of what was happening and how much damage he had inflicted on the enemy.

As the morning wore on, the crew of the *Taiho* worked to contain and repair the damage to the carrier. The forward elevator was jammed, and the operations of the flight deck would be hampered accordingly. But when repair crews tried to get in, they discovered the elevator pit was sloshing with aviation gasoline.

The concussion of the torpedo explosion had ruptured one of the gasoline storage tanks. Damage-control crews tried to find the source of the leak, and others brought in pumps to clear the spilled gasoline and pump the damaged tank dry. The damage-control officer decided that the best way to clear the gasoline fumes from the ship was to open all the ventilation on the ship and turn on all the power ducts to blow the fumes away. This was done, but the fumes seemed to linger. And instead of blowing away the vapor crept through the ship.

Admiral Ozawa did not notice any problem. His mind was impervious to such detail; just before noon another American submarine, the *Cavalla*, had discovered the Japanese fleet and torpedoed the *Shokaku*, pride of the Japanese carrier fleet, which had served so nobly from those opening hours of the war at Pearl Harbor. The *Cavalla's* captain, Lieutenant Commander H. J. Kossler, launched six torpedoes, and three of them struck the carrier. So at noon, when the planes of the first strike should be returning, the *Shokaku* was fighting for her life. Admiral Ozawa and his staff kept consulting their watches and looking anxiously at the smoke streaming from the *Shokaku*. Why did they have no reports on the battle? They had one disturbing report from their own force of oilers and service ships and protective destroyers. The planes of the second strike had passed directly over the ships, and the gunners had mistaken them for American. All the antiaircraft guns had opened up, and two of the planes had been destroyed and eight others damaged, so that they had had to come back to the carriers. Ozawa counted: eighteen planes of that second strike had failed to get past his own fleet perimeter, ten shot full of holes and eight suffering from mechanical failures that should never have been allowed. And still the radio was silent. The presentiment of a terrible disaster began to hang over the bridge of the *Taiho*. Shortly after noon, a handful of stragglers came limping back to Ozawa's three carriers of Division One. None could land on the *Shokaku*; she was maneuvering madly and her decks were aflame. They could and did land on the *Taiho* and the undamaged *Zuikaku*. And the story they had to tell, of being set upon by dozens of Hellcats before they found the American fleet, gave Admiral Ozawa part of the bad news, but not all of it. The pilots exaggerated wildly about their "success." Hardly had the planes come in when, with an enormous explosion, the *Shokaku* blew up. Several of the destroyers were still searching for the two submarines, and the thunder of exploding depth charges had been heard all morning long. (Both submarines survived the action.) This explosion aboard the *Shokaku* sent flames hundreds of feet in the air and was followed by more explosions. The ship began to list, she lost way, and finally she sank at 3:00 in the afternoon.

By this time Admiral Ozawa should have known that his second strike had also failed. There had been some damage. Anyone could expect that. The pilots came back telling of seeing their comrades zeroing in on American ships and sinking some. The reports were vague, but that was predictable. Too many pilots were still out. He must await their return to the carriers before they would be able to complete the picture.

The planes from the third raid, launched at 10:15 from Carrier Division Two, also returned—just a handful of them—but did not report failure. Then more began coming in, and finally forty of the forty-seven that had flown off the decks of the Japanese carriers were accounted for, either "returned" or "landed on one of the islands."

They had met with no success. They too had been intercepted by swarms of Hellcats before they could come up to the American fleet. But they did not indicate so much.

The fourth raid, which Admiral Ozawa had launched at 11:30, not knowing even yet that something was dreadfully wrong, had consisted of all the reserves available, from the *Junyo, Hiyo,* and *Ryuho* of the Second Division and from the *Zuikaku* of the First Division. Most of these planes did not even find the enemy, and headed for Guam as they had been ordered to do, to await instructions. So by 3:00 when the *Shokaku* blew up, Admiral Ozawa did not know that the day's action had been a failure. What he could not understand was the timidity of the Americans. From the enormous number of carriers, not a single plane had appeared over the Japanese fleet. Just now, he could be glad, for the damage-control parties of the *Taiho* were having difficulties getting rid of those gas fumes. The carrier was in no position to defend herself. As if to emphasize this point, half an hour later came an enormous explosion that seemed to spread all at once throughout the ship. A spark had ignited the gasoline fumes that had been blown into every compartment, and one explosion followed another until it became apparent that the *Taiho* could not be returned to operational condition. Admiral Ozawa hastily transferred his staff to the cruiser *Haguro*. Two carriers, the pride of the fleet, were out of action, and the American fleet had still not struck a blow. The loss of life had been very high, for both carriers had exploded. Nearly 4,000 men had been lost in one short day.

The end of the *Taiho* came in late afternoon, as the last of the planes from the Japanese carrier force were fighting for their lives over Guam. They had failed to find the American fleet and so were carrying out orders to jettison bombs and torpedoes and land at Oroto for new orders. The circling planes were spotted on the radar by the fighter directors, and American fighters of the Combat Air Patrol above the fleet were sent to Guam. Soon there were so many American fighters in the air here that Lieutenant Commander Gaylord Brown, leading the *Cowpens* group, said it was hard to decide which fighters had shot down which enemy planes. Brown began firing on one Zero and knocked pieces off its tail. The plane began wobbling and probably would have crashed, but as it came by Lieutenant (j.g) R. I. Raffman began firing, and the Zero began to burn, then crashed. Who had shot it down? Brown claimed the enemy fighter for both of them, and that was easy because they were both *Cowpens* pilots. In many cases planes were damaged by one pilot from one carrier, and then finished off by one or two more, from different carriers. So the count became thoroughly confused.

The Americans did not have it all their own way. Lieutenant (j.g.) M. L. Adams of the *Cowpens* was in the middle of the fight and helped shoot down one Zero. Then his guns began cutting out and he pulled up, trying to clear them. A few moments later along came a lone F6F, pursued by three Zeros. Adams had his guns working again, and he made a pass at the leading Zero, whereupon they broke off. Adams and the other F6F then pursued one, which fled down onto the deck. Adams shot it down. But Ensign G.L. Massenburg was shot down in another fracas with several Zeros, when one got on his tail. His wingmate, Ensign C.E. Eckhardt, went after the Zero and pulled the plane off Massenburg's tail, but the damage was done; the engine quit, and Massenburg landed in the sea. Eckhardt followed him down, saw him get into his rubber boat, and then circled until his fuel supply became dangerously low. He had radioed the position but by the time he had to leave, no help had come. That night Massenburg was listed as missing in action, so was Lieutenant F.R. Stieglitz, who was last seen attacking a Japanese torpedo bomber, then went into a *chandelle* turn and disappeared from the *Cowpens* group.

Commander C.W. Brewer of the *Essex* led a flight of seven fighters to Guam, and when they got there, at 6:00 in the evening, dusk was settling in. About twenty minutes of circling brought no action; there were no planes in the air above Orote field. But then suddenly they spotted a dive bomber and went after it, all seven of them. They shot down the dive bomber. Then from above they were attacked by sixteen Zeros. The American fighters were strung out in a very loose formation, which made it possible for the Zeros to choose individual targets. Commander Brewer and his wingman, Ensign T. Tarr, Jr., turned and headed into the enemy, with two other planes from the formation, piloted by Lieutenant E.W. Overton and Ensign G.E. Mellon, Jr. The Japanese came down in a coordinated attack, four Zeros to each of the four F6Fs. Commander Brewer began firing and hit the leader of the planes attacking him, which continued its dive into the ground on Guam, where it burst into flame and exploded. Ensign Tarr shot down another. Then the fight became general, and the other members of the squadron were too busy to see what was happening to planes outside their immediate vicinity. They did see one F6F nose up in what was apparently the start of a loop, and then shudder, fall off, and dive straight down into the ground. That was either Brewer or Tarr, and no one knew which. What they did know, after Lieutenant Overton led them home, was that both Brewer and Tarr were missing.

When they returned to the carrier for debriefing, it occurred to many of them that the dive bomber which had appeared so tantalizingly over Orote, all by itself, had been a Japanese plant to lure them into an attack, so they in turn could be attacked. It had certainly worked. The pilots of this formation claimed eleven kills on that mission, but the loss of two of their squadron dampened their spirits severely.

There were not many such tales to be told, for the Americans had overwhelming force available over Guam that afternoon. The result was that planes from the carriers shot down sixty percent of the Japanese planes trying to land, and the planes that did land were badly shot up either in the air or by strafing attacks. The Americans had put 300 planes in the air that day and lost 10 percent of the aircraft, but some of the pilots and aircrewmen were recovered. The Japanese had sent out 370 planes from the carriers, and less than a third of those returned to Admiral Ozawa's ships.

Admiral Kukita's attempt to assist Admiral Ozawa had been overwhelmed by the American bombing and strafing of his airfields and the hundreds of fighters in the air. At least fifty planes based on Guam had been destroyed, and others flown up from Truk and other islands had never made it to land. On the night of June 19, there were still many Japanese pilots on Guam, but their airfield had been bombed repeatedly during the day and most of the installations were destroyed or damaged.

In the flush of victory, the Americans would call the battle the Great Marianas Turkey Shoot, and if it was an exaggeration (at a turkey shoot the riflemen do not also get killed), still, it was an apt description of the apparently absurd ease with which the American pilots destroyed the Japanese air strikes. The Americans were better trained, and they had superior aircraft and an enormous advantage in numbers. They were not even forced to strain themselves to put fighters into the air, because the Japanese planes came in small enough groups to be dealt with before they broke the perimeter of the battle force. Only a handful of Japanese planes ever got through, all day long. One could not fault the Japanese for courage. They used their slender resources as best they could, and the trapping of the *Essex* fighter sweep was an indication of their war wisdom. But too many of their pilots were green, and too many of their aircraft were outmoded. So the result was a disaster for Admiral Ozawa. He had only one perplexity as he retired that night to the northwest, to reorganize and refuel for the next day's battle. Why had the Americans never attacked him from the air? Admiral Spruance's strange timidity was very hard for Admiral Ozawa to understand. He could only be grateful for small favors. He must have hurt the Americans sorely if they could not even reorganize enough to launch a single air strike.

17
MITSCHER STRIKES BACK

All day long, as the airmen fought their glorious battle, Admiral Spruance had kept the fleet heading eastward, away from Admiral Ozawa's carrier force. When the issue was no longer in the slightest doubt, at 3:00 in the afternoon, Admiral Spruance decided to attack. It was far too late to do so, and the American fleet had moved to within a few miles of Guam and Rota. Admiral Ozawa's force was completely out of range.

The Americans had finished up the daylight hours of June 19 in the belief that they had shot down or destroyed every aircraft in the Marianas. But that night the Japanese began sending planes up from an airstrip near Agana. Spruance had been his usual cautious self, and ordered night-fighter sweeps. They produced results. Admiral Harrill's group was detached from Task Force 58 and assigned to watching the islands. Harrill had night fighters, and they made several sweeps. At daylight on June 20 they hit Guam again and found what appeared to be about forty planes on the ground. These were strafed. Apparently the results were good, because enemy air activity in the Marianas was virtually stifled from that point on.

The other three task groups of Task Force 58 spent the evening steaming into the wind, recovering their aircraft. Then, at 8:00

in the evening, Mitscher headed west. He hoped to attack the
Japanese fleet the next day, and Admiral Spruance, although
cautioning that they must remember their primary task of pro-
tecting the Saipan invasion, concurred that an attack was possible.
But only if they could find the enemy, and this was an area of
activity in which the Americans had proved dismally inferior.
Although submarines had sighted Ozawa's force numerous times
in the past seventy-two hours, and two submarines had already
crippled the carrier fleet by sinking two of the finest ships in
Ozawa's command, Task Force 58 still did not know where
Ozawa was. The Japanese had turned northwest several hours
before Mitscher turned west. Mitscher had to travel at cruising
speed (about 23 knots) in order to save fuel in case they did get
into action the next day. And although he launched a search
early on the morning of June 20, it failed to find Ozawa. The
American carrier planes flew out 325 miles, which was just about
their limit. Ozawa was nearly a hundred miles farther to the
northwest of them, fueling. Once before, Pearl Harbor's radio
intelligence team had found the enemy for them, but now Ozawa
had nothing more to say to Admiral Kukita and he kept radio
silence.

The Americans steamed west without knowing what to expect
the next day. Aboard the carriers, the pilots were up half the
night, laughing and telling tales of their adventures of the day
with much zooming of hands and sound effects and grimaces.
The euphoria of having engaged in a major action and survived
had them firmly in its grip. Somehow it had all seemed so easy,
until they contemplated the missing faces, and these were, indeed,
relatively few. They were less than generous in describing the
behavior of the enemy. Most of the pilots felt the Japanese had
not pressed home their attacks on the fleet as hard as they would
have done.

On his bridge, Admiral Mitscher was torn between the desire
to send planes out to search at night, and the need to keep
moving if he was to reach a point where he could engage Ozawa.
For the weather gauge was against the Americans. To launch

planes for a search, a carrier would have to turn almost 180 degrees to get into the wind, and that would mean every carrier launching search planes would lose 40 miles in an hour, as the fleet moved on ahead. That 40 miles might make the difference between any carrier's capability of making an effective attack and inability to send a force out far enough to fight. By this time in the war, the Americans had brought night fighters into the fleet. The carriers had two dozen of them, but they were distributed among the carriers, which meant that several carriers would have to turn away to launch. Besides this, with all the pressure put on the land-based air force to conduct a search, Mitscher expected Admiral Hoover's planes to find the enemy for him. But they did not. Nor did the submarines come to the rescue, for Admiral Ozawa was both skillful and lucky in avoiding detection.

By noon on June 20 the prospects of locating the enemy seemed poor. Several officers on Mitscher's staff predicted that they would find the Japanese long gone, headed for home. Mitscher was persuaded to launch a search of a group of fighters equipped with belly tanks. They went out 475 miles, but never came closer than 150 miles from the Japanese. (Twice during the period from midnight to noon Mitscher had been within striking range of Ozawa by accident, but had not known it.)

Although Ozawa had lost two carriers and had only the most fragmentary reports on the air battle of the previous day, he had no hesitation about pursuing the attack. He had only a hundred planes left in his carrier fleet, which would give any commander pause, but he was not counting that way. He had no knowledge of the complete disaster in the Marianas. The Japanese had counted for so long on the effectiveness of the shuttle strategy that it did not occur to Ozawa that it might have failed. So he said, if he had a hundred planes, there must be 300 or 400 on the airfields of Guam and Rota, preparing to attack in the morning. That night, even if Ozawa had been willing to forget radio silence, he probably would not have learned much. The cruiser *Haguro* was not a command ship and was not equipped with the elaborate communications establishment an admiral needed. Aboard the remaining carriers the air intelligence officers interviewed pilots and got exaggerated answers. Some pilots claimed to have seen carriers sinking, and one said he saw six covered with smoke. They spoke of shooting down many "Grummans," as they called the F6F.

But on June 20, in Tokyo, Admiral Toyoda began to assemble intelligence reports from various points, and he realized that the attack of June 19 had failed completely. The sinking of the carriers *Taiho* and *Shokaku* were serious matters; the loss of so many aircraft was serious too, but that could be remedied in a matter of months, whereas new carriers took years to build, and Japan's resources were overstrained already. Toyoda ordered Admiral Ozawa to steam toward Okinawa when he had fueled, and, in effect, to break off the engagement. Ozawa, after the war, said he never did break off the engagement, but all that day as the Americans maneuvered fruitlessly but in his general direction, he was retiring. Early in the afternoon, he transferred his command to the carrier *Zuikaku,* whose communications were better than the cruiser's. He kept planes in the air, searching. From 7:30 in the morning on, Ozawa knew that the Americans were out looking for him, for many planes reported carrier planes in their search areas. But Ozawa did not find the American fleet this day. Had he done so early enough, he would have known that all the reports he had of sunken carriers and mortally damaged battleships were dross. He was undetermined about fueling. All day long he had rumors that the Americans were in striking distance. At noon he gave the order to fuel, but it was never carried out; the priorities of ships were mixed up and the tankers never seemed to get together with the warships.

The Japanese communications were extremely poor. The A-Go Plan had called for Kakuta to have 500 planes in action in the Marianas and Palau, and Admiral Ozawa had heard nothing to the contrary. Kakuta never told him that his reinforcements had been decimated. Kakuta did tell Ozawa that a number of the fleet planes had landed at Rota and Guam, and this was true, but Kakuta did not add that most of them had been so badly damaged as to be useless until repaired, and that many had been destroyed by American raids on the airfields.

Admiral Mitscher was still moving as rapidly as he could across the Pacific, still unable to travel at flank speed because of the fuel problem. At 1:30 in the afternoon another search was launched, and for two hours nothing was heard. Lieutenant R. S. Nelson had reached the end of his search pattern. He was 325 miles out from the carriers, and must in a moment turn back or he would never make the *Enterprise,* his base. Just as he was ready to turn he saw the Japanese fleet: carriers, battleships and some cruisers, oilers, and destroyers. He did not have time to count, but he radioed back that there they were, heading northwest at 20 knots. The news was passed excitedly through the U. S. fleet by voice radio, and this carelessness destroyed any hope of surprise, for the intelligence officer of *Atago* listened in and at 4:15 passed the word to Admiral Ozawa that they had been found by the Americans, who were launching an air strike. Ozawa stopped all attempts at fueling and ordered the fleet to increase its speed to 24 knots.

But the problem for the Americans all went back to the inefficiency of their search methods. Lieutenant Nelson's first report had been so garbled that the *Enterprise* was able to gather only that he had seen the fleet, but not where. It was nearly 6:00 before Admiral Mitscher had a corrected report from Nelson. Meanwhile, every carrier had been alerted, and the *Enterprise* had launched a dozen dive bombers, a dozen fighters, and half a dozen torpedo planes at 4:30. The problem was that they did not know exactly where to go, so they set off westward, to be corrected in their heading when the location of the Japanese was made clear. They were about 300 miles away, which meant at the outer limits of the American aircraft. The sort of prudence that Admiral Spruance had exhibited would have dictated a wait, for an attack this late in the day, from this distance, would be bound to lose Task Force 58 many aircraft. The planes would make their attack, and some of them would run out of gas before they came home, and some would get lost.

They would also have to land back on the carriers at night, and only a handful of the pilots had any substantial training in night operations. If the weather was perfect it would still be an expensive operation in men and planes. But if they did not strike now, the Japanese fleet might elude them entirely. Mitscher did not hesitate. He informed Admiral Spruance that he was going ahead, and he ordered the launch of 131 bombers and eighty-eight fighters.

18
OZAWA'S TWILIGHT

The sun was on the horizon when the American air squadrons sighted the Japanese fleet, and if they were to attack while it was still light they must strike immediately. The flight leaders, looking at their gas gauges and estimating the distance home, saw that there was absolutely no margin, so they abandoned all plans for a coordinated attack, and each squadron went in independently.

The Japanese were ranged in a tight circle, so that their antiaircraft fire could concentrate on the attacking planes. The Japanese carriers had launched seventy-five planes, and these circled and came to meet the Americans as they came down.

Lieutenant Commander J. D. Ramage led eleven dive bombers from the *Enterprise* in this attack. At 6:40 in the evening, they passed over the oilers, which had been left behind as the carriers and other capital ships moved away. They ignored the cargo ships and hurried on. In twenty minutes more they saw the Japanese fleet, and other American planes attacking. The *Enterprise* planes were at 16,000 feet. Ramage decided on two attacks, against two carriers he saw clearly in the gathering dusk. The first division was to attack the biggest carrier, of the *Zuiho* class. As the planes got within range, the Japanese antiaircraft guns opened up and five-inch shells began bursting. At first they were about 200 yards off to the right, but at the proper altitude, which was a little scary. But there was no time for worry. Ramage peeled off, and five planes followed him. At 9,000 feet they began their bombing dives, as Japanese fighters attacked them from above. Ramage and Lieutenant De Temple bombed first. Their bombs missed the carrier but struck just aft, and started fires on the hangar deck. Lieutenant Hubbard followed them, with a near miss on the port beam. Lieutenant Schafer's bomb-release mechanism failed, and Lieutenant Fife dropped off the port side. Lieutenant Schaal, the last to bomb, made a clean hit on the stern with an armor-piercing bomb. It must have exploded below deck. Smoke and flame began to emerge.

Squadron Leader Ramage came out of his dive and found himself under attack by a Zero, but when his rear gunner began firing the Japanese plane ducked into a cloud and did not come back.

The bomber division flew through intensive antiaircraft fire at low altitude to escape through the protective ring of cruisers and destroyers. It was every plane for itself at this point, but they all came safely through, and joined into formation.

They picked up the rest of the dive bombers of their squadron, and started home. Lieutenant Bangs, the leader of one section, did not appear. His division had bombed one of the smaller carriers. Bangs had bombed first, and his bomb had struck squarely on the after end of the flight deck, smashing half a dozen planes on the fantail. Several of them slid off into the water. Lieutenant Mester followed, and made another hit just forward of the first. Then down came Lieutenant Lewis, who put another 1,000-pound bomb just aft of the island, and then, like the others, strafed the deck as he came across at about 100 feet. Lewis saw a sheet of flame go out from the side of the carrier, and as he sped along he avoided most of the fire from the destroyers and cruisers that were spitting out antiaircraft shells.

As they gained altitude and looked back, the pilots could see the small carrier dead in the water, but they had time for just a quick look, for Bangs and Mester were jumped by a group of Zeros. One came in close and put a 20mm cannon hole in the wing of the dive bomber and twenty machine-gun bullets into the nacelle. Bangs felt the shuddering, but the plane continued to fly, and his rear gunner drove off the attack.

The final section of the *Enterprise's* dive bombers found a third carrier of the *Zuiho* class and dropped on it. But the bombs were all near misses. They strafed the deck, but there were no planes in sight. They jinked through the antiaircraft fire and came out on the far side to reassemble. A Zero attacked, but an F6F came out of nowhere and shot it down. Half an hour from the time the planes had sighted the carrier fleet their part in the attack was over, and they were going home. Only Lieutenant Bangs had failed to join the others.

The fighters of the *Enterprise,* led by Lieutenant Commander W. R. Kane, commander of the air group, split into divisions as they came to the Japanese fleet. Kane led a strafing attack on a big carrier, following the dive bombers down to protect them, and as he came out he observed the near misses and hit on the stern. A Zero appeared in front of him and he made a pass and fired. The Zero's right wheel came down, but Kane's speed carried him past. His wingman, Lieutenant Wolf, shot the plane down. Then they headed for the rendezvous point, as they were suppose to do, following approved tactics. The job of the fighters had been to bring the bombers to the enemy, and now was to get the bombers home again. There was no time for personal heroics. In a few minutes the dive bombers and torpedo bombers had assembled and the fighters had a protective cover over them. Commander Kane saw many Zeros and Hamps, but did not turn aside. The old-fashioned dog fight in which fighter planes squared away at one another like boxers had no place in Commander Kane's book. He observed that the Japanese pilots he saw this day were skilled, and whatever the weaknesses of their aircraft, they were more maneuverable than the F6Fs. The key to success of American fighter tactics was to stick together in sections and divisions, and present a united front. The Japanese fighters, about twenty of them, followed the American planes away from the fleet for a time. But every time a Zero or a Hamp peeled off for an attack, one or two Hellcats turned straight toward him, and the Japanese veered off against that firepower.

Among the other planes they were escorting were the torpedo bombers of the *Enterprise's* torpedo squadron. There were only five of these planes involved in the attack, for most of the squadron had been engaged all day long in fruitless air search for the enemy until Lieutenant Nelson had finally made contact that afternoon. Eight aircrews from the *Enterprise*, then, were entirely out of the action. They had finished their mission and landed on the carrier at 5:30 in the afternoon, too late to join up. So the five bombers represented *Enterprise* in the fight. They were led by Lieutenant Van V. Eason. They were not carrying torpedoes, however, but had been equipped for search missions with four 500-pound bombs on each plane. There had been no time to unload the bombs and load torpedoes if the bombers wanted to participate in the late afternoon attack. Commander W.I. Martin, the skipper of the squadron, held back from this mission for a potentially more dangerous one: he proposed to lead a second strike which had been authorized, a low-level night attack on the Japanese fleet.

When the torpedo planes arrived on the scene with the rest of the VC-10 contingent, they turned to attack the *Zuikaku*. But as they came up, they saw that carrier under attack by a swarm of dive bombers, so they again turned this time toward another smaller carrier that had appeared from beneath a cloud. They began diving at 12,000 feet and pulled out at 3,000 and 4,000, releasing their bombs. This was the same carrier that the *Enterprise* dive bombers attacked. The torpedo planes secured three hits forward, with one set of bombs going off to starboard and the next-to-last bomber dropping just off the port beam. The carrier they bombed was the *Ryuho*, and the American pilots' estimates of damage were no more reliable than the estimates of damage to the American fleet delivered by Japanese airmen. The *Ryuho* was hit in this attack, but she did not even have to go into port for repairs, the damage was so slight.

Four torpedo bombers from the carrier *Belleau Wood* took off at 4:20 and soon joined up with a group of *Yorktown*. When they sighted the three sections of the Japanese fleet, they were flying at 12,000 feet. The first group, off to the south, consisted of the oilers and protective destroyers. Lieutenant (j.g.) George Brown, who was leading the *Belleau Wood* pilots, ignored this small game. He also decided against attacking the second group, although he could see two small carriers and several battleships. But the third group,which contained the biggest carrier, attracted his attention. The *Yorktown* commander turned down the alley between the two groups and then headed toward the *Zuikaku*, the biggest fish of all. But Lieutenant Brown then broke away and led his three other torpedo-laden bombers to the second group. He had seen fighters and dive bombers already attacking the biggest carrier, and nobody was attacking the two small carriers. For a time as they made their diving approach, the Japanese fleet was obscured by clouds, but they broke out and found the two carriers. Three of the torpedo bombers had managed to stay together, but Ensign W. D. Luton's TBF had wandered, and he was approaching from another angle. The antiaircraft guns opened on the three planes as they approached the perimeter, and they spread out, Lieutenant Brown approaching from the port bow, Lieutenant (j.g.) B. C. Tate on the starboard bow, and Lieutenant (j.g.) W. R. Omark on the starboard quarter. As Brown began his final run, the torpedo bomber was hit hard by antiaircraft fire. One section of the left wing fell off. Several shells entered the fuselage and started a fire. The port wing tank blazed and filled the radioman's and gunner's compartments with smoke. Both bailed out and landed in the water, where they became spectators for what was to happen.

Lieutenant Brown bored on in despite the fire in the plane. The carrier maneuvered to avoid the attack and turned into the oncoming bomber. Brown launched his torpedo against the port side, but as the carrier turned, it struck the starboard bow. Brown pulled out and away, and as he turned, the wind blew the fire out.

Lieutenant Tate came in next to drop, but his torpedo missed the target. He flew off to head homeward. Lieutenant Omark's torpedo ran true and struck the carrier about a quarter of the distance back from the bow.

As the torpedo bombers retired, they came under attack by Japanese fighters. Lieutenant Tate's TBF had been severely damaged by antiaircraft fire. The top part of the joystick had been shot away, so he could not fire his wing guns. The turret gun jammed, so his defenses against fighters were almost nil. Two Zeros moved in, one on each side. One Zero made a pass, and Tate turned directly into him as if ready to open fire. The Zero turned away. The second Zero tried the same maneuver, and Tate made the same bluff. The second Zero also turned away. Tate escaped by flying into a cloud. Shortly afterward he saw a TBF flying very low, and wobbling. He went down. It was Lieutenant Brown. Tate led him back toward the ship, but Brown's plane kept wobbling and dropping, as if he was badly hurt. Finally Tate lost him and flew on.

Lieutenant Omark pulled out of his bombing run and was almost immediately attacked by two Japanese dive bombers and a Zero fighter. But Omark's turret gunner, Aircraft Machinist's Mate J. E. Prince, put a burst into one of the dive bombers, which went off into a cloud, and Radioman R. B. Ranes fired on the approaching Zero and hit it, so that the fighter also veered away. Omark then headed for the carrier without further attack. Just before dark he came upon a wobbly TBF flying close to the water. He dropped down to investigate. It was Lieutenant Brown, bleeding badly and apparently in worse shape than Tate had believed. The plane was blackened and torn by the fire, and the left wing was shaky. Omark tried to lead Brown with him, but the TBF wandered away. Its lights were gone, so Omark lost it in the gloom.

Ensign Luton's TBF was hit by antiaircraft fire so hard that he could not close the bomb bay doors after releasing the torpedo. Another plane joined him, and together they flew back toward the carriers. But Luton wondered if he would make it.

The open bomb bay doors added to the plane's drag, and that meant higher fuel consumption.

Behind them, the torpedo bombers of the *Belleau Wood* left two men in the water, Machinist's Mate Babcock and Radioman Platz. They were nearly run down by a Japanese battleship which was maneuvering to escape attack. They floated in the water, wondering what was going to happen to them. The darkness came down, the American attack ended, and the sea was silent, except for the death throes of the *Hiyo*, the carrier the *Belleau Wood's* planes had torpedoed. She had flamed immediately and fires broke out all along her length. After dark she was like a great torch, lighting up the sky. Smoke settled around her so she could barely be seen from the aircrewman's vantage point. Then came an enormous explosion, so strong it must have been a fuel tank or a magazine. It was followed by another explosion and another, each of them sending new fireworks high into the night above the carrier. By this time the rest of the fleet was gone, save one destroyer, which stood by to take off crew members and watch the end. The Japanese searchlight played a-round the water, looking for heads, but did not come as far as the Americans, who could hardly have been eager to be rescued by the Japanese if there was any alternative. At the moment an alternative seemed more than a little dim, but they were not forced to any decisions, as they rode in their Mae Wests in the water. The *Hiyo* was down by the bow, the last time the two Americans saw her, with her propellers clearly visible, sticking up at an angle above the water. Then the smoke, the clouds, and the darkness intervened and they did not see her again. The destroyer stood by for many hours, sweeping in a circle, looking for survivors. Then the destroyer too left the scene, and the quiet was complete.

The *Hornet* sent fourteen dive bombers against the Japanese fleet. The *Lexington* sent fifteen dive bombers and six torpedo bombers. The *Hornet's* planes attacked the *Zuikaku* and damaged her so seriously that Admiral Ozawa at one point thought he was going to have to abandon ship. The order was given, but as men were going over the side, the fires were brought under control by the damage-control parties, and the order was rescinded. *Zuikaku* lived to fight another day. The planes of the *Lexington* attacked the smaller carriers *Ryuho* and *Junyo* and reported many bomb hits on them, but neither ship was sunk.

Four torpedo bombers from the *Langley* joined in the attack, but carrying bombs, not torpedoes, and so did two from the *San Jacinto*. They too headed for the carriers, although some of the *Langley's* planes bombed the *Nagato*, the big battleship. The whole action lasted only about twenty minutes. At the end of it, the Americans had sunk one carrier and damaged three, the *Chiyoda, Junyo,* and *Ryuho.* They had damaged a battleship and a cruiser and sunk two oilers. The damage would have been much greater and the American victory much more spectacular had Admiral Mitscher been prepared to launch torpedo-laden bombers. But for two days those bombers had been making search missions and no one had expected that the Japanese fleet would be encountered under such difficult conditions, late in the day, at extreme range, with no time for rearming. As it was, Admiral Ozawa knew he was defeated, and he headed for Okinawa as soon as he had recovered the handful of aircraft remaining to him. Of the one hundred planes available that afternoon, half had been lost in action, deck crashes on landing at night, and water landings. The A-Go Plan had begun with high hopes for victory. It had ended in numbing defeat.

19
NIGHT RECOVERY

Late on the afternoon of June 21, Admiral Mitscher had asked
Admiral Spruance to release the battleships and cruisers to make
a night attack on the Japanese fleet. With his characteristic conservatism, Spruance had refused, and the American battle line
remained harnessed, with no chance to strike the enemy. The
Japanese were far less timid. Admiral Ozawa had instructed
Admiral Kurita, his battleship commander, to seek a night engagement, and at dark Kurita began charging toward the Americans. He launched ten reconnaissance planes to find the
American fleet and steamed ahead toward battle. But at 11:00
that night Admiral Ozawa recalled Kurita and ordered him to
turn about and follow the carriers back to Japan. Thus was
avoided a major confrontation of big warships.

Mitscher had wanted to finish the job and put the Japanese
fleet out of action. He could have done so, given a different
fleet commander. But Spruance was content to have destroyed
the threat to the Marianas invasion forces, and by dark it was all
over. As the strike ended, Mitscher canceled all plans for another.
It was too late, the enemy was retiring, and he still had the wind
working against him. In order to recover planes, he had to steam
directly away from them, and away from the Japanese. The

irony was that the planes, coming from the end of their range, were all short of gas, and a mile or two might mean the difference between a carrier landing and a splash in the sea. But there was absolutely nothing to be done about it; the wind this day had all been with the Japanese.

The returning planes were to be brought in by radio beams, and about 100 miles out they began to pick them up. But knowing where the carrier was and making it back to deck were two different matters this night. Darkness had set in before 8:00. The sky was overcast, which hampered the pilots more. Halfway back to the carriers, the planes began to ditch. The first to go down were those which had suffered damage in the fight, particularly those which had lost a wing tank or had gas tanks punctured. An hour after dark, the planes began to arrive over the carriers. But then the confusion began. Some pilots, unused to making night landings, plowed their planes into the barriers and fouled the decks. This was the situation that faced Commander Ramage and his dive bombers when they arrived over the *Enterprise*. They were ready to land, but they got a waveoff from the landing signal officer. The deck was fouled and they could not land. The planes had to find other carriers to take them, because they could not last very long with their gas supply almost gone. Ramage and the others did, except one. Lieutenant Bangs did not have enough gas to wait around. He came in on *Enterprise* in the landing pattern, got a waveoff, and before he could find another carrier, he ran out of gas. He ditched not far from his ship. When the plane went in, Bangs hit his head on the gunsight and split his forehead open. But he did not black out and escaped the sinking plane. He was in the water for thirty minutes, then was picked up by a destroyer. His head was patched up with six stitches, and next day he was delivered safe, and nearly sound, to the carrier.

Most of the *Enterprise* fighters were fortunate. A dozen of them had flown out under Commander Kane's supervision, and eleven of them landed safely aboard various carriers. Ensign J.I. Turner joined up with several other fighters after the strafing dives, and they ran into a pair of Zeros, which started shooting. One Zero attacked Ensign Turner's plane, and the bullets severed an oil line. In a few seconds the windshield was spattered and the cockpit was dripping in oil. Turner dove for the water, stayed down, and flew about 30 miles toward the American task force and then ditched. He got out of the plane without trouble, inflated his Mae West and the rubber raft that was kept under the seat, and waited.

The five torpedo bombers of the *Enterprise* had trouble. When they returned, Lieutenant Eason ran out of gas near the fleet and ditched. He and his crewmen were rescued by the USS *Cogswell*. Lieutenant Doyle came in with his wheels up and skidded along the length of the flight deck. He and the crew were safe, but the TBF had to be thrown over the side. Lieutenant Lawton landed safely aboard the *Princeton*, but Lieutenants Collins and Cummings ran out of gas and had to land in the sea. Two more TBFs were scratched.

As the planes came in in the darkness, Admiral Mitscher made the decision to light up the force so that the chances of an aviator making a successful first pass would be increased. The danger —and he knew it well—was that a Japanese submarine might get in among them and wreak havoc. But luck came back to Admiral Mitscher that night, and no Japanese submarine appeared. Part of the reason for that was the excellent search job already done in the area by destroyers and aircraft. At least two Japanese submarines in this sector had been destroyed several days earlier. But Admiral Mitscher had no way of knowing there were no submarines about nor any air elements that could damage him. The decision was brave and was remembered. If Mitscher had never done another thing in the war, he would still be beloved by his pilots for that gesture.

Unfortunately it did not help the pilots who were out of gas, except to give them an aiming point for ditching. When the planes of the *Belleau Wood* came back, Lieutenant Brown was missing. Somewhere out there he had fainted from loss of blood or the TBF had given up, for Brown was not seen again.

The *Bunker Hill* had sent out fourteen fighters, twelve dive bombers, and eight torpedo bombers to the battle. Half of them were badly shot up either by antiaircraft fire or by Japanese Zeros. Nineteen of them were lost, which meant that more than half the planes of this carrier's strike failed to return. A dozen of them made water landings and the pilots were rescued. But at the end of that long day, eleven pilots and aircrewmen of the *Bunker Hill* were either known dead or missing in action. Most of the planes that crashed or landed in the sea had been damaged in the action, and either suffered from excessive drag or loss of fuel. Commander R. L. Shifley, leader of the air group, made the rendezvous after the attack and tried to lead his planes home. Many were separated on the way, and he arrived with a small group. He circled for fifty-five minutes above the *Bunker Hill* and waited while the deck was cleared of crashed planes. He came in with 90 gallons of gas in his tanks, but that was a rare exception. The dive bombers took the worst beating: when the *Bunker Hill*'s contingent left the Japanese fleet, only one of the dozen dive bombers was not damaged, either by antiaircraft fire or fighters. Lieutenant (j.g.) Harwood Sharp's plane was hit in the propeller and carburetor. Gas fumes filled the cockpit and he had to put on his oxygen mask. His engine cut out five times on the way home, and each time he saved the plane from crashing by nosing over and pumping gas into the system. His engine vibrated violently all the way back, and his compass and most of his electrical gear went out. Lieutenant Arthur Jones found that his tail controls were shot out, and he had to guide the plane home without them. Lieutenant Warren Pilcher had his propeller stuck at 1,600 revolutions per minute, and he never managed to remedy the damage.

As the darkness closed in on them, they flew through squalls and heavy clouds, which made it even blacker. Many of the planes had lost their radios, and the circuits were overloaded with pilots asking directions of each other. Gradually the formation fell apart into twos and threes, and that is how the ones who made it as far as the carrier fleet struggled home. Of the dive bombers of the *Bunker Hill*, only one, that of Lieutenant (j.g.) Kenneth Holmes, managed to land on a carrier at all. He came in on the USS *Cabot* at 9:20 that night with 20 gallons of fuel left. The only reason he made it was that his plane was that single exception that was not damaged in the raid.

The *Bunker Hill*'s torpedo bombers were a little luckier. Three of them managed to land on other carriers, although one (Lieutenant Le Compte's) landed on *Enterprise* with a bump. When the plane had stopped and the crew got out, an "airedale" (plane handler) took a reading on the gas tank. It registered zero. Not one TBF from the *Bunker Hill* got back to its carrier that night. Four of them landed in the sea, and one crew of three parachuted rather than chance a water landing. Lieutenant (j.g.) Mason made four passes at the *Bunker Hill* and three at the *Wasp* before his gas gave out and he had to ditch. There were just too many crashes aboard.

Twelve of the *Bunker Hill*'s fighters managed to land on carriers, nine of them on their own. The thirteenth was seen to crash into the water just short of the carrier and explode. The pilot was not recovered.

The other carrier pilots had almost the same experiences. The fighters, with their wing tanks, seemed best equipped for the long haul home. The dive bombers, carrying heavy loads and without adequate gas supply, had the worst time of it. *Hornet*'s thirteen dive bombers were nearly wiped out; eight made water landings, and three crashed into the barrier on landing and were destroyed. Battle damage and fuel exhaustion were the causes, and they were not so serious for the fighters. The *Bataan*, for example, launched ten fighters only for the strike, and all but one returned safely and landed aboard their own carrier.

The fouling of the *Bunker Hill*'s decks, and those of most of the other troubled carriers, was a direct result of the fuel shortage and general confusion of the recovery that night. At 8:00 the carrier's combat information center reported contact with a large number of planes heading toward the task force. The normal precautions were taken, but everyone aboard expected it was the returning strike. Just before 8:30 Captain Jeter turned the carrier into the wind, and she was ready to land planes. Twenty minutes later a dive bomber from the *Hornet* started an approach. The landing signal officer gave the pilot a waveoff because the deck was already full of landed planes, but the dive bomber was out of gas, and the pilot landed anyhow. The bomber crashed into the barrier and nosed over, its propeller lodging in the wooden deck and sticking there. The airedales tried to move the plane, but it was stuck fast.

It was still stuck at 9:06 when a torpedo bomber from the *Cabot* started an approach. The TBF was waved off, but the pilot paid no attention and came in. As he landed he saw the crashed dive bomber in front of him and veered to the right to avoid it. This maneuver caused the torpedo bomber to hit a gun mount with its right wing. The wing tore off, and the bomber skidded into the crashed dive bomber, and then turned over on its back and crashed into the island. Commander W.O. Smith and two men were working to free the dive bomber when the TBF came hurtling in. They were all killed, because they were directly in the line of approach. Four other men of the *Bunker Hill* were injured. The pilot of the TBF was burned but survived, and rescuers got him out and into sick bay. The TBF and the dive bomber were both total wrecks and had to be jettisoned, and when the airedales went to the task they could not remove the body of one of the dead and it had to go over with the planes. It was half an hour before the *Bunker Hill*'s deck was clear again for landing. By this time, most of the planes that had come home low on gas had gone into the sea.

As Admiral Mitscher assembled the reports from the carriers that night, he learned that the task force had lost 100 of 216 planes sent out in the attack—almost half the force. By far the majority of planes were lost on the way home; only twenty could be identified as shot down in combat. But 209 men had gone into the water, and that night only 101 of them had been rescued. Pilots and aircrewmen were strung out at sea all around the carrier force, and all the way between Task Force 58 and the point of the attack. Having been deprived of the opportunity to strike the Japanese hard again, Mitscher turned his attention to the rescue of his pilots, and recommended a course of sixteen knots toward the scene of the battle. Spruance agreed, because they might find some Japanese cripples to destroy. His intelligence reports showed two carriers sunk in the attack, and two others damaged, one battleship damaged, one cruiser damaged, one destroyer sunk and two damaged, and three oilers sunk and two others damaged. So there might indeed be cripples—if his intelligence had been accurate, which it was not, by far.

That night patrol planes based on Saipan started searching for the Japanese fleet, and made contact 325 miles out. But at 16 knots, Task Force 58 would not catch the fleet. Just before six o'clock in the morning, Mitscher launched another strike toward the reported position and course of the Japanese, and a search at the same time. The strike found nothing. The search planes, carrying extra fuel tanks and no bombs, did make contact with the enemy, which was heading toward Japan at 20 knots. But the force consisted of battleships and destroyers. Farther ahead, they found three small carriers, but they did not find any more. All this led Spruance to believe the attack had been far more successful than it was, for Ozawa had preserved six of his nine carriers. But since the American searches throughout the engagement had been so sketchy, Spruance really never knew the size and components of the force he faced.

Spruance took the *Indianapolis* to join the fast battleships, which steamed ahead of the carriers, accompanied by the carriers *Bunker Hill* and *Wasp* for protection. They sped along all day but found no cripples, and finally turned back toward Saipan when they were 550 miles from the Philippines.

He arrived back off Saipan's shore on June 23—just in time to step into a hornet's nest.

20
SAIPAN, CONTINUED

On the morning of June 16, D minus one, it was apparent that at Saipan there had been some serious miscalculations about Japanese defenses on the part of the American high command. The plan had called for seizure of a line along the foothills a mile behind the beach from the northern edge of attack, about two miles south of Garapan, to Agingan Point at the southern end of the island. That was to be accomplished the first day. The second day the marines were to capture Aslito airfield on the southern end of the island and drive clear across to Magicienne Bay on the eastern shore. But the plan had not allowed for the extremely effective use to which General Saito put his artillery, or the excellent disposition and aim of the Japanese mortars which blanketed the beaches. As important as all that, at the end of the first day, prisoners and documents indicated that the Americans were facing a force perhaps twice as large as the one they had expected to meet here. As the landings began, Admiral Turner had been jaunty. He predicted that the objectives would be taken and Saipan would collapse in a week. He told Admiral Spruance he thought it was feasible to launch the Guam invasion on June 18. But by the morning of June 16 all had changed. Admiral Spruance had the word that Ozawa was out looking for him with

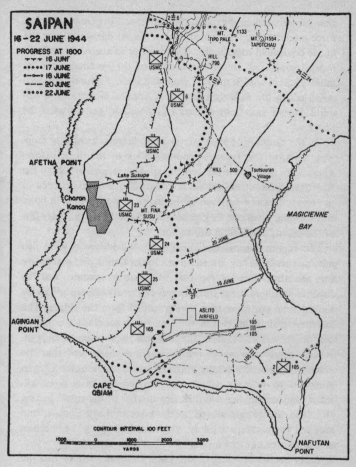

the Japanese fleet, and Admiral Turner and General Holland Smith had the bad news that their troops had not managed to get farther than halfway to their objectives on that first day. There would be no Guam invasion on June 18. The twenty-seventh Army Division, which had been established as the Saipan reserve, and which Holland Smith distrusted intensely, would now have to be committed to the battle, and the Guam invasion force would be kept as a further reserve for Saipan in case the battle continued to go badly. Those decisions made, and arrangements completed for the protection of the invasion force by more cruisers and destroyers from the fleet, Admiral Spruance sailed off in the *Indianapolis* to join Admiral Mitscher, and Admiral Turner and General Smith prepared to get on with the battle.

On the morning of June 16, the Sixth Marines were busy mopping up after the Japanese counterattack of the night before. There were many little pockets of Japanese resistance behind the American lines—stragglers who had not been able to get back to the ridge. It was a question of finding the Japanese in their holes and flushing them out by grenades and flamethrowers. Very few of the enemy survived in this sector.

The Eighth Marines and the Twenty-third Marines were also moving slowly. They linked up at Charan Kanoa pier that morning, and thus closed a gap that had been worrisome. But the Japanese artillery fire in this area was extremely effective. Troops moved into positions that were screened from the ridges. The Japanese had no aircraft in the air. Yet as soon as a troop concentration was established, the Japanese shells began coming in. It was nearly a week before the marines discovered that the enemy had placed a soldier in the tall smokestack of the Charan Kanoa sugar refinery, which had survived the naval bombardment, and the soldier was directing the fire of the guns. But on the 16th the troops moved to the edge of Lake Susupe, and stopped there. More artillery was landed all along the beaches, and more troops came in.

Early on the morning of the 16th, General Schmidt had the Fourth Marine Division moving in the south. Agingan Point was captured, and troops of the Twenty-fifth Marines managed to reach a point half a mile from Aslito airfield. But by the end of the day, Japanese resistance had been so stout that the Fourth Marine Division still had not entirely reached its first day's objective. The second day at Saipan proved that the battle would be longer and more intense than the American commanders had anticipated. They had lost the impetus of the invasion. The Japanese had not been concentrated here in a small area as at Tarawa and in the Marshalls, and so the shock value of the naval and aerial bombardment had been largely lost. The Japanese ability to stop the Americans at the ridgeline on the first day had encouraged the defenders, and their resistance was more fierce and effective on June 16.

General Saito decided that day that the time had come for an offensive, and he chose to launch it on the north against the Second Marine Division. The three marine regiments of the division were strung out on a ragged line that ran from the original invasion's left flank to Afetna Point. During the daylight hours of June 16 the fighting was minimal, with most of the active troops engaged in mopup operations that removed the enemy from within their perimeter. The objective that General Saito chose to capture was the Saipan radio station, in the middle of the Second Division's perimeter, a quarter of a mile inside the American lines. The radio station had been wrecked in the earlier bombardments, but its site was still plainly visible. General Saito chose Colonel Takashi Goto's Ninth Tank Regiment to lead the attack. The Americans had known the Japanese had many tanks on Saipan, and before the invasion they had expected to meet perhaps 200 of them in the battle. They did not know, however, that the tanks included new Japanese medium tanks, which mounted 47mm guns. Colonel Goto brought up forty-four tanks in the fading hours of daylight, and at dusk prepared to lead the attack. The tanks would drive inside the Sixth Marines lines to the radio station, and behind them the 136th Infantry Regiment would attack and take Charan Kanoa. At the same time, Lieutenant Commander Tatsue Karashima would lead the First Yokosuka Special Naval Landing Force south from Garapan along the coastal road to strike the flank of the Second Marines.

Late on the afternoon of June 16, marine observers, flying above the lines in their "grasshoppers" and in torpedo bombers from the escort carriers, noticed a concentration of tanks in the foothills, west of the Sixth Marines' line, but the tanks were not moving, nor did they give any indication of an impending attack, so there was no panic. The observers passed the word of the tank concentration to the ground troops, and the Sixth Marines took note of the fact that they might have to face tanks soon. Lieutenant Colonel William K. Jones of the Sixth Regiment's First Battalion made sure that he had marine tanks in the area, just in case.

At 3:30 on the morning of June 17, the marines in their foxholes on the perimeter of the First Battalion were roused by the almost simultaneous starting up of a number of heavy engines in a valley behind the ridgeline. They could not see what was occurring and called for starshells over the area. The guns provided the light, and Jones called for the Sherman tanks that had been moved up behind the line. The noise grew louder, and ten minutes later the starshells illuminated the first of the Japanese tanks as it rumbled around a corner of the ridge and bumped down toward the marine lines. The first tank was followed by others, and the marines could see Japanese soldiers of the 136th Infantry clinging to the sides of the tanks as they came. Besides the Sherman tanks, battalion commander Jones had several self-propelled 75mm guns, 37mm antitank guns, a number of bazookas and grenade launchers, and the usual complement of machine guns. All these began firing as the Japanese tanks came into the regiment's sector. Above, the starshells lit the battlefield. On the ground the air was alive with tracer and lead. A Japanese tank was hit and set afire. In the smoky light the marines could see another behind it and one alongside. For an hour the battle raged, with Japanese tanks overrunning the American positions, then being stopped by gunfire from front and rear. One tank after another was disabled. The Japanese infantrymen coming behind to consolidate the positions found themselves in the midst of the marines, but without the tank support that was supposed to make their task easy. They dropped to the ground and began firing their rifles, the marines responded, and the din grew.

In the north, Lieutenant Commander Karashima's special land-ing force was to coordinate with this attack, which spilled over into the right flank of the Second Marines, and hit the Second from the other side. But Karashima was slow arriving, and when he came there was no brave frontal attack along the road to split the marines and join up with the troops of the 136th. Perhaps Karashima could tell what was happening on the other side, for his troops never committed themselves. They held back and attacked the Second's flank with mortars, but there was no in-fantry drive. Lieutenant Colonel Jones could be thankful for that; he had his hands full with the Japanese tank attack, and it could have split the regiment and isolated the marines north of the radio station had it succeeded. By 5:30 it was apparent that the Japanese attack had been blunted. By 6:00 the surviving tanks were turning and heading back toward the ridgeline and their valley. By 7:00 the battlefield was still enough that the sound of single rifle shots could be heard as the marines hunted out little pockets of Japanese infantrymen who had become trapped behind the re-formed perimeter. Twenty-four Japanese tanks lay smouldering in the sand and brush. The Ninth Tank Regiment's striking force had been all but wiped out. Colonel Goto had few reinforcements; two companies of his tanks and part of a third—40 percent of his force—had been sent to Guam several weeks earlier. The dozen or so tanks that remained were all that was left of his unit. Colonel Yukitsume Ogawa counted the dead and missing from his 136th Regiment. He had lost 300 men. The attack had failed.

The Japanese did not know it, but they had mauled the ma-rines severely. The First Battalion of the Sixth Marines had lost almost the equivalent of a rifle company, and the regiment had lost many of its artillery pieces in the Japanese shelling that ac-companied the tank drive. The casualty list for the Saipan op-eration was over 3,000, and rising.

That night, General Holland Smith had ordered the Twenty-seventh Division to begin landing its troops, and it was apparent he would need these reserves if the marines were to move ahead.

The 165th Army Infantry was to help break out from the coastal plain and over the ridgeline that had stopped the Americans so far. The plan now called for the Americans to drive north to Garapan, and for other forces to push across to Magicienne Bay, thus sealing off the southern half of the island below Mount Tapotchau. The attack would be three-directional: the Second Marines would drive north, the Sixth Marines would move northwest toward Mt. Tapotchau, and the Eighth Marines would cross the marshes of Lake Susupe.

The Japanese tanks were still burning at 7:00 when the marines attacked. The Second Marines were to move halfway to Garapan, and then stop and dig in. They achieved their objective in three hours with very little fighting. The Sixth Marines also had the advantage of the blunted Japanese attack of the night before. They moved up to the foothills of Mount Tipo Pale, the mountain that jutted up in front of Tapotchau. By late afternoon they were on their assigned line, and had been reinforced. The Eighth Marines bore the burden of the attack this day. Those on the left, who faced sloping ground to the top of the ridge, had fairly easy going. Deprived of their tank support, the Japanese had fallen back in this area.

But in the swamps along the edge of Lake Susupe the enemy took advantage of the difficult terrain to move up snipers, who were most effective. The marines' equipment bogged down in the swamp, and as they struggled to free it they came under sniper fire. Movement had to stop while riflemen went out to find the snipers. The Japanese concentrated their machine guns and rifle positions in a grove of palm trees and along the edge of the ridge back of the coastal plain, above the swamp. The fire was effective, and the marines suffered many casualties. Four tanks came along the coastal road, and Lieutenant Colonel Rathvon Tompkins commandeered them for his fight. The tanks fired on the Japanese along the ridge and kept their heads down while the marines moved up the ridge and captured the position. The palm grove proved troublesome most of the afternoon, but after the ridgeline was secured, the marines tried to dislodge the enemy there. They brought up mortars and fired steadily, but the Japanese were obviously in prepared defenses, and the mortar fire did not end the resistance. As it was growing late, Tompkins dug in for the night, leaving the Japanese in possession of the palm grove. Since he did not know how many enemy there were in this place, he brought forward several 75mm self-propelled guns to protect against a possible night counterattack.

While the marines were driving along the island, Colonel Gerard Kelley's 165th Infantry was assigned the job of taking Aslito airfield, which lay south of the marine perimeter held by the Twenty-fifth Marines. The army men attacked with the usual army tactics, along a broad line, moving up slowly, and making sure of superiority before moving again. The Japanese defenses here at first were minimal, so the army troops moved relatively quickly. But as the direction of the drive became apparent to the Japanese, resistance increased. From Agingan Point, the 165th moved toward Cape Obiam, on the southern shore of the island. Beyond the cape, inland, lay the ridgeline back from the coastal plain, and beyond the ridge lay Aslito airfield, their destination. But before they could take the airfield they had to take the ridge, and the Japanese had the advantage of the high ground. Late in the afternoon, the 165th attacked up the hill, but the troops were driven back by a determined Japanese counterattack. On the north, another battalion of the 165th had moved within a few yards of the Aslito runways, but with its right flank pushed back, the regiment halted for the night and dug in, along a broad if wavering front.

North of the 165th, Colonel Batchelder's Twenty-fifth Marines attacked in marine fashion, which was to strike like an arrow for an objective. The differences in techniques could be seen very clearly in this action. The Twenty-fifth Marines moved forward in a column to a point 1,500 yards from their jump-off position, taking the ridge beyond the airfield and securing the north end from Japanese reinforcement. Batchelder discovered late in the afternoon that the Japanese had abandoned the airfield, and he informed Colonel Kelley. But the army, which might have occupied the airfield and straightened up the peri-meter, refused to move. The 165th had a good defensive position for the night and did not want to sacrifice it. Thus the marines were out on a limb with a gap between their ridgeline and the army back along the west side of the airfield.

Directly north of the Twenty-fifth Marines were the men of the Twenty-fourth, who had faced strong opposition from the Japanese all day, and some complications of their own. Japanese artillery at Nafutan Point had proved very troublesome in stal-ling the advance that was supposed to take the Twenty-fourth about midway along the north-south axis of the island. They were supposed to hit and dig in. On their left, the Twenty-third Marines had an even more difficult time on the 17th. A group of soldiers from the well-trained Japanese Forty-seventh Indepen-dent Mixed Brigade held the position they were supposed to take. They held it all day, in spite of repeated attacks. They were well entrenched, and they had a 3-inch gun and several 40mm guns. But the worst difficulty of the day came from the marines' own lines. At about 3:00 in the afternoon one unit of the Twenty-third called for help. The help proved to be quite sophisticated, coming from one of the new provisional rocket detachments which was equipped with heavy trucks on which rocket launchers were mounted. The rocket launchers came up and fired a wave of 4.5-inch missiles at the enemy. But the missiles were wrongly aimed, and they struck in the middle of the Second Battalion of the Twenty-fourth Marines, causing twenty casualties. It seemed hardly fair to have to face fire from behind as well as from the front, but the marines rallied and went on. A few yards farther along they saw their objective, the ridgeline ahead. They moved, and as they did so, from the face of a cliff came a shattering fire from machine guns and rifles. The ground on which the marines were moving was open land, with coral just beneath the surface. There was no way to dig a foxhole in this stuff, and they were trapped. There was only one answer—retreat—and they did till they found a point where they could dig in. The advance that day, of a little more than a mile, had cost the battalion fifty-seven casualties as compared to the seventy-two casualties suffered by the whole 165th Regiment in the same day's fighting.

As evening came and dusk descended on Saipan, the Japanese made their first effort to support Admiral Ozawa's A-Go Plan in the air. Half a dozen planes from Truk flew toward Saipan to attack the invasion forces. They found the transports containing the invasion reserves, later destined for Guam, and attacked them. The transports and their destroyers shot down three of the bombers, but one torpedo bomber got through and its torpedo hit an LCI, causing twenty casualties. In terms of the Japanese effort involved, it was a waste of a torpedo, although to the men of the ship it was a deadly matter. The LCI was taken in tow, but sank before it could reach port. It was the only casualty of the transports in the raid.

A much larger force from Yap attacked later that evening. The combat air patrols from the escort carriers shot down a number of the planes, but several bombers and torpedo planes got through to the carriers, which were operating as a group off the Saipan shore. The *Fanshaw Bay* was hit by a bomb that exploded below the flight deck, starting fires and killing and wounding a number of men. The fires were controlled, but the *Fanshaw Bay* could not operate, so she headed back to Eniwetok for repairs. The *Coral Sea* took several near misses, and so did the *Gambier Bay*. For most of the men of these ships, this was the first action. They comported themselves very well; there was a certain amount of confusion in the air, and some shooting by American ships at American planes, but a number of the Japanese bombers were destroyed by fighters, and several by the gun crews of the carriers.

With the usual aviator ebullience, the Japanese pilots returned to base talking of their exploits. They identified the "carriers" but confused them with the big fleet carriers of Admiral Mitscher's force. There was quite a difference: a fleet carrier, such as the *Yorktown*, carried eighty-six fighters and bombers; an escort carrier of the Kaiser class, which most of these were, carried about thirty planes. This improper identification cheered the Japanese commanders, and was partly responsible for Admiral Kurita's erroneous reports to Admiral Ozawa.

On the night of June 17, General Saito regrouped his forces for the defense. Apparently he expected a counter invasion from nearby Tinian, for the Aslito airfield garrison had moved to Nafutan Point, which was virtually surrounded by the Americans. The majority of the Japanese troops, however, fell back to a line that ran from Garapan down along the ridge line to Mt. Tapotchau, and then to the eastern shore of the island. The Japanese still occupied two-thirds of the island then, and abandoned the southern third to the invaders. The territory they held was far more rugged than anything the Americans had yet encountered, ideally suited for defense.

The difficulties that lay ahead were concealed on the morning of June 18, however, by the ease with which the Americans were able to advance. The army's 165th Regimental Combat Team took Aslito airfield without trouble. The marines moved swiftly across the island to Magicienne Bay. General Holland Smith had moved his headquarters ashore to Charan Kanoa on the night of June 17, and so had General Ralph Smith of the Twenty-seventh Infantry Division. The decision of Admiral Spruance to leave the invasion force had its first repercussions this day on the land battle. The 105th Army Infantry landed, but it was discovered that its supply train had been loaded aboard other transports, which had sailed by Admiral Spruance's order away from the beach to minimize the danger of Japanese aerial attack. So the troops were ashore but their equipment was not. Colonel Leonard Bishop did the best he could. He sent his men to round up and repair Japanese trucks, and they ran them for a week. But because the regiment's supplies were missing, General Holland Smith kept them at the rear of the Fourth Marine Division to guard against an enemy counterattack.

On the morning of June 18, it was apparent that the fate of the Saipan garrison was already determined, unless General Saito could receive troop support from Guam or some other island.

Colonel Robert Hogaboom, the operations officer on General Holland Smith's staff, reported that the Japanese defenses were weakening. On the night before, the Japanese had mounted a handful of small attacks, but they had been minor and easily repelled. The most serious threat had been an attempt to send about thirty landing barges from Tanapag to land behind the marines, but the navy had been alert to this and about half the barges were sunk by destroyers and gunboats and a few by marine artillery from the beach. The "invasion" failed and the troops of the 135th Infantry Division went back to Tanapag.

On the morning of the 18th, even Tokyo seemed aware of the course of the battle. Premier Hideki Tojo sent a message to General Saito on Saipan to inspire the troops. But the "inspiration" consisted of abjuration to do their duty and die for the emperor. It was hardly a victory message. General Saito's response was even more indicative of the state of affairs on the Japanese side of the lines. "By becoming the bulwark of the Pacific with 10,000 deaths, we hope to requite imperial favor," he radioed. Imperial favor they would have, but it would be lavished on them at the Yasukuni shrine where the military heroes of the nation were revered. General Saito knew that he would never need another promotion. The abandonment of Aslito airfield meant that within a few days the Americans would be able to operate land-based aircraft there, and that meant disaster. Already the Seabees were ashore, plugging the bomb craters in the runways and salvaging buildings and equipment.

The ease with which marine and army troops moved on the morning of June 18 was comforting, but it did not last. The moment they came to the ridgeline, they found the Japanese dug in and waiting. The Eighth Marines captured their coconut grove below the ridge, which had been largely abandoned, but when they got past that point they were stalled. The Twenty-third and Twenty-fourth Marines moved forward to the ridge, but could not get over it, and at nightfall had to move back to find defensive positions. The marines also moved to the shore of Magicienne Bay, thus isolating the Nafutan Point garrison completely. The Japanese mounted only one action that day. Two tanks came down from the ridgeline and moved along the American perimeter, firing. But when the artillery began shooting at them, they prudently retired. A sample of the coming pattern was given the marines on the east coast. The Twenty-fourth Marines came to a cliff that was dotted with caves full of Japanese defenders. There was no way to make a sweep; the Japanese had to be routed cave by cave. The job was given to the Twenty-fifth Marines, the Fourth Division reserve, and they spent the whole day at it. The demolition men brought up satchel charges. The flamethrowers were broken out, and each cave was scoured. Some caves were too deep to clear, and these were blasted so that the entrances were sealed, and the Japanese left to a particularly unpleasant death.

The marines had been critical of the 165th Army Regiment's failure to take Aslito airfield when it was discovered to be deserted on the evening of June 16. These frictions continued and were multiplied. Colonel Kelley did not know whether he was to continue to report to General Schmidt, the Fourth Marine's commander who had directed operations on that first day, or to General Ralph Smith, his own divisional commander, who had landed and set up a command post. Kelley telephoned Fourth Marine Division headquarters but did not get a definitive answer. He spoke to General Ralph Smith, who indicated that of course the 165th would now come back under army command. After conferring with Ralph Smith, Colonel Kelley attacked the Japanese along the ridgeline in his sector, without orders from the Fourth Marines. Since the Japanese had already written off the whole area, the attack was easily successful, so little was said, but General Schmidt did not like army colonels taking action in his command zone without orders. As night fell on June 18, the matter of command was still not resolved.

That night, General Saito elaborated on his defense plans. Seeing the work of the Seabees at Aslito airfield, he ordered the forward units to make a series of infiltration attacks, not to capture the airfield, which he knew he could not hold, but to destroy installations and prevent the Americans from using the field. He was still hoping for reinforcement: the A-Go Plan promised that, and as the Japanese fleet came forth searching for the Americans, Imperial General Headquarters sent messages of inspiration and hope. The great Japanese naval victory in a day or two would change everything. But at the Thirty-first Army's intelligence section, the Japanese officers began burning their code books and papers that referred to defense of other areas of the inner empire. "You will hold Saipan," said one exuberant message from Tokyo. "If Saipan is lost air raids on Tokyo will take place often . . . . therefore you will hold." Obviously there was some very intelligent observation going on in Tokyo, although obfuscated by the growing need to phrase every message of despair in euphemisms.

The going for the Americans had slowed down. General Holland Smith wanted those transports back off the beaches with their precious loads of ammunition and supply, before he launched any major attack. Admiral Turner, told that supplies on the beach were running low, said that he had his orders, and the transports were held back, except for those carrying supplies General Smith said were needed desperately, and would be unloaded immediately. The marines, seeing the transports leave and not come back, began to feel as they had at Guadalcanal, when Admiral Turner's supply ships had been forced to sail away, leaving them stranded, because of Japanese air and sea control of the island in the first days of the American invasion. So while the marines and the army did move on the 19th, they did not move far.

On the night of June 19-20, the Japanese began their harassing attacks. A unit of about seventy-five soldiers moved forward on the positions of the Twenty-fourth Marines, attacked the perimeter, fought for a time, and then retreated. A smaller unit in the sector of the Sixth Marines did the same.

Early on June 20, the Americans advanced again, to the high point of ground called Hill 500. They did not take the hill, but moved to be in a position to do so. That day, General Saito had some bad news from his operations officers. They told him that almost half of the Forty-third Division had been wiped out. It had lost two-thirds of its artillery. The Forty-seventh Mixed Brigade had lost all its artillery and was so scattered that the command could not even estimate the number of units still fighting. Three rifle battalions had been organized from among the stragglers stranded on Saipan, and these had been decimated. The engineers were down to half strength, and the antiaircraft artillery was too. About 20 percent of the total military force had been killed, wounded, or captured.

The attack on Hill 500 came in the middle of the morning of June 20. Colonel Batchelder's Twenty-Fifth Marines were assigned the task of capturing the hill. First the artillery laid down a smoke barrage and then the troops moved. Five hundred yards below the crest they stopped and reorganized, and then began the ascent. The Japanese were mostly concealed in caves on the hillside, and each of these had to be flushed out or sealed in. The task took all afternoon. When the fight for Hill 500 ended, the marines counted forty-four dead Japanese defenders, but they could not count the number dead in the caves. The marines had suffered about fifty casualties, far less than they had expected, because the Japanese had drawn back to a new defense line and did not seriously contest the terrain. The biggest surprise of the day was the explosion of a Japanese ammunition dump in the Twenty-fourth Marines' area, on the Magicienne Bay side of the island. Several marines were killed or wounded.

In the south, General Ralph Smith's Twenty-seventh Division army troops moved forward satisfactorily, moving forward about two-thirds of a mile. The big news of the day, as far as Admiral Turner was concerned, was the completion of the repairs to Aslito airfield. The first American planes arrived that evening. To Turner this meant the Army Air Force could move in land-based fighters and bombers, and the responsibility of the escort carriers for air protection was ended. That had been one worrisome aspect of Admiral Spruance's departure with Task Force 58 to meet the Japanese fleet. If the Japanese had somehow mounted

a sustained air attack on the ships of the amphibious force, the
hundred planes of the escort carriers might not have been able
to contain them. The 165th Infantry Division, which had captured the airfield, had exercised the usual prerogative of giving
it an English-language name. They chose to call it Conroy Field,
in honor of Colonel Gardiner J. Conroy, the regimental commander who had been killed at Makin in the Gilberts. The navy
demurred and promptly renamed the field Isely field, in honor
of Commander Robert H. Isely, commander of VT-16, the *Lexington's* torpedo squadron, who had been killed there on a pre-
invasion air strike. The navy name became official and stuck,
to the annoyance of the officers and men of the Twenty-seventh
Division.

At the end of June 20, the Americans had straightened out
their lines and held all of southern Saipan except the redoubt at
Nafutan Point, which was going to be left hanging on a little
longer since it did not threaten any position. The marines and
army troops were up against General Saito's new line of defense
and ready to attack.

On June 21, the marines reorganized. They brought supplies
up from the beaches to points closer to the line. Some units were
set to scouring the marshes around Lake Susupe; they killed a
number of Japanese holed up there, but some escaped. They
offered no threat except occasionally to come out and snipe at
passersby. They were, in other words, dangerous to individuals
but not to the command.

Troops of the Second Marines were engaged in scouting activities. They tried to ascertain the condition and extent of
General Saito's defenses, without much success. On Hill 500
the marines continued to try to close up every crevice. A few
Japanese were persuaded to surrender, but most fought to the
end.

General Holland Smith ordered General Ralph Smith's Twenty-
seventh Division troops to move up north of Aslito airfield and
go into reserve for the marines. One battalion of the division
could be left behind to clear out Nafutan Point, but the rest were

to join the general advance. When General Ralph Smith received that order, he met with his commanders. They argued that it would take a regiment to clear up Nafutan Point—the Japanese were holed up there in stout defenses since the army's style of fighting employed a large number of troops and lots of artillery and tank support to keep casualties down. Ralph Smith conferred and considered for five hours. Then he telephoned Holland Smith and asked that he be allowed to assign a regiment to the Nafutan Point task. Holland Smith concurred, as long as Ralph Smith would hold one battalion in reserve for Holland Smith's use elsewhere on the island.

Ralph Smith then ordered the 105th Infantry to hold the current line at Nafutan Point, with two battalions on the line and a third battalion in reserve. He said nothing to the regimental commander about keeping one battalion free for Holland Smith's employment. He said nothing about continuing the attack that day on Nafutan Point, as General Holland Smith had indicated in his order earlier. The 105th was to "hold" when it moved into position at 6:30 on June 22, replacing the 165th Army Infantry.

All this activity on the night of June 21 presaged a new American attack the next day. That night the Japanese prepared. Along the line they infiltrated and learned what they could about American movements. Back on the beach, a handful of Japanese holdouts who had concealed themselves for five days came out and blew up an ammunition dump on Green Beach 1. The cache exploded with a roar, and then fireworks continued all night long, sending streaks of light and flashes all across the island. It was a fitting overture for the next day. The initial American drive had ended with the capture of Aslito airfield and the flat ground that led to the mountains. The Americans were in control of the coastal plain. Now they would have to assault the secondary defense line, which was far stronger than anything they had yet seen on Saipan. General Holland Smith's command had suffered 6,100 casualties in six days of fighting, far more than had been expected in the planning days at Pearl Harbor. But fortunately the Guam invasion had been postponed, and so Holland Smith had those troops to back up his marines. On June 22, he expected the marines to advance about 2.5 miles, and capture Mount Tipo Pale and Mount Tapotchau. General Ralph Smith's Twenty-seventh Division troops were to be the reserve. General Holland Smith did not know how he might have to employ them, so he ordered Ralph Smith to select two routes, one leading to the Second Marine Division front, and the other to the Fourth Division. It might go either way. The Second Division moved out at 6:00 on the morning of June 22, toward the slopes of Mount Tipo Pale. They reached the slope early in the afternoon, having encountered only token resistance. The Sixth Marine Regiment advanced up the slope. One company of its Third Battalion moved around the entrance to a ravine and up the hill to the top. They could not go down the other side, however, because they were on a steep cliff, with a drop of more than 1,000 feet to the bottom.

Meanwhile a platoon of the Sixth Marines had investigated the bypassed ravine and found it alive with Japanese. They were dug into the sides of the hill, and the marines soon found the Japanese had interconnecting tunnels. Mount Tipo Pale was like a hand, with the ravine fingers deep into the hill, and the ravines were connected by tunnels through the fingers. This made it necessary to maintain a constant pressure on the base of the hill, and that meant employment of troops who otherwise would be moving ahead.

The Fourth Marine Division also ran into heavier resistance this day. General Schmidt had told his commanders to advance about a mile and a quarter to the base of Hill 600. But the terrain was not much like that indicated on the maps. One of the difficulties of the whole Central Pacific campaign had been charts and maps, because the Japanese had kept the area bottled up for twenty-five years and there simply were no proper maps in American hands. The Fourth Division's advance was to be made through four sets of ridges and valleys. At the first one they ran into a determined Japanese force that attacked them as they came up. When the fight was over the Japanese had lost ninety men killed, but the Americans had been hurt badly too. The commander of the Third Battalion's Company K was killed in the assault. His place was taken by another officer, and he was killed. His place was taken by another and he was killed. Finally that position was taken, but the story was repeated during the day, so that at the end of June 22, the Fourth Division had advanced just half as far as General Holland Smith had expected, and that only in part of the area. The Twenty-fourth Marines had gotten less than halfway.

Late that afternoon, when General Holland Smith discovered how the going was, he decided it was time to commit the reserves of the Twenty-seventh Division to the fight. He outlined a plan of advance for the next day that would put the Americans into the village of LauLau on the northeastern shore of Magicienne Bay, and across Mount Tapotchau in the center of the island, and half a mile south of Garapan on the west. To do this he would use the Twenty-seventh Division, which was rested. They would attack the next morning, passing through the Twenty-fifth Marines to take Mount Tapotchau. General Holland Smith did not know that along the line across the island General Saito had concentrated his defenses, nor that he faced 15,000 determined defenders.

On June 23 the Americans ran into trouble. The marines discovered that the supply road leading past Mount Tapotchau was dominated by a hill in Japanese hands. The Eighth Marines moved, but had to stop because the army 106th Infantry on their flank had not begun to move by 11:30 that morning. The army units had gotten mixed up in moving forward and had to be sorted out, and it was nearly noon before they came up. Then they ran into a very difficult piece of terrain, which was soon dubbed Hell's Pocket, and they were stopped again. On their flank the 165th Infantry did move ahead to the ridge called Purple Heart Ridge, which got its name that day. The Japanese fought the Americans here and stopped them, with many casualties on both sides.

The result, at the end of June 23, was that the American line had scarcely advanced and Nafutan Point, which was supposed to have been reduced, was still in Japanese hands. When General Holland Smith looked at his situation map that afternoon he was annoyed. He had given the Twenty-seventh Army Division two tasks to perform and they had not done either. He conferred with Major General Sanderford Jarman, commander of the army troops who formed the Saipan garrison and took over as the attack units moved forward. He told Jarman he was extremely displeased and asked Jarman to go forward and have a talk with Ralph Smith. Jarman went to the line and found General Ralph Smith. He told the Twenty-seventh Division commander that Holland Smith was very unhappy with the performance of the Twenty-seventh. Ralph Smith agreed. He was unhappy too and was just about to have a very serious talk with his regimental commanders. On June 24, he said, the Twenty-seventh Division was going to *move*, and he personally was going to make sure that it went forward. If the division did not move, then he, Major General Ralph Smith, should be removed from command.

General Jarman then went back to Holland Smith's command post and related the conversation, which seemed to placate the marine general, although the next morning he made sure Ralph Smith and the Twenty-seventh Division knew what he thought of the performance of June 23: "Commanding General is highly displeased with the failure of the Twenty-seventh Division to launch its attack as ordered . . . and the lack of offensive action in its failure to advance and seize the objective . . . when opposed only by small arms and mortar fire . . . . " His two marine divisions, he said, had been forced to stop and wait to prevent exposure of their interior flanks because the Twenty-seventh at the middle of the line had not moved.

This message from headquarters buttressed the words of Ralph Smith to his senior officers. The Twenty-seventh had done a very bad job and this could not be permitted to continue.

It was not quite true, however, that the Twenty-seventh Division had faced only small arms and mortar fire. Half a dozen tanks had attacked the division that night and been repelled.

Another half dozen had come up later in the night, and one burst through the lines of the 106th Infantry and set fire to an ammunition dump, which blew up and forced the whole Third Battalion of the 106th back several hundred yards. But those tanks had not been apparent during the daylight hours, and the two forces that faced the Twenty-seventh in the middle of the line—the Japanese 118th and 136th Regiments—were regiments only in name; the total number of defenders was fewer than 3,000, and these were strung out between the Twenty-seventh's front and the front of the Second Marines. So Holland Smith was right in his implication that the Twenty-seventh had stalled for reasons other than strong enemy defense.

On that night of June 23, as both Generals Smith demanded strong action from the Twenty-seventh Division, General Saito was making the same demands on his defenders along the line where the army division would attack. During the day, Colonel Russell Ayres, commander of the offending 106th Regiment, had probed a long ravine ahead of him and decided that it was too strongly defended for a major attack by his troops alone. Their first encounter had been with half a platoon of Japanese, but they had six machine guns, located in strategic positions and protected by rock and caves. The 106th called it Death Valley, and Colonel Ayres predicted that any unit going along that valley would be exposed to fire also from Mount Tapotchau on the left and Purple Heart Ridge on the right.

But Ralph Smith either did not share Colonel Ayres' view, or he felt it made no difference; the good name of the division must be retrieved, and he was going to retrieve it. The Twenty-seventh would move out next morning and capture its objectives. By nightfall General Holland Smith expected them to have moved to a line extending from Garapan, which the Second Marines would capture, then advance to overrun Mount Tapotchau. The Fourth Marines would head east to capture the Kagman Peninsula, which juts out from the main part of the island behind Purple Heart Ridge, and the Twenty-seventh, in the center, would move straight ahead to straighten out the line and push it forward about two miles. The Americans, at the end of the day, should control two-thirds of the island, and be prepared to launch a new drive through the mountains that would carry them down to the Tanapag Plain. After that, they would be in relatively flat country and the going would be much easier.

On the morning of June 24, the Second Marines moved up against Garapan, and by nightfall had taken the southern half of the town and were dug in. The Japanese sent seven tanks up that night, without any infantry support. What they were supposed to do was unknown; what they did was move into the fire of American medium tanks and self-propelled 75mm guns, which destroyed six of them and sent the seventh back to the Japanese lines full of holes. On the right side of the division, troops of the Eighth Marines moved forward satisfactorily along the foot of Mount Tapotchau, even though some of the terrain was a mass of tangled vines and deep forest.

In the middle, General Ralph Smith had promised that the army troops would move and move fast. But they did not. Colonel Kelley's 165th Infantry gained a position on the eastern slope of Purple Heart Ridge which was fairly satisfactory to General Holland Smith. Next day they should be able to take the ridge. But the 106th completely failed to make progress. Colonel Ayres sent his troops into Death Valley, and they did not penetrate beyond Hell's Pocket. They suffered casualties of fourteen killed and 109 wounded (very high by army standards), and they retreated to the original point of departure of the morning. No gain.

When General Holland Smith learned that the 106th had failed again he was furious. He issued a flat order to Colonel Ayres to go back into Death Valley and take the place. (Meanwhile, Colonel Ayres had convinced General Ralph Smith that the mission was impossible, and Ralph Smith had issued orders to Colonel Ayres to detach a battalion to contain the Japanese in Death Valley, and move the rest of his troops up Purple Heart Ridge and around the valley to Mount Tapotchau.) Holland Smith also issued orders that the Twenty-seventh Division troops left behind to take Nafutan Point, which they had not done, were to be put under the command of Colonel Geoffrey O'Connell, chief of staff of the Saipan garrison, and were to take the position the next day. Then General Holland Smith got into a boat and went out to the flagship. Admiral Spruance had just come back from the battle of the Philippine Sea. Smith wanted to talk to him and to Admiral Turner about what was to be done with the Twenty-seventh Division, which for two days had held up the whole Saipan campaign.

21
THE END OF
GENERAL SMITH (RALPH)

On the evening of June 24, General Holland Smith took his situation map and his anger and boarded the *Rocky Mount,* Admiral Turner's flagship. He went over the map with the admiral, pointing out how the Second and Fourth Marines had moved forward on both flanks of Saipan, and how the middle of the line had sagged. They could not move up the island until that line was straightened out and the marines could expect to have their flanks secure as they fought. As Admiral Turner already knew, General Holland Smith had been most reluctant to accept the Twenty-seventh Army Division at all, and he hoped to keep these troops perennially in reserve. Their performance at Makin and Eniwetok had been so poor that he simply could not trust them. But the miscalculation of Japanese strength back at Pearl Harbor had left Holland Smith with no alternative. There were too many Japanese defenders on Saipan, and they were fighting too hard for him to manage with only his two divisions of marines, no matter how experienced, dedicated, and tough they were. Holland Smith had found no alternative to the use of the Twenty-seventh at Saipan.

He had tried to use the Twenty-seventh in a way that would minimize the division's faults. Putting them in the middle with trusted marines on the flanks meant that the army men need not fear an attack by the enemy that would cut them off. But it had not worked, and on June 24 the troops of the Twenty-seventh Division were jeopardizing the success of the Saipan invasion, and they were costing many lives among the marines. Something had to be done.

There was no point in discussing the faults of the division. It was not a question of inferior men. The army soldiers had basically the same uniforms, the same weapons, and the same equipment as the marines. The soldiers were young Americans, just as the marines were. Their training, of course, had not been the same: the Twenty-seventh Division was extremely short on amphibious training. But the amphibious aspect of the battle for Saipan was over before the division was brought into action. Nobody was asking the Twenty-seventh's men to storm a beach. They *were* being asked to do what they had been trained to do, at least theoretically. Long before, however, Holland Smith had told Admiral Turner that his distrust of the Twenty-seventh was based on its background. The division was the greatest argument Holland Smith knew against the American National Guard system. For the Twenty-seventh was a National Guard division from the state of New York. The officers and men had known each other, in some cases, for years. The nucleus was the Seventh Regiment, a famous World War I organization, which had been maintained in the years after. In 1944 the Seventh Regiment had an armory on Park Avenue in New York City which was more like a club than a military training ground. The regiment was famous for its balls and parties, and the indoor polo played on the tanbark of the armory. It was, in effect, a rich man's club. When war had come, the young men and some of the not so young men had left their stockbroking offices and law practices and accounting firms and joined the colors on a full-time basis. From the famous Seventh Regiment, the Twenty-seventh Division had drawn many of its officers. As Holland Smith put it, the problem was "militiaitis," which to him was totally nonmilitary.

"Employer noncommissioned officers in the Twenty-seventh were sometimes commanded, if that is the word, by employee officers; there was sometimes a gentlemanly reluctance on the part of officers to offend the Old Seventh messmates through harsh criticisms or rigorous measures; in the eyes of many, especially the ambitious, there were reputations—New York reputations—to be made or broken; and behind all there was Albany, where the State Adjutant General's office allocated peacetime plums."

What should have been done, Holland Smith had said before, was to break up this gang of cronies and mix them up in the military service so they could be useful. It had not been done; even after Makin, General Richardson had been more concerned with maintaining the Twenty-seventh's reputation than with discovering what had gone wrong. The Twenty-seventh emerged from the Gilberts invasion covered with medals and citations that concealed the fact that if Makin had been as stoutly defended—or half as stoutly defended—as Tarawa, they could not have taken it at all without assistance from outside. For the trouble with the Twenty-seventh was not the men, but the leaders. Hell's Pocket and Death Valley were tough Japanese positions in front of Mount Tapotchau, but it was a tough war, and when the marines were assigned to take a piece of ground they took it and let the high command count the cost and pick up the pieces. The commander of the 106th Regiment had simply refused to do this; for two days he had not done it, and General Ralph Smith had not removed him. Furthermore, in the south, one battalion had been assigned to clean up Nafutan Point, and had not done it, the battalion commander complaining that he did not have the force to do so. The situation, from a command point of view, was intolerable.

After Turner had heard Holland Smith out, the two of them got into the admiral's barge and went to the *Indianapolis*, Admiral Spruance's flagship. General Holland Smith laid out his situation map again and explained the problem. Admiral Turner stood by and nodded as Spruance asked his questions. Finally Spruance asked the final question. What was to be done?

"Ralph Smith has shown that he lacks aggressive spirit," said Holland Smith, "and his division is slowing down our advance. He should be relieved."

Admiral Spruance looked at Admiral Turner. He nodded his agreement. "All right," said Admiral Spruance, "relieve him, then." They discussed the details: General Jarman would be placed in command of the division and see if he could not get it rolling. They discussed Holland Smith's plans then, and Smith and Admiral Turner left the fleet flagship, Turner to go back to the *Rocky Mount* and a good stiff drink, and Smith to go back to his command post and a very unpleasant task. For all three commanders knew precisely what they were doing and the hornet's nest that would be stirred up by the relief of an army general by a marine. General Richardson would bluster to Washington. General Marshall would order an inquiry. The result would be intensification of interservice rivalry, and it might even cost one of the three commanders his job and his future and his reputation. But aboard the *Indianapolis* all the ramifications boiled down to one decision. There was a war to be won, and it was not progressing in the hands of people who would not do what they were told to do. That was the final problem.

Back at the command post, General Holland Smith called for General Jarman to come up, and when General Jarman came, he told him what was going to happen—"one of the most disagreeable tasks of my career," he said.

General Holland Smith then drafted the papers, and the change was made. Major General Ralph Smith was put on an airplane and flown back to Pearl Harbor. There General Richardson appointed Ralph Smith commanding general of the Ninety-eighth Division. Richardson was furious because he had not been informed before the action was taken. What good that might have done, given the distance between Pearl Harbor and Saipan, was never explained. But in matters of ruffled feathers, the war seemed to take a back seat to career with some of America's commanders. In the inquiry that followed, General Ralph Smith was absolved of all blame by his army brethren. They had to admit that the Twenty-seventh was not doing its job, but the onus was placed on the commander of the 106th Regiment and the offending battalion back at Nafutan Point. No one said anything about the obligations of a divisional command. The buck was passed, and even the facts were obscured. Much was made of the difficulties the Twenty-seventh Division faced, and little of the failures. General Holland Smith came out of the hearings more tarnished than General Ralph Smith; it was decided by the army generals that Holland Smith had been tactless. Those hearings, held in the summer of 1944, were an indication of the state of the war. America was winning and there was time for recrimination and complaint against the men who were doing the fighting. The war had become politicized in the Pacific.

22

THE END OF
GENERAL SAITO

On the night of June 2, the bad news about the battle of the Philippine Sea was known at General Saito's headquarters. Admiral Ozawa had been defeated. The radio reports from Tokyo, claiming the destruction of eleven American carriers, were heard but not believed. For the purpose of the Ozawa strike had been to coordinate with the defense of Saipan and drive the Americans out. There had been absolutely no sign of the fleet, and since June 18, Japanese air activity over Saipan had been almost nonexistent. On the afternoon of June 23 one lone bomber had gotten through to the Americans and put a torpedo into the battleship *Maryland*, which had then been forced to raise anchor and return to Pearl Harbor for repairs. But that was hardly the destruction of the American invasion, and Admiral Nagumo knew that what had happened to him at Midway had now happened to Ozawa. General Saito knew that his war was about to end. But that did not mean the Japanese would stop fighting. Quite to the contrary, the resistance became stronger than ever.

On the 24th, the single battalion of the 105th Regimental Combat Team made no progress against the Japanese defenders of Nafutan Point. A halfhearted attack was launched that day, but it did not get anywhere. The talk was that there were thousands of Japanese holed up at the point; the fact was that there were about 500 troops, plus several hundred civilians and wounded. But the battalion commander was sure he needed help, and until he got it, he was not going to risk a major drive.

On the night of the 24th, as General Ralph Smith was moving out of the command post of the Twenty-seventh Division and General Jarman was moving in, the stiffened Japanese defenses made themselves felt. The previous night had been quiet. On the night of the 24th the Japanese air force showed itself again, with an attack apparently launched from Palau on the ships off Saipan. Bombs fell but no ships were sunk. Neither were any of the Japanese attackers shot down. On the line in Saipan the Japanese made several attempts to infiltrate the lines. The Second Marines faced a charge that cost them ten men, but left eighty Japanese dead in front of their positions. The Japanese artillery opened up that night, causing much discomfort among the Americans but no appreciable damage.

On the morning of June 25, in the best of all possible worlds the Twenty-seventh Division under its new commander would have risen to heights of glory and captured all the points assigned. But that did not happen.

The 165th Infantry was in motion; Colonel Kelley's troops captured the southern part of Purple Heart Ridge, but then stalled. One battalion which had been supposed to attack on the right flank was stopped by a pocket of Japanese, and Colonel Kelley decided to give up the position and move to the flank of the Twenty-third Marines. The 106th Infantry was supposed to circle to the right of Purple Heart Ridge and meet the Second Marine Division on the slopes of Mount Tapotchau. But once again the 106th was late, and by the time the men got into position the enemy was firing very actively and the attackers retired to the position of the day before in front of Death Valley. The Second Battalion of the 106th went into the valley that day and moved well inside but finally decided the resistance was too stiff and came out again. So General Jarman, whose will to fight was unquestioned, could not get the Twenty-seventh Division moving either. It was obvious by the end of the day that many changes were needed in the roster of senior officers of the division.

But on June 25, the marines made up for lost time. The Second Marines stood fast at Garapan, and the Sixth Marines attacked the Tipo Pale line. The Eighth Marines were attacking on four sides of Mount Tapotchau. Lieutenant Colonel Tompkins, who had taken over command of the First Battalion of the Twenty-ninth Marine Regiment, attacked along a ridgeline that was supposed to lead him to the summit. After two hours of heavy fighting the troops became bogged down, not by the Japanese as much as by the impassable terrain. But on their right, the Second Battalion of the Eighth Marines sent a patrol almost to the top of Mount Tapotchau, and there did not seem to be any Japanese up there. Tompkins then led two companies up the mountain toward the crest. As he was moving along a trail, the men in single file, the Japanese suddenly discovered that their enemies were about to take the highest point on the island without opposition. They launched a series of counterattacks at the marines all around the mountain. Their mortar fire was particularly effective against the Second Battalion, Eighth Regiment, and drove them back from a position on a cliff that they had attained earlier. By evening, as the sun was setting, the issue seemed to be in doubt but Tompkins and his men were still moving and ready to climb the mountain. He needed all the help he could get, and he was getting it. His own 81mm mortars were set to fire on the positions ahead. The mortars of the Second Battalion of the Eighth Regiment were also enlisted to fire from a different angle on all possible Japanese positions. The 105mm howitzers of the artillery were brought into play. Tompkins and his riflemen climbed the slope in the darkness. Not a man was lost and they achieved the summit.

Once up they had to dig in. They could expect a Japanese counterattack that night or by dawn for certain. But digging in was something else; most of the men found themselves on top of solid rock. A few discovered patches of earth and made foxholes.

The others had to scurry around to find loose stones and build up protective parapets. As expected, just before midnight the Japanese attacked. But the marines were ready for them and did not give an inch. The Japanese retired. Next morning the marines counted eighteen dead Japanese on the summit around them.

So the fighting on June 25 was more to General Holland Smith's liking. The Twenty-seventh division had not performed as well as he had expected, but he had not needed them. He had Mount Tapotchau, and on the right, the Kagman Peninsula had been captured by his marines.

That night, the Japanese made one last attempt to help General Saito with reinforcements. An infantry company set out from Tinian in eleven barges, heading for the east coast of the island. But the barges were discovered by the destroyer *Bancroft*. This ship and the destroyer escort *Elden* began firing on the barges, and sank one. The others turned and moved back to Tinian. There would be no reinforcement of General Saito.

On the night of June 25, Saito's position had become hopeless. He still had command of the 135th, 136th, and 118th Infantry Regiments, the Forty-seventh Mixed Brigade, the Seventh Engineers, the Third Mountain Artillery Regiment, and the Ninth Tank Regiment. But they were just names. The number of troops over which he had effective command was about 4,000; the others were isolated in pockets and it was merely a matter of time before they were wiped out. He had only three tanks left. The Third Mountain Artillery Regiment had *no* artillery. That night General Saito sent a radio message to Imperial Japanese Headquarters in Tokyo. "Please apologize deeply to the emperor," he said, "that we cannot do better than we are doing."

But in terms of trouble, the Japanese in the pockets were becoming more effective as the Americans advanced. At Mount Tipo Pale, the Sixth Marines bypassed a pocket, and regretted it when the Second Battalion came under fire that forced them to abandon an advance on June 26. On Mount Tapotchau, the

Americans held the summit, but the Japanese held the northwest part of the mountain. On the slopes below, the Eighth Marines were literally clawing their way through the heavy forest. Dodging grenades and mortar shells became standard procedure; the real problem was to get through the brush.

At Death Valley, the 106th was still given the task of cleaning out the Japanese. The First Battalion was to take Hell's Pocket. The other two battalions of the regiment were to attack along Purple Heart Ridge and then come up the middle, to bring that sagging line straight again. But once again, the 106th could not seem to get moving. Finally, in despair, General Jarman did what must have been painful but probably should have been done weeks before: he relieved the commander of the 106th Regiment and replaced him with Colonel Albert Stebbins, his own chief of staff. Had this been done that week before, it is conceivable that the relief of General Ralph Smith would have been avoided. But the fact that it was not done was an indication of the command difficulties within the regiment.

The 106th attacked again, and once more was thrown back. At Nafutan Point, where Colonel O'Connell, chief of staff of the island garrison force, had been put in charge of the operation against the Japanese strongpoint, the halfhearted attack of the battalion of the 105th Infantry had breached the outer defenses of the point, but done little else. On June 26 the attack was renewed, and supported by tanks, antiaircraft guns, and naval gunfire. The troops took Mount Nafutan, one of the main points of the defense. That night, the Japanese assessed their position. It had grown totally hopeless. The hoped-for reinforcements from Tinian had never appeared. Captain Sasaki, commander of a battalion of the 317th Infantry, now that all his seniors were dead, had fewer than 500 troops still fit to fight. They included the pitiful remnants of his own battalion, part of the Forty-seventh Independednt Mixed Brigade, and stragglers from naval units and artillery, engineers, and service units. Sasaki was out of communication with all other Japanese units. The last information he had received indicated that the Americans had seized Aslito airfield, but that his countrymen continued to hold at the line of Hill 500 on the northern edge of the field. He decided to make a breakthrough to join the defenders in the north. He issued orders: all those who were wounded or unfit to make the breakthrough must stay and defend Nafutan Point to the last. All those who could not help with the defense must now commit suicide. As for himself and his able-bodied men, they were going to fight through to General Saito. The password for the night would be *Shichi Sei Hokoku:* Seven Lives for One's Country.

At midnight Captain Sasaki led his men out. They passed undetected through the forward line. They came up against the command post of the Second Battalion of the 105th and waged a bloody fight in which the Americans suffered twenty-four casualties, and the Japanese left twenty-seven dead on the field. They moved then to Aslito airfield, where they destroyed one P-47 fighter plane and damaged several others. Then they crossed the field and moved toward Hill 500. When they arrived at the foot of the hill, however, instead of finding General Saito's men, they found the Twenty-fifth Marines. The surprise was mutual. In a few moments they were engaged in a fight, and before it was over Sasaki's men were dead. Some of them died fighting to break through the lines. But when it became apparent that they were trapped, and they were cut into small units and under attack, they began to commit suicide. The plan had all been settled back at Nafutan Point. By the time that the sun rose high, Captain Sasaki and his men were no more, and the vexing problem of Nafutan Point was resolved.

On June 27, the 106th Infantry finally got moving. Two rifle companies of the First Battalion circled around Hell's Pocket and took the ridge to the left. The Second and Third Battalions moved into Death Valley and stayed there for the first time. On the right the Fourth Marine Division made spectacular gains, to the north and west, and at the end of the day General Holland Smith was well satisfied. The assault on Saipan was back on schedule.

That night Japanese planes bombed Aslito field, and Charan Kanoa, where the fleet's invasion ships were at anchor. The Japanese were still trying to help from outside although their resources had been sharply reduced. Planes had come up from Truk and down from the Palaus to strike the Americans. The strikes were not effective—there was not enough strength in them—but they did serve notice that the war was far from over. Since June 16, Admiral Takagi's communications from Saipan to his Sixth Fleet of submarines had been cut off, and command had been assumed by Rear Admiral Noburo Owada at Truk. Admiral Owada had decided to form several sentry lines and attack the Americans in the Marianas. He sent two dozen submarines to the area, including *I-10*, which had specific orders to come in and evacuate Admiral Takagi and his staff. *I-10* never made it. On the night of June 27, Admiral Owada knew the submarine must be lost, and he assigned *I-38* to rescue Takagi. Despite the popular postwar idea that the Japanese abandoned their most senior officers in the fighting in the islands, the high command did its best to save as many as possible. Only when rescue or breakthrough became impossible did the Japanese commit suicide rather than face capture. The senior officers did so because of the tradition and regulations that surrender was a capital offense.

But throughout the Pacific campaign the Japanese made strenuous efforts to rescue the personnel deemed most valuable to their war effort, just as the Americans had at Corregidor. In the Marianas, it was apparent by the end of the third week in June that the battle was lost. The submarine *I-41* was sent to Guam to rescue all the pilots there who had been stranded by the American destruction of their planes. Pilots were at a premium in the Japanese forces, and Lieutenant Commander Mitsuma Itakura brought off this plan on June 22. Other Japanese submarines were dispatched to Guam carrying long tubes full of supplies for the troops there. It was the only way the Japanese could manage any resupply at all. The battle still raged, but the outcome was assured by the frustration of Admiral Ozawa at the naval battle of the Philippine Sea.

Japanese resistance never faltered. The marines and army troops moved, but only after cleaning out pocket after pocket. The bitterness of the Japanese resistance was indicated in the growing number of names for military objectives. To Death Valley and Hell's Pocket were added Flametree and Sugar Loaf Hill, the one named by the marines for a tree that stood atop a bitterly contested objective, the other for a "sweet" Japanese defensive position that took the marines a long time to capture.

On June 28 Major General George Griner arrived on Saipan. Back at Pearl Harbor, an angry General Richardson had moved as quickly as he could to protect his prerogative, the appointment of the commander of the Twenty-seventh Division. Griner came to assume that role, and General Jarman went back to his own job, to command the garrison forces. Under this new command, the Twenty-seventh really moved. On June 29 the soldiers burst through Death Valley and wiped out the Japanese at Hell's Pocket. They cleaned up Purple Heart Ridge, and the next day they joined the marines on a clean-cut straight line across the island. The task of the Twenty-seventh had been a hard one, and General Schmidt said that no one on Saipan had a tougher job than the army troops in the middle of the assault line. But how much of the difficulty and how many of the 2,000 casualties were the result of stiff Japanese resistance, rather than inept command, would never be settled. The investigations and the press scandal raised by the Ralph Smith relief produced much heat and virtually no light on the conduct of the war for Saipan. What was proved, by General Griner, was that the soldiers of the Twenty-seventh were as good as any in the American military force, if they had the proper leadership. That need having been fullfilled, the Twenty-seventh was doing its part.

By June 30, the Japanese had been pressed north into their final defensive line, and General Holland Smith now planned a series of strikes that would take him to the end of the island. By July 5 they had reached the Tanapag plain on the left, and the Twenty-seventh Division troops faced the last Japanese headquarters in what the Japanese called the Valley of Hell. The Fourth Marine Division, on the right, moved north along the

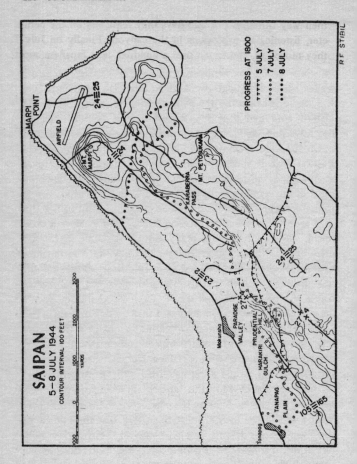

R F STIBIL

SAIPAN
5–8 JULY 1944
CONTOUR INTERVAL 100 FEET

PROGRESS AT 1800
▼▼▼▼ 5 JULY
○○○○○ 7 JULY
••••• 8 JULY

MARPI
POINT

AIRFIELD

MT. MARPI

24≡25

2≡24

KARABERRA
PASS

MT. PETOSUKARA

23≡2

24≡25

Matansa

27×3
PARADISE
VALLEY
PRUDENTIAL
HILL
O HILL

4×3

HARAKIRI
GULCH

TANAPAG
PLAIN

Tanapag

105≡165

plain. On its left came the Second division and on the far left
the Twenty-seventh. The Twenty-seventh's 105th Regiment
moved up the west coast, then, while the marines went up the
interior. On July 6, the Third Battalion of the 105th came to a
large canyon, 50 yards wide and 400 yards long, running east to
west in front of the troops. They attacked but could not force

their way through. For two days they remained on the perimeter, listening to explosions in the canyon. Finally on July 7 they moved in, and found over a hundred dead Japanese, most of them killed by grenades or other suicidal weapons. They labeled the canyon Harakiri Gulch.

By July 6, the Japanese were in desperate condition. General Saito's command post was a cave 1000 yards from the village of Makunsha in Paradise Valley or the Valley of Hell as the Japanese called it. The ragged, gaunt general and his half-starved staff clustered here in the shelter of a jungle hillside to make what plans they could. Every day their position was hit by artillery and naval gunfire. General Saito had been wounded by a piece of shrapnel. That night of July 6, the general made a new plan. On the following morning the Japanese would stage one last glorious attack on the invaders, and die proclaiming the everlasting life of their emperor. There was nothing to be gained by the attack—nothing remained to be gained; the Americans were everywhere. But they could not surrender, and he would not lie down and let the Americans run over him. "Whether we attack or whether we stay where we are there is only death," said Saito. What they could do for the emperor was exact seven lives for each of theirs, as high a price as possible to be paid by the invaders who had fouled the empire.

That night, General Saito ordered out the last of the stores, the delicacies he had saved. The staff ate canned crabmeat and drank sake in the cave. Then the general excused himself until the dawn, when he said he would personally lead the banzai charge. But he had no such intention. He was tired and he felt very old and very dispirited. Only one gesture could redeem his self-respect, and he went to make it. He went into seclusion in the cave, and committed seppukku, and died.

After midnight, Colonel Eisuke Suzuki, once commander of the proud 135th Infantry but now leader of a motley gang, made what preparations he could for the attack. He had about 4,000 defenders left to fight, most of them in this immediate area. Not all of them were armed; some would have to make do with handmade spears until they could capture arms from the enemy.

They would throw themselves against the Americans and kill as many as possible. That was all the plan consisted of; there was no military objective.

General Holland Smith was expecting just such a move at any time. The Tanapag plain was the most logical place for the Japanese to try such a maneuver, and the 105th Infantry was squarely in front. That night, General Smith planned to move the Second Marine Division through the 105th Regiment and press forward to the end of the island with the fresh marines. But at 4:00 in the morning, the men of the 105th were snapped awake by howling, screaming Japanese who came straight down the plain like a stampede of cattle. They were led by tanks, but soon most of these were shot out. They had machine guns, but they seldom stopped to put up a machine-gun position. They charged ahead. "They just kept coming and coming," said Major Edward McCarthy, commander of the 105th's Second Battalion. "I didn't think they would ever stop."

The first Americans to be hit were the outposts of the First and Second Battalions, 1,200 yards south of Makunsha. At 5:30 the area was alive with Japanese mortar fire. The two battalions had left a 300-yard gap between their outposts, and the Japanese had discovered it. This became their avenue, and they came down so thickly that they overwhelmed the defenders. There were too many of them to be stopped, although on the heights above the Twenty-third Marines saw them moving and began firing on them with mortars and machine guns. On the floor of the valley, the troops of the First and Second Battalions of the 105th had to take it. Lieutenant Colonel William J. O'Brien, commander of the First Battalion, found himself on the front line. He had two pistols, and he fired them both until he ran out of ammunition. He was wounded. He saw a machine gun whose gunners had been killed. He moved to the gun and fired steadily until a handful of Japanese rushed the position and killed him.

The Americans had been driving hard that previous day, and had been so careless as to leave that gap in their lines. Now they paid dearly for the error. By 6:30 that morning the forward positions of the 105th were overrun. The Japanese swarmed out in three directions: they struck the Twenty-seventh, they charged the Tenth Marines, who were ensconced on high ground above Harakiri Gulch, and they hit the artillery on the west side of the railroad just outside Tanapag. The Third Battalion of the 105th held on high ground near the gulch. The First and Second Battalions of the regiment were soon in desperate condition from lack of ammunition, water, and medical supplies. Just before Colonel O'Brien was killed he radioed the regimental command post.

"There are only 100 men left in the First and Second Battalions of the 105th. For God's sake get us some ammunition and water and medical supplies right away." Regiment tried to comply with the request, but four jeeploads of ammunition were thrown back when they tried to force their way through the Japanese fire. So soon the survivors of the banzai charge fell back into Tanapag and defended one house after another.

The forward battery of the artillery was hit at 5:15, as day was breaking, by about 500 Japanese soldiers with machine guns, rifles, and grenades. Most of the guns could not fire, because Americans were between them and the Japanese and the range was zero. Artillerymen of Battery H cut their fuses to four-tenths of a second; the shells exploded 50 yards ahead of the guns. One crew used a howitzer as an antitank gun, and blew the insides out of a tank that was approaching them from the rear. But the Japanese were shooting down the gunners at their guns, and the effectiveness of fire was soon limited. By 7:00 the positions were overrun, and the artillery men had to abandon their weapons and withdraw to an old Japanese motor pool across the road, where they dug in and fought with carbines and captured Japanese rifles. They held. Alongside, the Japanese overran Battery H and the service battery behind it. The Americans were driven back to the positions of Battery G, where they were joined around midday by some troops from the 106th.

The Japanese swept south of Tanapag, heading for the 105th's regimental command post, 800 yards from the town limits. But by this time, around noon, the Japanese were strung over a large area and were running low on ammunition. The drive could not continue long without supply, and there was no supply. So the attack slowed down. General Griner had ordered the First and Second Battalions of the 106th Infantry Regiment to come out of reserve and support the front line. The men were moving by 10:00 along the railroad from the south. They broadened their front at Tanapag and moved north along the line. By midafternoon, the Japanese attack was reduced to occasional bursts of fire and the popping of small-caliber rifles. By 6:00 in the evening, it was all over. A body count was made the next day, and 4,311 Japanese corpses were found. Some of these men had died before the attack, but not many. This package of death was General Saito's last gift to his emperor. The Americans had suffered heavy casualties: the Third Battalion of the Tenth Marines alone had lost forty-five killed and eighty-two wounded. But it was all over in the Tanapag area, and the headquarters of the Japanese defenses no longer existed. From this point on, the Americans would be fighting small groups of holdouts; there would be casualties, and all the pockets had to be cleared out, but the end was in sight.

Most of the units of the Twenty-seventh Division, which had comported itself gallantly under its new leadership, were put into reserve to get a rest and resupply. Only the 165th Infantry, which had been used sparingly, was employed. It moved through the canyons against some resistance, but reached the west coast on July 9. Paradise Valley, which was the American name for the area the Japanese called the Valley of Death, was bypassed and a battalion was left there to finish off any Japanese left from General Saito's last effort. The rest of the troops moved ahead. The Third Battalion stopped at the village of Makunsha, which was occupied by Japanese. By July 8 about all that remained to be taken was Mount Marpi, the airfield on the northern corner of the island, and Marpi Point, the cliff looking out over the sea toward Japan. Four marine regiments moved abreast up the island. They passed by Prudential Hill, "the rock" of the insurance company advertisements, or at least its double; Gibraltar was a long way away. At 6:00 on the night of July 9, Admiral Turner radioed Admiral Spruance that Saipan was secure. He did not mention the numbing sight the American soldiers saw as they came up to Marpi Point that afternoon. Hundreds, thousands of Japanese soldiers, sailors, and civilians went out to Marpi Point and jumped off into the sea. The Americans had made some broadcasts and other attempts to persuade the civilians that they would be safe, and some had surrendered. But this was Japanese territory, and these were Japanese civilians, and most of them had been inculcated with the spirit of *bushido* from childhood. So the marines watched as women took their children up to the point and pushed them off, and then jumped after them. One pregnant woman leaped into the sea, and when her body was found, the baby was half-born.

Saipan had been a costly adventure in terms of lives. The Americans had nearly 17,000 casualties, including about 4,000 dead. The Japanese dead were listed officially at about 24,000, but this record was woefully incomplete. Many bodies were never found, hidden in caves that had been sealed by dynamite, and many Japanese had cast themselves into the sea.

But in the war this cost was inevitable. The importance of Saipan was that it brought the war a little closer to the end. General Holland Smith, summing it up, said that it was the most important battle of the Pacific campaign. He had called Tarawa "a dreadful error," but Saipan, he said, was the "decisive battle." The Japanese agreed with him; General Hideki Tojo was forced to resign as premier, and a new cabinet was formed. It could not call itself "antiwar"—the Japanese military was still too strongly ensconced for this—but Emperor Hirohito was already talking about the need to seek a quick negotiated peace to end the suffering of his subjects. The emperor of Japan at that point was a captive of his own previous aggressiveness, and his generals and admirals outdid themselves in promising him a victory that all of them knew could not be achieved. The spirit of *bushido* demanded no less; they could not admit that their resources were exhausted, their armies depleted, their navy reduced to the point that it could not possibly survive in an encounter with the American Fifth Fleet alone. The Japanese future was already apparent there on Saipan, two weeks before the campaign for the island ended. On June 24 work began on the first B-29 airfield. Five months later, a hundred of the Superfortresses would take off from that field on one day to begin the saturation bombing of Japan. All this was anticipated by General Saito and by Tokyo. The hopelessness of the situation was illustrated by the fate of Admiral Nagumo, once the hero of Pearl Harbor, whom the Japanese navy could not even manage to rescue from Saipan. He committed suicide on the night before the last desperate banzai charge out of the Valley of Hell. His fate was a harbinger. The war had turned completely around.

23
TINIAN

Historically, the battles for Tinian and Guam seem anticlimactic, for as General Holland Smith said, with Saipan the Americans had what they wanted in the Marianas. But Tinian had to be captured, because it was only a few thousand yards across a narrow channel from Saipan. If it was bypassed, the Japanese could bring aircraft in to bomb the American airfields and might even launch an amphibious attack across the channel, which would harry the occupation force if nothing else. So Tinian must have its share of blood. The marines prepared to cross the 3 miles that separated Agingan Point on Saipan from Ushi Point on Tinian. The major target would be the island's airfields, which the Americans wanted to preserve and extend to accommodate the B-29 bombers that would be arriving from the United States in a few months. There were four airfields on the 12-mile-long island, and one of them was better than Aslito field on Saipan. Before the war Tinian had been an agricultural island of considerable importance in the Japanese economy. It was laid out in neat patterns of fields and pastures, which from the air resembled the farms of Ohio or Iowa. It was fertile land, 90 percent tillable, with wet and dry seasons that produced plenty of moisture and sunshine for crops. The principal crop was sugar, and Tinian was more important than

Saipan in this regard. The population was almost totally Japanese by 1944; the native Chamorros had been ousted and sent to the less valuable islands of the Marianas.

As a point of defense, Tinian was formidable. The island was encircled by coral cliffs, and only three areas of beach were possible landing places for the Americans, one near Tinian town at

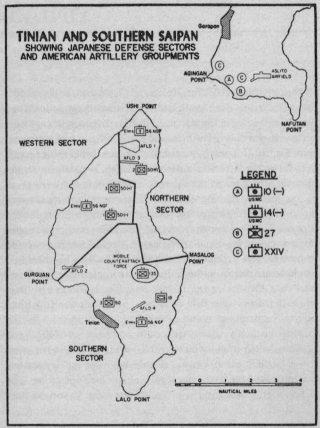

TINIAN AND SOUTHERN SAIPAN
SHOWING JAPANESE DEFENSE SECTORS
AND AMERICAN ARTILLERY GROUPMENTS

R F STIBIL

Suharon Harbor, one on the other side of the island on Asiga Bay, and one below Ushi Point. Colonel Keishi Ogata, the commander of Tinian's defense forces, was certain that the Americans would land either at Tinian town or across the island at Asiga Bay. He established a command post in a cave on Mount Lasso, the highest point of the island, and planned his defenses for landings at those two points only. He disposed his 9,000 men accordingly. The strength of the defense lay in the Fiftieth Infantry Regiment, of about 4,000 men, with three battalions of troops, and a number of guns that ranged from 75mm pack artillery pieces to 37mm antitank guns. The airfields also had many antiaircraft guns in place, which could be depressed and used for defense on land. During the battle for Saipan, the Tinian air defenses had aroused the respect of the American pilots after several were shot down. The Fiftieth Infantry was one of Japan's finest regiments. It had been brought down from Manchuria that spring, as the army faced up to the attrition of its forces in the South Pacific. One battalion of the 135th Infantry was also in Tinian; it had been undergoing amphibious training there when the Americans attacked Saipan, and on Tinian it remained. That accounted for about half the defenses. The other half consisted of naval forces and service troops. Admiral Kakuda, who had promised so much to Admiral Ozawa from his First Air Fleet, was the senior officer of the navy forces, but before Saipan fell, he transferred his headquarters to Palau, leaving Captain Goichi Oya in charge of the Japanese naval contingent. Theoretically Oya was responsible to Colonel Ogata. Actually, Oya had no intentions of taking orders from an army man. The long rivalry between the navy and the army extended even here, to the outposts of empire.

Colonel Ogata divided his defenses into three sectors, and assigned one battalion of the Fiftieth Infantry to each of them. In the sector where the small northwestern beaches lay, he withdrew all but one company of the assigned battalion and put the other companies in reserve, along with the battalion from the 135th, which he called his mobile striking force. The mobile force was to be prepared to move in any direction, depending on where the

American assault came. In Colonel Ogata's defense orders, he told his officers to "destroy the enemy at the beaches"—that was standard wording these days. But he also told them to be prepared to move two-thirds of their forces elsewhere, which indicated a fluid defense that was neither suicidal nor foolish.

The strongest weapons on Tinian were divided among the coast and the airfields. The harbors were defended by a number of 150mm coastal guns, fixed pieces of artillery that were valuable for repelling destroyers and cruisers, but not maneuverable. The airfields were ringed by those deadly antiaircraft guns. Along the shores, the Japanese had built dozens of pillboxes and machine-gun emplacements. A defense map, prepared before the American invasion, showed a formidable system of protection.

But by July 1944, when the Americans prepared to move in to the beaches, much of the defense had already crumbled. Tinian was so close to the sister island of Saipan that the American artillery could be used to fire on Tinian when not needed on Saipan. Thus Tinian had longer and more sustained bombardment from naval and land guns than any other objective of the Pacific war. Since June 13 the island had been bombed and bombarded every day, and on June 26 three American cruisers began systematic bombardment of specific targets, particularly in Tinian town. They used everything from armor-piercing ammunition to white phosphorus projectiles that were aimed to start forest fires. By mid-July, the Saipan battle over, General Holland Smith could turn thirteen battalions of artillery against Tinian, and did. The navy could use its battleships as well as its cruisers and destroyers against Tinian, and did. The small carriers had very little to do except strike Tinian. So by the time of the invasion most of the pillboxes were reduced to rubble, and the only installations that escaped harm were those artfully concealed from the spying eyes of the American cameras. Then, on July 19, an officer came up from the South Pacific to announce that the army there had developed a new bombing technique which involved napalm, a powder that produced a highly incendiary jelly when mixed with aircraft gasoline. The officer showed an Army Air Force film to

General Schmidt of the Fourth Marine Division and Admiral Harry Hill, commander of the amphibious forces for this operation. They authorized the use of napalm against Tinian, and in the third week of July, Army Air Force P-47s from Saipan ranged over the island burning the cane fields and underbrush around the beach areas. It was very satisfactory.

For two weeks after the capture of Saipan the marines and army troops of the three divisions were able to take it easy. A few guns still popped on the island, and occasionally a guard flushed a sniper. There were a few casualties, but no military action. The Fourth Marine Division would lead the assault, with the Second Marine Division in support. The Twenty-seventh Army Division was held in reserve. This looked like a very powerful force on paper, but in fact all three divisions had suffered enormously from casualties in the Saipan struggle, and virtually no replacements had been brought in. So General Schmidt, who was charged with the responsibility for the land actions because General Holland Smith was going off to supervise the capture of Guam, reapportioned his artillery and tanks and engineers so that as the time for the invasion came the command was a totally mixed bag.

For several weeks Admiral Hill and his staff considered the approaches to Tinian. The most direct route would be across the channel to the two narrow beaches on the northwest coast called Beach White 1 and Beach White 2. But they were so small that Colonel Ogata had already dismissed the possibility of the Americans landing there; as far as the space for amphibious tractors was concerned, Beach White 1 was only 60 yards wide and Beach White 2 was 65 yards wide. Could two divisions of troops be landed and supplied in such narrow confines?

To answer that question a detachment of marines was sent to the beaches accompanied by a team of navy underwater demolition experts. Their task was to actually measure the beaches and the land beyond, and the reef and surf, and to find any underwater obstacles the Japanese might have·put down. They went aboard the transport destroyers *Gilmer* and *Stringham* on July 9. They rehearsed that night off Saipan, and the next night they were taken to Tinian. The men aboard the *Gilmer* would check Asiga Bay. The men on the *Stringham* would investigate White Beaches 1 and 2.

In the dark of night before moonrise the men went ashore on the Yellow beach in rubber boats. The eight underwater demolition men found floating mines anchored a foot under water and many boulders and potholes that would hamper landing forces. On the beach the twenty marines found a double line of barbed-wire roll and very nearly ran into several Japanese parties building pillboxes. Captain Merwin Silverthorn, leader of the group, saw several Japanese sentries looking down at the beach from the cliff, and several times lights flashed around them, but they were not detected. The Yellow Beach did not look like a good target, given the mines and the obstacles and the high cliffs that boxed it on both sides.

The marines who were put into boats off the White Beaches 1 and 2 discovered the first difficulty of that area immediately: the current. The men who were supposed to land on White 1 were swept half a mile north, where there was no beach at all. The men who were supposed to land on White 2 landed on White 1. They did their job, but White 1 had to wait for the next night. When the results were in they were hardly appealing. White 1 was a sandy beach 60 yards wide, and though White 2 was twice as large, coral made just about the same amount of space actually available. The landing craft *could* negotiate these beaches, if they were willing to risk it.

All this information was gathered and given to Admiral Turner, and Admiral Hill and General Schmidt recommended the White Beaches. The alternatives were even less satisfactory; the Yellow Beach was stoutly defended, obviously. The Tinian town beaches were on the other side of the island, which made a supply problem. So White it was to be.

The invasion was set for July 24. It was to be something new: the troops would be carried to the beaches by landing craft from the beginning. The only big transports to be used were seven which would carry troops of the Second and Eighth Marines

for a feint off Tinian town's harbor on invasion day. The maneuver had not worked spectacularly at Saipan, but on Tinian it
was more likely to succeed, for obviously the Japanese expected
landings on the easier beaches. The landing ships were loaded
with tanks and artillery and men and moved across the channel.
For many days the artillery and the naval ships and the planes
had been smashing Tinian from one end to the other. The White
Beaches were hit often but not in a way to call special attention
to them. Indeed, the special attention was devoted to Tinian
Town. Destroyers and minesweepers moved ostentatiously off
the town in daylight, and underwater demolition men made a
minute inspection of the reef offshore while the minesweepers
combed the area. The battleships *Colorado* and *Tennessee* and
several destroyers and cruisers conducted a "prelanding bombardment" of Tinian town. Planes from four carriers struck the island on the day before invasion. Much attention was given to
that far side of the island, and just after daylight on July 24, the
deception began. The transports "landed" the troops—that is,
they put them over the side into landing barges. Navy planes
came across the town bombing and strafing in a "pre-invasion"
strike. The strike was real, but the troops who climbed down
into the landing barges on the cargo nets then climbed up again
—on the far side of the ships—and climbed down again, and back
up. From the beach it must have seemed that an endless stream
of Americans was moving into those boats. At 7:30 the landing
craft moved away from the ships and milled about. Soon splashes
were seen coming in, from shore, and since Admiral Hill had ordered the commanders not to jeopardize the men, the landing
craft moved offshore several hundred yards farther and "re-
formed." Once again the shells began coming in and several
landing craft were hit with shrapnel, but no one was hurt. The
boats moved to within 400 yards of the shore, and then turned
and moved back again. By this time it was 10:30. The landings on the White Beaches were supposed to have come at 7:30.
The time for deception had ended, so the boats went back to
the transports and the tired troops of the Second Division ended

their play-acting. Later that day, Admiral Hill heard how successful they were: Radio Tokyo announced that Colonel Ogata's brave men had repelled a landing at Tinian town involving more than a hundred landing barges.

But if that broadcast was good for a laugh, there was no question about the deadly seriousness of the undertaking, nor the skill of the Japanese defenders. The Japanese had placed three 6-inch naval guns behind the harbor. In all the bombings and all the shells that had been thrown at Tinian, those guns were untouched and so well concealed that their existence was unknown to the Americans. Certain that all big guns had been silenced, the captain of the battleship *Colorado* took her in close to the beach, just about 2 miles offshore, to do his shelling. When she was so close, the Japanese began firing on the battleship, and hit her twenty-two times in fifteen minutes, causing about 250 casualties. The ship itself was badly damaged, but managed to make it around the island and back to Saipan. The destroyer *Norman Scott* was brought between the battleship and the beach as the destroyer captain tried to protect the battleship. The destroyer was hit six times by those same guns and suffered about sixty-five casualties. This was not play-acting. This was war.

24

BLOOD ON WHITE BEACHES

Since Colonel Ogata had not expected any action on the White Beaches, there were no big guns in place. The battleships and cruisers of the bombardment force here were not fired upon at all. They fired on the beaches, trying to knock out some mines the Japanese had placed there, and did hit about a third of them. Just before the landings they switched to smoke shells and laid down a barrage between Colonel Ogata's command post in the cave on Mount Lasso and the beaches. It seemed a fine idea at the time, but the wind shifted just before the troops began to come in and the smoke drifted back to the beach, where it caused almost as much difficulty for the invaders as it had for the invadees.

But Colonel Ogata was surprised, there was no question about it. The first marines came in on Beach White 1, a space so narrow that only four LVTs could come right up to the beach. The other four tractors bearing Company E of the Second Battalion of the Twenty-fourth Marines had to land on ledges next to the beach and wade ashore. Had it been like Saipan or Tarawa they would have been decimated by enemy fire, but only a handful of troops appeared to contest the landings. Colonel Ogata's single company of the 135th Infantry was not going to be able to stop much of anything by itself. In less than an hour, the first defenses, in caves along the beach, were destroyed or sealed up. There was some mortar fire from thick brush and caves ahead, but the marines called the landing "a cakewalk." By 9:00 the reserve battalion was being landed at White Beach 1.

On White Beach 2 Colonel Ogata had taken a few more pains. His men had built several pillboxes which had survived the bombings and shells. They had put in more mines than the navy expected, and the pre-invasion shelling had not destroyed too many of them. So the going was more difficult here, but by 9:30 the troops were ashore. By 4:00 p.m. the Twenty-fourth Marines had moved nearly a mile inland and were on the edge of No. 3 airfield. But the line was ragged. The Twenty-fifth Marines on White Beach 2 were held up by Japanese fire and found several pillboxes that the artillery had not. They also encountered land mines and booby traps. The Japanese had been very thorough. Those tempting cases of Asahi beer next to the destroyed guns were mined. Most of the marines had been through this before at Eniwetok and Saipan, and they avoided the traps. But two amph-tracs were blown up just past the beach, and another when it came back and tried to turn around.

The engineers came in with mine detectors and then brought in the underwater demolition teams and bomb-disposal teams. Their efforts, combined, cleared the beach of mines by midafternoon. By the end of the day the marines occupied a beachhead about 2 miles wide. At the greatest depth it was not quite a mile inland. During the day there had been relatively light resistance from Colonel Ogata's force, but General Schmidt still thought it wise to bring the reserves onto the beach to face the counterattack that was expected. General Clifton Cates, commander of the assault, ordered the marines to stop moving at about 4:30 in the afternoon and dig in for such an attack. They emplaced barbed wire along the entire division front and brought up extra ammunition for the weapons. Machine guns and mortars were placed to create interlocking fields of fire and the mortars to reach all the declivities and beyond the high points. Bazooka teams were stationed at all probable points where the enemy might bring tanks against the line. The crews of the antitank guns were given armor-piercing and canister shells for the 37mm weapons. The Twenty-third Marines, which were in reserve, came in, and the First Battalion took position behind the Twenty-fifth Marines. Light tanks with flamethrowers were landed, and some medium tanks moved along behind the perimeter. By nightfall nearly 16,000 Americans were ashore on Tinian. As night came, they waited.

All morning, Colonel Ogata was bemused by the thought that Tinian town was really the target of the landing force. When the Americans turned back from the beach, at first he believed the report that they were driven off by his brave soldiers. The landing on the two northwest beaches seemed to be the feint—it must be, for he was perfectly convinced that no major amphibious assault could be carried out on those narrow beaches. So it was 10:00 before he did anything to change his troop disposal. Then he called for the mobile reserve battalion, the First Battalion of the 135th Infantry, to come to the Mount Lasso area. But he did not take the troops away from the Asiga Bay area on the east side of the island and move them west. He still believed the major assault would come on the east.

Communications between Colonel Ogata's command post and the White Beach area had been destroyed early in the day, but the Japanese defenders had their battle orders. They were to push the enemy back into the sea. The mobile force began to move toward the area from the Marpo radio station 2 miles northwest of Tinian town. Captain Izumi kept his men concealed; he marched them on roads through the trees, and left the road whenever an American plane appeared. The 1,000 men of the battalion moved to the west side of the island without being observed. By late afternoon a plan for attack had been worked out. About 1,000 naval troops from the Ushi airfield garrison would attack on the north. The 135th Battalion would attack in the center, and the First and Second Battalions of the Fiftieth Infantry, supported by half a dozen tanks, would attack on the south.

The tanks would roll north to meet the navy men, and the beach-head would be squeezed out of existence.

All day long it had been raining, not a steady downpour but a succession of showers. As night came, the clouds intensified until it was pitch dark, a situation which helped the defenders of the positions along the American line more than a little. The Japanese were expert at probing front-line positions, but this night they did not have much time and the weather was against them. Still, the attack must continue.

Around midnight the Japanese artillery from Mount Lasso to the sea began firing a barrage. One moment the shells were coming in almost lackadaisically, as if the gunners had been told only to keep the Americans from going to sleep. The next moment the fire had become purposeful and the heavy field guns back on the slopes were firing rapidly. From the defense positions near the shore the infantry added a steady fire from mortars. At 2:00 in the morning, 600 naval troops from the Ushi airfield were approaching the line on the left side. They had been badly briefed about the line and assumed it was much farther seaward than it was, so they marched down the coast road. The ratings were in their fatigue uniforms, but the officers were in dress with white gloves and swords. Quite suddenly they appeared in formation before the line of the First Battalion of the Twenty-Fourth Marines. They marched to within 100 yards. At that point the alarm was given along the line and the marines opened fire with rifles, machine guns, and automatic weapons. With the noise, gunners in the rear fired starshells, which revealed the Japanese naval force scattering for cover, the white gloves of the officers picking them out.

When they recovered from the surprise, the Japanese launched a rush on the prepared positions. Some were entangled in the barbed wire that they had not expected or seen in the dark. The marines were firing with 37mm guns, machine guns, and mortars augmenting the spitting of the M-1s. Company A of the First Battalion was in the center of this attack and began to take casualties. Some mortar shells, American and Japanese, tore holes in the barbed wire, and the Japanese came through. The fighting was close, but the defenses ordered by General Cates made the difference, and in two hours it became apparent that the Japanese would not break through here. By dawn Company A had been reduced to about a third of its strength, but those thirty men kept fighting.

As day broke, a platoon of marine tanks came forward to push the Japanese back. The marine artillery registered on positions just behind the attackers. They were caught in the squeeze, and as they realized they could not move a number of them committed suicide. The marines saw them stand up and hold grenades against their chests and then fall. By 7:00 on the morning of the second day the front of the Twenty-fourth marines was quiet.

Captain Izumi had managed to probe the center of the American line that evening before and found a weak point between the Twenty-fourth and Twenty-fifth Marines. This is where he would attack. When the Japanese barrage lifted at 2:00, Captain Izumi moved, his infantry supported by several tanks. The Twenty-fourth Marines had set up an outpost 400 yards in front of the line, and at 2:30 the telephone call came from the post, warning that the Japanese were advancing on them, heading for the boundary of the Twenty-fourth. The Twenty-fifth's command post was alerted and Lieutenant Colonel Justice Chambers ordered the men to begin firing. Meanwhile, Captain Izumi moved his main force into a swamp which was not covered by machine guns, since it had seemed impassable. The Japanese knew the terrain better than the Americans. In the swamp, Captain Izumi divided his force. One group set out for the artillery positions near the beach. The artillery men of the Fourteenth Marines were ready. They had set up .50-caliber machine guns, and these opened fire with devastating effect. The artillery called for infantry support of the guns, but when it came the infantrymen found that the attack had been stopped. Tanks arrived about dawn, but there was nothing for them to do. When light came, the men of the Fourteenth counted a hundred dead

Japanese out in front of their guns. Captain Izumi's second group had struck for the dividing point of the two regiments. They did get in behind the front line, through the swamp, and then turned toward the center. But the American positions were much deeper than Izumi had expected, and the Japanese ran into trouble immediately. Many of them were caught in the woods at the side of the swamp. The artillery had the woods spotted, and laid in a steady stream of fire that turned Izumi's attack into a rout, and sent a handful of stragglers back on the Japanese side of the line. When morning came the intelligence officers began checking. They found that the dead numbered about 400 here, many caught on the barbed wire in that first rush, and many others in the woods. Most of them were troops of the 135th Imperial Japanese Army Infantry.

On the south, the attack had been entrusted to two battalions of the Fiftieth Infantry Regiment, and they came up led by tanks camouflaged with leaves and branches. They hit the area guarded by the Second Battalion of the Twenty-third Marines around 3:30. The tanks came first, but as they came the Twenty-third called for support from the ships offshore, and the whole area was lit up by starshells. In the blue-white light the bazooka teams began firing from their foxholes and so did the 75mm half-track self-propelled guns and the 37mm antitank guns. Colonel Louis Jones, commander of the Twenty-third Marines, seemed to have been omniscient: he had reinforced the battalion with extra 37mm guns, as if expecting the attack to come just here. Six tanks had set out ahead of the infantry. They represented half of the Japanese tank force on all Tinian. They were light tanks, with 37mm guns and 7.7mm machine guns. But they were still tanks, and powerful enough to overrun infantry positions. Japanese soldiers were riding the tanks, and when they broke through they would jump down and scatter out to destroy the machine guns and mortars of the Americans.

That was the plan. The execution was something else. The three lead tanks came lumbering up abreast. The marines were firing with .50-caliber machine guns, bazookas, 37mm guns, and

75mm guns. One tank was hit and set afire. It began to smoke, and then the steel glowed red. The tank swerved into a ditch and was silent, its crew roasted inside. The second tank was hit in the side, knocking off a track, which disabled it and made it a sitting duck for American fire. The gunners swept the American lines until they were killed. A third tank was hit repeatedly and turned to retreat. But the bazooka teams blew it apart. From behind, these wrecks were overtaken by the second line of tanks, which fared no better. The first of these was hit by a bazooka rocket, which came in through the driver's visual port and killed him. The tank ground to a halt and the rest of the crew poured out, shouting and waving weapons. They were cut down as they hit the ground. The fifth tank was completely surrounded by advancing Americans; several bazookas turned on it at once set it afire and the crew died inside. The sixth tank, seeing what was happening, turned and made its escape into the woods.

In spite of what had happened to their tanks, the infantrymen of the Fiftieth Regiment surged forward against the American positions. But this was the place where the Twenty-third Marines had been brought into positions directly behind the line of the Twenty-fifth. So the Japanese who fought through the first line found themselves facing another line where the fire was equally impressive. Some of them carried antitank mines; their mission was to get through and destroy the American tanks. But not one American tank was knocked out that day; and as light came, one group of Japanese, surrounded behind the lines of their enemies, detonated one of the mines and blew themselves apart.

When the sun rose high on that morning of the second day, General Cates had the word that the line had held on all points, and that the marines had accounted for 1,241 Japanese soldiers and sailors during the night. It was a job well done, but General Cates knew that it was going to have to be repeated, over and over again.

25

TINIAN CAPTURED

On July 25, the Second Marine Division came ashore on Tinian and the Fourth Division headed across the island to cut Tinian in two. Then marines would drive north and south to clear out the defenses. By the end of the second day troops captured two of the four airfields. The fighting that day was centered around Mount Maga, a 400-foot hill that the Japanese had fortified. Colonel Batchelder sent his Twenty-fifth Marines around the hill and enveloped it. One side was cliff, and the Japanese had built pillboxes and caves from which they fought. The marines brought up tanks and mortars and silenced the defenses. The Japanese did not quit. Although they had only machine guns and mortars, they moved doggedly from one position back to the next, firing all the while. But there were too many Americans, too many tanks, too many self-propelled guns, and so by nightfall Mount Maga was completely encircled and the defenders had been reduced to a handful. That night U.S. naval and artillery fire on Mount Maga just about finished the job. Three 47mm guns near the foot of the hill were smashed and several fortified positions were destroyed. By noon on the third day there were no Japanese left on Mount Maga. The most serious Japanese countermove had been by the artillery on Mount Lasso. One of the guns there was

firing on the beach sent a 75mm shell into the tent that housed a
fire direction center of the American artillery. The shell exploded
on the tent pole and killed ten officers and men and wounded
fourteen others. But while tragic, this incident was minimal in the
picture on Tinian. The Americans would take casualties and
many Americans would die on the island, but the issue was not
in doubt and never had been. There was no way in the world that
Colonel Ogata, with perhaps 6,000 men left, could possibly prevent the American seizure of Tinian. All that happened, from the
moment that the Americans waded ashore on the White Beaches,
was waste.

The waste continued. That day Colonel Ogata turned the fire
of his artillery on Mount Lasso on the beaches, and destroyed
supplies and some incoming landing craft. The Americans were
surprised; intelligence had earlier told them that all the guns on
Mount Lasso had been silenced by the naval barrages, the firing
from Saipan, and the aerial attacks. But the reports had been
overoptimistic. Colonel Ogata's artillerymen were canny; they
did not fire long enough for the Americans to discover the location of the guns. A shell would come in, and then another, but
from different locations. By day's end the Japanese guns were
still intact.

On the third day, the Americans were moving fast. The Second
Division began edging south. The Fourth Division moved toward
Mount Lasso and the north. They expected to meet heavy resistance on Mount Lasso, but when they got there, the Japanese
had gone. Colonel Ogata had moved his command post and his
artillery down to Tinian town. There was not much left in the
town; the navy and the marine and army artillery had blasted
just about every building. But the Japanese set up the command
post and prepared to play out the game they could not win.

Most of the resistance after July 27 came from isolated groups
of Japanese who had rifles and machine guns and mortars with
which to fight. They also had grenades, and were expert at using
them. But such weapons could not stop a force three times as
large as their own. The American position grew ever stronger.

The artillery was moved over from Saipan and blanketed the island. As they moved forward on July 27 and 28 they found one position after another abandoned. There was resistance. At night, pockets of Japanese tried to break through the American lines, but the cost was always about the same as on the night of July 26, when a party of bypassed Japanese tried to break through the line of Company F of the Second Battalion of the Second Marines. They came from the American rear, obviously a party that had joined up and was trying to get through to Colonel Ogata's defense line. The Japanese attacked in the dark, and the Americans responded with a withering fire from all those guns, machine guns, mortars, rifles, tanks, and bazookas. When morning came 137 Japanese were dead around the company perimeter, and two marines were also dead and two wounded. That was the difference that firepower made.

As July drew to a close, it seemed that the major factor slowing the American advance across and south on Tinian was the weather rather than the enemy. The typhoon season had come, and on July 28 one storm brushed the Marianas. The result was wind and surf so high that unloading of supplies on the White Beaches had to be suspended, and for the following week supply became a major problem. The marines continued to move, but more slowly. The ground was wet, the rains came almost incessantly, yet by July 30, the marines were approaching Tinian town and could look down on it. Somewhere down there, reportedly in a cave about 2 miles from the town, Colonel Ogata had placed his new command post. General Schmidt expected a stiffening of resistance from this point on. But the resistance was remarkably slight, most of it coming from small units holed up in caves along the shore north of the town. In the middle of the afternoon of July 30, the marines entered what was left of Tinian town. It was almost completely flattened by their bombardments over the weeks. They pushed on to the airstrip, the fourth and last field on the island, and with its capture, after a scattered resistance by Japanese armed mostly with mortars, they controlled 85 percent of the island. The Japanese that remained had been pushed down to the southern end, toward Lalo and Marpi points. General Schmidt's orders were now succinct: "Annihilate the opposing Japanese."

Prisoners indicated that the Japanese still numbered around 4,000 troops. Colonel Ogata had ordered all troops to assemble in the wooded areas and high ground southeast of Tinian town for their last stand. The Americans know on July 31 that they would face trouble. The terrain was going to be difficult: a mile south of Tinian town the ground rose to a high plateau thick with brush. The approaches were blocked by cliffs and a rain forest. On the east the ground became cliff, so there was no flanking to be done. Through the middle ran a road, but it wound about, giving good view and weapons access from several points; and besides, said prisoners, it had been heavily mined. The west side offered the only sensible access, and this was also cliff, but cliff possible to scale.

As General Schmidt half expected, on the night of July 30 the Japanese staged an attack. Three tanks led about a hundred infantrymen against the lines of the Twenty-fourth Marines. One tank was destroyed, scores of Japanese soldiers were killed, and the attack dissolved. It did emphasize the difficulties, and as dawn broke on July 31, it came with the thunder of the artillery. The navy was called into action; its guns fired 600 tons of shells against the relatively small wooded area of the south. In spite of the difficult weather, carrier bombers and land-based bombers from Saipan and the Tinian airfields dropped 69 tons of bombs. The Japanese, cornered in this end of Tinian, found the bombardment dreadful. Indeed, for the few who survived, the major memory was of weeks of intensive bombardment and shelling; and this was quite a correct assessment, because never before had the Central Pacific forces used so much artillery and naval fire to reduce an island.

But someone had to take the territory, and that was the marines. They faced a difficult cliff on the left. General Schmidt ringed the cliff with troops of the Second Division, and told them to stay at the base, to prevent Japanese escape along the east coast. The road, dangerous as it might be, offered the only sensible approach to the bastion area. As the troops began to move, they were slowed by the emergence from the area of Korean and Japanese civilians who wanted to surrender. The Second Marines rounded them up. The Eighth Marines led the way in the attack, supported by tanks. As they approached the plateau they moved through flat cane fields along the railroad track. The Japanese resisted as well as they could. At one point fifteen soldiers rushed out from their hiding place along the embankment in a banzai charge against an American tank. In five minutes there were fifteen Japanese bodies on the ground, and the tank lumbered on.

As they came to the cliffs, and the road winding upward through them, the Japanese fire intensified. Riflemen and machine guns were hidden in deep caves and ravines, and as the first tanks and troops reached the edge of the rising ground, they began to fire. The rate and intensity of the fire were such that Lieutenant Colonel Gavin Humphrey, commanding the Third Battalion of the Eighth Marines, stopped: he must find some way to reduce the fire from the ground above. Medium tanks came to up turn their 75mm guns on the area. Their fire was not very effective; the Japanese simply retreated into their caves. Flamethrower tanks came up to try to burn away the vegetation that concealed the cave entrances. They were not very successful. The ground and the vegetation were too wet. Self-propelled 75mm guns were brought up, and they did no more to resolve the problem than the tanks had done. Humphrey suggested to the regimental command post that he be allowed to withdraw his troops 400 yards to the rear, and then bring down an artillery barrage on the whole area. It could not be done; the First Battalion of the regiment was on the right of the Third; it was growing late in the day, and to withdraw would leave a hole in the line that would invite a Japanese flank attack. So the marines dug in for the night at the bottom of the high ground.

The First Battalion actually fought its way up the road, and to the top. At least Company A reached the top and was followed by a platoon of Company C. Late in the afternoon, most of the battalion reached the high ground, but that did not mean they had captured it. The Japanese were all around them, and at 6:30 that evening, they attacked. A force of about a hundred riflemen came charging out of the brush. Most of them were killed, but as darkness fell, the American position was tenuous. The Eighth Marines were strung out along the road from bottom to top. Colonel Clarence Wallace, commander of the regiment, sent two platoons of his reserve company and two 37mm guns up to the top to reinforce the front position. It was here, he knew from experience, that he could expect the night assault that most surely would come.

An hour before midnight, the attack began. The Japanese came quietly forward until they were 20 yards from the American positions. They harassed the front line from there. At about 1:00 in the morning, the Japanese sent a force of about a hundred men to cut the road. They crossed, burned two jeep ambulances, and captured a number of vehicles. From the base of the cliff Major William C. Chamberlin led a counterattack up the road. They recaptured most of the vehicles and killed most of the Japanese. Twenty Japanese soldiers, isolated by this attack, were found next day, suicides by grenade.

At 3:00 in the morning, the Japanese attacked again, and were repelled. At 5:15 a group of more than 600 charged the Americans at the top of the hill. The 37mm guns began firing canister, which exploded and sent shrapnel over a wide area. The Japanese turned machine guns against the 37mm guns, and one 13mm gun tore large holes in the protective shield of one of the 37mm guns and killed the crew. But other marines jumped in to man the guns, and they kept firing. The two 37mm guns at the top of the hill made the difference; they fired steadily and kept the Japanese advance from materializing. In an hour of fighting, the marines suffered seventy-five casualties, but the Japanese left 200 dead in an area about 100 yards square. They retreated into the woods and cliffs southeast of the marine position.

On the morning of July 21, the tanks began to move again. They were stopped by high-velocity antitank fire that scored six hits on one tank in a few minutes. One of them penetrated the turret and wrecked it. But the tank was not destroyed. Its commander backed off about 15 yards and then fired smoke shells to show the area from which the high-velocity fire had come. The Japanese obviously had an antitank gun back there. The spotters, flying above the marines in their observation planes, gave the coordinates to the destroyers and cruisers offshore. Bazookas were brought up to fire into the area. More tanks came up and fired their guns toward the woods. They seemed to have destroyed the gun, for the area became quiet. The tanks moved forward with a new tank on the left flank where the one had been hit before. When they moved, the replacement tank had no sooner reached the spot where the first tank was hit than it too was hit six times in rapid succession. Then the tankers discovered the enemy gun in a fortified position 30 yards off to the left. Two tanks moved out to destroy the gun. One fired a smoke shell into the position. The other moved behind the position and fired into the concrete wall of the back. Smoke came out, and so did a few Japanese, who were killed by the guns of the tank in front. The tank men then stopped to look over their enemy: the Japanese had put a 47mm antitank gun into a concrete emplacement, enclosed on three sides. The weapon was trained on a fire lane about 10 yards wide, through which any tanks would have to pass along this route. It had been a very effective position, but again the sheer power of numbers had made the difference. Two American tanks had been damaged, but the Japanese had lost one of their few antitank weapons and twenty soldiers.

The road was the key to capture of the area. The Japanese knew it and defended it and made it dangerous with mines. The Americans took the road, and the engineers dug out the mines, and at night the Japanese infiltrated and laid new mines. At one point when a tank hit a mine that shattered its suspension system and injured three of the crew, the Japanese came charging out from the brush to finish off the tank. But other tanks came up to rescue the crew of the stopped tank, and infantrymen kept the Japanese back. As they retreated they saw the Japanese setting up a machine gun in the wrecked tank. They stopped, turned, and blew apart their own tank to prevent the enemy from using it.

On the morning of August 1 the drive continued. The Twenty-fourth Marines were moving down the coast from Tinian town. It was tedious business, involving a few yards of advance, discovery of a cave filled with Japanese, and then the difficult process of routing them out, firing into the cave with 75mm pack howitzers and flamethrowers, and perhaps finally having to seal the cave with a satchel charge before they could go on. Half the time they never saw the enemies they were killing. But the Japanese defenses were stout. In one area, a dozen yards wide and 30 yards long, which the marines had to traverse because of the rugged ground, the engineers cleared forty-five mines.

On the morning of August 1, three battalions attacked across the plateau that had been fought over so hard during the previous day and night. Resistance suddenly seemed to stop, and hundreds of civilians appeared. This was not surprising, for after the marines had watched with shock as women and children killed themselves on Saipan, they had launched a massive propaganda campaign on Tinian to prevent the same tragedy. On Saipan, the Japanese military had persuaded the civilians that they would all be murdered by the Americans, and they might as well die for the emperor. Thousands of leaflets dropped by aircraft on Tinian before and during the campaign promised the civilians good treatment, and also promised the military that surrenders would be accepted and the prisoners treated under the rules of the Geneva convention. So several thousand civilians, most of them from this southern part of the island and Tinian town in particular, began surrendering. The Sixth Marine advance was stopped that day by the surrenders. The civilians were passed back through the lines and herded into concentration camps in the rear, where they were fed and given clothing if they needed it. A few needed medical attention, but very few had been hurt by the bombing that had flattened their town. By August 2 about 4,000 civilians had surrendered, along with about fifty Japanese soldiers and sailors.

On the night of August 1-2 the Japanese began a series of *banzai* charges without any objectives at all, which indicated the approaching end of organized resistance. They attacked the command post of the Third Battalion of the Sixth Marines, and killed the battalion commander, Lieutenant Colonel John W. Easley, and several other marines. The Japanese were decimated. This pattern, however, was to continue. Many Japanese soldiers refused to quit. They hid out in caves or in the woods, waiting for a chance to strike some sort of blow against their enemies. Organized resistance ended in that first week of August, but resistance did not. Indeed, in its way it was more difficult and painful than Saipan. Colonel Ogata was dead, and his staff dead or dispersed, but individuals and little bands fought on, even as the Americans began building B-29 facilities on Tinian, too. The First Battalion of the Eighth Marines was left on the island to mop up. The process continued until the end of the year. More than 500 Japanese soldiers and sailors were killed in the next five months, at a cost of 38 marines dead and 125 wounded. The total casualties for the Americans in the capture of Tinian had been about 2,000 killed and wounded. No one knew exactly how many Japanese had died; the figure was somewhere between 5,000 and 9,000, but the caves and the sea alone could tell the story.

26
GUAM RETAKEN

When Admiral Spruance steamed over in the *Indianapolis* on July 20 to join the invasion forces heading for Guam, he was fulfilling a promise made two and a half years earlier, that the Americans would come back and repossess the first piece of American territory seized by the Japanese. The invasion of Guam was the most symbolic step yet taken in the Central Pacific campaign.

It was late in coming, first because of Admiral Ozawa's foray from the East Indies, which had upset the Marianas timetable, but even more important, because of the underestimation of the size of the Japanese defense force on Saipan. The Guam invasion had been planned for the employment of marines, but the Twenty-seventh Army Division had been the reserve. The Twenty-seventh had been totally committed at Saipan, and after the battle had suffered so many casualties that nothing short of desperation could have brought about the division's employment. Back at Pearl Harbor, Admiral Nimitz designated the Seventy-seventh Army Division to replace the Twenty-seventh as the Central Pacific force reserve, but the problem was then logistics. The Seventy-seventh, in intensive amphibious training (General Richardson could learn, after all), had to be supplied and organized for combat and transported to Guam. This all took time.

The III Amphibious Corps was to be the landing force for Guam; Major General Roy S. Geiger would command the troops ashore, and Rear Admiral Conolly would get them there with his Southern Attack Force. The troops came mostly from the Third Marine Division and the First Provisional Marine Brigade, which had absorbed a number of organizations, including the marine raider battalions. The raiders had been the marines' super-shock troops, and had fought at Guadalcanal. (Colonel Evans Carlson had led a raider raid on Makin back in 1942, which became more and more controversial and contributed finally to the disbandment of the raider battalions. The marines did not like "trick outfits" and by 1944 had decided to have no more of them.)

Guam, said all concerned, was going to be a different dish of tea from all these other Central Pacific islands. The Americans had been in possession of the island from 1898 to 1941, and so the problem of maps did not seem serious. They had plenty of maps and charts, since the days of the old coaling station which had been the navy's principal reason for wanting Guam in the first place. The governor of Guam, traditionally, had been a naval officer, and the navy and marines had the run of the place. Chamorros, the natives of the Marianas, were relatively well treated, and could be expected to show a loyalty to the Americans that had not been an aspect of any other island campaign to date.

But Guam presented a new sort of problem to the Central Pacific forces. It was the largest piece of land they had yet set out to conquer, the biggest island north of the equator between Hawaii and the Philippines—three times the size of Saipan. The terrain ranged from high plateau, mountains, and cliffs in the south, to a lesser plateau covered with hardwoods and dense tropical vegetation in the north. The Americans had been careless in the peaceful years, and had not prepared really useful topographical maps. Consequently when Guam was placed on the Central Pacific agenda, the intelligence officers began scurrying for information. Submarines were assigned to take profile photographs. The air photo services were sent to Guam to take a series of grid photographs. Old-line naval and marine officers who had served on the island

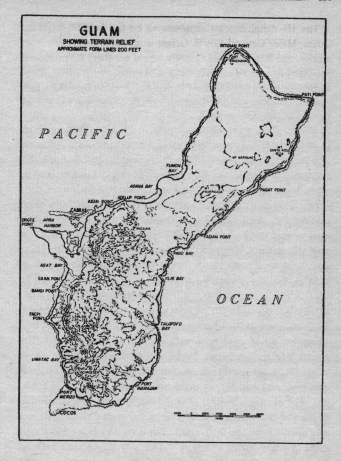

were brought out of retirement to draw maps and correct errors in others. By the summer of 1944 the planners at Pearl Harbor had a fair idea, but no more than that, of the topography. They did not know much about the coral reef outside, except that it virtually circled the island. They knew even less about the Japanese defenses. But the hiatus caused by the battle of the Phillippine Sea and the miscalculation of Japanese strength on Saipan worked to help the invaders of Guam. By July 14 the underwater teams were swimming around the island. They destroyed about 1,000 obstacles off Asan and Agat on the west side of the island, where the invasion would be mounted. The fact that there were so many man-made obstacles along the reef was an indication of the Japanese plans for defense.

Those plans were relatively new. After the Japanese seized Guam in 1941 they paid little attention to the island. A force of less than 200 naval troops was left to guard the installations. The army did not consider Guam important to the defenses, and besides, the army was not thinking about defenses, for it was driving forward on all fronts, and generals in Tokyo were talking about setting up in Sydney. But as it became apparent that the Americans were going to attack either the Gilberts or the Marshalls, as they did in the summer of 1943, Imperial Headquarters in Tokyo had some second thoughts. The Twenty-ninth Division of Manchuria's famous Kwantung army was assigned to Guam, and before its officers began to prepare they were warned by Tokyo that their job was vital to the defense of the empire: "Loss of these islands signifies Japan's surrender." The division, which had been operating on the old lines with strict division of authority between infantry, engineers, tanks, and service troops, was reorganized along the lines of the American regimental combat teams; each regiment had its own engineers and artillery. Then, in February 1944, the Twenty-ninth Division was brought down from Manchuria, where it had been training for war against the Soviets, and outfitted for war in the tropics. The division was loaded aboard three big transports at Pusan, Korea. The Eighteenth Infantry boarded the *Sakito Maru;* the Fiftieth Infantry boarded another *maru* of the same size, and the Thirty-eighth Infantry and division headquarters boarded a third ship. They all sailed for the Marianas in February. Just two days out of port the *Sakito Maru* was spotted by the American submarine *Trout,* which sank her, with a loss of more than half the 3,500 men aboard, including the regimental commander. The regiment also lost its artillery, tanks, and heavy equipment. So before any fighting had been done the Thirty-eighth was reduced to scattering in the Marianas. One battalion stayed on Saipan, where it was lost almost to the last man. The other two battalions and headquarters went to Guam. They had two companies of tanks, but only about 1,300 men. The Fiftieth Regiment had gone to Tinian, where it suffered the fate of the Saipan defenders. Division headquarters went to Guam with the Thirty-eighth Infantry, adding another 3,000 men to the defenses. Then, because of the disaster that had befallen the *Sakito Maru*, Imperial Headquarters dredged up another force from the rapidly dwindling resources of the Kwantung army. Parts of the First and Eleventh Divisions were detached, and assigned a new name: the Sixth Expeditionary Force. But in spite of the big name, when the troops arrived in Guam, there were about 3,000 of them, and they were again reorganized into the Forty-eighth Independent Mixed Brigade and the Tenth Independent Mixed Regiment. Altogether, by June 1944 the defense force had been raised to 11,500 men. Commander of the whole defense was Lieutenant General Rakeshi Takashima. General Obata, commander of the Thirty-first Army, was in overall charge, but Takashima ran the Guam defenses. The navy also had a large force on the island, about 2,500 men under Captain Yutaka Sugimoto, who had been commander of the island before 1943. So, adding up navy, army, and odd units of survivors from various disasters, the total military presence on Guam in July 1944 was around 19,000.

With the capture of Saipan, a good deal of information about Guam defenses fell into American hands. The Japanese were expecting invasion by four or five American divisions on the west side of the island. The problem of defense was the paucity of artillery. General Takashima had a few 150mm guns, but the preponderance were no larger than 75mm, and there could never be enough of these. Beginning in the fall of 1943 the naval battalions and civilian construction crews had built a network of defenses—pillboxes, spiderweb trench systems, and all the refinements they could muster. A central communications system was planned for construction underground, and work was begun. The delay in

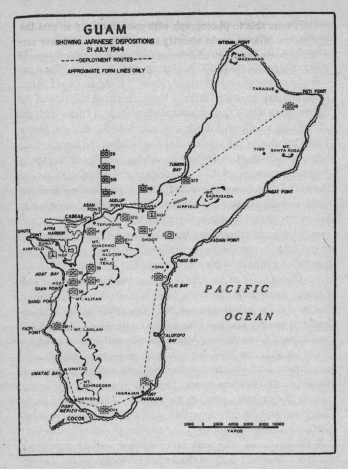

GUAM
SHOWING JAPANESE DISPOSITIONS
21 JULY 1944
— — — DEPLOYMENT ROUTES — — —
APPROXIMATE FORM LINES ONLY

invasion, then, worked not only for the Americans, but probably
even more for the Japanese. Aerial photographs in the early spring
had shown little defense. Those taken in the early summer
showed fifty-one artillery emplacements, thirty-six antiaircraft
positions, and 141 machine-gun and mortar posts—all fortified.
And these were only the unconcealed positions that the American

aviators were able to photograph with enough clarity so that the intelligence officers could identify them. There were many surprises, including a system of defenses that was built to deny access of the Americans to the northern half of the island, and particularly to Orote Peninsula, which juts out into Apra Harbor, the principal port of Guam.

Off and on, since early June, the Americans had been bombing and shelling Guam. The systematic bombardment of the island began on July 8, and continued day after day. All that had gone before, in the Marshalls and at Saipan and Tinian, was less than what came here. The bombardment was so intensive and so continuous that it virtually stopped Japanese work on the defenses during the daylight hours, and hampered it at night. As bad as this was, the effect on the morale of the troops was worse. The constant noise and surprise of shells coming in played havoc with the men's nerves. It was "near the limit bearable by humans," said several of the survivors.

As the Americans were ready to invade, they were satisfied that they had knocked out all the major Japanese defenses; more than 50 percent of the installations they could see from the air or along the shore were destroyed. Aircraft coming in from the carriers and from land bases kept the Japanese troops movements down to night maneuvers. But the bombardment was so widely scattered that it was not until July 16 that the defenders had a real idea where the Americans planned to land. On that day the whole force was turned along the west coast, and particularly around Tumon Bay, and then General Takashima knew that the Americans were coming to this area.

Having learned from the Saipan experience, the Americans assembled a strong force for the capture of Guam. In July, 37,000 marines and 19,000 army soldiers were ready for the fight. They would land on the two best beaches of the island: Asan, north of Apra Harbor, and Agat, across Orote Peninsula south of the harbor. Admiral Conolly, the bombardment expert, said at the outset that it was his aim to get the troops ashore standing up—which meant that he intended to destroy so much of the Japanese shore defense that there would be no killing on the beach. In the week before the invasion, he had tried his best to do just that. On July 21, at 5:30 in the morning, four battleships off Orote Peninsula opened fire, each using a dozen 14-inch guns, and inside Agat Bay the old *Pennsylvania* fired at the cliff line. Other ships, cruisers and destroyers, joined the fire on the beaches. It was all planned; each ship was firing in a selected zone, and at selected targets for the most part. Forty-five minutes after the barrage began, from the carriers came a dozen fighter planes, nine dive bombers, and five torpedo bombers. They had permission to hit any targets that seemed worthy, and their first strike was at buildings and guns on Cabras island north of Apra harbor. At 7:15 came an even more spectacular display: eighty-five fighters, sixty-two dive bombers, and fifty-three torpedo bombers from the carriers flew along the beaches, bombing and strafing. For the first time, the planes came in successfully during the naval bombardment. The experience at Eniwetok and Saipan, where planes had been damaged or destroyed by "friendly fire," had led to an experiment—the naval gunners adjusted their trajectories so that no shell rose above 1,200 feet, and the fliers pulled out of their runs at 1,500 feet. It worked very well.

The landing force was already assembling. The First Marine Provisional Brigade would land on the Agat beaches, the Third Marine Division on the Asan beaches. The procedures followed the well-established pattern; Guam was, after all, the Central Pacific forces' tenth amphibious landing. First came the barrage from the ships, then the gunboats, and then 360 LVTs. At 8:00 in the morning as the assault boats moved toward land, the air observer flying over the island to spot for the Third Marine Division saw no signs of Japanese activity. There was no sign of Japanese on the beaches; not a shell came out from the shore toward the ships. In the First Brigade's area one gun was observed firing, so the 14-inch guns of the battleships were turned on Yona island, where the fire was coming from. But as the marines came to those last few yards of water that separated reef from beach, suddenly the situation changed. Several amphibious tractors were disabled by underwater mines that blew up in the faces of the men. The beach defenses, supposedly destroyed, came to life. Off the northern shore, guns ranging from 75mm to 37mm suddenly opened fire. Several amphtracs were hit; marines jumped and began wading in to the beach. Admiral Connolly's hope of getting them in with dry feet was ended. The Japanese were firing armor-piercing shells and bullets, and the LVTs were hit. As the marines came out of them, the Japanese machine guns fired on the beaches. In that first and second wave, dozens of LVTs were hit, and ten were destroyed. In the south, the First Brigade's area, ten more were destroyed. One by one the guns of the ships found the enemy positions and began shelling them. But the defenses on Guam were the most secure that the Americans had yet encountered. One effective gun position was located on Gaan Point inside a coral hill. It had not been seen from the air, but when the invasion troops landed its effect was known almost immediately. Embedded in four feet of rock, one 75mm gun and a 37mm gun fired down on the beach.

Colonel Carvel Hall's Third Marines were to secure Adelup Point, Chonito Cliff and the high ground on the left flank of the division. The Twenty-first Marines would move inland, and on the right the Ninth Marines would take the low ground and Cabras Island. On the south, the First Provisional Brigade would land on the other side of the Orote peninsula. The Twenty-second Marines would occupy Agat, with the Fourth Marines on their right flank and the 305th Marines turning north to seize the Orote peninsula and link up with the Third Division in the north.

Before the landing, the naval officers had been congratulating one another on the smoothness of their operation—the best yet. But as the marines came ashore, and began to fall on the beaches, it was apparent that the Japanese had been more clever than the intelligence officers had believed. Dozens of guns and machine guns had survived the barrage and bombing by the carrier and land-based aircraft. At Adelup Point, the fire on the Third Marines was "ominously heavy," as one observer put it. An observer counted twenty disabled amph-tracs in the water off the beach. Still, by 8:30, the marines were ashore and moving along the beach, firing their weapons.

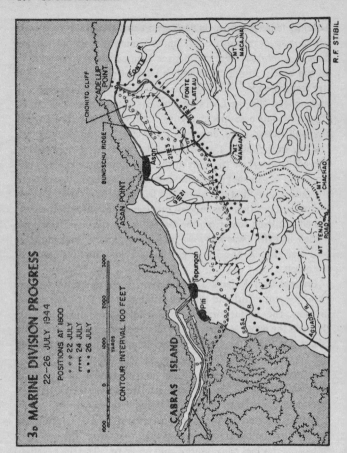

The Third Marines had the hardest going. The Japanese had retreated during the bombardment to caves and shelters on the reverse slopes of the hills. But when the guns lifted to let the marines land, the Japanese came out of their caves and over the hill to
man the prepared positions on Chonito Cliff, which overshadows

the beaches and ground to the south. They manned field guns, mortars, and machine guns that were sighted in on the reef and beaches, and the Third Marines took many casualties. Soon the cry of "corpsman" began ringing in the air, and the number of litters allocated was used up. The marines began making litters from poles and ponchos to carry their wounded back to the beach.

The Japanese had built one strongpoint that ran between Adelup Point and Chonito Cliff. They had dug a tunnel system 400 yards long, with guns covering a concrete bridge and the beach road. From their positions they could fire on the beach, and if the marines got off the beach and came to the road they could fire on the vehicles as they tried to move south. The Third Battalion of the Third Marines faced this fire. Company L was stopped by the Japanese at the draw that led inland to the road. Company K crossed the bed of a dry stream and started up Chonito Cliff, but the Japanese fired down on them, and when the marines lobbed grenades uphill, the Japanese rolled them back down. Lieutenant Colonel Ralph Houser, the battalion commander, called for flame-throwers and tanks. They came up and began firing into the caves. One by one the positions were destroyed, with the Japanese moving on to the next. By noon, the Americans had taken Chonito Cliff. In the afternoon, they took Adelup Point. But the advance was snagged by a band of Japanese inhabiting a rock pile 200 yards square and 400 feet high. Company A of the First Battalion ran squarely into this position. Aboard ship, as the plan was laid out for the troops, this bit of real estate had been christened Bundschu Ridge, in honor of Captain Geary Bundschu, commander of Company A. On the morning of July 21, he might have declined the honor, for coming in to shore his troops had been hit hard by fire from the position. But they moved ahead, two platoons assaulting and one in reserve. At 9:20 the two lead platoons were pinned down in a gully below the ridge by Japanese machine-gun and mortar fire. The support platoon was sent around to the east side, on the left. The casualties were so heavy that Bundschu called for more corpsmen and stretcher bearers from the rear. On the right of the hill Company B was a little better off, but not much. Five men were killed from that company that day. When resistance on Adelup Point stopped, the 81mm mortars of the First Battalion were turned over to this area, but when the mortar men moved up to the ridge, they were almost immediately pinned down by Japanese fire from above. The gunnery sergeant and four men were hit within a few minutes. By 3:00 in the afternoon, the attack was stalled. Colonel Hall committed the Second Battalion to the area.

Captain Bundschu of Company A could not move at all. At 2:00 he had asked for permission to disengage, draw back, and try another approach. But Colonel Hall denied the request. The company was right in the middle of the line, and its movement back would jeopardize the troops on either side. So Captain Bundschu turned back to the enemy and led a charge up the hill. The Japanese machine guns began to rattle, and the mortars spat their charges high into the air. Captain Bundschu fell dead as a handful of his men reached the crest of the hill. Colonel James Snedeker, executive officer of the Third Marines, was sitting on a sand dune with a portable radio, spotting for the 40mm antiaircraft guns that were being used to support the troops (in the absence of Japanese planes). He saw the marines falling down the hill, and he saw little puffs of sand rising all around his dune as the Japanese fire intensified. As night fell, the Japanese still held Bundschu Ridge and their fire from it kept up all night long.

Elsewhere the situation was not too different. The arc of hills around the Asan beachhead had been sternly defended by the Japanese. As night came, the Americans found themselves with two separate operations ashore; the Third Marines and the First Brigade had not been able to link up. The Japanese still held Orote Peninsula.

The Twenty-first Marines had encountered the same sort of difficulties as faced the Third Regiment. They came to call the ridge for which they were fighting Banzai Ridge. By nightfall they had a slender hold on one bit of ridge top and were in contact with the Ninth Marines on their right; the Ninth had not encountered such enemy resistance and had made the most progress of all the division, through dry rice paddies to the ridge that extends from Asan

Point to the mouth of the Nidual River, and toward the Tatgua River. By dark, the troops had dug in 400 yards from the bank. The amount of territory taken and the speed were deceptive. The Ninth had been lucky enough to have easier terrain, but paid a dear price for its advance. Twenty officers were killed or wounded and 211 men. The commanders of two companies of the Third Battalion were among the dead. By the end of the day, the Third Division had suffered 105 men killed, 536 wounded, and fifty-six missing in action. The division held a beachhead 2.5 miles wide and about a mile deep at its point of farthest penetration. But even this picture was illusory, for all through the area the Japanese still held high points and could still fire down on the beachhead to harass and kill men coming ashore. But the marines had come to stay, they said, and to prove it Major General Allen Turage set up his divisional command post ashore.

In the south the First Brigade had much easier terrain to take, but the Japanese resistance was also stronger. In spite of the naval barrage, dozens of pillboxes stood intact, and from them and the intricate trench system came a wave of fire as the marines came ashore. The tanks began to fall into traps. Still, by noon, the Twenty-second Marines advanced to high ground 1,000 yards inland. Here they were out of range of the guns firing on the beach, but they faced a new danger: artillery fire from the hills. It got stronger as they moved inland. The Second Battalion moved around noon to seize the first day's objective, a line that included the village of Agat. But Japanese guns stopped them, and when the commander of the battalion ordered an air strike from a carrier, the bombs fell on Company F, killing and wounding a number of men. The attack had to be junked, and the battalion dug in for the night instead of meeting the First Battalion at Agat. The First Battalion took the rubble of the village, but then the men of Company C ran into real trouble. They were getting fire from a concealed Japanese position 50 yards away on a small hill. They had to withdraw to a series of Japanese trenches below the hill, and they were pinned down there, still not knowing where the machine guns were. They dug in there as darkness came. Then, after

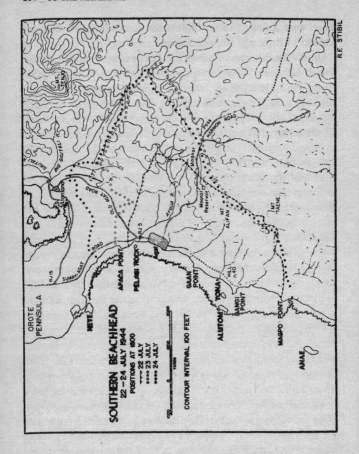

R.F. STIBIL

SOUTHERN BEACHHEAD
22–24 JULY 1944
POSITIONS AT 1800
▼▼▼ 22 JULY
○○○ 23 JULY
●●● 24 JULY

0   500   1000
YARDS

CONTOUR INTERVAL 100 FEET

dark, down a trail leading to the trench marched a dozen Japanese soldiers, carrying three heavy machine guns and a light machine gun. These were the guns that had stopped the company all afternoon, and the Japanese were apparently moving them forward in the belief that the Americans had retreated back to the beach. The riflemen of Company C began shooting, and all twelve Japanese were killed. "Those Nips were so heavy with slugs we couldn't lift them," said one marine.

In the Twenty-second's area life had been complicated all day, and continued that way. The heavy Japanese fire on the beach had wrecked many amphibious tractors and delayed the bringing of supplies and reinforcements. A shell had hit an aid station, destroying medical supplies and killing or wounding all the members of the party. The night was spent trying to catch up.

The Fourth Marines came in on flat ground after they hit the beaches and were soon 700 yards inland. By noon they had reached their first objective. In the afternoon they moved toward Mount Alifan and before nightfall reached the foot of the mountain and dug in. Casualties had been about 350 men killed and wounded. They had no idea about Japanese casualties; they saw very few bodies. The same was true in the north; the Americans had very little idea of what they faced. But they were ashore. The 305th Marines, in reserve, came ashore in the afternoon and evening. At the end of the first day the invasion was established.

The Japanese had suffered more casualties than the marines could find. The Thirty-eighth Regiment had been hard hit. Two companies of the First Battalion in the Agat beach area had been wiped out by noon by the Fourth Marines. The Second Battalion had suffered many casualties in trying to hold Agat, and had failed to hold the town, so as Colonel Tsuentaro Suenaga, the regimental commander, pondered the course of the battle that evening in his command post on the slope of Mt. Alifan he saw that the Americans had moved far inland and threatened to take the whole sector he was entrusted to defend. The only answer was a counterattack to regain the lost territory and drive the marines back to the beach. It must come that night, before the marines had a chance to bring more men and more tanks and guns. He sent out orders to the platoons and squads of the First and Second Battalions: prepare for counterattack. Then he telephoned General Takashima to ask permission to attack. The general refused: the regiment had been badly hurt during the day and was in no condition to make such an attack. But Colonal Suenaga said it was now or never; in the morning the marines would drive forward again, and he could not hold long against such overwhelming power. So the general was persuaded to allow an attack he knew would fail. His last words to Suenaga were to be sure to reassemble his men to continue the defense of Mount Alifan. What he meant was to remember that whatever was left must go to Mount Alifan to die. Suenaga obviously knew what was coming, for he burned the regimental colors to be sure they were not captured by the enemy.

As darkness became total, the word was passed along the marine line to be ready for a *banzai* charge in any and every section. The artillery zeroed in on all the avenues of approach. Offshore the ships took position to support the troops. Just before midnight mortar shells began falling on Company K of the Third Battalion of the Fourth Marines. The Japanese came charging forth. Flares were sent up, and they showed scores of screaming Japanese coming at full tilt, with bayonet and sword. Six marines in forward foxholes were overrun and bayoneted to death before the fire could intensify and drive the Japanese back. All along the line the story was repeated; the Japanese charged, they killed marines, and then the artillery and the machine guns found them and they were killed, or driven into retreat. Some Japanese with explosives wormed their way to the beach, and blew up two weapons carriers and three LVTs before they were surrounded and killed by marines. The Fourth Marines' tank company also was a target. The Japanese came in to destroy the tanks, and the marines killed twenty-three of them, without losing a tank.

At about 2:00 in the morning, the marines of the Fourth Regiment's Second Battalion heard the rumble of tanks along the beach road. They sent out a call for help, and marine tanks came up. Half an hour later a line of Japanese light tanks came up to the battle line. Starshells from the ships offshore illuminated the area in greenish light, and the Japanese tanks were clearly visible. The bazooka men began firing, at point-blank range, and so did several 37mm antitank guns. The first two enemy tanks were hit by one bazooka gunner. He was killed by return fire. The 75mm guns of the Sherman tanks hit two more tanks, and they began to burn. The tank assault had failed.

All along the marine line, the attack was repeated. The First Battalion of the Fourth Marines took a beating. Company A pushed back one charge after another by Japanese troops rushing down the wooded slopes of the mountain. One rifle platoon was reduced to four able-bodied men. The brigade lost fifty men killed and a hundred wounded, but the commander estimated that the Japanese had lost four times as many men. And the result, sad for Colonel Suenaga to contemplate, was that the Thirty-eighth Regiment of the Imperial Japanese Army had ceased to exist as a fighting force. General Shigematsu of the Forty-eighth Independent Mixed Brigade had taken control of most of the troops in this area, and that night they staged other attacks. The general set up his command post in a quarry off the Fonte river valley road, and as reinforcements came up, he sent them to join the battle. Everywhere, the marines held, and in the morning, the Japanese Tenth and Eighteenth Infantry Regiments had suffered losses. In the most serious thrust, made against the marines at Chonito Cliff, some of the Japanese attacked frontally and others went down the dry streambed between Adlup Point and the cliff. They came around to climb the slopes behind the marines. But the marines of the Third held, too, with the help of a company of the Twenty-first marines that came up, and support from LVTs on the beach. By 8:30 in the morning the attack was sealed off, and the Japanese attackers were being picked off one by one.

On this second day, July 22, the marines had scheduled an advance, but they could not drive forward because the Japanese still held Bundschu Ridge. On the right, the Ninth Marines did advance into the flats beyond Asan Point, and took the villages of Tepungan and Piti, and the Piti navy yard. They moved to Cabras island at the mouth of the harbor. The Japanese let them land unopposed, but the marines almost immediately ran into thick brush and mines.

Bundschu Ridge was the major problem. General Turnage's men fought all day long to gain control of the height, but they did not manage to do so. The defense positions had been carefully planned, and everywhere the marines moved the Japanese were able to fire on them and keep them from advancing. As night came down, General Turnage began planning an all-out assault on the ridge. The Japanese helped him inadvertently, because Lieutenant Colonel Hideyuki Takeda wanted to make a showing against the marines and, if possible, push them back farther, off the slopes of the ridge. He was operations officer of the Twenty-ninth Division, and this was his job. He instructed the 321st Independent Infantry Battalion, which was working the Bundschu area, to make an attack that night. The plan called for the Japanese to sneak up to the American line, blast the line with grenades, and then withdraw in the confusion, having routed the Americans out of their positions. But when the Japanese came up, their officers grew over-enthusiastic at the thought of attack, and charged the American lines, their troops behind them. Machine guns, mortars, and field guns behind the marine lines began firing. In the morning, when the Japanese attack here ended, Colonel Takeda could count only fifty survivors of the 500-man battalion.

By the morning of July 23, the Japanese position had deteriorated more than it might have seemed in terms of numbers. There remained thousands of troops on the island, brave and ready to give their lives. But the best fighting men, the troops of the Twenty-ninth Division and the Forty-fourth Independent Mixed Brigade, were dead. The Japanese field hospital in the valley below Mount Majacina was overcrowded with wounded men. The Fonte River, usually a source of drinking water, could not be used because it was fouled by rotting bodies. General Takashima knew all this, and on the 23rd he made the decision to stage a major attack before his reserves were exhausted by this sort of fighting. At the moment it continued, the marines advancing in small spurts. It was not until the fourth day that they had closed the gaps in the line of the Third Division. On July 22 the attack on Orote Peninulsa began, since it must be cleared to consolidate the lines of the Third Division and the First Brigade. The plan was to move across the neck of the peninsula and seal it off. The advance was stoutly contested by the Japanese, and so the Seventy-seventh Army Division was brought in from the ships.

The 305th and 306th Regimental Combat Teams began to land. By July 25, the Japanese decided to move to prevent just such a sealing off. The Ninth Marines and the Twenty-first Marines bore the brunt of a Japanese counterattack near the Mount Tenjo Road. By the end of July 25, the marine reserves were completely exhausted; every man of the First Battalion of the Twenty-first Marines, for example, was actually on the line, in a combat position. They were nearly exhausted after four days of constant fighting.

And it was this night that General Takashima chose to stage his major counterattack. The first move came at midnight against the Reconnaissance Company of the Third Marines. General Takashima had planned to have tanks move up, then the infantry would breach the line and charge through, and turn and seal off the whole flank of the American force. But the tanks did not manage to get there—they got lost! Naval troops of the Fifty-fourth Keibetai (assault battalion) were led forward by Captain Yutaki Sugimoto, the senior Japanese naval officer. He was killed in the assault, and so were hundreds of his men. The Japanese did breach the lines, and did destroy some American equipment behind them, including a tank, but again there were too many reserves, too much material, too many guns, too much support from the Americans on the beaches and at sea, and there was no way the Japanese could take and hold positions in the American rear.

That night, Japanese attacked the American hospital near the Nidual River and killed and wounded many of the already wounded and the hospital personnel. But by morning that too was over. In the work of the night, the marines estimated they had killed more than 3,000 Japanese. What they did not then know was the serious blow that had befallen the enemy in the deaths of many of the senior officers of the Japanese command. General Shigematsu, the commander of the Forty-eighth Brigade, was killed when marine tanks blasted his command post. The commander of the Eighteenth Regiment was killed leading his troops. Both his batallion commanders were killed after they had led troops behind the American lines. On July 26, this mournful news was sent to Tokyo by a dispirited General Obata who

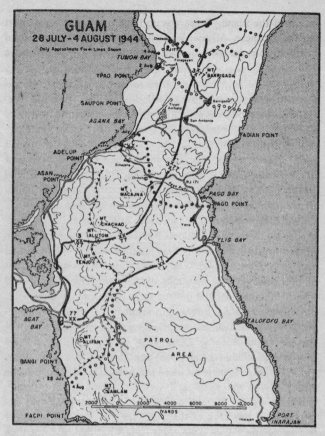

radioed the words that Imperial General Headquarters now knew to be a signal of impeding disaster:

"I will defend Mount Mangan to the last by assembling the remaining strength . . . ."

So Tokyo knew the battle was lost and it was simply a matter of time; 95 percent of the officers in the action had been killed, and 90 percent of the weapons lost. The Orote Peninsula defense force was wiped out, and the Americans now held the whole Agat sector of the island. There was no hope of naval or air support for the Japanese. All that was left for them was a campaign of attrition, to make the American recapture of Guam as expensive as they could.

On July 29 the American flag was raised on Guam for the first time since 1941, above the ruins of the old Marine Barracks on Orote. Planes began landing on the Orote Peninsula airfield. The marines and army troops moved out, fanlike, to secure the island.

The major Japanese forces moved into the northern half of the island after they were defeated at the Orote Peninsula. General Obata, the military commander for all the area, who had been caught on Guam by the offensive, moved his headquarters to Ordot, just above the center of the island. General Takashima, commander of the Twenty-ninth Division, was trapped in a cave in the Fonte area, and escaped by jumping off a cliff and running between two tanks. Later on July 28 General Takashima was shot down by a tank machine gunner as he reached the foot of Mount Majacina. General Obata then assumed tactical command of the Guam forces for the first time.

For several days, General Geiger stopped to rest and reorganize his troops. The very size of Guam made this campaign different from all those that had preceded it, for although the Japanese were on the defensive and retreating, there was plenty of space into which they could retreat, and even in the south and central parts of the island, hundreds of Japanese stragglers were holed up, which endangered every American movement. On July 30, as the Americans reorganized, they counted the cost. They had suffered 6,000 casualties in this battle for Guam, and the island was only half won. The Japanese dead they could account for came to over 6,000. They had taken only fifty prisoners, a grim reminder that Japan would not be defeated easily. If the terrain to the south had been difficult, that to the north was far worse; the rolling hills were covered with dense brush and underbrush. But the marines and the army troops moved out on July 31 to strike against Agana, the capital of the island. By nightfall they held the town plaza and the shattered buildings around it. They bypassed many Japanese in the hills and gullies, who did not know they had been passed. As usual, when the American units encountered Japanese, the latter fought, and usually had to be killed to the last man.

The troops moved along the roads, and they took the villages, and the Japanese continued to occupy large parts of Guam in between. Stubbornly, the Japanese yielded ground, moved back, fought, and fought again. There were fights around Mount Barrigada, Mount Mataguoc, and Mount Santa Rosa. General Obata ordered his men to fight delaying actions at every one of these points. General Geiger wanted artillery support, but in the thick jungle the shells of battleships and cruisers were of limited assistance. Saipan-based B-25 medium bombers and P-47 fighters flew in to bomb and drop napalm. The army and marine artillery moved up behind the troops, and the Americans slugged their way northward on Guam.

The nature of the fighting was indicated on August 3, in the area occupied by the Third Battalion of the Twenty-first Marines. They had reached the Finegayan-Barrigada road, and a crossroads where those roads from Agana and Barrigada met. As long as they kept to the road north and did not stray into the jungle alongside, they encountered relatively few Japanese. The enemy was posted at significant points, and it was here that fighting usually occurred —such points as road crossings and villages. On the afternoon of August 3, when the marines reached the Finegayan-Barrigade junction, they stopped because this presented new problems, and Major Jess Ferrill, commander of the Third Battalion of the Ninth Marines, had no contact with the army troops on his right. The men of the Third Battalion of the Twenty-first Marines were then sent up behind the Ferrill unit, and they dug in for the night. Major Ferrill wanted to know what existed along those side roads, and an armored reconnaissance force was organized that afternoon. Lieutenant Colonel Hartnoll Withers of the Third Tank Battalion brought up several Sherman medium tanks, two half-tracks, four radio jeeps, and several truckloads of troops, including a mine-clearing detachment and Company I of the Twenty-first Marines. The patrol unit went out on the road, and on its way back, got sidetracked onto one of the small market roads that honeycombed central Guam, a road that led east to Liguan. Four hundred yards past the crossroads, Japanese forces on both sides of the road ambushed the American vehicles. For two hours the force was cut off from retreat. For the most part the Americans could not see the enemy, who had field guns, machine guns, mortars, and many riflemen. The jungle prevented the Shermans from maneuvering. The half-tracks were nearly as badly off. The trucks could not turn around. So the Americans dug in and fought. Finally, they knocked out a Japanese tank and a pair of 75mm guns and managed to break loose and retreat, leaving behind one wrecked half-track and one truck, and carrying with them fifteen casualties. This was a pattern of fighting repeated many times. Also, the Americans had the night attacks to harry them. That night at 10:00 two medium Japanese tanks came down that Liguan road and into the American positions, firing steadily, went right on through, firing all the while, and sped westward up another road, escaping in spite of return fire from every sort of American weapon.

The soldiers of the Seventy-seventh Division had an even rougher time in some ways. There were few roads in their sector, which meant they moved northward over rough terrain. Yet tanks paved the way, and bulldozers came up behind, making roads over which supplies could be brought forward. They surrounded Mount Barrigada, and on the afternoon of August 4 the American forces were abreast, ready to drive northward again. The Japanese retreated north and east, fighting furiously. Their tanks were extremely effective, particularly at night. In one encounter on August 6, similar to that of the Liguan road, the Japanese sent two medium tanks and a platoon of infantry clattering into a position held by the 305th Infantry Regiment. In spite of fire from American guns, they sped down the trail, firing on both sides, ran into a Sherman tank and damaged it, backed off, crushed a jeep, and raced back the way they had come, leaving fifteen American dead and forty-six wounded, without any apparent casualties of their own.

One of the worst aspects of the fighting on Guam was the ease with which the Japanese could elude their pursuers in the jungle.

This made the snipers more deadly than ever, and the Japanese snipers caused heavy casualties, particularly among key personnel. They preferred radiomen, jeep drivers, and officers as targets. On August 6 a sniper shot down Colonel Douglas C. McNair, the chief of staff of the Seventy-seventh Division, as he was setting up a new command post. At one moment the colonel was looking over the ground. The next he was dead from a bullet, and the jungle from which the bullet had come was silent.

The Americans took the Liguan road, of course. They took Mount Barrigada and the roads that led past to Mount Mataguac and Mount Santa Rosa. Bombers and the naval artillery concentrated on these points ahead, and the Japanese who defended them (and survived) said, as had those at Tinian and Saipan, that the constant bombing and shelling was almost more than they could bear. But they did bear it. And they fought on. On August 7 the Americans cleaned out the area around that Seventy-seventh Division command post where Colonel McNair had fallen, and they discovered that they had put their headquarters in the middle of a Japanese stronghold. Not 500 yards away was a company of Japanese troops, totally unobserved until the American riflemen and tanks came upon them in the search. It took six hours of close fighting before the last shot was heard, and the Americans counted their casualties: thirty-three dead and wounded.

The Americans moved forward, sometimes swiftly, sometimes haltingly, but they moved. The Japanese counterattacked time and again, but never successfully. All they could do was fight a delaying action and cause casualties, but this they did very well indeed. Their tanks came out at unexpected moments, seldom more than one or two of them, made a foray, and retreated. They lost tanks and they lost men. The attrition worked both ways.

On August 8 the Americans of the 305th and 307th Infantry Regiments took Mount Santa Rosa. The Japanese had moved out. As they were compressed into an ever-smaller area, they became more savage. The Americans encountered the battered bodies of many Chamorros, beheaded. They had been work-men pressed into building the Japanese defenses, and apparent-ly the enemy had killed them to prevent them from talking to the Americans. By August 8, Mount Mataguac had fallen, and the last Japanese strongpoint lay in the Third Marine Division's zone of the island. It included tanks and many troops. The marines were told that Admiral Nimitz was coming to take a look at Guam and that they were to hurry with the cleanup. They did. They moved into the area, knocked out some Japanese tanks, established a "straggler line" across the island from Fadian Point to a point north of Tumon Bay (about a third of the island), and declared Guam secured. On August 10, General Geiger so said.

That afternoon Admiral Nimitz arrived by air at Orote air-field. It would not have done at all to have it otherwise for his visit. And of course in sense of control, the island was secure, but General Obata was still alive north of the straggler line and thousands of Japanese soldiers were still alive around the island. On the morning of August 10, as Admiral Nimitz was flying toward Guam, General Obata sent his last message for Japan, containing the now-predictable personal apologies to the em-peror for the loss of the Marianas. On the 11th, he said, he would engage in the last desperate battle on the slopes of Mount Mataguac, where he would die with his soldiers. On the morn-ing of August 11, the troops of the 306th Infantry attacked be-hind tanks and moved steadily along the slopes of the moun-tain. The Japanese simply did not have the guns and tanks to resist the American armor. Sometime during the morning, Gen-eral Obata committed *seppukku*. In the only way he knew, he had atoned to his emperor for the failure to defend the islands.

But if Guam was "secure" on August 11, 1944, it was not a very comfortable sort of security. An estimated 10,000 Japan-ese were still alive on the island. True, they had relatively few heavy weapons, and they were scattered in groups of not more than company size. As the days went on, they suffered from lack of supply, for there was absolutely nothing for them anywhere. The Chamorros, by and large, were their enemies; the Japanese had abused them over the past three years and even changed the name of their island, so the natives of the place had no love for Japanese. Literally, the Japanese starved. In the months to come, the Americans used Guam as a "live ammunition" training center. The mopping-up gave combat troops new skills. But what was to be done? The Japanese would not surrender. When they saw Americans they shot at them. Perhaps a massive propaganda campaign would have produced some results, but it is doubtful. Long after the war ended, Japanese stragglers were still being unearthed from the jungles of Guam, and some managed to survive for years there.

By mid-August, however, the war had taken an entirely new turn, and Guam was to play a role. It would become the advance headquarters of the Central Pacific forces, and Admiral Nimitz would move there to direct operations. Inside a year, Guam would house 200,000 American troops.

Finally, the casualties of Guam were counted. In twenty-one days of battle the marines, who bore the assault in the beginning, had 7,000 killed and wounded. The army suffered about 1,000 casualties. The Americans counted 11,000 Japanese bodies, but many more were sealed in caves. The propaganda campaign of later months did bring some Japanese out of hiding; by the end of the war, 1,250 Japanese had surrendered, most of them starving. But finally the Americans counted 18,500 Japanese dead on Guam, which meant that another 8,000 soldiers and sailors had starved or been killed after the island was lost.

For several reasons, the Marianas operation marked a major change in the American approach to the Pacific war. While General Holland Smith and his commanders were taking the Marianas, General Douglas MacArthur went to Pearl Harbor to meet with President Franklin D. Roosevelt and Admiral Nimitz in a historic conference. At Pearl Harbor, General MacArthur managed to convince the President to follow a war program that the Joint Chiefs of Staff had rejected—to move to the Philippines, not to

Formosa or China as Nimitz and Admiral King wished to do, and then to move against Japan. On the military side, MacArthur's argument was strengthened by the sort of war that had been waged in the Marianas. These were larger bodies of land than any the Central Pacific forces had assaulted earlier. The assault on a large land area demanded different techniques; the marines' fierce driving on the smaller islands would not work here. The slower army advance, along a broad front, was what would be wanted. And while General Holland Smith had led his men successfully so far, the quarrel with General Ralph Smith emphasized a major problem within the armed forces. The army was deeply resentful of the relief of Ralph Smith, and that resentment was felt throughout army Washington.

In the end, however, it was the politics of war that turned the direction of the Americans in the Pacific. President Roosevelt saw the political advantages of redeeming General MacArthur's promise to return to the Philippines—advantages to be reaped in the war effort and on the home political front. Roosevelt was the consummate politician, just as General MacArthur was the consummate political general. The Pearl Harbor meeting ended with the President deciding that the army and General MacArthur would lead and that the Central Pacific forces would move into a position of support. It was a bitter pill for Admiral King to swallow, for he had hoped to have the navy lead the way to Tokyo. Admiral Nimitz was disappointed, but cheerfully moved into what would become a new role. Admiral Spruance would not lead the way, and the fleet would become a fleet once more, and not a major military command.

All this had been decided by the time that Admiral Nimitz came to Guam in August. Spruance was relieved and the forces were turned over to Admiral William F. Halsey, and called the Third Fleet. Actually most of the ships were the same—the new battleships, the fast carriers, and the cruisers and destroyers. Halsey would prepare for the invasion of the Palau Islands, which had been indicated as the new Japanese command area for the outer empire. In fact, the Palaus would turn out to be a "paper tiger," the Japanese having withdrawn to the Philippines and Okinawa and Formosa. The war would go on in the Central Pacific, and the navy would carry a big load. But with the capture of the Marianas, the Central Pacific forces ceased to be the prime element of the American effort, and their role would never again be the same.

If there is a lasting value to this history of Central Pacific operations, it is to show the development of the Pacific war, and the reasons that it took the direction it did after July 1944, when the high command reversed its policy and decided to move through the Philippines instead of China. What would have happened if Nimitz and King had been victorious in that debate at Pearl Harbor makes for interesting speculation. The Chinese had armies in the field, both on the Nationalist side and the Communist side, and some of those troops were very effective. By going into the Philippines, the Americans secured some native support, but the Philippines had been in reality an occupied country, whereas China, even on the coast of the China seas, was never better than half occupied, and the Chinese were far more antipathetic as a whole to the Japanese than were the Filipinos, who numbered among their ranks many cooperators with the greater East Asia Co-Prosperity Sphere.

Overall, the Central Pacific campaign foreshadowed the future. It became apparent at Saipan and even more so at Guam that the Japanese would continue to resist ever more stoutly (if that was possible) as the Americans approached the inner core of empire, and the American casualties would be heavier as they went along and Japanese pockets of resistance harder to eradicate as the Japanese were given more territory in which to operate. All this became painfully apparent at Guam, so that what was to happen at Okinawa, in particular, could have come as no surprise at all to those who knew.

NOTES AND BIBLIOGRAPHY

The primary sources for research for *To the Marianas* was the Operational Archive of the U. S. Navy historical section in the Washington Navy Yard. The primary documents were the War Diaries and action reports of the U. S. Fifth Fleet for Operation Forager, as the Marianas invasion was called, and Operation Flintlock, as the Marshalls invasion was called. I also used the Action Reports of the U. S. carrier force in the Philippine Sea Battle (NRS 1977-17), which included the individual carriers and the aviation commands aboard those carriers. Also available were the individual records of the various carriers and squadrons in the winter and spring of 1943-44 and the summer of 1944. Some materials came from my own *How They Won the War in the Pacific* (Weybright and Talley, 1968), for which I had studied most aspects of the command activities of the Central Pacific forces. *To the Marianas* is a sequel to *Storm over the Gilberts* (Van Nostrand Reinhold, 1978), and some of the research materials acquired for the first book have been useful for the second, including Marine Corps records and naval records. The U. S. Marine Corps' *History of Marine Corps Operations in World War II*, Volume III, was most valuable. So was Samuel Eliot Morison's *History of United States Naval Operations in World*

War II, Volume VIII. Vice Admiral George C. Dyer's biography of Admiral Richmond Kelly Turner, *The Amphibians Came to Conquer* (U. S. Government Printing Office, undated) was very useful. I also used Stanley Smith's *The United States Marine Corps in World War II* (Random House, 1969) and *Battles of the Philippine Sea* by Charles Lockwood and Hans Christian Adamson.

Some notes from the Saipan and Tinian operations came from research conducted earlier for *The Men of the Gambier Bay* (Eriksson, 1979), the story of an escort carrier's activities in this and subsequent campaigns. I used various volumes of *History of United States Army Operations in World War II,* particularly those dealing with the Gilberts and Marshalls operations, and some on logistics. Andrieu d'Albas' *Death of a Navy* (Devin-Adair 1957) gave some indication of Japanese activity in the period, and so did Ito and Pineau's *The End of the Imperial Japanese Navy* (Norton, 1956) and Zenji Orita and Joseph Harrington's *I Boat Captain.* Saburo Hayashi's *Kogun,* the story of the Japanese Army in the Pacific war, was useful. So were various reports of interrogations of Japanese officials and prisoners, including the *U. S. Strategic Bombing Survey* conducted in Japan at the end of the war, and various reports by naval and marine intelligence sources disseminated during and after the war. Interviews with various figures also were the basis of some material, particularly those with Captain (later Rear Admiral) Charles J. Moore, Admiral Spruance's chief of staff; Vice Admiral Harry W. Hill, who led the amphibious forces in several of these operations; and Admiral Arleigh Burke, who was Admiral Mitscher's chief of staff.

Holland Smith's *Coral and Brass* (Scribner's 1949) tells his side of the Smith vs. Smith quarrel. More is told in Dyer's book about Turner. The army history is extremely restrained in this matter; what is apparent is that the Twenty-seventh Division, as it was constituted, had no business in battle—a problem that was remedied at Saipan, but only, unfortunately, after Ralph Smith had been removed from command. How Ralph Smith came to be a commander in the Pacific at all seems to be something of an anomaly; he was regarded in military circles in the 1940s as the leading American expert on the French army. Perhaps after the fall of France the Washington seers decided that specialties had no further place in American planning, in spite of General de Gaulle and the Free French. The tragedy of Smith vs. Smith was that it was inescapable—that Ralph Smith was victim of circumstances he could not control, and Holland Smith had no recourse but to do what he did, in spite of the hornet's nest predictably aroused in Washington.

INDEX